KU-175-264

John Lescroart was born in Houston, Texas and brought up in Texas, New York and Northern California. On graduating from U.C. Berkeley, he did various jobs before becoming a full-time writer, including working as a singer in Europe, a bar tender in an Irish pub in San Francisco and associate director of the Jewish Homes for the Aging in Los Angeles. After doctors estimated he had two hours to live when he contracted meningitis, John Lescroart decided, on his return to health, to take the risk of writing full-time. Two years after that decision, his novel THE 13th JUROR hit the *New York Times* bestseller list and stayed on the *Publishers Weekly* bestseller list for three months.

John Lescroart lives in Northern California, with his architect wife and their two children.

Nothing but the Truth

John Lescroart

HEADLINE
FEATURE

Copyright © 1999 John Lescroart

The right of John Lescroart to be identified as the Author of
the Work has been asserted by him in accordance with
the Copyright, Designs and Patents Act 1988.

First published in hardback in 1999
by HEADLINE BOOK PUBLISHING

First published in paperback in 2000
by HEADLINE BOOK PUBLISHING

10 9 8 7 6 5 4 3 2 1

All rights reserved. No part of this publication may be reproduced,
stored in a retrieval system, or transmitted, in any form or by any
means without the prior written permission of the publisher, nor be
otherwise circulated in any form of binding or cover other than that
in which it is published and without a similar condition being
imposed on the subsequent purchaser.

All characters in this publication are fictitious and any resemblance
to real persons, living or dead, is purely coincidental.

ISBN 0 7472 5976 3

Typeset by Avon Dataset Ltd, Bidford-on-Avon, Warks

Printed and bound in Great Britain by
Mackays of Chatham plc, Chatham, Kent

HEADLINE BOOK PUBLISHING
A division of the Hodder Headline Group
338 Euston Road
London NW1 3BH

www.headline.co.uk
www.hodderheadline.com

To the Big Cactus and the little Gambas

No mask like open truth to cover lies,
As to go naked is the best disguise.
William Congreve

PART ONE

1

At the tail end of a dog of a morning, Dismas Hardy was beginning to fear that he would also be spending the whole stiflingly dull afternoon in municipal court on the second floor of the Hall of Justice in San Francisco.

He was waiting – interminably since nine a.m. – for his client to be admitted into the courtroom. This would not have been his first choice for how to celebrate his forty-eighth birthday.

Now again the clerk called out someone not his client – this time a young man who looked as though he'd been drinking since he'd turned twenty-one and possibly for two or three years before that. Maybe he was still drunk – certainly he looked wasted.

The judge was Peter Li, a former assistant district attorney with whom Hardy was reasonably friendly. The prosecuting attorney was Randy Huang, who sat at his table inside the bar rail as the defendant went shuffling past. The public defender was a ten-year veteran named Donna Wong.

Judge Li's long-time clerk, another Asian named Manny See, read the charge against the young man as he stood, swaying, eyes opening and closing, at the center podium. The judge addressed him. 'Mr Reynolds, you've been in custody now for two full days, trying to get to sober, and your attorney tells me you've gotten there. Is that true?'

'Yes, your honor,' Donna Wong declared quickly.

Judge Li nodded patiently, but spoke in a firm tone. 'I'd like to hear it from Mr Reynolds himself, counsellor. Sir?'

Reynolds looked up, swayed for a beat, let out a long breath, and shook his head.

'Mr Reynolds,' Judge Li raised his voice. 'Look at me, please. Do you know where you are?'

Donna Wong prodded him with her elbow. Reynolds looked down at her, up to the judge and his clerk, across to Huang sitting at the prosecution table. His expression took on a look of stunned surprise as he became aware of his surroundings, of the Asian faces everywhere he turned. 'I don't know.' A pause. 'China?'

But the courtroom humor, such as it was, mingled uneasily with tragedy and the sometimes cruel impersonality of the law. Twenty-five very long minutes after the drunken Mr Reynolds had been removed from the courtroom, another case had been called, another defendant – not Hardy's – brought in. He was beginning to think that his own client wouldn't get his hearing and that another entire day would have been wasted. This was not all that unusual an occurrence. Everyone bitched about it, but no one seemed to be able to make things better.

The new defendant was Joshua Bonder, and from the Penal Code Section read out by the clerk, Hardy knew the charge was dealing amphetamines. But before things got started, Judge Li wanted to make sure that the three material witnesses in the case were in the building and ready to testify.

Hardy was half nodding off, half aware of the jockeying between Judge Li and the attorneys, when suddenly the back door by the judge's bench opened. At the sound of rattling chains – shades of the Middle Ages – Hardy looked up as a couple of armed bailiffs escorted three children into the courtroom.

The two boys and a girl seemed to range in age from about ten to fourteen. All of them rail-thin, poorly dressed, obviously terrified. But what sent an almost electric buzz through the courtroom was the fact that they were all shackled together in handcuffs and leg chains.

Joshua Bonder, whose own handcuffs had been removed for the hearing, screamed out, 'You sons of bitches!' and nearly

4

knocked over the defense table, jumping up, trying to get to the kids. 'What have you done to my children?'

Hardy had seen many murderers walk into the courtroom on their own, without any hardware. He thought he'd seen most of everything here, but this shocked him to his roots.

And he wasn't alone. Both of the courtroom bailiffs had leapt to restrain Mr Bonder, and now held him by the defense table. But Judge Li himself was up behind the bench, his normal calm demeanor thrown to the winds at this outrage.

'What the hell is this?' he boomed at the guards. 'Uncuff those children at once!' His eyes raked the room, stopping at the prosecution table. 'Mr Vela' – the assistant DA who'd drawn Joshua Bonder – 'what is the meaning of this?'

Vela, too, was on his feet, stammering. 'Your honor, you yourself issued the body attachments for these children as witnesses. We were afraid they would flee. They wouldn't testify against their father – he's their only guardian. So we have been holding them in youth guidance.'

'For how long?'

Vela clearly wished the floor would open up and swallow him. 'Two weeks, your honor. You must remember . . .'

Li listened, then went back to shouting. 'I remember the case, but I didn't order them shackled, for God's sake!'

Vela the bureaucrat had an answer for that, too. 'That's the mandated procedure, your honor. When we transfer inmates from juvenile hall and we think there's a flight risk, we shackle them.'

Judge Li was almost stammering in his rage. 'But look at these people, Mr Vela. They're *children*, not even teenage—'

The father's attorney, a woman named Gina Roake, decided to put in her two cents worth. 'Your honor, am I to understand that these children have been at the YGC for two weeks?'

Vela mumbled something about how Ms Roake shouldn't get on her high horse; it was standard procedure. But Roake was by now truly exercised, her voice hoarse with disgust. 'You locked up these innocent children in the company of serious juvenile offenders? Is that what you're telling me, Mr Vela?'

'They are not innocent—'

'No? What was their crime? Reluctance to testify against their father? That's all? And for this they're shackled?'

Vela tried again. 'The judge ordered—'

But Li wasn't having any part of that. Exploding, he pointed his whole hand at the prosecutor, now booming at the top of his voice. 'I ordered the least restrictive setting that would ensure the children's return to court. *Least* restrictive, Mr Vela. You know what that means?'

The smallest of the three kids had started crying, and the girl had moved over, putting her arm around him. As the bailiff moved in to separate them, Gina Roake cried out, 'Don't you dare touch them. Your honor?' A plea.

Which Li accepted. 'Let them alone.'

A moment of relative quiet ensued. Into it, Gina Roake inserted a heartfelt reproach. 'Your honor, this is the inevitable outcome when children are drawn into the criminal justice system. There has to be a better way. This is a travesty.'

At long last, it was Hardy's turn.

His client, a 32-year-old recent Dallas transplant named Jason Trent, made his living laying carpet and was now in custody charged with three counts of mayhem and inflicting grievous bodily injury pursuant to a fight in the 3Com Stadium parking lot after a Forty-Niner game.

Trent's story, and Hardy believed it, was that a trio of local boys had taken exception to his Dallas Cowboys attire and, after the 'Niners had been soundly thrashed, thought they would work out some of their frustrations by ganging up on the lone cowboy. This, in common with most of the other Niner decisions on the field during the game, turned out to be a bad idea for the home team.

Jason Trent had black belts in both karate and aikido and had also been a Golden Gloves champion in his teens back in

Fort Worth. After being sprayed with beer and pushed from two directions at once, and all the while warning his assailants about his various defense skills, Jason had finally lost his temper. In a very short fight, he put all three boys on the ground. Then – his real mistake – he'd gone around with a few more rage-driven punches, in the process breaking two arms, one collarbone, and one nose.

'You should have stopped when they were down,' Hardy had told him.

To which Jason had shrugged. 'They started it.'

Even so, the story probably would have ended there had not one of the three 'victims' been the son of Richard Raintree, a San Francisco supervisor and political ally of District Attorney Sharron Pratt. Raintree contended that Jason Trent had overreacted to what amounted only to good-natured hazing and was himself drunk on beer. Sharron Pratt agreed – she'd ordered Jason arrested and charged. Now Hardy addressed Judge Li. 'Your honor,' he said, 'this is my client's first alleged offense. He has no criminal record, not even a parking ticket. He holds a steady job. He's married and has three young children. He shouldn't even be here in this courtroom. His alleged victims started this fight and he was forced to defend himself.'

Li allowed a crack in his stern visage, glancing over at the bandaged and splinted victims at the prosecution table. 'And did a good job of it, didn't he?'

Hardy kept at it. 'The point, your honor, is that Mr Trent was pushed to this extreme by three punks who were ganging up on him. For all he knew, they were planning to kill him.'

This woke up the prosecutor, Frank Fischer, who objected to the use of the word punk. 'And further, your honor, the victims were on the ground at the time of the attack. They posed no threat to Mr Trent at that time.'

'They are the reason anything happened at all, your honor.' The odds were that he was whistling in the wind, but Hardy felt he had to go ahead. This was San Francisco in the Nineties.

The ultimate responsibility for any action only rarely got all the way back to a prime mover – there were always too many victims in the path who could claim stress or that their rights had somehow been violated.

The law said that Jason Trent had gone beyond simple self-defense. Trent himself admitted that he'd been driven to loss of control. He wouldn't pretend he didn't do it. He'd hurt these slimeballs on purpose because they'd hurt and threatened him first. Whose fault was that? he wanted to know.

So, law or no law, Hardy felt that for his client's sake he had to make the point. 'Mr Trent didn't do anything wrong here, your honor. The law recognizes self-defense as a perfect defense. These young men scared and outnumbered him. He felt he had no option but to immobilize them until he could get away.'

'Even after they were down on the ground?' Li asked.

Hardy nodded. 'He wanted to make sure they wouldn't get up until he could remove himself from any further danger. He didn't use anything like deadly force, which he very well could have, your honor. He used appropriate force to stop a vicious and unprovoked attack.'

Hardy noted vibration at his belt, his silent beeper going off. He glanced down at it – a message from his office. Well, he was almost done here. Finally. The judge had heard his little speech, and now would set bail and assign a trial date, and then . . .

But Li, no doubt still simmering in his earlier fury with the DA's cavalier style, suddenly had a different idea. After he listened to Hardy's argument, he allowed a short silence to reign in his courtroom. Then he looked over at the prosecutor. 'Mr Fischer,' he said, 'do the People concede that Messrs Raintree *et al.* assaulted the defendant here, Mr Trent, without provocation of any kind, other than his choice of clothing?'

Fischer was a nondescript functionary in his mid-thirties. By his reaction, this might have been the very first time that a judge had surprised him, or even spoken to him in the course of a proceeding. Now he stood up slowly, looked down at his notebook, and brought his eyes back up to the judge. 'Your honor, there was an exchange of words and insults. We have witnesses who . . .'

Li interrupted. 'Who hit who first?'

Fischer scratched at the table before him. 'Regardless of whatever instigated the fight that resulted in . . .'

Li's face remained placid but his voice hardened. 'Excuse me, Mr Fischer, I asked you a simple question. Would you like me to repeat it?'

'No, your honor. That isn't necessary.'

'Then would you do me the kindness to answer it?' Li repeated it anyway. 'Did Mr Raintree and the others start this fight?'

Fischer looked over at Hardy. Finally, he had to give it up. 'Yes, your honor.'

Hardy thought he saw a momentary glint in the judge's eye, and was suddenly certain he knew what the judge was going to do next. He wasn't supposed to do it, but Li obviously had had enough and didn't care. A couple more seconds of thought, then he tapped his gavel and stunned the courtroom with the words, 'Case dismissed.'

2

Hardy had no time to savor the triumph. He thought he'd just quickly call his office, pick up his message, and then go have a celebratory birthday/freedom lunch with Jason Trent. Enjoy a rare midday Martini. Maybe two.

But the phone message ended all thought of that. It was the call all parents fear. His receptionist, Phyllis, told him that Theresa Wilson from Merryvale needed him to get in touch with her as soon as possible. Merryvale was where his children – Rebecca and Vincent – went to school, and Theresa Wilson was the principal there. It was one thirty, a Thursday afternoon in the middle of October.

'Are the kids all right?' He blurted it out. Hardy had lost a son, Michael, twenty-five years before and that wound still hadn't completely healed – it never would. Now any threat to his children blanked his mind and brought his stomach to his throat.

'They're fine.'

He closed his eyes and let out a breath of relief.

'But no one's come to pick them up.'

'Frannie hasn't called?' No, of course she hadn't. That's why Mrs Wilson was on the phone with him. He flicked a glance down at his watch. 'How late is she?'

He knew it sounded lame. He wasn't in charge of taking care of the kids – that was Frannie's job – so he wasn't certain what time school got out. Somewhere in the back of his mind he recalled that they had one early dismissal day every week. It must be Thursday.

'About an hour.'

An hour without even a call? Frannie liked to say that if a

10

punctual person was a lonely one, then she was one of the loneliest people on earth. 'Have you heard from Erin? I mean Mrs Cochran? She's on the call list.' This was Rebecca's grandmother, who often picked up the kids at school when Frannie had other errands.

'That was my first call, Mr Hardy, to Erin. But I just got an answering machine. I thought I'd wait a few more minutes before calling you at work – maybe somebody got caught in traffic.' She hesitated. 'Your son's pretty upset. He wants to talk to you.'

Hardy heard his third grader, Vincent, trying to be brave, but his voice was cracking, frayed. He responded with a hearty confidence. 'It's OK, bud, I'll be down to pick you up in no time. Tell Rebecca it's all right, too. Everything's fine.'

'But where's Mom?'

'I don't know, Vin, but don't worry. I'm sure it's just a communication mix-up. That or she's running late from something.' He was selling himself as well as his son. Maybe Frannie had arranged for another parent to pick up the kids and that person had forgotten. 'She'll probably show up before I get there.'

Although he didn't really believe that. Frannie would have told the children if someone else other than Erin were going to pick them up. They had strict rules about not going home with anybody other than Mom, Dad or Grandma unless the arrangements had been approved in advance. 'You be a big guy,' he said. 'Everything's OK, I promise.'

Hardy made a quick call back to his reception desk and questioned Phyllis – was she sure Frannie hadn't left a message earlier? But Phyllis was an efficiency machine. If his wife had called, she told him icily, she would have told Hardy. As she always did.

He checked his watch again. It had been less than five minutes since he'd talked to Mrs Wilson.

Undoubtedly there was a simple explanation. Even in this day of ubiquitous communication, there were places that didn't have phones, or access to them. Frannie might be at one of them, stuck, trying to reach him.

He got the answering machine when he tried at his home. Where could she be? If she were not picking up the children, something was wrong.

Perhaps she'd been in an accident? Hardy's fertile brain played with the possibilities of what might have happened, might be happening, to his wife. He didn't like any of them.

A few minutes later he was in his car, negotiating the downtown traffic. He tried to remember something about Frannie's day, her plans. For the life of him, he couldn't retrieve anything, if in fact she'd told him.

Truth was, lately she probably wouldn't have mentioned anything about her daily schedule and even if she had, it might not have registered with him. More and more, the two of them were leading separate lives. Both of them knew it and admitted that it was a problem, but it was the toll of day-to-dayness, and neither of them seemed able to break the cycle. Hardy knew about as much of his wife's routines as he did of his children's school day, which was precious little.

Though it was cold comfort, he told himself that it was just the way things had evolved. The family dynamic had changed, gotten more traditional. He was overwhelmed with the simple mechanics of making a living. Frannie volunteered for everything, never said no, and was always there to support the other moms, her circle of friends. All of it – Frannie's very existence, it seemed – revolved around their children. As he supposed it should – that was the job she'd wanted. He made the money and helped with discipline. That was the deal.

Finally, beyond Van Ness the traffic started to move along out toward the Avenues. With luck now he'd be to Merryvale in ten minutes.

By the time he got home with the children and searched the house for some kind of a note, he was really worried. His wife didn't simply disappear with no explanation.

12

He sent the kids to the backyard and got on the phone. His first call was to Erin Cochran but he got another answering machine. Next – a flash of insight – he called Moses McGuire, Frannie's brother, bartending at the Little Shamrock.

'She probably left you. I would have long ago.'

'She wouldn't have left the kids, Mose.'

'Well, that's probably true, you're right.'

'I don't know where she is.'

Moses took a minute. 'I wouldn't worry about it, Diz. She'll turn up.'

'Well, that's heartening. Thanks for the input.'

He hung up. Big help from the brother front. While he sat at the kitchen table contemplating his next call, the phone rang and he snatched at it.

'Are you really worried?'

'Some.'

'You really don't know where she is?'

'No. I'm kidding you. Actually, she's right here next to me. We just thought it would be fun to call you and say she was gone – see how you react.'

Moses got serious. 'When did you last talk to her?'

'This morning.'

'You guys fight or anything?'

'No.'

The line hummed with silence. Then, 'I'd try Erin.'

'I already did. She isn't home.'

'Maybe they went somewhere together and got hung up.'

'Maybe,' Hardy agreed. He didn't want to alarm her brother any more than he already had. Moses had raised Frannie. He often said that of the ten things he cared most about, Frannie was the first eight. 'Either Erin or one of her other friends.'

'But she didn't call you?'

This, of course, was the nub of it, but Hardy played it down. 'Phyllis might have lost the message. Happens all the time,' he lied.

13

'I'll call Susan,' Moses said, referring to his wife. 'Maybe she's heard something.'

'OK.' Hardy looked at his watch. Two fifty. 'I'm sure she'll be home anytime. I'll call.'

Forty-five minutes later, the phone had rung twice more, but neither one was Frannie.

First had been Susan, checking to make sure that Moses had not misinterpreted what Hardy was saying. Was Frannie really missing? Hardy didn't want to say that, not yet. She just wasn't home yet. He'd call Susan back when he heard from her.

The second call was Erin Cochran, home from a long weekend that she and her husband Ed had spent in the Napa vineyards. No, she hadn't talked to Frannie in a week. Mrs Wilson's call on her machine had told her that Frannie hadn't gone to pick up the children, then she'd gotten Hardy's message. What was going on? Was Frannie back yet?

She tried to hide it, but the worry in her voice was unmistakable. It was now nearly three hours since Frannie should have picked the kids up at school and Hardy *still* hadn't even heard from her? Did he need help at home? Erin could be right over.

Hardy admitted that maybe that wouldn't be a bad idea.

He'd put off making the next call for as long as he could, but now – nearly four thirty, with two red-eyed children at the table listlessly pushing around some Graham crackers and milk – he punched in a number he knew by heart.

'Glitsky. Homicide.'

Lieutenant Abe Glitsky, the chief of San Francisco's homicide department, was his best friend. Being in the criminal justice system, Glitsky could circumvent a lot of bureaucracy.

'Abe, it's Diz.'

This was so different from their usual obscene or ironic

greeting that it raised Glitsky's red flag. 'What the matter?'

Hardy told Abe to hold a minute, then stood up with the portable phone, and told Rebecca and Vincent he was talking to Uncle Abe – adult stuff – he was just going into the living room for a little privacy. He'd be right back. They should keep eating their snacks.

'Frannie's running about three hours late,' he whispered from the front of the house. He cast his eyes up and down the street out front. No Frannie.

'Three *hours*?'

'I thought you might check around.'

Hardy's casual tone didn't camouflage much for Glitsky. He knew what his friend meant by check around – accidents, hospital admissions, or the worst, recently dead Jane Does – unidentified women.

'Three hours?' Glitsky repeated.

Hardy looked at his watch, hating to say it. 'Maybe a little more.'

Glitsky got the message. 'I'm on it,' he said. Hardy hung up just as Vincent let out a cry in the kitchen.

The Cochrans – Big Ed and Erin – were the parents of Frannie's first husband, Ed, who was the biological father of Rebecca. Their son had been gone a long time now, but Ed and Erin still doted on their granddaughter and her brother Vincent. They loved Frannie and her husband. Hardy and his wife, with no living parents between them, considered them part of the family.

Now, after getting the word about Frannie's absence, they had come to Hardy's house. Erin was shepherding the kids through their homework at the kitchen table, trying to keep their minds engaged. Hardy and Ed were making small talk, casting glances at the telephone, waiting.

Hardy was on the phone before the ring ended. It was Abe Glitsky with his professional voice on. 'She back yet?'

Hardy told him no, and endured a short pause. 'OK, well.

The good news is nobody's dead, not anywhere. I checked Alameda, Marin, Santa Clara' – the counties surrounding San Francisco – 'and it's a slow day on the prairie. Barely a fender-bender. No reports of anything serious. Nothing in the city at all.'

Hardy let out a long sigh. 'So what now?'

'I don't know. We hang. She'll . . .' He stopped. Glitsky, who'd lost his own wife to cancer a few years before, wasn't one for stoking false hopes. 'She driving the Subaru?'

'I'd guess so. If she's driving.'

'Give me the license and I'll put it out over the dispatch – broaden the net.'

'All right.' Hardy hated the sound of that – broaden the net. It was getting official now. Objective. Harder to deny, even to himself.

Where was his wife?

3

Earlier that morning, Scott Randall was hosting an informal bull session with some law clerks in his tiny cubicle of an office on the third floor of the Hall of Justice. Even his most ardent admirers among these clerks would admit that Scott was the near embodiment of well-dressed, post-Gen-X arrogant disdain. But none of them viewed this as a negative. Indeed, the trait had allowed Scott, though only thirty-three, to rise to homicide prosecutor in the DA's office, an eminence to which they all aspired.

This morning, Scott had a theme and he was rolling. 'Listen up,' he told the acolytes. 'You are looking at someone who has gotten convictions on his first three murder cases – and I don't need to tell you how difficult that is in our compassion-driven little burg.' No false modesty for Scott Randall.

'But do you know what those three convictions have done for my career? Or what the same kind of cases will do for yours?' The question was rhetorical and he breezed ahead. 'Zero, zilch, nada. You know why? Because no one cares about the people in them. Look.' He held up a finger. 'One, a motorcycle gang brawl over one of their common-law women; two,' – another finger – 'a drug dealer killed by an addict he'd tried to cheat; three, a bum stabbed after he'd stolen another bum's grocery cart. This is not stuff over which newspaper readers salivate, believe me.'

One of the young men spoke up. 'So what do you do?'

'I'll answer by way of an example. I think you'll all have heard something about the murder of Bree Beaumont.' He reached for a manila file that sat atop his desk and from it extracted a couple of eight by ten glossy photographs, holding them up.

'Exhibit A, on the left,' he began – Scott spoke a precise legalese even in private – 'is a picture of the deceased. Bree Beaumont, very pretty, a player in the big-money oil business. Also married, two kids, and,' he paused for effect, 'rumored to be dating Damon Kerry.'

This was a trump that had been kept from the media and Scott enjoyed the reaction. 'Perhaps our next governor, that's right.'

Scott raised the picture in his right hand. 'Exhibit B is Bree Beaumont's body lying in the enclosed patio area underneath her penthouse apartment, where she landed after a long fall. As you've read in the papers, there were shards of glass in Bree's hairline. They didn't find glass where she landed, none in her apartment. So someone conked her on the head and threw her over. She was six weeks pregnant, too.'

Scott cocked an eyebrow. He had their interest. 'This is high profile, career-making stuff. You can't let these cases get away and if they start to slide, you've got to go pro-active.'

The first male clerk spoke again. 'How is it getting away?'

'It's been three weeks, and our friends in the police department don't have a suspect. After that amount of time, the odds say they never will. That's how.'

One of the female clerks checked in. 'But they must be looking? Isn't it just a matter of time?'

Scott conceded that sometimes it was. 'But in this case, the original inspector, Carl Griffin, was working solo and got himself shot to death – apparently unrelated – just a few days after Bree was killed. The new guys – Batavia and Coleman – haven't found anything and it doesn't seem like it's bothering them. And until they bring us a suspect, we've got no job.'

Scott let them absorb the facts for a moment. 'So if you're me and you want this case, I mean you *really* want this case, what do you do?'

This was the kind of information the clerks came here to lap up. They were rapt as he continued. 'I'll tell you what I *did* do. I went to Ms Pratt' – San Francisco's District Attorney,

Sharron Pratt – 'and told her, *promised* her, that if she gave me my own investigator, I would bring the case before the grand jury to get an indictment.'

The second young woman spoke up. 'How?'

Scott flashed a grin. 'I'm glad you asked that question, Kimberly. And here's the answer: the grand jury is your friend. You know how it works – no defense lawyers allowed, no judge in the room. You present your case to twenty average citizens, and do it without worrying too much about legalities. If you're not brain dead, you get your indictment.'

'But if the police don't have a suspect, who do you call as witnesses?' Kimberly asked.

'Everybody I can think of, including Kerry, his campaign manager Al Valens; Jim Pierce, this Caloco oil vice president who was Bree's old mentor. Then I go after the personal connections – and remember that no matter what else might be involved, murder is usually personal.

'So I subpoena Bree's husband Ron, Ron's friends and friends of friends, her professors, colleagues, lab partners. Somewhere I'm betting I'm going to pull a break.'

'So it's a fishing expedition,' the first clerk commented. 'But we've always been told not to—'

Scott was brusque. 'Forget the garbage they taught you in law school. Here's Real Life One-A. There's lawyers who win in front of juries, they've got careers. All the others wind up pushing paper or crunching numbers. Your choice. So I'm going to take this murder of Bree Beaumont and get my name on the marquee. The grand jury's my vehicle. I'm riding it and taking no prisoners.'

Scott's eyes were bright. 'This time next week, mark my words, this case is front burner. And it's mine.'

Scott had served his witness, a Mrs Frannie Hardy, at her home on the previous Friday. The subpoena had instructed her to call if her time on the witness stand presented a conflict or hardship. If that had been the case, Scott would have rescheduled – he'd done so with several other witnesses. If Mrs Hardy had called, he would have told her how long he expected her to be on the stand and what kinds of questions he was likely to ask.

Scott had no indication that the witness had ever met Bree Beaumont. He got her name from Ron, Bree's husband, who'd said that he and Mrs Hardy had been having coffee together on the morning of Bree's death. So she was Ron's primary alibi and as such Scott wanted to talk to her. But it wasn't going to be the Inquisition. Frannie Hardy was not a suspect. If she'd called to discuss anything, Scott would have reassured her.

But no call.

So this morning, when Mrs Hardy had arrived late at the grand jury room, ten minutes after it had gone into session at nine thirty, Scott had already begun talking to James Pierce, a senior vice president and Caloco's community relations officer. He had worked closely with Bree before she'd left the company and had known her since she'd been recruited from Cal. If there were any bones in her closet, Scott thought Pierce would know where they were hidden.

Ironically, Scott's initial plan had been to take Mrs Hardy before Pierce, thinking that hers was probably going to be a much shorter questioning – Scott hadn't wanted to hang her up for the whole day. But when she hadn't been there on time and Pierce had, that was too bad for her – she'd brought it on herself.

So now Scott was going to let Mrs Hardy sweat it out. No, he'd told her during a break in Pierce's testimony. He didn't know how long it would be until he got to her. No, she couldn't come back another day. He trotted out his favorite phrase. This was not a parlor game. This was a murder investigation.

'I know all about murder investigations,' she told him. 'My husband's an attorney, too.'

'Then you know how serious this is.'

Mrs Hardy did not seem convinced. 'I know how important

20

you all think it is,' she said mildly. 'Look, Mr Randall, I'm just trying to find out how long this will be. I've got to pick up my children at school. If I'm not going to be out of here by one o'clock, I'm going to have to make some phone calls.'

'I think that's a good possibility,' he said with conscious ambiguity.

She didn't think it was too important, did she? Well, she'd find out.

As it developed, he began with her just before noon. She had just decided to make her phone calls when Scott called her to testify. She thought it couldn't be too long. She'd have plenty of time. There was no need to call.

After he administered the oath that she tell the truth, the whole truth, and nothing but the truth, Scott had her identify herself, and then started right in. 'Mrs Hardy, were you acquainted with the deceased, Bree Beaumont?'

'No. I never met her.'

'But you did know her husband Ron?'

'That's correct.' Mrs Hardy was sitting at a table in the front of the room, facing the twenty jurors. Now she looked up at them and explained. 'Ron is the full-time parent in their family, so we saw each other mostly at school and other child-related events.'

'And how long have you known him?'

'I don't know exactly. A couple or three years.' Another explanation to the jury. 'He's kind of an honorary mom. We tease him about it.'

'We?'

'You know, the other moms at school.'

Scott was just fishing, talking about whatever came up. Here before the grand jury, strict relevancy wasn't much of an issue. 'Did he seem to resent this role?'

'What do you mean?'

'I mean, being Mr Mom? Did he ever talk about resenting that his wife worked and he didn't?'

21

Mrs Hardy gave that a minute's thought. 'No. I don't think it bothered him.'

'Did you find that strange?'

'What? That he took care of the kids or that he didn't resent taking care of them?'

'I don't know. Both. Either.'

Another beat while she reflected. 'Not any more than anybody else.' Mrs Hardy broke a smile to the jurors. 'I think sometimes our little darlings get hard for anybody.' Then, back to Scott, more seriously. 'But with Ron, he seemed fine with it. His wife did her job, he did his. He's a good father.'

'She made the money and he didn't?'

'That's right, Mr Randall. It happens here in the Nineties.'

'And that didn't bother him? Being the man and not making any money.'

'I just said that. It didn't seem to.' Her voice took on a sharp edge. 'I don't know what you're trying to get at.'

'I'm trying to find out who killed Mrs Beaumont.'

'Well, it wasn't Ron. He was with me when she died. We were having coffee at the Starbucks on 28th and Geary, near Merryvale School.' This seemed to remind of her something and she glanced up at the wall clock, pursed her lips.

Scott Randall pushed ahead. 'And how did that come about?'

'What?'

'Having coffee.'

'I don't even understand that question. We just decided to go get a cup of coffee. There wasn't anything sinister about it.'

'I didn't say there was.'

'Well, it seems to me you implied it. We met at school dropping off the kids, and Ron said he felt like a cup of coffee and I said I thought that sounded good. So we both went.'

Again, she glanced at the wall clock. 'Look, I'm sorry, but are we almost done here? I've got to go pick up my kids pretty soon.'

'When we're done,' Scott replied. 'After we're done.'

22

Scott did not view himself as a cruel person, but a woman's tears on a witness stand were as unimportant as the temperature in the room, or the lighting. Sometimes you had to deal with them, that was all. But you had no feelings about them one way or the other.

Frannie Hardy, on the stand before him now, crying, did not make his heart go all soft. True enough, she was quite lovely, well dressed, with striking green eyes and bright red hair, and if he'd been anywhere but in a courtroom with her, he might have had other thoughts. But not now. She'd brought her troubles upon herself and now she was paying the price.

She wasn't sobbing. Scott was sure these were tears of anger. He didn't care.

'You have to let me make my phone call.'

'No, ma'am, I'm sorry. You're staying here.'

'You told me we'd be finished by now.'

Scott shrugged. 'I said we might be. It was possible. I thought we would be, but you're not answering my questions. That's slowing things down.'

It was already half an hour past when she was supposed to have left to pick up her children. She'd been on the stand for two hours.

'Let's go over this one more time, all right?'

'I'm not saying anything until you let me use the phone.'

It had devolved into a pitched battle of wills, and Scott held the high ground. He made the rules in this room, and Mrs Hardy was going to play by them.

Scott had long since abandoned the casual approach. He was standing at one end of the front table so he could look now at Mrs Hardy and now at his jurors.

'Mrs Hardy, you're putting me in an awkward position. As it stands now, if you don't answer my questions you're going to force me to go to a judge in the Superior Court and get a contempt citation issued against you. You might very well get thrown in jail. Do you understand that? If that happens, if it gets to there, then you'll get your phone call to your attorney. But I'm not letting you off this stand in the middle of your testimony. We can be finished here in ten minutes if you cooperate, but if you don't, it's going to be a long afternoon.

'Now,' Scott pressed her. 'Let's try again one more time. You have testified that you knew – Ron Beaumont had confided in you – that his relationship with his wife was in a difficult stage. Isn't that true?'

'Yes, he told me that.'

'And did he tell you the nature of these difficulties?'

'A little bit.'

'Did Mr Beaumont tell you anything that suggested he was unhappy or angry with Mrs Beaumont?'

Frannie shook her head. 'No, I wouldn't say so. But really I have no idea how he felt. We didn't talk about them.'

'But he did tell you he was having difficulties?'

'I would say so.'

Scott Randall turned over a few pages on his yellow legal pad. He looked at the jury, then back to the witness. 'Mrs Hardy, do you find Mr Beaumont attractive?'

Her lips went tight. 'I have never thought about it.'

Scott conveyed his disbelief clearly to the jury. 'Never thought about it? You obviously had a relationship with him, a close relationship – isn't that true? And you didn't notice if he was attractive or not?'

'I may have noticed, but I didn't think about it. We were friends, that's all.'

'And yet he chose you, and you alone, to confide in about his marital problems.'

'I don't know that. He might have confided in other people. I don't know if it was only me.'

'Were you two having an affair, Mrs Hardy? Is that it?'

Frannie Hardy was biting down hard on her lower lip. She clipped out the words. 'I've already told you, we were friends.'

Scott Randall remained matter-of-fact. 'That's right, that's what you told me. But friends have affairs all the time. Did his wife find out about you – was that it? Was she going to make problems for the two of you?'

'I'm not going to dignify that with an answer.'

'Well, you'd better dignify *something* with an answer, and pretty soon. You're digging yourself into quite a hole here – don't you realize that?'

Frannie was shaking her head back and forth wearily. How had it all come to this so quickly? She closed her eyes and forced her voice to remain calm, rational. 'Look, Mr Randall, what do you want me to say? I'm late picking up my children, that's what I'm thinking about. I'm not having any affair with Ron Beaumont, and never did. I never met his wife. I don't think Ron's problems with his relationship led to his wife's death.'

'Let us decide that, Mrs Hardy. You've admitted that the problems existed. Just tell us what they were.'

Frannie didn't know it, but Scott Randall and the grand jury had already heard Ron Beaumont say that Bree and he were getting along fine and there were no problems between them. Scott thought it might be a good time to mention this to Frannie. She sat still, her face a blank now.

'Mrs Hardy?'

'I promised him it would remain between us and I wouldn't tell anybody. I gave him my word.'

Scott sensed an opening. 'Mrs Hardy, let's be realistic. No one believes that promises are that sacred anymore. This could be a crucial element in a murder investigation. Are you sure you haven't mentioned what Mr Beaumont told you to your husband or one of your girlfriends?'

She was staring at him, trying to keep her anger in check. More tears threatened. A drop escaped from her right eye. 'I promised,' she repeated. 'I gave my word.'

Scott looked back out to the jurors. He took a beat and sighed. 'All right, Mrs Hardy,' he said, 'You don't leave me any choice.'

* * *

25

By four thirty, Superior Court Judge Marian Braun had already had a long day on the bench presiding over an unusually depressing murder trial. Members of a gypsy clan had convinced several wealthy old people that they were their friends. They had persuaded them to sign over their assets, and then poisoned them with 'magic salt' – digitalis. The magic salt was a big yuk – the defendants had giggled as they sprinkled it on. Marian Braun was used to bad people committing heinous crimes, but this one got under her skin.

Today had been particularly dispiriting because a dozen or more very tough-looking relatives of the defendants had put on a show of force by appearing in her courtroom just in time to intimidate the state's main witness, another of the clan who hadn't been able to live with her conscience and who'd been promised immunity from prosecution in return for her testimony. But the thugs in the courtroom got their message across – the woman suddenly couldn't remember witnessing any of the defendants sprinkling salt on anything. Now it seemed possible that these heartless killers were going to go free.

When Judge Braun's bailiff came to her chambers and told her that Scott Randall had a contempt citation for her at the end of her already lousy day, she grabbed her robes, breathing fire, and strode impatiently through the hallways to the grand jury room.

'No, ma'am. As Mr Randall has explained to you, you don't have a choice unless you're claiming a Fifth Amendment right. But you've told me that your testimony will not incriminate yourself, which rules out that option. You've got to tell him what you know.'

Frannie Hardy shook her head. This had been going on for so long that all her patience was used up. 'I can't believe this is the United States.' She scanned the faces of the jurors, went to Scott Randall and finally rested on Marian Braun. 'What's the matter with all you people? You all ought to be ashamed of yourselves. Don't you have any real lives? I haven't done anything wrong.'

This line of discourse turned out to be a tactical error. Judge Braun wasn't about to have the validity of her life and work called into question by some nobody witness. She snapped out her reply. 'First, in this room you address me as "your honor". Next, as to doing something wrong, you are refusing to cooperate in the investigation of a murder case. Like it or not, that's a crime. Now for the last time, young lady, you answer the question or you go to jail.'

'I'm not your young lady.' A pause. 'Ma'am.'

Braun slapped at the table. 'All right, then, I'm ordering you held in the county jail until you decide to answer Mr Randall's questions.' Judge Braun half turned. 'Bailiff . . .'

But Frannie was on her feet now, her voice raised, color high. 'You want to talk contempt? I hold you in contempt. God help the system if you cretins are running it.'

Braun's steely gaze came back to her. 'You just got yourself four days before this grand jury citation even starts to run. You want more, young lady, just keep talking. Bailiff.'

The guard came forward.

4

Hardy got Frannie's call at six twenty and made the half-hour drive downtown to the Hall of Justice in seventeen minutes. On the way, he stopped fuming long enough to think to call Abe Glitsky on his car phone, to see if he could work some magic. The county jail and the Hall of Justice were on the same lot. Maybe Glitsky could get the ball rolling.

But the lieutenant was waiting for him by the back door of the Hall, at the entrance to the jail. He wasn't wearing his happy face.

Hardy came up at a jog, slacks and shirtsleeves, no coat, knowing before he asked. 'She still in there? She's *really* in there?' Though he never doubted she was. This wasn't the kind of funny birthday prank Frannie was likely to pull on him.

'Yep.'

Barely slowing, Hardy swore and turned in toward the jail's entrance. Glitsky reached and caught his sleeve, stopping him. 'Hey!'

'Let me go, Abe. I'm getting her out of there.'

'Not without a judge you're not. I couldn't.'

When Glitsky let go of his arm he stayed put, glaring in the dusk. The night had turned windy and cold. The lawyer in him knew that his friend was right – it wasn't a matter of summoning some patience. They had to find a judge, the night magistrate, somebody. To facilitate night-time warrants and other late business, the judges rotated magistrate duty so that there would be one judge on call every evening.

Even as Hardy said 'Where's Braun?' he was moving again, toward the Hall, Glitsky on his heels.

But though they had no trouble getting by the night guard and into the building, after they took the stairs to the second floor they couldn't get into the area of the judge's chambers, which were behind the courtrooms. Hardy banged on doors all the way down the hallway. No answer.

A clerk, working late in one of the rooms, opened her door and poked a head out. 'It's closed up back there. Everybody's gone home.'

Hardy kicked the door and the sound echoed off the walls. Then, suddenly, just as they turned to head back downstairs, the door opened. 'What's all this goddam racket?'

Leo Chomorro wasn't Hardy's favorite judge, although he was glad enough to see him now. It didn't appear to be mutual – Chomorro was scowling. Then, noticing Glitsky, he nodded more genially. 'Evening, lieutenant. What's going on here?'

Glitsky laid it out in a few words. They needed a judge to vacate a contempt citation and get Hardy's wife out of jail.

'Your *wife*?'

'Yes, your honor. There's been some kind of screw-up.'

Chomorro's scowl deepened. 'What was she doing down here? She's not an attorney, too, is she?'

'No. She got called before the grand jury and the next thing she knew she was in jail.'

Chomorro looked like he wanted to ask some more questions, but he'd heard the magic word – grand jury – and knew nobody was allowed to discuss anything about its proceedings. They'd already told him the charge was contempt, though – he might pursue that. 'Who issued the citation?' he asked warily.

'Marian Braun,' Glitsky said.

Making a face and no promises, Chomorro got a few more details, then finally said he'd put in a call to Braun and get some answers if he could. But he told them they shouldn't expect much – any communication about grand jury proceedings was prohibited. If they wanted to wait . . .

29

Glitsky stayed with the judge, but Hardy decided he had to see Frannie.

He'd been to the jail dozens of times and knew the routine, so within minutes he was in the attorneys' visiting room, waiting for his wife.

He hadn't really prepared himself. With other clients, he made it a point to pre-visualize their entrance into this room. It was often the first time he would see them in the jail's orange jumpsuit, and the reality of someone he'd known in civilian life dressed for the slammer was always something of a shock.

In this case, the first sight was more in the order of a physical assault. Frannie, always petite, looked positively gaunt. In the room's institutional glare, his wife's cheeks were ghostly – the washed-out, faded yellow-gray of ancient paste. Her beautiful red hair had already lost its luster and now hung flat and drab.

A glance reconnected them and they crossed to each other, nearly falling into an embrace. Frannie clung to him, her face buried in his chest, repeating, 'Thank God, thank God,' over and over.

He held her.

Finally, their hands enfolded on the table, they began to get to it, Frannie trying to explain away the subpoena, and the fact that she hadn't told him about it. 'I didn't think it was anything, that's why.'

Hardy shook his head. This wasn't tracking right. 'No,' he said, 'you thought it was *something*, Frannie. If you thought it was nothing, you *would* have told me about it. You would have said, "I got this subpoena today to go testify in front of the grand jury. I wonder what it's all about." Instead, you kept it to yourself.' She was silent, biting at her lower lip. After a minute, Hardy prompted her. 'Frannie?'

'All right,' she admitted.

'All right, what?'

Pulling her hands away from his, she crossed her arms over her chest. 'Now you're cross-examining me. I think I've had enough of that for today.'

Hardy kept his voice in tight control. 'I'm not doing that.' He brought it down to a whisper. 'I don't know why you're here. I'm confused. I don't know what's going on. You want to help me out with this? I'm on your side.'

Closing her eyes, she let out a breath. 'OK,' she said. She reached again for his hand. 'I know I should have told you. I mean, I know that now. It's just we've had such different lives lately. I didn't want you to misunderstand, I guess – to have to deal with it at all.'

'Deal with what?'

She met his eyes, taking a long moment before answering. 'Ron.'

'Ron,' Hardy repeated, his voice hardening in spite of himself. 'I don't believe we know a Ron.'

'Ron Beaumont,' she said. 'Max and Cassandra's dad.'

Hardy knew the children a bit from their visits with his kids, from sleepovers. The older one, Cassandra, had become one of Rebecca's good friends, maybe even her best friend, although he wasn't sure of that. Hardy had some vague sense, a dim memory, of a charming, vivacious child, although the 'kid thing,' as he called it, had been pushed off – banished from? – the front burner of his life. But he had never met the father. 'Max and Cassandra's dad,' he repeated, his voice flat. 'Ron.'

Frannie looked at him and he saw desperation, even despair, in her expression. And, behind that, maybe a disturbing hint of defiance. 'He's a friend of mine. Like you with the women in your life.'

This was a sore point. Hardy often went to lunch, or sometimes even dinner, with other women, colleagues who he worked with, got along with. Even his ex-wife Jane, too, once in a while. He and Frannie finally had to put a moratorium on questions about who they all were, the various personal and professional relationships. They were all just friends. They'd leave it at that.

But on the other foot, Hardy discovered, the shoe cramped him up.

He suddenly had to get away from what he thought he might be hearing. Walking across the room to its doorway, he stood looking out through the wired glass opening into the hallway of the jail. Finally, he turned. 'OK, we'll leave it where you want. But I've got to remind you that you brought all this up. I never heard of Ron Beaumont until two minutes ago and you're in jail because of some subpoena involving you and him. I don't think a little curiosity is out of the question.'

'His wife was murdered. He's a suspect.'

By the door, Hardy stood stock still. 'And the grand jury decided it had to talk to you about him?'

She shrugged. 'I was with him – drinking coffee,' she added quickly, 'on the morning she died. In public.'

He waited.

'So they wanted to see if my alibi matched his.'

Hardy was still trying to figure out the logistics. 'Did you ever talk to the police about this, before today?'

'No.'

This wasn't making sense. If Frannie was the alibi of one of the main suspects in a murder case, the police would have interrogated her as a matter of course, if for no other reason than to have her words on the record. He'd have to remember to ask Abe why they hadn't, if Abe knew. And if it were true.

But first, he was here. 'OK, so you got the subpoena you didn't tell me about . . .'

'I thought it would be a quick hour in the middle of the morning, Dismas. There was no need to bother you with it.'

Hardy didn't want to start down that road again. There were lots of facts he wanted to know. When they got home and out of this environment, things would seem different. They'd be able to talk until they got somewhere. Here in the jail, time

32

pressed on them. 'All right, so I assume you verified Ron's alibi.'

'I did.'

'And after that?'

'Well, this lawyer, the prosecutor – do you know a Scott Randall?'

Hardy shook his head. 'I've heard the name. He's the guy who put you here?'

She nodded. 'He asked if Ron had told me about any problems between him and his wife that might have something to do with what happened to her.'

'Why would he have told you that? Why did this Scott Randall think to ask that?'

'I don't know, but he did.'

Their eyes met across the room again, and this time Hardy left the doorway and came back to the table, sitting on a corner of it. 'So what did you say?'

'I said he had.' She shrugged. 'So Mr Randall asked me what it was, to tell the grand jury what Ron had told me.'

'And?'

'And I couldn't do that.'

'Why not?'

'Because I'd promised Ron I wouldn't.'

'OK, so what was it, this big secret?'

She looked up at him imploringly. 'Dismas, come on.'

At this moment, before Hardy could respond, there was a knock at the door and the guard admitted Abe Glitsky, who was a study in controlled rage of his own. Stealing a quick look at Frannie, his eyes narrowed for a millisecond and the scar between his lips went white. Then he focused on Hardy. 'It's not happening,' he said. 'Braun's not budging.'

Instinctively, forgetting their disagreements, Hardy reached a hand out on the table and Frannie took it. He looked down at her and her eyes were brimming. He didn't blame her.

'I can't stay here, Dismas. Abe?'

Miserable, the two men looked at each other. They didn't

33

have to say anything. Jail was a reality in both of their lives. When a judge ordered it, people wound up staying all the time. Finally, Hardy let out a breath. 'So what's left, Abe? What are our options?'

The lieutenant was shaking his head. 'I don't know. I could talk to the desk – maybe get her in Adseg.'

'What's that?' Frannie asked. 'I'm right here, guys. Don't third person me.'

'Administrative segregation,' Glitsky explained to her. 'Basically it's isolation, a nicer cell. Keep you away from the general population, which you want – trust me on this.'

'This can't be happening,' Hardy said.

'Evidently,' Abe went on, looking at Frannie, 'you broke the first rule of the courtroom – you don't insult the judge.'

'She's a pompous ass,' Frannie retorted. 'She insulted me first.'

'She's allowed to insult you. It's in her job description. What did you say to her?'

'I told her I held *her* in contempt, that this whole thing was contemptible . . .'

Hardy was shaking his head, believing it all now. When Frannie got her dander up, watch out.

'It got her four days,' Glitsky said.

'*Four days*?' Hardy gathered himself for a beat. 'This isn't about some secret?'

'What secret? Not that I heard from Chomorro. It's about Braun.' Glitsky changed to a hopeful tone. 'Maybe she'll talk to you tomorrow, Diz.'

'No maybe about it,' Hardy said. 'I'll tackle her in the hallway if I have to.'

Frannie reached across the table. 'Dismas, you can't let them keep me here. The kids need me. This is some horrible mistake. It just started with this stupid promise. That's all they wanted.'

'So what is it? Tell me – I promise, *I* won't tell anybody. You can hire me as your attorney and it'll be privileged.

Nobody will ever know and maybe we can use it as a chip. I'll go wake up the judge at her house, explain the situation . . .'

Glitsky butted in. 'I wouldn't do that. What secret?'

Frannie ignored Abe. 'They could just ask Ron. You, Dismas, could ask Ron. Go to his house and wake him up. Call him from here even. If he knew I was in jail, he'd tell them what they want to know. He wouldn't let this happen to me.'

'What is this secret?' Glitsky asked again.

Frannie finally raised her voice. 'The secret isn't the issue!' Her eyes pleaded with her husband, trying to tell him something, but what it was remained shrouded in mystery.

Then she shifted her glance quickly to Abe. 'I promised Ron. I gave him my word. It's *his* secret. Dismas, maybe if you could call him or go to his apartment and tell him what's going on . . . I'm sure he'll tell you. Then you come back and get me out of here.'

5

Abe was sifting through an armful of files he'd brought in from one of the desks in the homicide detail. He found the file he wanted and pitched it across his desk to Hardy. 'As you recall from your days as a prosecutor, the address is there on the top right. Broadway.'

Hardy glanced down, then looked up. 'No phone number? A phone number would be nice.'

'A lot would be nice in that file, Diz. There's next to nothing there.' He sighed. 'My first inspector got himself killed about a week into the case. You might remember him – Carl Griffin?'

Hardy nodded. 'Yeah. He got killed how?' He didn't want to talk about any dead policemen, especially to his best friend the live one, but this might bear on Frannie and he had to know.

'Some witness meeting went bad, we think.'

Sergeant Inspector Carl Griffin didn't know it, but when he got up from his desk in the homicide detail on the fourth floor of San Francisco's Hall of Justice on Monday morning, 5 October, it was for the last time.

He was the lone inspector working the murder of Bree Beaumont, a 36-year-old environmental and, recently, political consultant. He'd been on the case for six days. Griffin had been a homicide inspector for fourteen years and knew the hard truths by now – if you didn't have a murderer in your sights within four days of the crime, it was likely you never would.

Carl was a plodder with a D in personality. Everybody in homicide, including his lieutenant, Abe Glitsky,

36

considered him the dullest tack in the unit. Loyal and hardworking, true, but also slow, culturally ignorant and hygienically suspect.

Still, on occasion Carl did have his successes. He would often go a week, sometimes ten days, conducting interviews with witnesses and their acquaintances, gathering materials to be fingerprinted and other physical evidence, throwing everything into unlabeled freezer bags in the trunk of his city-issued car. When he was ready, he'd gather all his junk into some semblance of coherence, and sometimes wind up with a convictable suspect.

Not that he often got assigned to cases that needed brains to solve. In San Francisco, nine out of ten homicides were open books. A woman kills a man who's beating her. A jealous guy kills a wandering girlfriend. Dope deals go bad. Gang bangs. Drunken mistakes.

Low-lifes purifying the gene pool.

In these cases, homicide inspectors collected the evidence that a jury would need to convict the completely obvious suspect and their job was done. Carl was useful here, connecting the dots.

Once in a while, since homicides came in over the transom and got assigned to whoever was on call, Griffin would draw a case that had to be worked. This hadn't happened in over two years when the call came in about a politically connected white woman on Broadway, so Glitsky really had no choice. It wasn't apparent at the outset that the case was high profile and if the lieutenant had suspected that it would go ballistic, he would have assigned other inspectors and Carl's feelings be damned.

But as it was, Griffin got the Beaumont case, and he was in his sixth day, and he hadn't made an arrest.

After receiving her doctorate from UC Berkeley in the early eighties, Bree had run that institution's environmental toxicology lab for a couple of years before leaving academia to

37

consult for the Western States Petroleum Association, and later to work for Caloco Oil.

Only a few months before her death, though, she'd abandoned the oil company and changed sides in the volatile wars over the multi-billion-dollar gasoline additive industry. Going public with her opposition to what she had come to believe were cancer-causing additives in California gasoline, Bree had aligned herself with the state assemblyman from San Francisco, Damon Kerry, now running for governor.

The central plank of Kerry's platform played on the public's fears that these petroleum-based gasoline additives, particularly a substance called MTBE – methyl tertiary butyl ether – was seeping into California's groundwater in alarming amounts. It was dangerous and had to be outlawed, but the government wouldn't move on it.

When Bree, the oil industry's very photogenic baby, had agreed to join his campaign, it had given Kerry a terrific boost. And now, after her death, radio talk shows hummed with theories that the oil companies had killed Bree Beaumont, either in revenge for her defection or to keep her from giving Kerry more and better ammunition to use against them.

With the election four weeks from tomorrow, Kerry trailed his opponent by half-a-dozen points. Bree's death had become big news. And every time someone mentioned her name, Damon Kerry came up as well.

But Carl Griffin wasn't troubled. He had a plate full of active homicides and knew the suspects in three of them. He was simply assembling the packages.

On Bree Beaumont, he was confident he was close to asking for a warrant. There was just one piece of information he had to verify and he'd have it tied up. And wouldn't that just show Glitsky and the rest of them who thought he couldn't get anything done on this kind of case?

That's why he never told anybody about his progress or lack of it. He wasn't good with criticism. It rankled when *other inspectors second-guessed him about what they'd do differently, where they'd look, why they wouldn't talk to the people Carl was talking to.*

Carl didn't take this as good-natured ribbing, and maybe it wasn't. He considered that he was an old-fashioned cop, a dog sniffing where his nose led, discarding anything that didn't smell, following what did. His nose told him he was about a step away on Beaumont.

He stood in Glitsky's doorway on his way out of the office. He wore his black Raider's windbreaker over an orange and blue Hawaiian shirt that he tucked into a shiny pair of ancient black slacks. The shirt billowed over his belt. He looked about halfway to term.

Griffin was telling his lieutenant that he was going to be seeing a snitch on a gang-related in the Western Addition first thing this morning. He was late for it now, which didn't matter because the snitch would be late, too. Then, depending on how things broke with the snitch, if he got time, he planned to try to find the knife in the Sanchez case – the crime scene investigators hadn't been able to locate it in the house, but he'd bet it was somewhere on the block, so Griffin was going to poke around the shrubs and see what he came up with. His guess was she got out of the house and threw it somewhere and then came back before she dialed 911. Anyway, then . . .

Glitsky interrupted him. 'How we doin' on Beaumont?'

'Pretty good.'

Glitsky waited.

'Couple more days.'

'You writing it all up?'

Griffin lifted his windbreaker to show Glitsky the notebook tucked into his belt. He patted it. 'Every word.'

There was no point in pushing. Griffin would tell him when he had something and he'd write it up when he got to it. Meanwhile, it sounded like he was moving steadily on at least two of his other cases. It would have to do for now.

But if Beaumont didn't close in a couple of days, Glitsky

39

knew he would have to pressure Carl to share his discoveries – he was starting to take heat about it.

'All right.' Griffin started to turn and for some reason, Glitsky said, 'Watch your back, Carl.'

A nod. 'Always.'

'Griffin wasn't the brightest light in the detail,' Abe said. 'You ever meet him?'

'Couple of times, yeah.'

'So you know. Anyhow, we figure he arranged some kind of sting, putting the heat on one of his witnesses. Guy might have been on something and didn't like the way it was going. Anyway, he didn't respond well under pressure, felt he was getting double-crossed, and shot Carl, something like that.' Glitsky made a face. 'We may never know for sure.'

Hardy clucked in commiseration, then gestured down at the file he was holding. 'So who's got the case now?'

Glitsky nodded at the stack of folders he'd just gone through. 'I got these off Tyler Coleman's desk. That one doesn't look much like it's been worked.'

'Why not?'

Glitsky shrugged. 'It's their sixth active. Time they got it – the thing's already over a week old. Priorities.'

Hardy knew. Homicide inspectors didn't want to waste their time – when the kill was no longer fresh, the scent disappeared. Suddenly, Hardy pulled the telephone around and punched for information. A minute later he hung up. 'Unlisted, of course. If it were listed, I could just call and save myself an hour, but I wouldn't want to do that now, would I?' He was on his feet. 'I've got to go. Are you going to be around?'

Glitsky checked his watch – nine o'clock. 'I was thinking about seeing Orel.' Glitsky was a widower with a fourteen-year-old son at home. He tried to make some time for him every day. Some. Now he looked across the desk into the worried face of his friend. 'You get something, call me at home. Fair?'

Hardy pointed a finger – they had a deal – and hit the door running.

As Hardy drove out to the site of Bree Beaumont's death, he realized that it was going to take some kind of miracle to get Frannie out of jail tonight. Even if he convinced this guy Ron, Frannie's *friend* Ron, to divulge his secret, then what?

Glitsky had counseled him against calling on Judge Braun at her home, and he was right. It would only make matters worse, and perhaps get Hardy his own contempt citation. He had to put it out of his mind and take things one step at a time.

But he kept getting distracted. He couldn't understand it. How could Frannie have let this happen, degree by degree? Now the family truly had a problem that was going to impact both him and their children in a major way. And all because Frannie had simply gotten her back up. At any point, she could have done something differently and avoided this mess.

But she hadn't and that had something to do with Ron, something personal.

He didn't want to follow that train of thought, which of course made it irresistible. What about if Frannie was simply a novice at covering her tracks, at making excuses? She'd never had to learn those tricks before because she'd never cheated before. They'd always told each other everything. But now, suddenly, with Ron (whoever the hell he was), with his dead – no, his *murdered* wife – things had changed.

Frannie hadn't even mentioned the subpoena?

Hardy couldn't imagine getting a subpoena to appear before the dogcatcher, to say nothing of the grand jury, and not discussing every detail of it with his wife. What had he done? How was he connected? How should he act? What did it mean?

And yet Frannie had been summoned, *days ago*, to be a witness in a murder investigation and hadn't mentioned it to him even in passing?

Didn't want to bother him with it? He didn't think so. He didn't think that was it at all.

Something else was in play here.

He missed his left turn on to Broadway, immediately swerved – not in time – and, swearing, slammed his hand on the wheel so hard that he thought he might have broken it. Finally, his insides curdled, he made the next left that presented itself five blocks later.

Why had he left Frannie at the jail? Allowed himself to be conned out to ask Ron Beaumont about his damned secret? He and Frannie had each other's trust or they had nothing. Something was very, very wrong with the picture, with Frannie's actions as well as her explanations for them. How could she have done this to all of them?

And, perhaps more fundamentally, what exactly had she done?

He opened his window to breathe in some of the cold, sea-scented air. It wasn't just anger after all. He brought his hand to his chest and pressed. His heart was beating strongly all right, but he felt as if a piece of it had been nicked away.

When it gets down to North Beach, Broadway is famous for its strip shows and tawdry tourism. But after it moves out of the old Italian neighborhood, through the city's longest tunnel, then across Van Ness Avenue, it begins to define the ridge of the escarpment that falls steeply down to Cow Hollow and the Marina. At this point, the avenue boasts some of the most impressive residential structures in San Francisco.

The palazzos of power brokers share the street with consulates and private mansions and estates. The mayor lives on Broadway; so do one of the state's US senators, the bestselling author west of Mississippi, the head of the country's most profitable fashion house, and the managing partner of the city's largest law firm. Broadway is the legal address and occasional residence of the heads of three of the ten most wealthy families in California. Overlooking, from a great height, the spectacular panoramic view of the Bay and both of its famous bridges, Broadway – particularly its north side – seems as far removed from the mundane cares of working people as it is possible to get. And yet, Hardy reflected, this is where Bree Beaumont had been murdered.

He had gotten his emotions back in check and was in the grip of what he knew to be a dangerous calm – he was sure it was his body's natural defense to his tendency to feel things too deeply, to fall prey to his emotions.

He would sometimes get this way at trial, his concentration focused down to a single point. He was going to do what he had to do and do it right. Later he'd reflect on it, curse himself, drink too much, laugh, get sick, whatever. But not now.

Now he'd act.

Double-checking the address, he pulled up and parked at the curb. Aided by his glance at the police report in Glitsky's office, he was recalling the story he'd followed in the newspaper after it had broken. He'd known that the woman, Bree, had been Max and Cassandra's mom, so it had been more than ordinarily compelling. But Frannie had – even then – never mentioned Ron.

What Hardy remembered was that the mother of some of his kids' classmates had been killed. Talk of politics. Big oil. Which meant big money. A beautiful young victim.

And somehow his wife was now in the mix.

The Beaumonts lived on the top floor of this monster, the penthouse – twelve floors up. The brass surrounding the glass double-door entry was polished to a shine. Inside, the expansive marble foyer which opened on to the elevator banks seemed to shimmer under a couple of enormous chandeliers.

But there was no getting in – the doors were locked, as Hardy realized he should have expected at this time of night. There was a night bell to one side of the door, which he pressed, but nothing happened.

He suddenly noticed a light flickering over one of the elevators. Somebody was coming down. Turning away, he walked about halfway back toward his car, then did an about face and waited until the couple came out of the elevator. He got to the door at the same time as they opened it going out and thanked them as he passed inside.

He rang another bell, this one from a bank next to the elevators, marked 'Beaumont,' and waited. And waited. It was a school night at half past ten. The family should be home, if this were in fact home anymore after Bree's death.

The elevator stood open before him and he stepped in, pressing the penthouse button. He didn't really believe anything would happen – in luxury residences such as this one, the elevator doors on the upper floors would often open directly into a living area. You needed a card or a key to go with the button. Much to his surprise, though, the doors closed and he started up.

He stepped out into a dimly lit lobby, ten feet on a side, with a hardwood floor covered by a Persian throw rug. Through a west-facing window, he could recognize the blinking lights on a tower of the Golden Gate Bridge. There was only one door in the lobby, and he was standing in front of it. But no one answered his ring, his knock. In a last gesture of futility, he grabbed at the handle.

And the door opened. 'All right,' he whispered. 'The kid gets a break.'

Behind him he heard the elevator door close, but he couldn't force himself forward immediately. He wasn't fooling himself. This wasn't a deserted residence. Aside from being a recent crime scene (although there wasn't any police tape), it was somebody's home, and entering it without invitation was trespassing. If he went in, he was putting himself at great risk. He might get himself confused for a burglar – always bad luck. If he got caught, he could be disciplined by the state bar, and perhaps lose his license to practice law. Unlawful entry was a very serious matter.

But there were times that called for risk and this, he told himself, was one of them. His wife had never been in jail before either. If Ron Beaumont came home – or a building superintendent or security guard for that matter – while Hardy was inside, he would explain the situation. Technically, he wasn't there to steal, so it wasn't a burglary. Hardy would say he was worried there might have been another crime. But really, he didn't care – he needed to find out where Ron might be, and the sooner the better.

In any event, fortified by his rationalizations – it was always good to have *some* story – he pushed the door all the way open, stepped over the lintel, and switched on the lights.

His first sight of the place stopped him cold. He thought he remembered from the newspapers that Bree Beaumont had been a professor at UC Berkeley who'd gone into industry. That may have once been true, but if the first glimpse of their abode were any indication, the Beaumonts had left academic privation far behind.

He closed the door behind him and was standing in an enormous sunken living room out of *Architectural Digest*. Wealth seemed to infuse the air around him. Framed modern original art graced the walls, each piece tastefully illuminated by recessed lighting. There were two seating areas – couches in leather and wing chairs in brocaded silk. Elegant end tables, coffee tables, a writing desk, a pair of matching marble pieces on pedestals. Along his right side, floor-to-ceiling windows displayed the glittering city below.

Following his eyes, he stepped up into a formal dining area – a granite table and six tubular chairs under an ultra-modern lighting device. A spacious gourmet kitchen was to his left across a bar of a dark space-age material.

Beyond the table – the wine racks, the little seating area off the formal dining room – Hardy got to the drapes covering the back wall. He pulled them back a foot or two, the dim light from the living room now all but lost behind him.

French doors gave on to a balcony. He opened them and stepped out, noticing the red Spanish tiles, a small, round outdoor dining table and chairs, and several plants. The balcony was neither large nor small, but the view made it magnificent. Facing due north, it was unimpeded for a hundred miles, especially on a night like tonight when a brisk breeze scoured the sky free of fog and haze.

It suddenly hit him – this was where Bree Beaumont had gone down. Walking to the edge of the balcony, he leaned out over the substantial cast-iron railing and looked down into what from this height appeared to be a square of light – the enclosed garden where she had lain undiscovered, apparently, for several hours. Stepping back, he sensed rather than felt a gust of wind out in front of him – it didn't even rustle the plants on the ledge, though it did raise the hairs on his neck.

But he was wasting time out here, taking in the sights. He had to get something to lead him to Ron and then get out if he was to do Frannie any good, if tonight wasn't already a wash.

He came back through the drapes into the sitting area off the dining room. In a moment, he'd passed through the kitchen into a hallway he'd ignored on his first pass. It led off the sunken living room to another wing, and on the first step in, he turned on the lights.

The room on his left had a blinking light that caught his attention. On a desk sat the telephone answering machine. It was an office, and as such, it might have what he needed. Crossing the room, planning to check first the messages, then the rolodex, then the computer, he heard a creak.

Frozen, he stood listening. A step back toward the hall. An unmistakable sound now, the front door opening. There was a shift in the light coming out of the living room into the hallway.

He had company.

6

There was no other option. Hardy cleared his throat loudly and went out to face whoever it was.

'Hold it right there!'

'I'm holding it.'

He was standing in the hall's entrance, his hands wide apart, palms out before him at chest height. He was looking at a man about his size wearing black slacks, tennis shoes, and a green windbreaker. The man was holding a gun as though he knew what to do with it, and this got his complete attention.

'You're Hardy?'

'Guilty.' He kept his hands in the air. It would be a bad time for a sudden movement to get misunderstood. 'I generally let the guy with the gun talk first, but maybe I should explain why I'm here. Are you Ron Beaumont?'

The man looked down at the weapon, then put it back into its shoulder holster. 'No. I'm Phil Canetta, a sergeant out of Central Station.' He came forward. 'You're Glitsky's pal.' It wasn't a question.

Hardy nodded.

'I was at the station when he called – he said somebody might want to keep on eye on you. You were on your way over here, and might need some help.' An aggressive look. 'I didn't expect you'd be inside.'

'The door wasn't locked. I tried it and it opened. I've got to find the guy who lives here. Do you know him? Beaumont?'

'No. I saw him the day of the murder, that's all. I did meet her a couple times.' Hardy must have changed expressions, since Canetta went on to explain. 'I do some moonlight security – convention work, parties. Caloco does a lot of that.'

47

'And Bree would be at these things?'

He nodded. 'Yeah.' Then. 'And when she was around, you noticed.'

'I saw her picture in the paper. Good-looking woman.'

Canetta almost angrily shook his head. 'Didn't come close.' Hardy wondered a little at the strong response, but Canetta was going on. 'So where is everybody?'

'I don't know. I hope they didn't run.'

'Were they close to bringing him in, the husband?'

'I think it's crossed their minds. Are you helping out on this murder somehow?'

He'd touched a nerve. 'Are you kidding? Station cops don't investigate murders. This is my beat, that's all. The day it happened, I got the call and showed up here, and secured the scene until Glitsky's people showed. The professionals.' He almost sneered the word, but then, maybe remembering that Hardy was Glitsky's friend, he got back to business. 'They must be at a movie, out to dinner, or something.'

The wall clock read almost eleven. Hardy shook his head. 'It's getting late for kids on a school night. But I don't want to just assume Beaumont's on the run, not when there's so many other alternatives. Maybe this place freaks out his kids. Maybe they're all with relatives.'

'Does he have any?'

Hardy wished he'd copied the file that Glitsky had given him. It might contain some of these details. There was one other avenue, but Hardy wasn't sure how to bring it up. He only knew he hated to leave before exploring it. 'You know,' he said, 'there's an answering machine in the office down that hall.'

'Eight calls,' Hardy remarked.

'Popular guy.'

'Either that or he hasn't been here in a while.'

Canetta nodded. 'I was going to say that next.' He pointed to the machine. 'Let's hit that thing, see what it says.'

Hardy pushed the button.

Whatever else was going on, Ron Beaumont either hadn't checked or hadn't erased his messages since one oh seven p.m. on Tuesday, two days ago. It was one of those systems that announced the date and time of the calls, so Hardy and Canetta could place them exactly. The first was a man named Bill Tilton who wanted Ron to call back about insurance and left his number.

Canetta had come up beside Hardy, borrowed a pen from its holder on the desk, and was scribbling into a spiral pad. Hardy thought this was a bit odd, but maybe the sergeant wanted to be an inspector someday, get beyond station work. He also might simply want to solve a murder and rub it in homicide's nose.

The machine kept talking. A woman with an Asian name – Kogee Sasaka? – called to remind Ron about their appointment, although she neglected to leave her number or the time or place of it, or what it was about.

James Pierce from Caloco. Asking Ron to call him back. There were some questions about Bree's effects and he'd like to come up sometime and . . .

Another woman: Marie. Just calling to say hi.

Moving through Tuesday afternoon. Al Valens. Something about Bree's files, some new data she had been working on.

'Both sides of the fence.'

Hardy pushed the pause button. 'What's that?'

'The first guy, Pierce, and this new one, Valens. He works with Damon Kerry.' The candidate for governor. 'His campaign manager.'

Hardy turned back to Canetta. 'For a station cop, you've got a pretty good handle on this case, don't you?'

A defensive shrug. 'I read the papers. Whatever they say downtown, there's no rule says we're not allowed to think.'

'So what do you think about these guys, sergeant – Pierce and Valens?'

A moment of hesitation, seeing if Hardy was playing with

49

him, then deciding he wasn't. 'Something with Bree's work, I'd guess. They're on opposite sides in these gas additive wars.'

'So what would they both want with Ron?'

A moment's consideration. 'He must know something.'

'About her work?'

'I don't know. Maybe. That's what I read. It was her work.'

'That got her killed? That means it probably wasn't Ron.'

'I don't know. Maybe not.' Canetta shrugged with what Hardy thought was an exaggerated nonchalance. 'Which brings us back. Maybe Ron knows something.'

'I wonder if he knows what it is.'

Canetta nodded. 'Or finally figured something out. If it was her work. Maybe that's why he ran, if he did.'

Hardy knew next to nothing about gas additives or the wars related to them. His concern was limited to his wife at the moment. But if Canetta needed to air his theories, it wouldn't hurt to listen. He pushed the play button again.

They'd gotten to Wednesday morning now, yesterday. *Déjà vu* as Hardy heard Theresa Wilson's voice again, from Merryvale. The Beaumont children hadn't yet arrived at school and she was calling Ron to find out why, where they might be.

Hardy hit pause. 'So if we assume the kids were at school and got picked up Tuesday, he left right after that.'

Next up was Marie for the second time.

Then the last voice. 'Hi Ron. You know I told you about this subpoena I got? I'm worried. I'm sure they're going to want me to talk about you and Bree. We need to get together to keep our stories straight. But don't call here after about six thirty. I'll try to reach you again when I can talk. Are you there? Ron?' The tape went silent.

' "Keep our stories straight," ' Canetta said into the vacuum. 'That doesn't sound very good, does it?'

Hardy turned to him, his voice flat. 'That was my wife.'

Canetta fixated on Frannie telling Ron that they had to keep their stories straight. To Hardy, the most telling line had been

50

when she told him not to call after six thirty – not to call, that is, after Hardy might be home. Again the truth jolted him – it had been no simple oversight that had kept her from mentioning the subpoena to him. She wanted to keep her relationship with Ron hidden and this realization, though maybe predictable, hit him like a jab to the solar plexus.

But it wouldn't be smart to share his reaction with Canetta. The point was that there were no hints about Ron's disappearance on the answering machine. Hardy wasn't going to locate him, not tonight, and that meant he wasn't getting Frannie out of jail.

To Hardy, it was obvious that Canetta was consciously resisting the urge to talk about Frannie's involvement. The sergeant cursorily rearranged a few items on the desk. When he'd stalled long enough, he straightened up, turned around, and cleared his throat. 'Well, since we're here, we might as well make sure nobody's dead in the other rooms. What do you say?'

They walked down the hallway and turned into the first of the bedrooms, a child's room with a twin bed made up neatly with a white lace bedspread. There was a collection of dolls on the bed and a decent-sized pile of beanie babies in the corner. On the wall, stenciled roses in half-a-dozen colors bloomed on the powder-blue sponge-painted wall.

Canetta walked directly across the room and opened the top dresser drawer. 'Look at this.' Hardy came up behind him. Except for a couple of pairs of socks, there wasn't anything to see. 'They're gone,' Canetta observed. 'We'd better be, too.'

On the way out, Hardy made sure the front door was locked behind them. The two men rode down the elevator in an awkward silence, then crossed the lobby and stepped outside.

'What's your plan now?' Canetta asked.

Hardy didn't know. It was late and nothing had worked. He shrugged. 'Try to find him. See if his kids are in school. If not, tell Glitsky, I suppose. If he's on the run . . .'

A silence fell and Hardy sighed.

'Your wife?'

A nod. 'They've got her locked up at the county jail. The two of them, Frannie and Ron, he told her some secret . . .' Again, he just trailed off. It sounded so lame. 'She told me he'd never let her stay down there if he knew she was in jail, but it was his secret to tell, not hers. She promised him.'

Canetta had no solace to offer. Hardy could see what he was thinking and, worse, didn't blame him. 'Well, good luck.'

He drove around for a while, trying to decide whether to visit the jail again, go home and sleep, or wake up a judge. Everything felt wrong. Finally he wound up on Sutter Street, in front of David Freeman's building, where he worked.

Upstairs in his office, Hardy called and woke up Glitsky at home. The lieutenant agreed that Ron Beaumont's disappearance – if that's what it was – increased his profile as a murder suspect. It didn't help Frannie either. Finally, Glitsky promised that he would get in early tomorrow and talk to Scott Randall, maybe try to pull a string or two at the jail, but he didn't hold out much hope.

After he hung up, Hardy thought a moment and seriously considered a night raid on Braun's house, maybe getting David Freeman to accompany him, to make his case to the judge. But he knew he'd only make things worse with any kind of spontaneous act in the mood he was in.

He had to think, develop a plan, stay rational. But the thought of his wife lying on one of the jail cots, surrounded by scum, terrified and unprotected, made this a tall order.

It took very little imagination to see her there, curled under the thin fabric of the institutional blanket. Smells of disinfectant, sounds of desperation. Wide-eyed and sleepless on the unyielding mattress, wondering what she'd done, how it had happened. What tomorrow would bring.

Four days! Hardy suddenly sat upright with the realization. Braun had given her four days. She couldn't do four days, even in AdSeg. He knew his wife, or thought he did. Four days in jail would cause a lot of damage that would be a long time healing.

He sat trying to come up with something, anything. But it was the middle of the night, and the world was asleep. At a little after one o'clock, he accepted that he'd failed. He wasn't getting his wife out of jail today. If he didn't get at least a little rest, he wouldn't be any good for her tomorrow either.

There was nothing to do but go home.

But his night wasn't over yet.

His house was a railroad-style Victorian – a long hallway down one side with rooms coming off to the right – about fifteen blocks from the beach, well within San Francisco's belt of nearly perennial fog. He'd run into the wall of it, and by the time he'd reached his street, his windshield wipers were beating a steady rhythm. Of course there was no available street parking, but tonight he decided to take the risk and left his car in a no-parking zone right around the corner on Clement. He figured he'd be up and out before dawn anyway – most days the parking enforcers didn't get rolling until well after that.

The house sat between a brace of four-story apartment buildings and was set back maybe forty feet from the curb. Hardy couldn't see it until he was right in front. As he opened the gate through the white picket fence, he couldn't see Moses, either, sitting on the darkened porch with his back against the front door. 'Where is she?'

The surprise of the voice out of the dead night fog almost knocked him backwards. When he got moving again, he didn't waste any words. 'Still locked up. Let's go inside.'

Erin sat in her bathrobe, her feet up under her in the window seat, the blinds closed against the night and the fog. Moses paced in front of the fire's embers. Ed Cochran snored gently in Hardy's favorite recliner, so Hardy had pulled in one of the dining-room chairs and now straddled it backwards. After

53

twenty minutes of regaling them with the highlights of his frustrating night, he'd just asked if either one of them had heard Frannie talk about Ron Beaumont, his kids, Bree's death, or anything that might relate.

Moses stopped walking, folded his arms, and scowled. He loved his sister, but between his work as owner of the Little Shamrock bar and his family, they didn't spend a lot of time sharing special moments.

Hardy's eyes went to Erin. She shifted where she sat and looked somewhere off into the middle distance. 'Erin?' he prompted her. 'What?'

She came back to him. 'I don't know. I'm not sure it's anything really. She never mentioned anybody by name.' She hesitated and Hardy forced himself to wait until she figured out how she was going to say it. 'From the way she talked, I assumed it was another woman, one of the mothers from Merryvale, but it could have been part of this.'

'What?'

Erin sighed, hating to betray her own confidences, if that's what this turned out to be. 'This is all nebulous, but one of her friends – it might not have been this Ron or Bree – evidently had had a marriage go bad a long time ago, years. Now they had a new life here and suddenly this person was afraid the old spouse was going to show up and start causing problems.'

'What kind of problems?'

Erin shifted again, and picked at some thread on her bathrobe for a few seconds. 'Custody problems, I think.'

'But how could that be? Divorces don't get final until all the custody issues are settled. How did this come up, anyway? If this is her giant secret, I don't know why—'

'I didn't say it was, Dismas. I don't know if it had anything to do with this. That's about as far as it went anyway, then suddenly she didn't want to talk about it, maybe as though she remembered she couldn't.'

'That could be it,' Moses said.

Hardy wasn't so sure, but at this point he'd take anything.

'How did the whole thing come up in the first place?'

Erin shook her head, as though she were unsure herself. 'We were just sitting watching Rebecca and Vincent in the backyard here – it couldn't have been more than a couple of weeks ago. They were having one of their great afternoons, just playing and laughing and being wonderful.

'Anyway, suddenly, really out of the blue, Frannie said she couldn't imagine maintaining any kind of normal life if she thought someone were going to try to take away her kids. I told her she didn't have to worry – why was she thinking about that? So she started to say something about this friend of hers, just what I've told you, not anything really. She didn't mention a name, but now tonight when you asked, it occurred to me it could be this Ron.'

Moses piped in. 'It might explain why he ran.'

Hardy was desperate for answers, but he didn't think this was one of them. 'We don't know that he did run, Mose. He might be staying at Grandma's house for all we know.'

'Well, how can we find that out?'

Hardy was done in. 'I'm working on that,' he said.

7

On his best day, David Freeman would never qualify as debonair and charming, and this wasn't close to his best day. He sat now in the pre-dawn at his ancient kitchen table which was laden with yellow legal pads, pencils, wads of Kleenex, open and closed lawbooks, and a dozen or more unwashed (perhaps from the look of them never washed) coffee mugs. He wore the frayed remains of a maroon bathrobe that had been new during the Nixon years. Gray chest hairs peeked out the top of a similarly graying T-shirt. Of course he hadn't shaved – Hardy had buzzed him awake only five minutes before. His jowls hung, his hair rioted, and for good measure he was chewing the stub of last night's cigar.

'You know, David, if the law business ever fades out on you, I think you could go into the movies, become a leading man, maybe marry Julia Roberts—'

'Who?'

Hardy shook his head. 'Never mind.' If it didn't have to do with the law, Freeman probably didn't know about it and certainly wasn't interested.

And Hardy wasn't much in the mood for witty banter himself. He'd slept less than three hours before rolling out of his bed, which last night had been his front-room couch. He'd given his bed to Ed and Erin – and God bless Erin. She was taking care of the kids, getting them to school, covering all those essential bases. This was a great relief even though the situation filled him with guilt.

But Hardy couldn't waste energy thinking about the time he wasn't spending with his children. Frannie was still in jail. 'So I thought you'd talk to Braun.'

Freeman's lugubrious face didn't offer any solace. 'It's always a pleasure to chew the fat with Marian, Diz, but if you think she's going to let anybody out of jail on my personal say-so, you've got our relationship wrong. How did your sweet wife get herself in so deep?'

Hardy outlined it briefly. David shifted the cigar butt to the other side of his mouth. Hardy started to say something, ready to stand up for Frannie's integrity, to explain away her insult to Marian Braun, but the old man held up his hand. 'It doesn't matter what she did, Diz, or why. You ought to know that by now. Just wait. Let me think a minute.'

Freeman was justly famous in San Francisco as much for his courtroom theatrics as for his knowledge of the law. The point was that he got results in an extraordinary number of cases and he didn't care how. As a defense attorney, his legal mandate was to provide the best defense the law allowed, and whether that included arguing some arcane legal point or standing on his head and spitting wooden nickels, that's what he'd do. He was damn proud of the fact that he had no pride.

And now he was thinking strategy. Frannie might not be his client, yet, but he'd gotten lots of folks out from behind bars in his time, and at base that's really what Hardy was asking him to help with. 'It seems to me that we've got two separate contempt charges – the secret, then getting smart with the judge. Am I right?'

Hardy nodded.

'OK.' Freeman pondered. 'I don't think we've got a *habeas* on the secret. Randall's got every right to throw her in jail if she won't spill it. Talk to Susan McDougal.' Hardy thought it was typical of Freeman to show no interest in Ron Beaumont's secret. 'But if she'd apologize to Marian, say maybe they were both having a bad day – would she go there?'

Hardy wasn't sure – a lot of things involving Frannie were in doubt lately – and he said so.

'Well, if she would that might get us to first base. Then maybe we hit Randall, or Pratt, but that'll be a tough nut, too.'

'Glitsky's already working on that.'

Freeman shook his head. 'You think a police lieutenant is going to persuade Randall to let somebody out of jail? A lieutenant, I might add, who somehow got himself out of the loop on this particular homicide, and didn't even know the grand jury had convened over it? I think you're whistlin' Dixie. Obviously something's going on here between the DA and the police. Glitsky's not the way. Randall will stonewall him.'

'How do you know? You know Randall?'

'I caught a couple of his closing arguments for fun. He's a hell of a trial lawyer, but I don't know what he's made of inside. I can't imagine jailing an otherwise good citizen over this unless he knows it's the key to a murder conviction. It wouldn't be trivial. It would help to know if he's got political ambitions.'

'Why's that?'

Freeman regarded Hardy as though he were a slow five-year-old. 'If he is, we use the media. Call a press conference and make him look like an unreasonable, detestable, miserable son of a bitch keeping a good mother from her loving family. But there's a flaw with that, too.'

'Which is?'

'Your typical prosecutor, it makes his day to keep mothers from their families. As you know.'

Hardy used to be a prosecutor and he remembered. It wasn't exactly that he had wanted to separate mothers and children, but he'd never shed a tear over sending someone he'd convicted off to jail, even if a relative or lover was sobbing horribly behind him in the courtroom, which happened quite frequently. So Freeman was right – Hardy shouldn't put any hope in a media campaign with Scott Randall. 'But Pratt might be different,' the old man said. 'She's got to care about public reaction, about votes, right? We've got an election here in a couple of weeks.'

'Unfortunately, not Pratt's. She's got two more years no matter what we do now. Still, we can try it,' Freeman conceded,

58

though it was plain he considered it a long shot. 'Of course, after her night in jail, Frannie might have decided that this precious secret of hers isn't the hill she wants to die on. Especially when she learns her friend may have left town.'

Hardy was at the jail at six forty-five, and they let him inside at seven sharp. Freeman was going to talk to Marian Braun, and try to make some apology with which Frannie would go along. He hoped. He also knew that Glitsky would light a fire under the homicide inspectors working the Beaumont case to find Ron.

But first there was Frannie. He had to see her again, get some sense of what was happening, and to that end he was here.

The door to the visitors' room opened and she stood still, as though afraid to move forward, perhaps afraid of him. The guard shot a questioning look at Hardy. 'This OK? You ready?'

And as the door closed behind her, Frannie took one step into the room.

'He wasn't home.' Hardy was using his 'I've got bad news' lawyer voice, uninflected and neutral. Reciting facts. 'Ron wasn't there. He's moved out.'

She didn't look any better than she had the night before, but she didn't look worse, either. Maybe she'd slept a little. The worst thing was this tension that seemed to keep her from moving forward. Hardy had spent so much time punishing himself for his inability to get her sprung out of jail that it had never occurred to him that she might be harboring similar self-loathing feelings for what she'd put him and the kids through.

Something in her look – and that thought struck him now. He would take the first literal step, reaching for her. With a heart-rending sob, she fell into his arms.

'I couldn't tell you last night, Dismas. Abe was there, remember. He came in just as we got to it, or started to.'

'So tell Abe, too.'

She shook her head. 'I couldn't do that. I told Ron that I couldn't promise not to tell you, that I told you everything, but Abe wouldn't be the same thing at all.'

'Couldn't you have just asked him to leave last night, step outside for a minute?'

'No, not in front of you. Then he would have known I'd told you something, wouldn't he? And what could that be except Ron's secret? He wouldn't have let it go. You know Abe. It's not a matter of trust, but he's a cop. He's always a cop first, even with you.'

Hardy knew she was right. A couple of years before, he'd had a case where he'd gotten confused on that point, and Abe hadn't talked to him for several months. If Abe knew that Hardy was holding a secret that related to one of Abe's cases and didn't tell him about it, it would be tricky at best. Frannie had saved him from having to deal with that.

She sat next to him, her hands holding his on her lap. She was still in jail, but at least they were talking now, man and wife again. What he really wanted to know about was the relationship between her and Ron, but he wouldn't ask that specifically. It shouldn't matter. She was his wife and she needed his help. That was today's issue; when she was out of this situation, he'd deal with the rest of it.

Also, he told himself that if it did matter, if something threatening to their marriage was going on, then she should tell him – she *would* tell him, wouldn't she? He knew that the betrayal of failing to tell would be worse than anything she might have done. She would tell him.

But he couldn't ask directly. He'd go general and see how she went with it. He put on his lawyer face, and asked in his least aggressive tone, 'So what's this all about?'

Frannie was using his hands as a pair of worry beads. He noticed she was shaking and took off his nylon jacket. He put it over her shoulders.

The guard knocked and said she was going to miss breakfast

if this meeting didn't end, but Hardy with his vast legal expertise finagled a couple of cups of coffee and this morning's food unit, biscuits and gravy, for which they waited a few minutes in an uncomfortable silence.

Why doesn't he ask me? she was thinking. Can he really care so little that he doesn't even ask? If it were me, that's the only question I'd have, about me and Ron.

He's been in this business too long, that's it. It's changed him so fundamentally. Now he sits there so cold and clinical and he's got another *case*, another problem to solve. Never mind if his wife's been unfaithful. He just wants to know what *happened*. Just the facts, ma'am – but it wasn't a Joe Friday joke with him. It was his essence.

Please, Dismas, would you just care enough about us to ask?

She tried to will him to talk, but he only sat at the table, patient and understanding, waiting for her breakfast to be delivered. Occasionally he would squeeze her hand, the way he might comfort any female client.

She wanted to punch him.

When the tray arrived, Frannie took a few quick bites. She was famished. She had been so upset last night that she'd been unable to get down any of her evening meal. Finally, she put the plastic spoon down and sipped at her coffee. 'OK.' She spoke to herself in a near whisper, as though afraid that even in this private room, someone would hear. 'But this has to stay between us.'

'This secret that can get you out of jail? You want me to know and not use it?'

'That's the only way I can tell you, Dismas. That's what I promised Ron. I can't tell you as my lawyer, especially not as my lawyer. Only as my husband. You'll understand when you hear what it is.'

Hardy wasn't sure this would prove to be true – he wasn't

understanding much of this as it developed – but he knew he had to know, and to know he had to promise not to tell.

He wasn't comfortable with any part of the idea. And beyond his own personal reservation, there were two other basic, professional reasons for his reluctance to make this promise. As a licensed attorney, he was an officer of the court, obliged to cooperate with law enforcement in a whole slew of public matters.

The second reason was even more fundamental – if Frannie told her secret to him as her lawyer, it would be protected under the attorney-client privilege. No court could make him reveal it – it was a shield. What Frannie was asking was fraught with danger. As a private citizen, he could very easily find himself called before the grand jury and in the same position as his wife, unable to testify, tossed into the clink. Beyond that, if he got into any investigation about Ron Beaumont, and he couldn't claim privilege, then he could very easily picture himself having to lie about what he did or didn't know to the very people – Glitsky, Canetta – who might be helping him. It was ugly in all respects, and he tried to explain it all calmly to Frannie.

But she wasn't budging. 'No,' she still spoke in a near-whisper, but her voice was firm. 'What will happen is that you'll trust the privilege.'

'And? What's your point? That's how it works.'

'But sometimes it doesn't. Sometimes the system doesn't work.'

'Uh oh,' Hardy said.

'What?'

'The system doesn't work. That oldie but goodie greatest hit of the sixties. Except I get nervous when I hear it. Because I'll tell you what – sometimes the system does work.'

'It didn't in Ron's case. It betrayed him.' Her eyes had some of that old spark back in them, although Hardy wasn't especially delighted to see it. She reached out toward him and her voice softened. 'Dismas, you have to believe me on this.

Ron had a reason not to trust lawyers, you'll see.'

'I don't doubt that,' Hardy said. 'I don't trust too many of them myself. But this is me.'

'You the person, not you the lawyer.'

He hung his head and shook it from side to side. His wife had her hand on his knee. He drained the last gulp from the plastic cup of tepid coffee. 'All right,' he said, 'I promise. It's between you and me-the-person, me-the-son, and me-the-Holy-Ghost. Let's hear it.'

Frannie took a last look back toward the door to the room, making sure no guard lurked to overhear. Then she came back to Hardy, took a breath, and began. 'Ron and Bree had been fighting a lot over this change in her jobs.'

Hardy didn't like this opening. 'I really hope that after all this preamble you're not going to tell me, "Oh, yeah, I remember. He did kill her after all." '

The concept wasn't all that funny, but she forced a smile. 'He didn't kill her. He was with me when she died.'

Whether or not this was good news remained a question, but he wasn't saying anything about it right now. 'All right. I'm listening. What were they fighting about?'

'Well, her old job with the oil company was evidently pretty great. Anonymous but big money. She did her research and wrote her papers and nobody paid too much attention out in the real world. She was kind of a star in-house. I mean, she played a big role paving the legislative way for this three-billion-dollar industry, but she wasn't really a public figure.'

'But when she signed on with Kerry, that changed?'

'Right. She started getting a lot of press right away about all the problems with these oil additives.'

'So why was this an issue with Ron? I mean, if she was the one working, why did he have any say in it?'

'Same reason I have some kind of input on what you do, the clients you take. At least I think I do, don't I?'

This was true. Frannie wouldn't want him to defend, say, the tobacco companies, or a mass murderer, and if he decided he had to/wanted to/needed to, they would certainly have words on the topic. But this whole area didn't need to be aired, not this morning on top of everything else. Hardy glossed over it. 'You're right. But we're not talking about me and you. We're talking about Ron and Bree, and they were arguing, right?'

'Right.' She was tightening up, as clipped as he was. But he had to keep pushing her. He had to know.

'OK, and what were they arguing about? Politics? Money?'

But Frannie surprised him. 'No, nothing like that. It was the kids. Ron's kids. Max and Cassandra.'

'They weren't her kids?'

'No. Ron was already divorced once. They're his from that time.'

'OK. And?'

'And what?'

'How was this new job going to affect the kids?' Suddenly Hardy remembered the discussion he'd had with Erin and Moses last night. 'Is this the custody thing you mentioned to Erin?'

A look of chagrin, her own carelessness coming back to hurt her. 'How did Erin connect that with Ron? I never mentioned him.'

She didn't even mention him to Erin? This news – more secrets – didn't make his heart sing. But Hardy had a craggy smile he could trot out for juries, and he employed it now, a deflection when something really bothered him and he didn't dare show it. 'I think some crafty lawyer might have helped her. But I'm missing the connection here. Job and fights, OK, but how does that relate to custody?'

Frannie wasn't ready to say exactly, not just yet. 'Ron thought she was sacrificing the safety of *his* children for some vague notion of all future children.' At Hardy's uncomprehending gaze, she pressed on. 'She had come to believe that these gas additives were ruining the water supply. She was all worried about cancer clusters and deformed babies.'

'And St Ron didn't want her to expose all of this? Why not?'

She frowned. They were getting to the crux of it. 'Because the more Bree became a public figure, the better the odds that Ron's ex-wife found out where he was.'

'And why would that be a problem? For the children, I mean? Was she a stalker, something like that?'

'Not exactly.'

He waited, then had to prompt her. 'Frannie.'

It sounded to Hardy as though she were trying the words out for the first time, to see how they flew. 'She was abusive.'

'Who? The ex-wife?'

A nod. 'Dawn. Her name was Dawn. She was' – Frannie seemed to be stumbling over the words – 'uh, she was starting to try to make money off the kids. Ron found some pictures.'

'Are we talking kiddie porn here?'

Frannie nodded.

Hardy blew out a long breath. 'Jesus.'

'So he filed for divorce, but even before it got to court, she started accusing him, saying *he* took the pictures. And the judge believed her and she got custody.'

'But he's got them now.'

'I know,' she said. 'He had to take them back.'

'What do you mean take them back?' It took a beat for the meaning of it to sink in. 'Are you saying he kidnapped his own children?'

Frannie didn't like that terminology. 'Maybe technically, but that wasn't what it was. He was saving them. And then, after he'd gone through all that, Bree was going to threaten the whole—'

He held up a hand. 'Wait a minute, wait a minute! Forget about Bree. You're telling me Ron lost the custody battle in court and then he took the kids? When was this?'

'About eight years ago.'

Hardy sat riveted to his chair, barely hearing her.

She continued. 'He managed to get set up out here, change

65

his name, get together with Bree. And everything was going along fine until she got involved with this Kerry ...' She stopped.

Hardy couldn't hold back the sarcasm. 'Everything was going along fine except that he was wanted for kidnapping?'

'But that wasn't a real problem—'

'Yes it was, Frannie. I don't care what he told you.'

But she was shaking her head. 'No. That was over. Nobody was looking for him anymore. There wasn't a problem until he and Bree started fighting, and he thought even that would blow over until—'

Hardy cut her off again. His earlier, patient, and understanding persona was taking a beating. 'Until she had the bad grace to get herself killed.' He dragged his palm across his forehead. 'So where is he now?'

'I don't know.'

He tried to keep his voice modulated, but wasn't entirely successful. 'You realize of course that if the police get anywhere on this, they're going to come to the conclusion that he killed her. The truth is, *I* think he killed her.'

'He didn't kill her, Dismas. He's desperate. He's trying to save his children.'

'He kidnapped his children to save them. Maybe he killed his wife to save her. Or here's a thought – maybe he killed his wife to save the kids again. Maybe he'll kill you next.'

'He didn't kill anybody. He's not going to kill anybody.'

Hardy would have said that he was at the end of his tether when he'd arrived at the jail. Now there was no doubt about it – he was completely wrung out. Frannie's hollow denial gonged in his ears, but he knew he was powerless to convince her of anything but what she already thought. Not today in any case, not now.

He consciously reined himself in, sought a different path. 'So Ron's gone and you're here. Telling the grand jury what you know can't make any difference now to him.'

'Of course it can. If they search for him and find him,

they'll take his kids. But they're not even trying to locate him yet – you told me that.'

'They will be, Frannie. He's going to be their prime suspect as soon as he's officially missing, which is going to happen like two minutes after Abe starts looking for him. By Tuesday morning when it meets again, the grand jury's going to indict him for Bree's murder, you wait and see.'

This hard fact – and Hardy believed it was the whole truth – finally seemed to get through to her. She slumped back in her chair, hugging his jacket around her. When she looked up at him, the fight had gone out of her. Still, she wasn't backing down. She said it flatly. 'He didn't kill her, Dismas.'

He sighed. 'All right, let's go with that. Either way, what do you want me to do now?'

8

Lou the Greek's was a dark bar/restaurant in the basement of a bail bondsman's building across the street from the Hall of Justice. When Hardy was at court, he'd often stop into the place for some kind of lunch or a drink at the end of the day. Lou the Greek had married a Chinese woman and every day she would put together her own version of California–Asian cuisine.

All over the city, celebrity chefs were making their reputations and fortunes by marrying the finest ingredients from the Pacific Rim and creating stunning masterpieces – lobster ravioli in a lemon-grass-infused beurre blanc, tuna sashimi over tuscan white beans with thyme and wasabi mustard. Here at Lou's you'd get stuffed grape leaves with sweet-and-sour sauce, fried squid floating in a bowl of dip made from garlic, cucumbers, and yoghurt. Surprisingly, most of Lou's wife's stuff tasted pretty good even if the architecture of the plate, as they called it, left a little something to be desired.

But it was still hours from lunchtime, and Hardy wasn't there to eat anyway. He was tucked into a corner booth around a mug of coffee, waiting for David Freeman.

After leaving Frannie, he'd gone by Glitsky's empty office, leaving a note about Ron's disappearance, then went down to the third floor to confront Scott Randall personally – physically wasn't even out of the question.

Even though it was well past eight o'clock, there wasn't a soul in the entire DA's wing. And they wondered why their conviction rates were in the toilet. Convictions, hell – they didn't even *charge* crimes in San Francisco at the same rate as in other counties.

So Hardy went to Lou's to wait, perhaps to try and think. He'd all but forgotten about the existence of the drinking breakfast crowd – guys and girls who were here when the door opened at six a.m. and had a couple of beers or a Bloody Mary. He recognized half-a-dozen fringe players from around the Hall and wondered how many of them recognized their need for a morning pick-me-up as any kind of danger sign.

But being a supercilious bastard was an easy game to play. At the moment, he didn't feel he had much of a leg up on any of them. His wife was still in jail and all of his training, discipline, sobriety, and connections weren't doing her any good at all.

For half a second he considered downing a couple of shots of something, put himself into creative mode, and out of his linear head until some great idea presented itself. Except that those great wet ideas, and he'd had plenty, never seemed to make the cut after the hangover.

Lou was silent with a surly edge this morning, and that suited Hardy to his toes. He pushed his mug toward the side of the table and got it topped up just as David Freeman slid into the booth across from him. 'Hey Lou, give me one of those fast, would you? Three sugars, black. Christ, it's dark in here. You ever notice that, Diz?'

'The food looks better that way. What did Braun say?'

Freeman wasn't in any hurry to get to it. He fiddled with his jacket for a minute, and squirmed down into the leatherette seat. 'Marian. You know I took her out a couple of times when we were both starting out. Everybody called her Marian the librarian of course. Great legs.' Freeman sighed, remembering, then clucked sympathetically. 'She used to be a lot more fun.'

'We all did, David.'

'Not true. Take me, for example. I'm in my prime. Have been for a while, actually.'

'I'm happy for you,' Hardy replied. 'What's the opposite of prime? That's where I am. What did Marian say about my wife?' Freeman had his hands folded on the table between them. Lou was back with his coffee and Freeman pulled it over in front of him, blowing on it, stalling. 'David?'

A glance over the mug. 'Truth is, and she didn't make any bones about it, she's not too happy with her.'

'Truth is, I'm not so much either.'

A pause. 'So I gather she didn't tell you the big secret?'

Hardy shrugged that off – he didn't even want to start trying to explain this mess to David Freeman. If he got even a taste of the bone he'd gnaw it to dust. 'She says it's a matter of honor. She gave her word and she can't tell.' He made a face. 'But that wasn't the issue with Braun anyway.'

'No,' Freeman agreed. 'Though that might have been better. If it was only a matter of law . . .' He let it hang there.

'She's pissed?'

'Very.'

Hardy swore. 'Would it help if I talked to her? Got Frannie to apologize? Did you tell her there are young children involved here?'

'I brought out the heavy artillery, Diz. She doesn't – how can I put this? – give a shit. She said Frannie's done it to herself. Braun's never in her career had anybody show such disrespect for the bench.'

'That's got to be an exaggeration.'

'It doesn't matter if it is if that's how the judge feels.' Freeman shrugged. 'The two of 'em got into a cat fight, Diz, that's what happened.'

'But Frannie didn't *do* anything, David. She's going along living her life, *our* life. She's not a criminal, not even a suspect for anything—'

'Material witness.'

'Not even that, not really.'

Again, Freeman's maddening nonchalant shrug. The law was the law. You could rant about it all you want, as people complained about the weather, and to about as much effect. 'It's the grand jury, Diz. You know as well as I do. Hell, you've even used it.'

Hardy couldn't deny it. Grand juries had awesome power. When he'd been a prosecutor, going before the grand jury had been one of his favorite pastimes. He would take a recalcitrant witness, put him in front of the panel without his attorney present, no judge to keep things on point, and keep that poor sucker up there for hours, often without a food or water or bathroom break, asking leading questions, doing whatever it took to get his evidence on to the record, because that's what the grand jury was for.

And though Scott Randall was certainly abusing it now, Hardy had to remember that the grand jury had come into existence, and still functioned, as a vehicle to protect civil rights. Because of its secrecy provisions and the teeth with which infractions against them were enforced, the grand jury was the only place where prosecutors could get answers from scared or recalcitrant witnesses, where the truth could come out. Nobody could ever know you were even there or what you might have said. You were safe – from your enemies, from corrupt officials, from the prying media.

In theory, anyway.

But now Frannie. He would not have dreamed this could ever happen to someone in his personal life. And never to his wife. Frannie wasn't living on the edge of the law. She wasn't like the others. Except that now, to Marian Braun and Scott Randall, it appeared that she was.

Even after all of his experience with the law, this perspective hit him with almost a concussive force. The law could happen to anybody. Again, Freeman's analogy with the weather. A hurricane had just swept Frannie up, and now she was in it.

But Freeman was resolutely moving ahead, as he did. Problem-solving. 'Have you talked to anybody yet who's found the husband, what's his name?'

'Beaumont. Ron Beaumont. No, Glitsky wasn't around. I left him a note. I'm going back up after we're done here. But let's not leave Frannie.'

'I'm not leaving her. I think we ought to go to the newspapers with this after all. Even if Randall and Pratt don't fold, Marian might be responsive to that kind of pressure. At least it's worth a shot.' He drank some coffee. 'But I think we need to consider cutting our losses.'

'Which are?'

'The four days. Unless they locate Mr Beaumont and can get him to talk, she's got herself a bigger problem than four days.'

Scott Randall was sitting in a folding chair, his legs crossed comfortably. With him in the large but spartan expanse of Sharron Pratt's office were homicide lieutenant Abe Glitsky, homicide sergeants Tyler Coleman and Jorge Batavia, and Randall's own DA's investigator Peter Struler. Randall was having himself a fine morning. At last, things were moving along on Beaumont, and all because of this Frannie Hardy woman.

Sometimes, he reflected, you just had to take prisoners.

And if it got to that, as it had here, then invariably you alienated some people. In this case, it was Glitsky and his sergeants. Well, Randall thought, maybe next time they got a hot homicide they would try to keep their investigation alive even if there happened to be a crisis in the department. For now, they just had their noses out of joint because Randall and Struler had actually made progress on a case they considered all but closed. Turf wars. Too bad for them.

But Glitsky, as head of the homicide detail, naturally had to put a different face on it. Now he was barking at Pratt. 'I *know* this woman, Sharron. She is a close personal friend. She watched my kids for a month after my wife died. She should not be in jail.'

'Evidently Judge Braun doesn't agree with you, lieutenant. I'm not sure I do, either.'

Pratt didn't like Glitsky. She thought the police were out to undermine her authority, and make her look bad whenever and wherever they could. For her part, the DA took every opportunity to criticize the force. She'd run for office on a platform of stomping out police brutality – nowhere near the greatest of the city's many problems. The Police Department union had supported her opponent and she wasn't likely to forget it.

She would often choose not to have her office prosecute a suspect that the police had already arrested because she didn't believe in so-called victimless crimes. So at least every week or two she'd simply set free suspected prostitutes, druggies, and other assorted misunderstood persons.

But she wasn't going to release Frannie Hardy. No siree. There were legal principles involved here. She was standing her ground. 'Isn't this woman,' she asked, 'isn't her husband the attorney? He used to work at this office, didn't he?'

Randall spoke up. 'Until he got fired.'

Glitsky shot him a look. 'He quit.'

Randall didn't rise to it. 'Check the record,' he retorted mildly. Back to Pratt. 'Dismas Hardy, and he was fired.'

Pratt's mouth turned up a millimeter, a beaming smile for her. 'Ah, yes. I've tried to work with him before.'

Glitsky noted the emphasis on the word 'tried' and Pratt's use of it didn't bode well for the Hardy camp. But he wasn't through fighting for Frannie, not by a long shot. 'Look.' He summoned up a conciliatory tone. 'Sharron. We don't have any evidence at all that connects Ron Beaumont to this murder. We're looking at him, sure, but by all accounts he was in fact out having coffee with Mrs Hardy when his wife was killed. Even Mr Randall doesn't dispute that.'

But Scott wasn't going to let Glitsky put words in his mouth. He piped right up. 'It's a big window of time. Actually, there's a lot of room for doubt.'

But this wasn't where Glitsky wanted to pick his fight, so he resisted the urge to snap back. Instead, he rolled his eyes and pressed on. 'And if we find that Mr Beaumont fits into that window of time, we'll probably get closer to a warrant.

But that's my point. Right now the investigation is nowhere and—'

'Precisely why I took it over and gave it to Senior Investigator Struler here.'

Glitsky tried to ignore Randall, to direct himself to Pratt. 'The original investigating officer *died*, Sharron. There wasn't any intentional foot-dragging.'

'I haven't heard anyone make that accusation, lieutenant.' Pratt smiled again, thinly. 'But the point, my point, is that Mr Randall was conducting his own investigation due to the . . . unfortunate lack of progress that yours was making.' Glitsky started to open his mouth, but she stopped him, holding up a hand. 'And in the course of his investigation, Mr Beaumont became a suspect for the murder, and so his associates became relevant targets for interrogation.'

'OK,' Glitsky conceded, 'and Frannie Hardy didn't answer a question.' He turned to Randall. 'Do you have any idea how often our witnesses don't answer questions, Scott? If we locked any percentage of them up, *any percentage*, one two per cent, we'd have to rent the whole city of San Bruno just for the warehouse space to hold 'em.'

Randall wasn't hearing it. 'But this a murder case, Abe. We're not looking for some shoplifter here.'

Glitsky all but exploded. 'What do you think I'm talking about? I'm *in* homicide. All I see are murder cases, and I don't get a witness in a hundred who'll tell me what time it is if there's not something in it for him and his dog.' He modulated his voice again, feigning a calm rationality that fooled no one in the room. 'What I'm getting at, Sharron, is that this may have been an over-reaction on all sides. Frannie should have been given a day or two to go home and think about what she would be comfortable—'

'Comfortable!' Randall's turn to let go. 'I don't care if she's comfortable. I don't want her to be comfortable. She knows something critical to a murder case—'

'You don't know that!'

'– and until she tells what that is, we've got a murderer walking around on the streets—'

This time it was Batavia who interrupted. 'You're out of your mind, Randall. You got nothing. You're nowhere here. She's probably just fucking the guy and doesn't want her husband to find out. The lieutenant's right. You got nothing on Beaumont. No motive, no means, opportunity. Forget it. Let the lady go, would you? Jesus. I got to go to the bathroom.' And with that, he was out the door.

'Charming gentleman,' Pratt said.

'Good cop,' Glitsky responded.

Randall came forward in his folding chair. 'I don't care if he's the king of England. He's not giving me any suspects, so I develop my own and build my case. And from where I'm sitting, Frannie Hardy's right in the middle of it.'

Glitsky caught the eye of Batavia's partner, Tyler Coleman, gave the secret sign, and they both stood up. 'I wish you'd think about it some more, Sharron. This is really wrong.'

She looked him right in the eye. 'I will, Abe. I promise.'

While Glitsky and Coleman were waiting for the elevator, Batavia emerged from the hallway behind them. 'If assholes could fly,' he said, 'that place would be an airport.'

Glitsky himself tried to limit his profanity to a word or two a year, but he appreciated a well-turned phrase. The scar between his lips tightened in amusement. But Coleman was still seething – implicit in everything that had just transpired in Pratt's office was the accusation that he and his partner had booted one. 'If there's such a fire under this one, Abe, why didn't we hear about it?'

The elevator door opened and they squeezed in amid the rest of the clerks, cops, lawyers, and citizens. Glitsky had at one time decided that it could be an instructive display of authority to talk in a crowded elevator, and he answered Coleman as if they were alone in his office. He also thought it wouldn't be all bad if some spy from the airport – he hoped that Batavia's new nickname for the DA's office would have a long life – heard him taking Mr Scott Randall to task for his misguided enthusiasm. Maybe he'd also drop a little rumor about Scott's ambitions that his boss wouldn't appreciate all that much.

'Randall wants a high-profile case, that's all, Vince. He wants out of this low-rent office, into the big private money. This building's not big enough for him, so due process takes a powder.'

Batavia was also immune to elevator squelch. His voice boomed in the enclosed space. 'But he doesn't have a goddam thing, Abe. Like I said in there.' The doors opened and they stepped out. 'What's this window of time shit, anyway? Everything we've read or heard, the guy was dropping the kids at school, going for coffee.'

But here, though he hated it, Glitsky had to admit that technically, Randall wasn't all wrong. He had to give Coleman and Batavia his reading that even if Frannie's alibi was righteous, Ron Beaumont still could have killed his wife. Bree's body hadn't been discovered in the patio for several hours, and the coroner hadn't been able to fix a precise time of death. 'It could have been three hours plus or minus,' he concluded. 'We're going on around eight thirty on the theory that Ron left the house a little before that and says she was still alive.'

'The kids say it, too. How about that?' Batavia wasn't ready to give anything to Scott Randall.

But Glitsky knew that the homicide cop's worst enemy was imprecision. Well, maybe second worst after jumping to conclusions, but certainly way up there. He corrected Batavia. 'I hate to say it, Jorge, but the kids were a little vague.'

Coleman popped in. 'Hey, it's two days after their mom *died*, for Christ's sake, and they didn't remember what she had for breakfast. I don't blame 'em. Hell, I don't remember what I had for breakfast today. I don't even know if I *ate* breakfast.'

'Donuts,' Batavia said. 'Remember, Lanier brought up—'

'Guys!' Glitsky stopped at the door to the homicide detail. 'The point is, Ron's not eliminated, OK?'

Batavia wasn't letting it go. 'The kids said the mom was there, Abe.'

Glitsky shook his head. 'Ron prompted them. Read the one transcript Griffin got around to getting typed. Carl didn't get the kids to talk to him with their father out of the room, and not to speak ill of the dead, but I do so wish he had. And let's not forget that Ron has left his home and gone to parts unknown.'

'All right. Shit.' Batavia had a habit of dismissing himself. He was turning now on his heel, on his way to his desk.

'Jorge!'

It was his lieutenant. He had to stop.

'We're not done here. This is still our case. Randall hasn't charged anybody.'

He took a step back. 'I thought you just said—'

Glitsky cut him off. 'I didn't say it was Ron. I said he wasn't impossible. But one thing's for sure – he's Randall's guy, isn't he? I mean, the DA's committed to Ron Beaumont now. Nobody else. You hear what I'm saying?'

Coleman did. He looked at his partner. 'Anybody else would be, like, a teeny tiny embarrassment, don't you think?'

Glitsky watched his inspectors, making sure they both got it. As Batavia's face broke into a smile of comprehension, he pointed a finger. 'Go,' he said.

'But I've got to find Ron,' Hardy said. 'How about your guys find Ron first, then they start on everybody else?'

It was a long-standing tradition in homicide that the lieutenant's desk held a stash of peanuts. Glitsky was taking advantage of this naturally occurring phenomenon, eating a hearty breakfast of donuts, peanuts, and tea. He broke a shell thoughtfully. 'You got any ideas where we look to find Ron?'

'No. But he's got to have some family. Maybe somebody

at the school, who he'd want them to notify in case of emergency . . .'

A reluctant sigh. 'OK, that's not bad. We can try that. I'll send a squad car back to his place, too. Couldn't hurt. But I wouldn't hold my breath, Diz. If he took his car and he's gone – what did you say, three days already? – then he could be in Chicago by now. If he flew, it could be anywhere.'

'OK, but if he flew, especially with the two kids, there's a record of it.'

Glitsky was shaking his head slowly, sadly. His friend hadn't gotten much sleep and it was showing. 'Diz, you know I'm feeling for Frannie. I just went a few rounds with Pratt over it. But we can't go large on Ron. We don't have the personnel and if we did they'd have better things to do.'

'Abe, the guy's a murder suspect—'

'Maybe, maybe. But he came in and talked to the grand jury when they asked him, and answered all their questions. They were done with him. Nobody gave him a thought as a suspect until Frannie mentioned their little secret.' He threw a peanut into his mouth and grabbed for his tea. 'Randall didn't even tell him not to leave town. Maybe they went camping, or to Disneyland. Who knows? The mom just died, Diz. They feel squirrely where she lived. It's weird there. This stuff happens. What's up with Frannie?'

Hardy shook his head. 'She's not talking.'

Glitsky did his still-life imitation. After a few seconds, he cracked another peanut. 'Braun cut her any slack?'

'Nope.'

Another long moment of nothing. Finally Glitsky spread his hands. 'Well . . .'

Hardy stood up. 'This can't be happening,' he said.

Glitsky had lost his own wife to cancer a few years before. That couldn't be happening either. He nodded. There wasn't anything left to say.

78

9

Hardy finally got finished at the Hall and the jail – his latest frustrating and unproductive visit with Frannie. After that, he had stopped by his office to check on Freeman's progress, if any, and then, waiting for Freeman to return from court, had nodded off. When he awoke from the two-hour nap on the couch in his office, nothing had changed.

He couldn't sit still any longer. He had to make something happen.

Glitsky had promised him that he'd send a squad car over to Merryvale to try to get an indication of Ron Beaumont's whereabouts, but that wasn't going to be good enough. It would fall under the category of ordinary business – Hardy doubted whether Glitsky would even send homicide inspectors. Some uniforms could take the information and pass it along upstairs. Well, Hardy decided, why should he wait when he could do the same thing himself?

Merryvale's principal, Theresa Wilson, was a no-nonsense, handsome woman in her mid-forties. She was standing as Hardy was shown into her office. Her handshake would have been impressive in a linebacker and her smile under a close-cropped henna mop appeared at the same time to be both genuine and professional, also impressive. She didn't hide behind her desk, either, but met him by the door, leading him to a small corner grouping of upholstered chairs. 'Mr Hardy. I hope your being here doesn't mean bad news for your wife? Please, sit down.'

The bare-bones explanation took less than a minute. It was a misunderstanding about some point of Ron Beaumont's alibi on the morning of his wife's death, and somehow Frannie had gotten in the middle of it.

'But that's terrible! She's not under any kind of suspicion herself I hope?'

'There's no sign of that so far.'

Mrs Wilson read between the lines of that. 'So how long might this continue? Until they let Frannie out of jail?'

A shrug, downplaying the drama of it. 'Best case, it might only be a couple of days. She thinks Ron Beaumont's gone camping or something with his kids and when he gets back and finds out what's going on with her, he'll come in and straighten out the whole mess.'

'But you don't think that?'

'No.'

'What do you think?'

'I don't know if Ron killed his wife, but my guess is he started to feel some heat from the police investigation and decided to take his kids and run.'

'But I thought . . .' She paused.

Hardy read her mind. 'The alibi with Frannie was solid, but evidently the time of death opened another door. He thought he was going to be arrested. At least that's my opinion.' He leaned back into the chair's cushion. 'And it's why I've come here to you.'

She looked him a question.

'I realize you're probably not allowed to give out any information about your students, but I was hoping you might be able to tell me if you know I'm wrong.'

'How would I?'

'Well, say, if the Beaumont kids have been in school the last couple of days, if Ron's given some kind of excuse . . .' Hardy gave her a weary smile. 'It looks like he's moved out of his home, probably Tuesday afternoon. I'd like to know if you've heard anything from him since then.'

As he expected, she was torn between his dilemma and her duties as principal. 'Ron Beaumont is a wonderful man, Mr

Hardy. He volunteered here all the time. Really. I don't believe he's any part of this either.'

But that wasn't Hardy's dilemma. He had to give it more urgency. 'Please, Mrs Wilson. I want to be clear that I'm not asking you to tell me where he is, if you know. Also, if you're protecting the children, OK, I understand. They must be having a rough go of it no matter what's happening. But if you've heard nothing, then I think that increases the chances that Ron is on the run, either that or' – a sudden, new possibility – 'or something's happened to him.' He stopped, elbows on knees, hands spread. 'Please,' he repeated. 'If I don't find him, Frannie stays in jail.'

After an excruciating minute, Mrs Wilson stood up and crossed to her desk, where she reached over, grabbed at a folder, opened it, and withdrew a sheet of paper. Another beat of hesitation. She turned around, crossed back to Hardy, and handed him the paper.

'I'm really not allowed to discuss any details of the children's lives without the parents' consent, as I know you understand.'

It was a list of about twenty names under the heading 'Absentees' and the day's date. There were asterisks next to four of the names, and two of them were Beaumont. There was also the number three in parentheses, which Hardy took to mean number of days running. At the bottom of the page, an asterisk indicated that the absence was unexcused.

Mrs Wilson hadn't heard a thing. The children were gone without a trace.

'You don't think something's happened to Mr Beaumont and his children, too, do you? Maybe the person who murdered his wife . . .?' A startled expression at the unthinkable that had just surfaced. 'You don't think it could have been him after all, do you?'

'I sure hope not, Mrs Wilson. Let's not think that, OK?'

Hardy was waiting by the curb outside Merryvale when the

81

bell rang to end the school day. Vincent was in the car almost before Hardy saw him. Ginger-haired after his mother and freckly, he was the all-American ten-year-old boy. 'Where's Mom now? Why are *you* here?'

He was sure that his son didn't mean it to sound so accusatory, so unwelcoming, but there it was. He'd better deal with it, since he had a feeling it was going to get worse after his daughter arrived. Rebecca had developed an impressive knack of late, pushing his buttons, not letting anything go.

Driving down on his way to the school, he'd decided how he'd break the news, on his precise phrasing. 'Your mother's down at the jail.' This had a decidedly familiar ring in the family – since Hardy himself was often visiting clients who were behind bars, his children were accustomed to hearing the words. They wouldn't, by themselves, produce trauma. He hoped.

And when he tried them on Vincent, they seemed to go down well enough. 'What for?' he asked, still calm.

Hardy went for the noble spin. 'They wanted her to tell a secret that she'd promised not to, and now—'

'Where's Mom?' Rebecca had the back door open, throwing backpack and lunch pail into the car in front of her. 'She promised she'd be helping paint our class's Hallowe'en booth – she *promised* – and it was today and—'

'Beck, hold it! Hold it.'

'She's at the jail,' Vincent piped into the silence. He appeared to be delighted with the news, and definitely happy to be the one to break it. Finally he got to tell his sister something she didn't know.

Although for a moment it didn't register. 'Well, she promised me *first*. There were two other moms waiting and waiting and she didn't even call and so here I am with my friends and their moms showed up, and I'm all embarrassed—'

Hardy snapped his fingers and pointed directly at her. 'Stop it! Right now!' His daughter glared sullenly back at him. 'Did you hear what your brother just said?'

82

She turned to Vincent, easier pickings. 'What?' she snapped.
'Never mind anyway.' Power play of the fourth graders.

Hardy thought he'd better get driving so he wasn't tempted to thrash his children right there in front of the school where everybody would see.

The Beck's teasing, na-na-na voice. 'I don't care. I heard you anyway.'

'Oh yeah? So what did I say, braceface?'

'Vincent!'

'You said she was in jail, stupid.'

This brought the wail. 'Da-ad! You heard that. The Beck just called me stupid.'

'*He* called me braceface first.'

'Tin grin!'

In the back seat, something was thrown, something connected. Vincent was screaming and swinging.

'Hey, hey, hey!' Hardy knew his face had gone crimson. Somehow he'd pulled over to the curb again and turned around in his seat, at the top of his voice. 'Stop this stupid, stupid bickering and fighting. Stop it right now!' Another finger pointed, this time at Vincent. 'And don't tell me I'm not supposed to say "stupid." *This* is stupid! Don't you two ever think about anything but yourselves? I said your mother's in jail, and you're screaming at each other about *nothing*, just to hear yourselves scream.'

'You're the one screaming.' The Beck had self-righteous indignation down to a fine art. She was right and that was just too bad for the rest of humanity.

'You didn't say "*in jail*,"' Vincent wailed as hysteria mounted. More tears broke. 'You said she was down at the jail, not in jail.'

So much for Plan A.

At last, Rebecca seemed to hear. 'Mom's *in* jail? What do you mean, *in jail*? How could Mom be in jail?'

Vincent: 'When does she get out? What did she do? Are we ever going to see her again?'

Now they were both crying.

'Daddy,' Beck asked, anguish through her tears. 'How could you let this happen?'

Finally, finally, after they got home, he and Erin and Ed succeeded in convincing the kids that Frannie was going to be OK. This was a funny glitch in the legal system, which they were always hearing Dad talk about anyway, right? This time it had just happened to their family.

Mom was sticking up for a friend of hers and Uncle Abe was there, working right across the way, taking care of her. And sure, she might be gone for a few days, but she was all right, in a really nice cell – 'a country club,' in fact. It was kind of like a vacation for Mom, and the Beck and Vincent got to stay with Grandma and Papa Ed for the weekend. It would be fun, an adventure. There wasn't anything to worry about.

10

Hardy, alone on Friday evening, pacing his home front to back, was trying to come to some – any – conclusions and develop a plan. All he knew for sure was that he would go back and see Frannie again tonight, freshly armed with the news that Ron hadn't simply gone fishing or something. If that had been the case, he would have told Mrs Wilson and there would have been no asterisk.

But he knew that this information wasn't going to sway his wife. She would tell Hardy that of course Ron had had to disappear. Because of his children, he couldn't let the law get involved with him. He would have had no choice.

And, fool that he was, Hardy had promised Frannie that *he* wouldn't reveal what she had told him, whether or not he believed a word of it. Never mind that he'd lost his claim to attorney-client privilege; he realized that he'd done something that was potentially far more debilitating. He couldn't talk to anybody about this – not Glitsky, Freeman, Moses, Erin, nobody. He shouldn't ever have promised Frannie, but now that he had, if he wanted to keep faith with her, he was stuck.

The telephone jarred him from these thoughts. Sometime before he must have stopped pacing because he was sitting at his kitchen table, a cup of coffee untouched and cold in front of him. The light had changed as another afternoon's load of fog had settled outside. He stood and picked up on the second ring.

'It's going to be on the five o'clock news.' Freeman wasn't much of a preamble kind of guy. He heard Hardy's voice and he was talking. 'I called a press conference and it must be a slow news day. Everybody came. You should have been here.

This is where the action is. What are you doing home anyway?'

'I'm picking out new curtains for the bedroom,' he said. 'What's going to be on the news? Frannie?'

'And Braun. And Randall. They loved it, they ate it up. I wouldn't be surprised if it hit the national wires. If I were you, I'd expect some calls myself pretty soon. Play up the wife and mother torn from her family part.'

'What other part is there?'

Freeman hesitated. 'Well, there's probably going to be some reporters with dirty minds, too. You might take this as a heads up, not blow off on them.' Then, back to strategy. 'I really think this might get to Pratt, persuade her to pull the rug out from Randall, and get him to reconsider. What do you hear about Bree's husband?'

'He left town.' Hardy told him about checking at Merryvale. The kids being gone.

'Do the cops know this?'

Hardy realized with a shock that they probably didn't. He hadn't thought to call Glitsky because the lieutenant had told him he wasn't really interested in Ron Beaumont as a suspect. But Freeman was right. His running changed that. 'I'll call as soon as I get off with you.'

'You ought to get to Frannie, too. She discovers that he's really run, he looks like a murder suspect, she might want to change her mind about protecting him.'

'That's a good idea,' he said, biting his tongue. 'I'll do that.'

'Check the news first,' Freeman said. 'Starts in about five minutes, channel four.'

'I'm on it. And David, thanks.'

Freeman laughed. 'Are you kidding? This is what I live for.'

He thought the idea of calling Glitsky was a good one. Although his inspectors would be happy if they found a suspect other than Ron for the murder of Bree, the fact that Ron had apparently fled the jurisdiction would have an impact on Abe. He'd have to do something.

'Why is that?' the lieutenant asked, exasperation starting to leak out. 'What do you want me to do?'

'Find him, Abe. He looks a lot better for the murder now. You've got to admit that.'

'Maybe a little better, but Scott Randall's already out beating the bushes trying to find him. The feeling here is that it might be fun to watch him for a while.'

'And meanwhile Frannie's rotting.'

Hardy could hear the patient exhale over the telephone line. Another beat. 'Have you made any progress with Judge Braun? Did Freeman?'

'No.'

'Well, then it looks like Frannie's in for four days no matter what, doesn't it?'

Hardy had no ready answer for this. It was the truth.

Glitsky went on, logical and detached. 'Ron could walk in here tonight with a signed confession including everything Randall wanted from Frannie, and my understanding is that it wouldn't make a hill of beans difference. Am I wrong?'

Hardy knew he wasn't. Frannie was in jail on two, separate contempt charges. Even if she talked now, she would still have to complete paying her personal four-day debt to Marian Braun. And on the other hand, even if Braun rescinded that citation, Frannie would remain in jail on the secret until Scott Randall said she could go.

Hardy knew all this, although it wasn't any solace. 'Look, Abe, maybe I can still get Braun—'

' "Maybe" is the key word here. Look, Diz, I've pleaded with Pratt, I've tried to bully Randall, I've been over to see Frannie twice and make sure they're taking care of her, which it seems like they are. I don't like this any more than you do.'

'I know, Abe. I'm not saying you're not—'

'But anything to do with Ron Beaumont isn't the issue for the next three days. Your immediate problem is with Braun.'

'But if you found Ron, put out a warrant, got other agencies looking . . .'

'Then what? That's going to happen when the grand jury reconvenes on Tuesday anyway. They're going to indict him unless my guys find somebody else and then the whole world will be looking for him. So they'll probably find him. But even then, if he's a killer he's not going to say anything. Then what's Frannie going to do?'

'I don't know, Abe, I just don't know.'

'Lord.' The cop voice softened. Abe clearly felt for him, was even trying to help on several fronts, but there just wasn't anything he could do. 'What do you think, Diz? She give you a hint what this is this all about? You got any ideas at all?'

He had to force the words. 'Not a clue, Abe,' he lied. 'Not a damn clue.'

Fifteen minutes after the news ended, he had his coat on and was walking out the door when the telephone rang again. He was sure it was the beginning of the onslaught of the reporters, and was going to let his answering machine get it while he drove downtown. But then he remembered that it might be Erin or the kids, so he decided to monitor the call and stood listening at the hallway extension.

'Hello?' An unfamiliar voice, probably a reporter, and one who was good enough to have scored Hardy's unlisted number. He sounded obviously disappointed that it hadn't connected with his interview. Well, Hardy didn't want to talk to reporters. He got to the front door, on his way out. The voice continued. 'I'm trying to reach Dismas Hardy. My name is Ron Beaumont and I just saw the news report on—'

Hardy grabbed at the phone and said hello.

'Mr Hardy, how are you?'

'Well, not so good, to tell you the truth. You know they've got Frannie in jail?'

'That's why I called you. It was on the news and I thought I might be able to help.'

88

'You could. Where are you now?'

A pause. 'Uh, I'd rather not say. Not too far away. I thought it would be smarter to get away before the police decided I was their suspect.'

'The police haven't decided that. It's the DA.'

A dry laugh. 'Same thing to me. I can't afford to get in their sights. Did your wife tell you about . . . about the situation here? With me?'

'Yeah. We talked.' Hardy knew he sounded furious, impatient. He was. He didn't feel compelled to dissemble for poor Ron the prime mover. 'The thing is, Frannie's in a pretty damn bleak way right now. She's already done a night in the can.'

'I know. I feel terrible about that. That's why I'm calling, to find out if there's anything I can do.'

'You want my recommendation?'

'Yes.'

Hardy gave it to him straight. 'You come see me now, give me a note to take to Frannie at the jail and tell her she's got your permission to talk to the grand jury. She takes this word-of-honor stuff pretty seriously.'

'Obviously you do, too.'

Hardy didn't answer that. He wasn't sure how far his nobility would go if Frannie stayed locked up much longer. But for the moment, let Ron think whatever would help Frannie. 'The point is, she needs to tell the grand jury. Or you do.'

A long silence. Then, 'You must know I can't do that.'

'Sure you can. You give Frannie permission to talk, then go back to wherever you are now. You said you're still local. You can just—'

'I didn't say that.'

Hardy wasn't going to get into semantics with him. He'd said he wasn't far away, and that was good enough for now. 'OK, you're not local. But wherever you are, you want to help Frannie, right? Isn't that why you called here?'

'But I can't—'

'Look, you can. I'm a lawyer. I can broker this thing through the courts—'

'No, you don't understand, that's not happening. Last time I tried to play by the rules and do things through the courts. I had a good lawyer, then, too. You know what happened? The courts gave my kids to their mother. You hear what I'm saying? The rules don't give the kids to the father. I can't have that again. I can't take the risk.'

'There doesn't have to be a risk. It doesn't have to come up at all. All they care about is if you killed your wife. If you didn't, you go back to your normal life.'

'No, I don't think so. That's what I'd like, but I don't see normal life in this picture anymore.'

Hardy took a beat, lowered his voice. He was sweating in the cool house, his hands white around the receiver. He let out a breath, spoke softly. 'Then I really don't understand why you called. I don't know what else you can do to help Frannie.'

After another pause, Ron Beaumont finally said, 'I'll try to think of something. I'm sorry.'

'No, wait! Maybe we—'

The line went dead.

'He wouldn't even write you a damn note, Frannie. How about that?'

His wife didn't let it faze her. 'I know he wants to help.'

'Oh yes,' Hardy dripped with sarcasm. 'He's all for helping. He just doesn't want to do anything.'

Arms crossed, her body language swearing at him, she spoke through tight lips. 'What could he do? What can he do that wouldn't threaten his kids?'

'How does it threaten his kids to let you talk? He stays hiding. Besides, tell me why they're not threatened right now.'

'You've said it yourself. Because he's not a suspect. Even Abe said it on TV. The police aren't looking for him.'

That had been, Hardy had to admit, one of very few sweet

moments in an otherwise disastrous day. Glitsky would undoubtedly wind up paying hell for saying that there wasn't any evidence to arrest Ron Beaumont for murder. The DA would complain to the chief. They'd foot drag even more than they already did on his cases. Even so, to Glitsky it was probably worth it.

But that wasn't why Hardy was here. 'How about *our* children? Don't you see that they're a little threatened here? How can you not see that?'

'Don't you dare patronize me,' she snapped. 'Of course I see that. Don't you think this is . . .' Her eyes flashed with fire and tears of rage. 'This is *impossible*! Don't you think I see that, I feel that?' She whirled in the small space behind the table in the attorneys' visiting room. Nowhere to run. 'But what do you want me to do?'

'That's an easy one. I want you to give him up.'

'And his kids?'

'It's either his or ours, Frannie. Doesn't seem like that tough a call to me.'

'Just give him up?'

He thought that maybe, at last, she'd heard him. With an effort, he reined in his temper. 'He's gone anyway, Frannie. He's on the run. It's going to look like he killed Bree as soon as that gets out. Then he's really in the news and the whole story – kids and all – comes out anyway. Then what's all this been for?'

Her face remained set. 'It's not there yet.'

'What isn't where?'

'Nobody's going to look into Ron's life. Not unless he gets charged. Ron isn't anybody's focus.'

'Yes he is,' Hardy said. 'He's mine. He's Scott Randall's.'

'Oh, that's real nice. That's swell, Dismas.' Frannie spit the words out at him. 'Side yourself with my pal Scott Randall.'

'I'm not siding with Scott Randall. Jesus Christ. I'm trying to get you out of here! I'm trying to put our family together again and all I get from you is poor Ron fucking Beaumont.

Because I'll tell you something, Frannie. He and his kids, they're gone.'

She looked up at him defiantly. 'You always think you know everything. You've got everything figured out. Well, I'll tell you something. No they're not gone. He called you an hour ago. He doesn't want to run. He wants to go back to his normal life. Don't you see that?'

Deflated, Hardy rested a haunch on the corner of the table. 'Don't you see that that's not going to happen?' he asked wearily. 'It's not going to happen no matter what.'

'It will if they find who killed Bree.'

Hardy shook his head. 'Not true, Frannie. That's just not true.' He forced a persuasive tone. 'Listen, on Tuesday, the grand jury is going to reconvene and by then Scott Randall – even without Glitsky's help – is going to discover that Ron has cut out. That's going to be enough to get him indicted. After that he's high profile. Then it all comes out.'

'OK, that's Tuesday,' she said. 'If somebody, maybe Abe, can find Bree's killer before that, some real evidence—'

'Unlikely.'

'Why?'

'Because it's already been three weeks. The case is dead. You're talking three *days*? It's not going to happen.'

'What if Ron helps? What if he tells everybody what he knows about Bree?'

'Tells who? Like Abe?'

But, infuriatingly, she shook her head. 'He can't get involved with the police.'

'Oh, that's right. I almost forgot. And while we're at it, are you saying he didn't tell the police all he knew when they asked last time?'

'No, I'm not saying that. And you don't have to be such a bully. He answered their questions—'

'But just sort of forgot to volunteer anything interesting he might have known about his own *wife's* murder? Give me a break, Frannie. This is ridiculous.'

She slammed her fist on the table pathetically. 'It's not ridiculous. Don't you see the tragedy of all this? Don't you care about anybody else? Don't you have any feelings anymore?'

'Oh, please . . .' He was up now, spun around on her. 'I've got more *feelings* than you can imagine right at this moment. I *feel* like killing the son of a bitch, for example. I *feel* like what's going to happen to our kids without their mother, what's going on with our marriage for that matter.'

He glared at her, but she said nothing. No denial, just a cold stare back at him.

'Shit,' he said, and walked as far away as he could, up against the glass block wall, and stood there.

Her chair scraped. A second later he felt her behind him, although their bodies didn't touch. 'Help him,' she whispered. He couldn't think of a thing to say and she spoke into the vacuum. 'You've told me I'm in here for another three days anyway, no matter what, isn't that right? That's got nothing to do with the secret.'

Glitsky's distinction, but what was Frannie's point? 'So?'

'So if you're right, they won't indict Ron until Tuesday. Which means that the kids – that whole thing – it won't have to come out until after that, and never if he doesn't get indicted. That means you have three days.'

He turned. '*I* have three days.'

'Yes.'

'For what?'

'To save some lives, Dismas.'

'And how do I do that?'

'You find Bree's killer.'

He hung his head. His wife had no idea what she was talking about. 'Oh, OK. I'll just run out and do that. Why didn't I think of that before? It's so simple.' He turned. 'Any bright idea of where I might begin?'

'With Ron,' she said. 'I told you he wants to help.'

'Well,' Hardy responded. 'Old Ron didn't get around to

telling me where I could find him. Maybe next time he calls—'

'I might know,' she said.

There was a hole in the floor, a so-called 'Turkish toilet,' against the back wall, a block of concrete with a mattress on it, and on the mattress a sheet and two gray woolen blankets. There was no sink. The walls were padded because the administrative segregation unit was where they put the bona-fide crazies before they got medicated.

The door closed behind her – she hardly realized and certainly wasn't grateful that it wasn't bars but a true door with a peephole and a place to slide food in on the bottom.

She stood, numb and mute, without moving for a minute or more.

At some level, she was aware of the cold coming up through the paper slippers she wore. Everything was cold.

Overhead, there was a light, recessed behind wired glass. The light would go off sometime soon and plunge the cell into darkness.

There was no control anywhere.

She alternated between not letting herself feel anything, or reacting to everything. Last night, when the light had gone off, she'd cried for nearly an hour. Tonight, the darkness itself would no longer matter. She could tell that already.

She was trying to feel her children, to imagine them with Erin, at least warm and safe. But the connection was gone for now. In its place was only the physical stuff here – the bed and the padded walls and the smell of disinfectant.

Maybe, she told herself, her emotions had played them-selves out. But an aura of panic seemed to shimmer around that thought, as if maybe her emotions had been cauterized so deeply that now they had been completely burned away, and she'd never let herself feel anything again, not at a certain level anyway.

And then her husband. Every time he came, all she felt she could do was fight and argue and explain. When all she wanted was the understanding they used to . . .

But she wouldn't be weak. Weakness would leave her helpless, unable to make decisions for the kids if it came to that.

What was it going to come to?

No, she would just put feelings away for now. Dismas was on her side – she would believe that. He was working for her interests, as well as his own and the children's. Though their intimacy was lost, perhaps irretrievably. It certainly felt that way. She knew she bore some of the blame for that.

For all of this.

She had never planned to do anything wrong and now all she had done had gotten her to here. Why did she still feel as though she should defend herself, that it was all defensible? Everything felt wrong. Every decision and act had cost her and her family dearly.

Would anyone ever forgive her? And why should they?

Abruptly, the cell went dark.

An undetermined period of time passed during which she remained motionless. Finally, she reached for the bed, found it, and pulled the blankets to her chin, holding them fisted against her chest.

She couldn't imagine her babies – where they were, if they were sleeping. And this, finally, brought the blessed tears.

11

In another lifetime, when Hardy had been a prosecutor with the very district attorney's office that he now despised, he sent people to jail all the time. Because his first wife, Jane, had been worried that some of his convicted and dangerous felons might get back to freedom with a chip on their shoulders, Hardy had applied for a CCW – carry a concealed weapon – permit. In the normal course of events, this would have been denied, but Jane's father was a Superior Court judge, and it got approved and, through some combination of politics and inertia, got renewed every year.

Over the years, Hardy had had occasion to take one of his guns out with him twice. Neither time did he have to fire at anyone, although once he had enjoyed letting off a round for the immediate and gratifying effect.

Yet tonight, in a kind of cold fury, grabbing for a weapon didn't feel strange at all. It was a little past dusk, and he was taking his Colt .38 Special out of the safe where he kept it since the Beck had been born. He hadn't even held the damn thing in a couple of years, but when he'd last taken it to the range, he'd cleaned, oiled, and wrapped it carefully in its cloth before putting it away.

Now he lifted it out and unwrapped it. A wipe with the rag and the finish shone. He checked to make sure that it was unloaded, then spun the cylinder and worked the action several times.

On the way back from his visit with Frannie, he had decided – if that was the word; the impulse had been more spontaneous than cerebral – to carry the piece. He probably couldn't have said why – surely not to shoot the man who might be sleeping with his wife. If he had a thought about it at all, he would have said that the gun might be persuasive in moving Ron to do what Hardy asked, whatever that might turn out to be.

So he wasn't going to be home for long. Frannie had told him where Ron had once told her – she remembered after she found out he'd fled – where Ron's first stop might be if he needed to run.

Hardy hadn't told Frannie that he *was* going to confront Ron. No more impetuous promises. And his wife, perhaps having erroneously concluded that Hardy had been converted all the way to Ron's side, hadn't demanded any.

Wearing jeans, a blue shirt over a rugby jersey, and a pair of running shoes, he stood in the dim light in the back room behind the kitchen and slid the bullets where they belonged. He stuck the gun into his belt, pulling the blue shirt out over it. He put the rest of the box of bullets back into the safe, carefully closed the door, and spun the lock.

On the way out, he grabbed a jacket from the peg near the front door.

It hadn't taken five minutes and he was back at his car. Ready.

Ron Brewster.

Now he was Ron Brewster. Frannie had explained it all to Hardy, thinking she was making points for Ron, showing her husband the lengths to which this great guy was willing to go to protect his children.

But the excuses and lies that he ran into every day in his criminal practice had honed Hardy's natural cynicism into a sharp-edged and profound skepticism that cut a swath through normal human feelings, at least whenever the law was involved. Although he fought it in his home life and with his few close friends, he found that he didn't take much at face value anymore. He tended not to believe interesting stories – there was always something else that didn't get said.

Frannie's explanations of Ron's behavior – his easy skill

with name change, for example; his successful kidnapping of his own children – only convinced Hardy that he was dealing with a very intelligent and resourceful criminal. One who had at the very least conned Frannie, and at the worst much more than that.

As if he needed more fuel to fire his rage.

They were at the Airport Hilton. Hardy had seen it before in people who were fleeing – the first instinct was to go to ground. Stay close. See which direction your pursuers took and then light out the other way.

Fifth floor, room 523. A 'Do Not Disturb' sign was affixed to the doorknob.

Hardy checked his watch. It was precisely nine sixteen. The sound of a television came from behind the door. Canned laughter.

He felt for the gun in his waistband, felt its reassuring presence, and left it where it was. He knocked.

Within a second, the television was turned off. And now behind the door there was only silence. He knocked again, almost tempted to call out, 'Candygram.' Instead, he waited, giving Ron every chance to do it in his own time.

Ron Beaumont held a finger over his lips, telling his children to make no sound. He crossed to the door of the hotel room. He, too, had a gun with him, but it was packed now in the false bottom of a suitcase.

He had to pray it wasn't the police, or, if it was, that it was only one man. Then he might be able to talk himself a couple of minutes, enough time to get to his suitcase, do what he might have to do.

Hardy gave it another knock, harder. 'Ron! Open the door!'

Another couple of seconds. Then, from behind the door, a firm voice. 'We're trying to sleep.'

Hardy leaned in closer, spoke with controlled urgency. 'This is Dismas Hardy.'

Finally the door opened, but just a crack. Ron had turned off the lights inside the room and left the chain on. Hardy had to fight the impulse to slam his shoulder into the door and break the chain free.

Hardy spread his hands wide. No threat. Just open the door and let's talk.

Ron Beaumont was a handsome man, though Hardy hated to admit it. Strong, angular features and clear, brown eyes set in cheekbones so chiseled that now, with his evening stubble, they looked like you could strike a match on them. An aquiline nose with a high bridge was perfectly centered over what Hardy supposed would be called a generous mouth. The full head of dark hair had a streak or two of gray at the temples, although the unlined face made that seem premature, or even dyed. Almost exactly the same height as Hardy's six feet, he weighed at least ten pounds less, and none of it was soft.

The door was open and he moved to the side to let Hardy in.

All the way down from the Avenues to the airport, Hardy had indulged in fantasy, savoring the moment of confrontation when he, goddamit, *made* Ron 'fess up to his responsibility to Frannie, to the damage he'd done. The other stuff, too, whatever it might have been – the true nature of their relationship, the alibi, whatever story they'd had to 'get straight.'

Max and Cassandra skewed the dynamic immediately.

Ron's kids as human beings in the center of this drama hadn't made center stage before the lights went on in the hotel room. Before that, he was aware of their existence, of course, but they had been mere pawns in the chess game Hardy had been playing. The fact that they were *here*, *now*, taking up the same physical space as Ron whatever-his-last-name, changed everything.

Cassandra lit up when she saw him. 'Mr Hardy. Hi.' Natural as can be. Surprised and delighted at his appearance. Suddenly the name clicked with the face for Hardy, too. Cassandra was no longer a half-remembered presence in his daughter's life, but one of the really good ones – polite, funny, able to speak in whole sentences.

He glanced at the boy, Max, now placing him as well. They'd both been to the house several times to play with his children, although Hardy hadn't engaged either of them in meaningful dialogue.

It threw him to see it, but even now in this stressful environment, both remained obviously well-cared-for children, newly bathed and wearing pajamas.

'Are you here to help us?' Cassandra asked. She turned to her father, explaining. 'Rebecca says that's what her dad does. He helps people. He's a lawyer.'

Ron didn't seem as impressed with it as his daughter was, but the statement seemed to play into his plan and he didn't miss the opportunity. 'That's right,' he responded easily. 'He's here to see if he can help us out.' A sideways glance, tacitly asking Hardy's complicity at the outset, which Hardy couldn't think fast enough to deny.

'He's trying to get us back home. It's time you guys turned in, OK?'

A couple of minutes of small talk finally dwindled down before Hardy got strong handshakes from both of them as they were heading off to bed. And – the acid test – they both looked him in the eye.

It was a bit disorienting for Hardy to realize that these were well-adjusted children who appeared to love their father. If they were a bit reserved, Hardy had to remember that it was near their bedtime, they were in strange surroundings, and their stepmother had been murdered only three weeks before. He wouldn't have expected giggling high spirits.

But he didn't pick up any scent of people-fear, either of him or of their father, and that was always the inevitable companion to abuse.

It threw him off his stride. Whatever he'd been expecting, it hadn't been this cozy domestic scene with father and loving children.

The gun rode heavily inside his belt, a stupid, clumsy, macho pretense. What had he been thinking? Shifting uncomfortably, pulling at his jacket to cover the gun, he felt a wave of disgust for himself.

Who was he kidding? He wasn't some kind of gunslinger. It had been two decades since he'd been a cop. Now he was a lawyer, a paper pusher, a persuader. Words and strategy, the tools of old men like David Freeman.

And now Dismas Hardy.

All this was the thought of an instant, though. Ron was keeping things moving. 'OK, you've told Mr Hardy goodnight enough times. Now march!' Firm, good-natured, in control.

Amazingly, there was no argument. *Chez* Hardy, bedtimes were often the most difficult time of the day. Impatient, depleted parents struggling to get their exhausted children to admit that they were even remotely tired. The exercise would wind up turning into a war of wills that left all sides defeated.

But Max and Cassandra were up and moving. Another polite goodnight, stalling for that last precious second, both of them telling Hardy they were so glad he was here.

For the first time, Hardy noticed that they were in a suite, with a separate room for the kids, and Ron said he'd be back in five minutes, after he'd tucked them in and gotten them settled. But Hardy hadn't come all the way down here only to have Ron and the kids slip out another door. So, feeling foolish, he nevertheless went and stood in the doorway to the bedroom, where he could watch in case the good father decided to bolt and run with his children.

But the bedtime rituals made it immediately obvious that this wasn't on the night's agenda. Apparently Ron had decided to accept Hardy's unexpected presence and work within these new parameters.

Hardy finally went back to the other room, sat in the chair at the desk, and half listened to the familiar goodnight noises.

The gun remained an uneasy presence, the unyielding pressure in his side. His stomach roiled with the unspent rage, the tension and hunger. A rogue wave of fatigue washed over him so powerfully that for a moment, snapping out of it, he was disoriented.

Out over the Bay, the huge planes on their airport approach floated down out of the darkling, cloud-scudded sky.

'So what do you intend to do?' Ron had closed the door to the kids' room and pulled over a wing chair. 'You want some coffee? A beer? Anything? The room's got everything.'

'I don't want anything except my wife out of jail.'

'Yeah, I can see that.' Ron sat. 'Look, I don't blame you for being mad. I can't tell you how sorry I am, but nobody could have seen this coming.'

'You saw it enough three days ago that you left your apartment and took your kids out of school.'

'That was when I learned they were going to talk to Frannie.' Hearing his wife's name used with such familiarity rekindled some of the flame of anger. Hardy fought it – it wasn't going to get him what he needed, not now. But Ron was going on, explaining, rationalizing how none of this was entirely his fault. 'That's when I realized the investigation was coming back to me. I couldn't hang around and let that happen.'

'No. It was better to let them come after Frannie.'

'I didn't foresee that.'

'You just said you knew they were talking to her. What did you think was going to happen?'

'I had no idea. I told them I had been drinking coffee with her. I thought they'd probably want to make sure.' He leaned forward in the chair. 'I don't know if you realize it, but the grand jury had already questioned me. I answered everything they asked me.'

'But obviously lied about fighting with your wife.'

Suddenly the floor seemed to hold a fascination for Ron. Finally, he raised his eyes. 'What was I supposed to do, put myself on their A-list?'

'The theory is you tell them nothing but the truth. That's the one Frannie went with. You might have told her she could tell your little secret.'

'I thought all they wanted was corroboration on the alibi. You've got to believe that. The other stuff, I never thought it would come up.'

'Well, it did.' But this was old news and Hardy was sick of it. 'So why didn't you just take off when you knew they'd started looking? You had three days. You could be in Australia by now.'

'The kids uprooted again. No insurance income from Bree's death. The police after me.'

'They're after you now.'

'That's not what I hear. Not yet.'

Macho or no, Hardy almost reached for the gun, to put an end to this stupidity. Take the man in and let the chips fall.

But then he remembered the three innocent, shackled children from Judge Li's courtroom. An example of what could happen – something similarly terrible almost inevitably *would* happen – to Cassandra and Max. Furious as he was, he couldn't be responsible for putting them into the criminal justice system. Not yet, anyway. Not if there were any other way.

Ron was leaning forward, tight-lipped and earnest. His elbows were on his knees and his hands were gripped, white-knuckled, together in front of him. 'Look, I know this is bad for you. Horrible. But my first responsibility has to be to my guys in there. I know you understand that.'

Hardy couldn't say anything. It galled him, but the fact was that it was true – he understood it completely.

Ron was going on. 'And we're not absolutely committed to running away either, not yet anyway. If this passes, the kids are back in school next week with a little unscheduled vacation and no one thinks a thing about it. The original plan was we'd take a few days off and see which way the wind was blowing.' He let out a deep breath. 'Maybe we wouldn't have to go after all.'

'Go where?'

'Wherever. Anywhere.'

'And do what?'

Ron hung his head again for an instant and brought it back up. 'Start over. Again.'

If this was a not-so-subtle play for sympathy, it was misdirected. Hardy snapped out. 'And meanwhile what happens to Frannie?'

'I release her. She gets out.'

Hardy didn't like the sound of that, either. 'You release her?'

A nod. 'From the promise.'

'I got an idea, Ron. Why don't you do it now? Like right now, this minute?' Hardy's voice had picked up some heat. He snatched up the pen and telephone pad from on the desk, held it out to him, once again considering the gun.

Ron was shaking his head no. 'The minute she talks, we have to run, we have to relocate. Don't you see that?'

Hardy looked around the suite. 'What do you call this? This isn't running?'

The pen was still out there in the air between them. Ron stood up slowly, took it, sat at the desk, and wrote for a minute.

When Hardy had read what he'd written, though, it didn't strike him as nearly enough. The note was brief and specific, telling Frannie that the next time she went before the grand jury, she should feel free to reveal his secret if she felt she needed to. But Hardy's problem was that the grand jury wasn't meeting until next Tuesday morning, which left Frannie exactly where she was right now. In a cold fury, Hardy raised his eyes and spoke. 'What the hell kind of good does this do?'

Ron sat on the edge of the bed and spoke with a desperate calm. 'My understanding from the television – am I right? – is that poor Frannie's in jail down there for four days no matter what happens with me.'

Hardy nodded. 'That's how it looks, but—'

Palm out, Ron stopped him. 'Please. May I? So my hope is that I won't have to do all this again – move my family, start over. I've already done it once, as you know. But the idea of doing it again . . .' He drew in a breath. 'I'd rather avoid that, and maybe I can.'

'How's that?'

'If they find who did it.'

This was what Frannie had suggested only a few hours earlier, but Hardy was damned if he was going to make the same argument he'd made to her. He could be a lot more straightforward here. He heard his volume going up. 'And what if they don't, Ron? How about that?'

'Then on Tuesday, the kids and I, we go. And Frannie can talk.'

'She can tell the grand jury you've kidnapped your kids?'

'I don't see it that way, but yes.'

'Put the FBI on your ass?'

A weak smile. 'They've been there before. They won't find me.'

'And Frannie gets out of jail? She tells them everything?'

'Yes. You have my word. Meanwhile, if Bree's killer is found' – he indicated the kids' bedroom – 'those guys maybe get to go back to a normal life. That's all I want, really.'

And here was Frannie's impetus in deciding to ask her husband to help her maybe-lover. Save some lives, she'd said, and he'd let himself be persuaded that she was talking about their own family.

But no.

Again, it was Ron. His kids.

Hardy knew nothing of the truth about Ron and Frannie, about Ron and his earlier marriage, the custody battle, Bree or her life or any of the political issues surrounding it. Three days wasn't enough time, even if he had an entire police department working with him, even if he was motivated to do it.

Which he wasn't.

105

He couldn't use his cop friends, his lawyer connections, or any of his personal channels because he'd sworn himself to secrecy. Finding a likely suspect for Bree's murder was a ridiculous notion. And why would he want to anyway? Ron Beaumont might not be anything he appeared right now. It might all be an act.

Help the man? Hardy still didn't feel as if he'd completely ruled out killing him.

Hardy glanced at the note a last time, folded it over, and jammed it into his pocket.

Ron, seeing this, picked a bad moment to comment. 'We can do this,' he said, all sincerity.

And Hardy suddenly lost all his patience, slapping a palm loudly on the table in front of him, raising his voice in a rage. 'What is this "we" shit? There's no "we" here. There's me and what I need to do for my family. Then there's you. And don't kid yourself – they're nothing like the same thing!'

Not trusting himself to keep his anger checked any further – he might pull that gun out after all – he got up and abruptly strode across to the door.

'You're not leaving?'

This wasn't Ron's voice and Hardy's surprise at the sound of it whirled him around. It was Cassandra, standing in the doorway to the suite. It was obvious that she had been crying, though now she had gotten herself back under control. 'Please, Mr Hardy, you can't leave.' At her father. 'We do need help, Daddy. He can help us. Rebecca says that's really what he does. That's why he can almost never be home, because he's helping other people.'

The innocent, unintended stab slashed deeply across Hardy's insides. But Ron kept to the point, not the subtext, answering his daughter calmly. 'I think he can, too, honey, but it's not my decision.'

There was a tentative knock from the children's door and now Max stuck his head through the crack. 'I'm sorry. I covered my head with the pillow, but I still couldn't help hearing you yelling.' He looked from Hardy to Ron. 'Are you all mad at each other?'

Cassandra reached back and put her arm around her brother. 'We're scared, Daddy. What's going to happen?'

'It's all right, hon, there's nothing to be scared of. Daddy's right here.'

Ron cast a glance at Hardy and went to stand up, but his daughter had advanced a step into the room, trailed by Max who now held on to her hand. The little girl's face was set with determination. Another step and she spoke right to Hardy. 'Mr Hardy, didn't you come here to try to help us? Is that true?'

Hardy stammered. 'Well, I . . .'

'Because we can't go back to Dawn. They can't make us do that. Even Max remembers . . .' The tears had begun again. 'We just want to stay with Daddy and have everything be like it was again.'

Max piped in through his own tears. 'And Bree back, too, please. I want Bree back.'

'Oh, guys . . .' Ron went to stand up.

But Cassandra didn't move toward him. She had her eyes on Hardy. 'Do you have to be our lawyer to help us? Is that how it works? How do you become our lawyer?'

Hardy crossed over near her, went down to one knee, and tried a tired smile. 'It's not that. It's that I don't know what I can do, Cassandra. It's complicated. Rebecca's mother's in a lot of trouble, too, and I've got to help her. She's got to be my first priority. You can understand that.'

But the girl was persistent. 'Maybe you could do both, though? And Daddy isn't sure what to do right now.'

Ron reached out to her. 'Oh, sweetie, come here. Both of you guys.' Ron was holding out his hands and the kids went to him. He enveloped them both in his arms, in a strong and soothing fatherhood. 'Come on, now, come on. There's nothing to be scared of. Let's say goodnight to Mr Hardy and go back to bed. It'll all look better in the morning.'

But Cassandra turned. 'Please, Mr Hardy, if you can.'

12

*I*t was Monday, October 5, less than a week after Bree Beaumont's death. In fact, it was the day she was to be buried. Baxter Thorne, a portly man with a gray goatee, a soft-spoken manner, and a gentle disposition, nervously paced the floor behind his computer banks in his office on the thirtieth floor of Embarcadero Two. Outside his inoperable windows, it was a gloriously clear day, with boats on the Bay and Treasure Island a nine-iron pitch across a mile and half of blue water. But Thorne had no use for the view. He'd told the cop – Griffin – he'd be here first thing in the morning. He had no idea what the man might have found, but the fact that he knew of Baxter Thorne's existence at all was a very bad sign.

The sign on Thorne's door announced that these were the offices of the Fuels Management Consortium – FMC. In fact, the organization was the center for the lobbying efforts of one of the country's two multinational farming conglomerates. Spader Krutch Ohio, SKO, along with its chief competitor Archer Daniels Midland, ADM, was one of the country's leading producers of ethanol. But while ADM was colloquially known by the benign nickname of 'Supermarket to the World,' SKO's reputation was somewhat less savory.

SKO had been having a rough time in the last several years, and Thorne had been assigned to California to direct a campaign on behalf of its interests – he'd proven himself as a creative media consultant.

SKO might be Thorne's biggest client, but the quiet, well-mannered gentleman with the goatee worked to please himself. He had a persuasive way with words, true, and could sway opinion with his pen. If his clients believed that his silver

108

tongue and lucid prose alone were converting the multitudes, Thorne was happy to let them. But in reality, he knew better.

Sometimes, to be effective, you simply had to shake things up.

And this was his real love – operations, wet work. It had lots of names. Thorne got his own personal jollies by pursuing an extra-legal agenda all his own. And it was far more extensive and dangerous than anything any of his clients would ever order or even, if they became aware of it, tolerate.

For example, two years before, SKO had been getting a lot of bad press. The company's CEO, Ellis Jackson, was fighting off charges of illegal campaign funding, gift-giving, and influence peddling. Because of this, the Senator from Kansas got cold feet and – reluctant to be identified with SKO – threatened to renege on his support of ethanol subsidies. This support was finally guaranteed by a donation of a million dollars to the Senator's campaign fund, but without Thorne it is doubtful that the Senator would have found a way to accept the gift.

On his own, Thorne had discovered the man's weakness for other young men. Then, Thorne had seen to it that one of these men had been on the corporate jet on the junket to Hilton Head. Finally, Thorne had decided precisely where to position the cameras.

But while Thorne loved his own covert operations more than anything else on earth, he didn't shrink from his nuts and bolts work – information management and spin control. In fact, the Fuels Management Consortium produced reams of paper every month for dissemination to radio shows, newspapers, think tanks, consultant firms and lobbyists.

In addition, Thorne's company produced campaign leaflets for political candidates who supported ethanol, or opposed MTBE, which amounted to the same thing. The most prominent of these was Damon Kerry, running for governor of California.

Unfortunately, in Thorne's view, Damon Kerry was a man who did not appreciate the big picture. Like the Senator from

109

Kansas, he didn't want to be publicly associated with SKO, with its questionable lobbying history. Damon Kerry was pure – he wasn't proposing the use of ethanol. He wasn't being bought by any special interests, no sir. He was merely opposed to the cancer-causing alternative, MTBE.

So Damon Kerry's campaign was in the thick of the gasoline additive wars. Except one of the generals was ignorant of where he got his army.

Baxter Thorne came to California to bolster Kerry's campaign, but Kerry had rejected his advances. Fortuitously, Kerry's campaign manager was a young man named Al Valens. Greedy, unscrupulous, devious, and skilled, Valens was more than happy to accept Thorne's help as well as a little personal financial support. In the role of Kerry's best friend, consigliere, and strategist, Valens in fact was a double agent. His role was to keep his candidate focused on the evils of Big Oil.

All things considered, and up until last night, when the cop called, Thorne had believed that things were going pretty well. Kerry had come from nowhere to get within spitting distance of his opponent, and with a couple of good spins and perhaps a trick or two, Thorne was confident he could eliminate that gap and bring his boy home.

But suddenly, there was a problem. The damned Beaumont woman, and some homicide cop with an alleged connection to the Fuels Management Consortium that he wanted to talk about.

Thorne looked at his watch for the fiftieth time. He was on time. Where was Griffin? What the hell did he think he knew?

From long experience in the political arena, Thorne had learned to distrust first impressions. There were a host of fat, slovenly, boorish elected officials in this country who were powerful, decisive, and dangerous. He wasn't sure where he was going to place Griffin just yet. From all appearances, the inspector was unimpressive, but the fact that he was sitting here at FMC meant that he'd made some unsettling

110

connections. Something might be going on between the man's ears.

So Thorne was playing it close, as was his inclination in any event. He smiled in his benign fashion, and spoke in kindly and professorial tones. 'I'm afraid I don't see anything sinister in Bree Beaumont having some of our literature at her apartment. She was in the combustion business, wasn't she?'

Griffin had stuffed himself into one of the secretary's rolling chairs and now was hunched forward, one leg awkwardly crossed over the other, rocking as though maybe he thought the chair was a rocker. But Thorne didn't think this was nerves. Under the working-class nonchalance, Griffin was intense as a surgeon. He didn't bother with returning any smiles. 'Yeah, we got your letterhead at the scene,' he said. 'I got that. But then I got Valens.'

'Al Valens?'

This did bring a smile. 'Don't bullshit a bullshitter, Mr Thorne. Al Valens. Your guy with Damon Kerry.'

This was truly alarming, and Thorne had to struggle to retain his equanimity. There was no way anybody official – much less this oafish flatfoot – should know about Thorne's relationship with Al Valens. If that became public, if Damon Kerry discovered that he was being deceived by his campaign manager, it would be the end of months of work, of a program that was on the verge of success.

So, his brain now on full alert, Thorne smiled again and leaned back in his chair, bringing his fingertips together over the tweedy vest that buttoned over his stomach. 'How do you conclude that this Mr Valens is my guy, as you put it?'

'I got a better one,' Griffin replied. 'How about if I ask the questions since that's what I'm here for? In exchange I don't bring you downtown.'

Thorne tried a little humor, to soften things here. 'I've always considered that these offices were downtown.'

Griffin's face was a slab of meat. 'What do you know about Valens' relationship with Bree Beaumont?'

There was nothing to do but stonewall until Thorne discovered a little more about what Griffin knew as well as the source of it. 'I don't know anything about his relationship with Bree Beaumont.'

'But you admit that you do know him? Valens?'

'I didn't say that.' He certainly wasn't ready to admit it, and Griffin had just cued him that he was fishing. Thorne reminded himself – the flip side of first impressions – that sometimes people looked and acted stupid because they were. 'But you've obviously heard that I do.' He ventured an educated guess. 'Jim Pierce?'

Pierce was an executive vice president of Caloco and, Thorne had heard, ex-lover of Bree Beaumont. When she'd left the oil company to join Kerry, there'd been hard feelings all around. Pierce had the money and the motivation to discredit Kerry, and to make Bree see the error of her new ways and come back to him and Caloco.

Griffin looked at his notepad, and this verified Thorne's suspicion. Poker wouldn't be this inspector's game. 'Because if it was Pierce, you've got to seriously consider the source.' He held up a hand. 'Now I'm not telling you what to think, but Jim Pierce? Jesus.'

'What about him?'

'He's Big Oil, is what.' Thorne sighed. 'Look, sergeant, I'm a consultant in this business. I know the players. And Pierce is a very big player. So here's what happens. If Kerry gets elected, which isn't looking too bad right now, Pierce's people, the petroleum folks, they're going to take the big hit on . . . you know about MTBE?'

Griffin nodded. 'Lately, yeah, I've heard of it.'

'Well, take my word on it, that's what this is about. Three billion a year goes down the drain if Kerry wins, so Pierce is trying to disrupt the campaign.'

Griffin seemed to remember what his original position had been. 'So you're saying you're not involved with Valens? That's your story?'

Another avuncular shake of the head. 'I don't have a story, sergeant. All I know about Bree Beaumont's death is what I've read in the paper. I'm especially saddened because, frankly, she was starting to make a real difference in the public's perception of the dangers of MTBE, which are substantial. Also, quite honestly, several of my clients stood to benefit from her recent work. As did Kerry and probably Valens. Not only is there no motive there, there's a positive disincentive.'

Thorne was fairly certain he'd deflected Griffin again from pursuing his own relationship with Valens. But he thought he could push things even further. 'Look, sergeant, I don't mean to speak out of turn, but let me guess what Mr Pierce told you – he said that Al Valens hated Bree, didn't he? That Al was jealous of all the attention Kerry was giving to Bree. Something like that, am I right?'

An ambiguous shrug.

'And who's the guy who tells you all this? Only the guy whose business is in the crapper if Bree succeeds, who by the way just got dumped by her personally.'

Griffin finally showed a spark. 'You know that?'

'Word on the street.' Thorne returned Griffin's open look – he'd answered his questions, been straight with the police. If there was anything more, he'd continue to cooperate. But his message was clear – Griffin was barking up the wrong tree here.

Finally, the sergeant straightened his body and grunted his way up out of his chair. 'I know where to find you,' he said.

A last smile. 'I'm not going anyplace.' Thorne extended a hand and after a beat Griffin took it.

'Listen to me, Al. The man was here. I don't know for sure what Pierce told him, but it wasn't news to him that you hated the woman.'

Al Valens swore. Then. 'Did he mention the report? Did he know anything about that?'

'No. I don't think he'd know what it was if it bit him. But

he'd obviously been to her place and gone through her papers, some with my letterhead.'

'How'd she get those?'

Thorne's voice took on a mild tone of reproach. 'Well, Al, I was going to ask you the same thing.'

Valens took it in silence. 'So where'd you leave it?'

'I sent him back to Pierce.'

Valens was silent for a long moment. 'How close was he to us?'

'Way too. But now he's looking at Pierce, who had every reason. More than every reason.' Thorne smiled thinly. 'I think Sergeant Griffin will come to the conclusion that Mr Pierce must have done it. And with no physical evidence, he'll have to go to the strongest motive.'

But Valens didn't sound convinced. 'What if he comes back to us, though? After all we've—'

Thorne cut him off. 'Al, he wants to catch a killer. Our arrangement is not his area of interest. He won't be looking this way.'

Valens' voice betrayed the panic Thorne knew he must be feeling. 'But what if he does, Baxter? What if he does?'

Thorne spoke in his most soothing tones. 'Then he'll have to be managed, that's all.'

The limousine bearing the Democratic candidate for governor pulled up to where a crowd of perhaps a hundred citizens waited in the chill by the Union Square entrance to the Saint Francis Hotel.

In the back seat, Damon Kerry nodded appreciatively at the man next to him. 'Good job, Al. Nice turnout.'

Valens wore a distracted air. There was no doubt that the crowd here would be satisfactory. You tell semi-indigents that you'll pay them twenty bucks to go someplace and stand around for fifteen minutes, and you can generally get some good percentage of them to show up and do it. And since both sides did it, neither could snitch off the other to the media.

Five months ago, Damon Kerry had unexpectedly taken the primary after the two other Democratic contenders had vilified each other to death in a series of TV debates. Since that time, Valens found himself more and more coming around to the opinion that the system could be improved by simply eliminating the middle men and paying people directly to vote.

In a cynical moment – and there had been hundreds lately – he'd amused himself doing the math. He'd concluded that for about the same amount of money they'd already blown through on this campaign, they could have paid every registered voter in the state twenty bucks to go into the booth and mark the 'X' next to Kerry.

If he took the number of citizens who actually voted – somewhere near thirty per cent of California's adults – and only wanted to ensure a simple majority of fifty-one per cent, he could up the ante to nearly a hundred dollars per vote. With that kind of incentive, people would take the whole day off with pay to 'vote.' That was the way to do it. Hell, they'd even make money on the deal.

'What are you thinking about, Al? You're not here.'

The limo had stopped at the entrance. He couldn't very well answer honestly, but since that wasn't an issue with him at any time, it didn't slow him down now. A quick shift of the mental gears and he was back to strategy, the campaign, life, or his anyway. 'Oh, sorry,' he said distractedly. 'Bree, I suppose. This new angle with Bree. The woman in jail.'

The television news had broken the story about Frannie Hardy only hours before, and it was already clear it was going to become large. Anything to do with damn Bree Beaumont was going to continue to have an effect on the campaign. Valens couldn't get away from it. It had surprised Al to see how Bree had come from out of nowhere to be such a focal point in the campaign. Certainly it had never been Valens' intention to get Bree and Damon together. She had been with the enemy. But then, after a radio program they had both appeared to defend their respective positions, things changed.

Bree had always viewed herself as a pioneer against pollution. She took pride in the fact that her MTBE was really doing a great job of cleaning up California's air. It wasn't just science to her. She *cared* that she was doing good. She was, it appeared, altruistic. She wanted a better world. In this way, she was very much like Damon Kerry, more so than Valens could have ever imagined.

Valens didn't understand principled people at all, but these two – the candidate and the scientist – connected to each other in a big way. Damon Kerry, passionate and personally charming, hadn't attacked Bree on the program. He'd been either smart or lucky enough to zero in on their common concern – keeping poisons out of the environment.

And what he'd made Bree do, which even Valens at the time had thought was brilliant, was direct her attention down, into the ground.

Before this one radio show, Bree's entire scientific life had been directed into the atmosphere. She had been cleaning up the air, defending how she did it. And that had kept her busy enough that she hadn't looked too carefully at the ground. She assumed, and the corporate culture in which she'd been immersed had aided the assumption, that her stuff – MTBE – in the ground would act like regular gasoline. Eventually it would dissolve or evaporate out. Reports – even scientific reports – to the contrary were paid for by the ethanol industry, by SKO. Bree considered the source, and discarded the facts.

So in her mind she had always been on the side of the angels, doing good work.

And then, suddenly, Damon Kerry had made her see it all differently. And in the immediate aftermath of that conversion, she'd been the greatest thing for the campaign since the battle of the front-running mudslingers.

But soon afterward, from Al Valens' perspective she became a substantial liability. Something personal started going on with Damon Kerry. Before Valens knew it, Bree was showing up everywhere with his candidate. Late dinners, early lunches, fundraising breakfasts.

By the time of her murder, Bree had mutated from occasional irritant to constant influence. Kerry was paying more attention to her than to Valens – giving more credence to Bree's idealistic, stupid advice than to his own campaign manager.

As the relationship evolved, Valens saw that it was only going to be a matter of time before the opponent's camp – to say nothing of the media – got wind of the story and used it to ruin everything he'd done. Valens had had nightmares about the headline: 'Candidate in Affair With Married Mother of Two.'

No, it wouldn't do. Bree Beaumont's death was not at all a bad thing for Damon Kerry, although it would probably be a while before he would see it.

Now, in the darkened back seat of the limousine, Kerry's face grew grave.

In the immediate aftermath of Bree's death, he'd gone into hibernation for three days. Valens had had to cancel all of his appearances, pleading a virus, the flu, something. For one terrifying moment, it had even looked as though Kerry was going to stop campaigning altogether, to give it up.

Valens had had to employ all of his wiles to get his client back on track, invoking Bree's sacred name. *Bree* would never have wanted him to quit. He had to hold on, and win the governorship for *Bree* if for nothing else. Fight the oil companies who had used *Bree* for their own evil purposes. If he didn't go on, *Bree* would have died in vain. All that nonsense.

But ultimately, it worked.

Now Valens leaned forward, rolled the connecting window down, and spoke to the driver. 'Peter, take it around the block one time, will you? We're a little early.'

This wasn't true, but Kerry wouldn't know that, and now that he'd mentioned Bree, it wouldn't hurt to solidify the spin. No doubt someone would question Kerry about it at the

Almond Growers' Association cocktail party tonight, and it would be bad luck to give an answer upon which they hadn't already agreed.

Valens laid a protective hand on his knee. The message bore repeating. 'She and Ron were happy, Damon. The marriage was a good one. He had no reason to kill her. You have to remember that.'

Kerry turned his face to the tinted windows.

Valens continued. 'If Ron and Bree were unhappy, she never mentioned it to you, OK? Right?'

For an answer, Kerry blew out a long breath.

'Look,' Valens pressed on, 'let's concentrate on the good news from this front. Look what's happening on the talk radio shows.'

Kerry snorted. 'I hate those people.'

'I know. I agree with you. But they don't hate you. And Bree in the news is good for you.'

Throughout the campaign, the talk radio campaign against MTBE had been one of his strongest weapons. Never mind that it was funded by Baxter Thorne's client, SKO, or that several callers linked themselves to groups that had targeted oil refineries and corporate offices with bombings and other vandalisms. Valens didn't mind terrorists, so long as they were *his* terrorists.

Valens patted Kerry on the leg. 'But like these folks or not, Damon, they are doing you a lot of good right now. They're getting your message out.'

'My message isn't just about gasoline additives, Al. It's about the public trust, public safety.'

Valens bit back his reply. There were worse things than a sincere candidate, he supposed. He tried to recall the great line – was it George Burns? – 'The politician's best friend is sincerity. Once you can fake that, you've got it licked.' Instead, he said, 'Yes, of course. I agree with you. Public safety, public trust. But the public has a handle on MTBE. They're nervous around it . . .'

'They should be.'

'Granted. But my point is that these people are keeping the issue hot, and it's *your* issue. You're against this bad stuff.'

'Damn straight.'

'And the oil companies are making it.'

'To the tune of a three-billion-dollar-a-year industry, Al. When only five years ago—'

'Agreed, agreed.' Valens had to stop him or he'd go into his whole speech right there in the limo . . .

. . . about how the oil companies had gotten together and decided that hey, maybe it was dirty-burning gasoline that was causing air pollution after all. They should do a study and if that radical theory turned out to be true, they should – out of the goodness of their corporate hearts – do something about it.

And sure enough, that's what the study – draft written by Bree Beaumont, Ph.D. – had found. Gasoline wasn't burning cleanly enough. It needed an 'additive' to burn more comp- letely away the hydrocarbons that contributed to smog. The California legislature and the US government's Environmental Protection Agency fell all over themselves passing laws that mandated the use of this magical additive, if a good one could only be found.

Valens had to admit Kerry was good at this next part. He'd heard it from dozens of podiums up and down the state and it always played beautifully, the great American public hating rich corporations as it did.

'So guess what these noble oil companies did? They spent lots and lots of their own money developing the very additive that their own gasoline needed to become clean and efficient – our old friend MTBE.' Here, Valens was pleased to note, there was often if not always a chorus of well-orchestrated 'boos.'

After which Kerry would continue: 'And then, as it turned out – just a coincidence, my friends, I assure you – it turned out that the oil companies found that their production of MTBE, made of a by-product of gasoline refining that they had earlier been throwing away – well, would you look at that? Here's a surprise! MTBE started to bring in a yearly income of *three billion dollars*!'

More boos.

'Oh, and darn, they forgot to tell us one last little detail.' A moment of suspense. 'Wouldn't you just know it? The dang stuff causes cancer and respiratory degeneration. Actually, the oil companies didn't really forget to tell us that. What they did was tell us the opposite – that MTBE was nearly medicinal in its impact on human health. The air so much cleaner we'd have a new Eden. Why, read the initial reports' – again, drafts by Bree – 'and you'd almost come away believing it's so safe you could drink the stuff.

'Except for one other problem.' And here Kerry would turn his most serious. 'Except it makes water taste like turpentine. It leaks out of holding tanks and jetski engines and everywhere else liquids leak out of. And once it gets into the groundwater, the wells and waterways of our great state, it never comes out. Never. Ever. It doesn't evaporate. It doesn't break down chemically. Ask the city of Santa Monica, which had to shut down five of its wells – that's half of its water supply – because of MTBE contamination from local corner gas stations.

'And even now, ladies and gentleman, even today as I'm talking to you, this stuff is added to every gallon of gasoline sold in California at a rate of up to fifteen per cent per gallon. That's fourteen point two million gallons of MTBE every single day.'

This statistic usually stunned the crowd into silence.

The candidate would wait as long as it he could, then hang his head a moment. His timing was excellent. He'd look up, sometimes even able to summon a tear. 'It can't go on. For our children and our future, it's got to be stopped. My name is Damon Kerry and I'm here to stop it.'

'So, bottom line, we can't comment about Ron and Bree. We have to stick to the issues. We've been through this all before, Damon. It's only a couple more days.'

'I know, but . . .'

But Valens knew there couldn't be any 'buts.' 'Listen,' he said with intensity. 'Every day in every major city in this state, the callers to these shows are spreading the word that the oil companies killed Bree to punish her for betraying them – changing her mind and campaigning *against* MTBE because she changed camps and came over to your side.' Valens stopped any reply, a hand up. 'Look, Damon, here's what I'm saying. You know it as well as I do – people love conspiracies, they love to hate these oil guys. This helps you.'

'But I'm not accusing the oil companies of—'

'And that what's makes it so brilliant!' Valens knew that his candidate could see this clearly, so why did he have to keep explaining it? 'Damon, you're Mr Clean. But your worthy opponent, who favors pumping MTBE until more research can be done? Guess what? He looks like he's with the oil interests—'

'Which he is.'

Lord! Valens couldn't get over Kerry's fascination with the literal truth. 'Yes, of course he is, but what matters for you is that we couldn't *buy* the radio time they're giving us. If we get them thinking about Ron Beaumont as a villain, it all gets diluted.'

'I don't know, Al. I wish they had would come up with *some* villain, some suspect. Somebody to take the heat off.'

'Take the heat off who?'

'Who do you think, Al? Me.'

'What about you?'

'And Bree.'

'You had a professional relationship. What's to talk?'

Kerry gave him a look. 'This would be a bad time for somebody to find out, though, wouldn't it? She's back in the news, the story's no longer dead, reporters start digging.'

'And find nothing. Do you hear me? You have to relax. They find nothing.'

The limo had pulled to a stop. Kerry hated to keep his crowd waiting. He needed to get out and press the flesh, keep connected to his voters. He reached for the door handle. 'All right, Al, I hear you. I hear you.'

13

Abe Glitsky lay awake, trying to ignore the television noise in the next room. His housekeeper/nanny Rita loved the TV as much as Glitsky hated it. She'd been living with them now for almost five years and was a treasure, especially with Orel. Abe needed her so badly he knew he would tolerate much worse in her than an unfortunate taste for popular dreck.

Still, tonight, with Frannie Hardy in jail and an unsolved high-profile murder starting to get renewed media attention, the inanities soothed like a buzz saw. Finally, he pulled off the covers and sat up.

Five minutes later, fully dressed, he was out of the house, walking down Lake Street on his way to where he'd parked his city-issue car about six blocks away – the closest parking space he could find.

He was telling himself that maybe it wasn't the television after all. What had gotten him up and moving was the sudden bolt that Frannie and his unsolved, high-profile murder were one and the same case. Not that he hadn't known it before, but he'd been viewing them as more or less separate problems, and suddenly it struck him that maybe they weren't.

One other thing was certain – he hadn't woken her up. From the looks of her eyes, she hadn't slept yet in her cell.

'Abe. Hi . . .?' A quick look around the walls of the interview room although there was no place anybody could hide. Glass block and light-green stucco. The question was all over her face – where was her husband? What was Abe doing here by himself in the middle of the night?

The door closed behind her and she took a little half-step

hop, jumping out of the way of something, the sound. Then a pitiful smile, embarrassed. 'I'm not good at this.'

Abe was standing close. 'Who is?' He came up and put his arms around her for a second. She felt almost dangerously insubstantial, all tiny bones. He pulled back and looked at her, swimming in the orange jail jumpsuit. 'Are you eating?'

She shrugged, no answer. 'Is Dismas coming in? Is he out there?'

'No, it's just me, checking on how you're holding up.'

Frannie crossed her arms, the ghost of her old self trying to appear, a dance in her eyes. 'No, checking on how I'm holding up was last time, before you went home. This is something else.'

The scar stretched between Glitsky's lips. His own beaming smile. His head bobbed appreciatively. 'You should be the lawyer.'

'I'll pass, thanks.' Boosting herself on to the table, she looked up at him. 'So what is it? The deal?'

Glitsky's brow furrowed. 'What deal?'

'It's not that? I thought they must have come and asked you—'

'I don't know any deal. What deal? Who offered you a deal?'

'Scott Randall, that bastard. He wasn't here an hour ago. Doesn't understand why I don't feel all warm and fuzzy about him, like he really didn't get it.' She was watching Glitsky's face. 'You really haven't heard about this?'

'Nothing. What did he want?'

'He wants Ron.'

'And how was he going to get that from you?'

'He said he'd drop the contempt charge and stop worrying about the secret. I wouldn't have to tell that to the grand jury.'

'In return for what?'

'For where Ron was. He thought I'd know where he was.'

'But you don't, right?'

Frannie was studying the wall over his shoulder.

'Right?' Abe repeated, but he already knew. 'Damn it,' –

the rare profanity came out with slow deliberation – 'what are you doing, Frannie? I've been on your side up to now, trying to get you out of here, because I have known and loved you for years, and I know you're not involved in any murder. Am I at least right on that?'

She nodded, met his eyes. 'I swear to you, Abe.'

He sighed heavily, perhaps reassured. 'All right, then. What else did Mr Randall want?'

'Just that. He wanted to get his hands on Ron and question him. He said he knew that's where the answer was. With Ron.'

'And where is that?'

Sitting on the edge of the table, Frannie hung her head and swung her feet back and forth like a child. Finally, she looked back up. 'Abe, he left the house and she was alive. When he came back she was dead. Somebody killed her.'

Glitsky started to respond, but she put her hand on his arm, stopping him. 'I know, I know. You told me, remember? The time of death. Technically, he could have done it before he left to take the kids to school.'

'I like that eye-roll thing you do.'

'Come on, can you picture it? Ron takes the kids down to the car, then says to himself, "Hey, here's an opportune moment. I think I'll just nip back upstairs, kill my wife, throw her off the balcony to make it look like a suicide, clean up the glass from whatever convenient murder weapon I find up there . . ." ' She was shaking her head. 'Please. I was with him that morning, and he was fine. He was normal. We just had a cup of coffee and kvetched about life, about children. You know how you do. You've had kids.'

'Still do.'

'You know what I mean. School age. Little guys.'

Glitsky nodded. 'OK, but he told you a secret so important that you're here in jail?'

'No, he didn't, Abe.'

'What do you mean?'

'I mean not that morning. That morning was nothing.'

125

'But Scott Randall gave me the impression—'

'I know. And now everybody assumes Ron told me something that morning. I'm telling you that's not what happened. I don't even remember if we mentioned Bree at all, not on that day.'

'Then why are you here?'

'Because I wouldn't tell what Ron told me.'

'Which had nothing to do with Bree's murder, so far as you know?'

'That's what I said on the stand.' Frannie had been admonished that revealing anything about what happened inside the grand jury room was a separate contempt of court. At this point, she couldn't have cared less. 'I said I didn't know. I didn't think so, but I wasn't sure.' Finally, she pushed off the table and got back to her feet. 'But I'm telling you, Abe, listen to me.' She had grabbed at his arms, the sleeves of his leather jacket. 'It doesn't matter even if he did have an incredible, compelling reason to kill her, which he didn't. And forget that he's just not the kind of person who would ever, ever kill anybody. Forget that. The point is that even if he wanted to, he couldn't have done it. *He wasn't there*. Why is this so hard for everybody to understand?'

Glitsky the cop almost found himself believing her, for the practical reason that what she said, particularly about the timing of the murder, made sense. If Ron Beaumont had killed his wife in the morning before taking the kids to school, while they were still hanging around or even waiting in the car, and managed to hide it from them, he had to admit that had been one hell of a party trick. Not that he couldn't have done it – and Abe had only recently argued that it was in fact possible – except that in the real world, possible didn't mean likely.

But there were still questions. There were always questions. 'So why is he on the run?'

'How do you know he is, that he hasn't just gone fishing or something to get away for a day or two?'

This was the wrong answer and Glitsky clucked in

frustration. 'Your husband told me. He went by the school.' A meaningful glance. 'I know that Diz also told you that, which brings up the question of why are you pretending you didn't know. It also brings us back to why he ran.'

'Maybe because he was scared, Abe. People get scared, even when they haven't done anything wrong.'

'That's true,' Glitsky conceded. 'They also get scared when they think they're going to get caught for what they did. I've seen it happen. Also, I notice you didn't answer the first part, why you're pretending you didn't know.'

Suddenly her eyes really flashed. 'Because there's things I don't have to tell anybody, that's why. Even you, even Dismas. I've got a right to a little privacy, Abe, just like you do. How about that?' She took a few steps away, then stopped abruptly and turned back. 'And while we're on questions, I've got one for you – what did you come down here for? It wasn't to check on me and you said it was. Why did you lie to me?'

Glitsky held out his hands. She was right. She was Hardy's wife, one of his closest friends in her own right, and being in jail didn't make her a criminal, a suspect, or anyone he had to deal with professionally. She was still the woman who'd cared for his boys for a month after his wife had died. 'I'm really sorry.'

She relented. A little. Arms still crossed, though. 'Sorry's good. Sorry's a start.' But she wasn't giving up on her questions, either. 'So why did you come down here?'

'I couldn't sleep. I thought maybe you could tell me something I didn't know about Bree. It occurred to me that with everything else going on, nobody's thought to ask you.'

'But I don't know anything about Bree.'

'You don't have any ideas about who killed her? Ron didn't have any?'

'I'm sure nothing he didn't already tell the grand jury.'

Glitsky tried to smile. 'I'm on your side, Frannie. Always. How about if I ask you some questions, to see if they point me toward anybody else?'

Her shoulders slumped, the fatigue showing everywhere. 'How about if we sit down?'

They'd been at it maybe twenty minutes, Glitsky feeling that he'd barely begun when the guard knocked and the door opened, and Dismas Hardy appeared. 'Party in Room A,' he said. But he didn't look like he was partying, Glitsky thought. More like he'd been through some kind of sleep torture.

Frannie got up and walked to him. Glitsky stood, realizing that his interview was over for tonight. He came around the table. 'OK you lovebirds. I can take a hint.'

'Abe, that's OK, we're just—'

But he was at the door. 'I know what you're doing. Diz, I'll be in my office for awhile.' He turned to go, then remembered something. 'Oh, and Frannie?'

'Yes?'

He pointed a finger at her. 'Eat.'

Then they were alone, holding each other. Hardy had come straight from the Airport Hilton, wanting to fill her in. He gave her Ron's note, which seemed to make almost no impression. And really, he reasoned, why should it? It would have no effect, if any, for days. More than that, though, Frannie was far more concerned with another issue. 'Before anything else,' she said, 'this thing about me and Ron.'

'OK.' His breathing had stopped and that was all he could get out.

'We liked each other, like each other.' A pause. 'Maybe a little more than that.'

Hardy tried to keep any hurt or recrimination out of his voice. 'How much more?'

His wife sighed. 'I think for a while I was infatuated with him. He seemed to feel the same way about me.' She read something in his face and let go of his hands. 'Now you're going to hate me, aren't you?'

'No,' he said. 'Nothing's going to make me hate you. I love you.'

She stared at him for another beat. 'We didn't . . .' She stopped. 'But he was *there*, Dismas. He was a friend. He listened. I just want you to understand.'

'I don't listen?'

'Yes. I mean no, you know you don't. Not about some things. You glaze over – the kids, school life, all those what you call mindless suburban activities. And I don't even blame you, not really. I know it's not the most exciting stuff in the world, but it's my life, and sometimes it's just horribly lonely and mind-numbing, and then suddenly there was this nice man who didn't think all of this was tedious to listen to.'

'So he'd listen, did he, old Ron?'

She nodded, going on. 'Ron and I, we were just having so many of the same issues with the kids . . .'

He couldn't hold it any longer. 'Wait a minute, Frannie. What about us? I seem to remember we're doing some of the same things, too – live in the same house, do the kid thing, have friends over, like that. That stuff doesn't count?'

'I know, I know, you're right.' There was pain in her voice, too, perhaps some faint overtones of the desperation she must have been feeling. 'But you know how things have changed with us. We're different. I hope you're still committed—'

'Of course I'm still committed. You think I'd be sitting here listening to all this if I wasn't pretty damn committed?'

'OK, I know that. But the romance . . .' She stopped. They both knew what she was getting at. The romance, and there used to be plenty, had been all but swallowed by the maw of the mundane.

And Hardy knew why. 'We're both working now. We work all the time.'

'Well, whatever the reason, we both know we're not the way we used to be. There's whole areas of each other's lives that we don't have the time or energy for anymore.'

Hardy brought his hand up to his eyes, all the fatigue of the past hours suddenly weighing in. Everything Frannie was saying was true. Nobody's lives were the way they used to be. But the accommodation he'd reached was to put it out of his mind. He had his job, making the money. She had hers, the house and the children's day-to-day activities. They shared the children's discipline and some organized playtime. They weren't actually fighting; they were both competent, so there wasn't much to fight about. This was adulthood and it was often not much fun. So what?

But she evidently had reached another conclusion – she needed something he wasn't giving her and she'd gone out and found it. 'What are you thinking?' she asked. 'Talk to me.'

'I'm thinking everybody . . .' He started over. 'I mean, married people . . . I don't know.' He rubbed at his burning eyes. 'I don't know.'

'We all get further apart?'

He shook his head. 'Maybe. But I've been trying to support us all here for the last few years. It takes a little bit of my time. Hell, it takes all my time. You think I'm OK with no leisure in my life? You think I don't miss it, too, the fun? But what's the option? Live poor, let the kids starve . . .?'

'Nobody's going to starve, Dismas. It's not that. You know that.'

'Actually, I'm not sure that I do know that. It feels like if I stop working, somebody might. The world might end.'

'But you never talked to me about that, did you? That fear?' He shrugged and she pressed him. 'Because you don't talk about those kinds of things, not anymore.'

He shrugged that off. 'I never did, Frannie. Nobody wants to hear about that, all those nebulous fears.'

'Yes they do. And nebulous hopes, too, and little insignificant worries that just need to get aired out, and the occasional dream that's just a dream, like we used to have all the time. What we were going to do when we got older, when the kids have moved out?'

'Frannie, you're talking a decade, minimum. We don't even

know if we'll be alive in a decade. Why talk about it?'

She folded her arms. 'That's exactly what I mean. We don't know something for sure and therefore it's not on the Top Forty list of acceptable topics.'

'But Ron does, is that it? You've got hopes and fears you can share with Ron, but not with me?' He was hurt and mad and starting to swing pretty freely, maybe rock her with a roundhouse. 'So what kind of dreams did you and Ron share and talk about?'

'I didn't have any dreams with Ron, Dismas. I only have dreams with you.'

That stopped him. Her eyes were beginning to well up. He reached over, pulling her to him. 'I don't want to yell at you,' he said. 'I don't understand this right now. I'm trying.' He pulled back so he could look at her. 'I've been trying with our whole lives, too, you know. I do try to be there for you and the kids. I haven't been distant on purpose.'

'I know. I shouldn't have let Ron even be friends, not that way. That's all it was, really, but I ... it seemed innocent, really, starting out. You know, connecting finally to somebody.'

Hardy knew. Just before Vincent had been born, he'd had the same experience – connection, infatuation. Fire that he had ducked away from before it had burned him and Frannie. He knew.

'I shouldn't have let him get important,' she said. 'I should have seen it and stopped, but we were just talking. It didn't seem it would hurt anything.'

'Except it's put you here.'

That brought them back to where they were, although of course they hadn't gone anywhere. It was almost midnight and the next morning their own children would be waking up at Grandma's with neither of their parents around.

Frannie, shivering now, looked down at her orange jumpsuit. This time the tears did well over.

'I'm so sorry, Dismas. I'm so sorry.'

He pulled her back to him, and moved his hand up and

down over her back, feeling pretty damn sorry himself.

Glitsky was at his desk, sipping from a mug of tepid tea, trying to get a take on what Frannie had told him, which wasn't much that he hadn't already known. Bree and the oil wars. But so what? He'd been a homicide inspector for a long time and the idea that this was some sort of business-related slaying was, for him, almost too far-fetched to consider.

When he got back to basics and asked himself who stood to benefit from Bree's death, he came up with Ron. So regardless of how much he'd prefer Sharron Pratt and Scott Randall to be wrong, he was thinking he'd be wise not to forget entirely about him. It might be nice to find an alternative suspect, but if homicide took the road less travelled and found no one on it after the DA had shown them the way, he had a hunch he'd be hearing about it for a decade or two.

He was vaguely aware of two inspectors writing reports out in the open homicide detail. Suddenly there was a shadow in his doorway and he looked up.

'I was half expecting you not to show.'

'Which half?' Hardy asked. He stepped into the office and crab-walked around the desk, which barely fit into the room, to one of the wooden chairs wedged into the tiny space that was left. 'Frannie told me you two had a nice talk.'

The lieutenant was twirling his mug around and around, wrestling with something. 'I'm not too happy about what I heard, Diz. I'm thinking it may be Ron after all.'

Hardy was poker-faced, keeping it casual. 'How could he have done it? I mean like when and where?'

'I know. There are problems with it.'

'Like he wasn't there? Would that be one of them?' Low-key. But the last thing he needed now was to get homicide on Ron. Because they would have a good shot at finding him, which would put him and his kids back in the system. It would eliminate Hardy's own private agenda – the only one, he believed, that could produce a satisfactory conclusion to this mess. So he asked, 'What do you have on Bree? What did Griffin get?'

The mug stopped halfway to Glitsky's mouth, then came back down. Glitsky's normal expression was something between a frown and a scowl, and now it moved a few degrees south. 'Carl might have had the case closed in two hours if he hadn't died. Or he might have been nowhere. Either way, he didn't get to writing up his reports. Paperwork wasn't his strong point.'

'What was?'

Glitsky narrowed his eyes. 'What are you getting at?'

'Well, he must have done something. Just because there's not much in the file doesn't mean there's nothing.' He had Glitsky's interest now and he kept going. 'Was Griffin married? Did he talk to his wife? Anybody in the office here? Who supervised at the crime scene? They must have gotten some kind of physical evidence at Bree's place. I mean, Griffin was in this, right? He had to have something.'

Hardy found it a lot easier getting into the penthouse with the key that Ron had given him.

Once inside, he turned and locked the door behind him, then switched on the lights. Nothing obvious had changed since he and Canetta had walked out together last night, but Hardy felt a dim charge as he started for the office with the answering machine.

What was it?

Stopping completely, telling himself that it was probably the difference between being merely tired, which was last night, and semi-comatose, now, he still took a minute getting his bearings, casting his eyes around the periphery of the rooms.

While he'd been visiting downtown with Frannie and then Glitsky, he'd left his gun stowed in his trunk. When he got back to his car he'd tucked it back into his belt. Now, feeling stupid about it for the second time in five hours didn't stop him from pulling it out again.

The paintings, the view, the dining area, all the same. It was nothing, he concluded. He was the walking dead at the moment, seeing ghosts, maybe playing with them.

But suddenly there it was.

He'd gone out to the balcony last night, and to do that he'd pulled the drapes aside a foot or two. He remembered it specifically because from the inside of the house, where he stood now, he hadn't been able to see the French doors leading out to the balcony from which Bree had been thrown. He hadn't known that the doors were there.

And now they were covered again, the drapes pulled closed.

He crossed the living room again, the dining area with its seating nook, trying to remember, growing more sure of it. Neither he nor Canetta had come anywhere near this area last night. And as Hardy was leaving, he'd glanced back at the room one last time – the French doors stuck in his mind, and that meant the drapes hadn't been pulled closed.

Moving them aside again, he pushed open one of the doors and stepped back out on to the balcony, over to its edge. It still was a long way down. Fighting vertigo, he backed up a step. Nothing had been moved, nothing had changed.

So somebody had pulled the drapes against the unlikely event that he would be seen moving around twelve floors up at the scene of a murder.

A last glance and Hardy was inside, this time pulling the drapes behind him. He still had the gun in his hand. 'Hello,' he called out. 'Anybody here?'

Silence.

Flicking the hall and room lights on before him, he took a tour of the back rooms, as he and Canetta had done last night. Nothing looked disturbed. Even the office, presumably the location of Bree's important files, was as he'd last seen it.

Except for one thing. The counter on the answering machine, which last night had read '8,' now was a zero.

All the messages had been erased.

134

PART TWO

14

Saturday morning in an empty house.

Gradually over the past several years, but chronically it seemed in the last few months, Hardy wasn't happy at home. Kids constantly underfoot, Frannie with her women friends, talking about kids mostly. Kids fighting, discipline. Kids' sports, games, school, homework, lessons, meals they didn't eat, pets they didn't care for. Kids kids kids.

Whenever anyone asked him directly, he always said he loved his own kids, and he thought he did. But if he had it to do over, being honest with himself, he had doubts.

When they'd started out, Frannie and he had read all the books about marriages coping with the changes of a growing family. Hardy had often wondered since why somebody hadn't written the real book, called '*Children? Don't!*'

Because he'd come to believe that having a family didn't simply change things – it *ended* that earlier existence. You might go into it thinking you were retaining the essentials of the old life, merely adding to its richness and variety. But in a few years you had a whole new life, and it felt as if none of it was really yours.

He'd come around to accepting as absolute fact that paradise would be sleeping in on a Saturday and waking up to an empty, quiet house. Maybe one that would stay that way.

Now, doing it, suddenly he wasn't so sure.

The sun was in his eyes. He threw a forearm over them, then squinted out his bedroom window over the city. Where was he, anyway? It came back to him – he'd slept in his clothes, crashing on the bed. The gun was on his reading table, where the clock read eight thirty. He must have been a zombie on wheels. He didn't remember anything about driving home, where he'd parked, letting himself in.

God, it was quiet.

Bones creaking, he forced himself to sit up, saw the gun and reached for it.

He got up and went into the bathroom, throwing cold water on his face, trying to wake all the way up. Through the rooms, then to the front door, which he'd locked, then back down the long hallway to the kitchen. The house felt hollow, as though the soul of it had been sucked out. The kids, he realized. Frannie.

It struck him forcibly – a revelation. Standing by his sturdy, rough-hewn table in a well-equipped and beautiful kitchen on a fantastic Indian summer morning, he felt nothing but an underlying sense of terror, a vast pervasive unease.

This was the alternative.

But he had work to do, and yesterday had been a reminder that the engine wouldn't work without fuel. His black and ancient cast-iron pan was in its place on the back burner. No matter what he cooked in it, nothing ever stuck. He cleaned it only with salt and a wipe with a rag. Since Hardy had first cured it, the pan had never known detergent or water, and now its surface was a flat black pearl.

Turning the gas on under it, he threw down a thin layer of salt from the shaker, then crossed to the refrigerator. He grabbed a couple of eggs. Evidently Frannie had been marinating filet mignons for Thursday night when the grand jury session had intervened. Hardy picked one of the steaks from its ceramic bowl and dropped it into the pan, then broke an egg on either side of it.

There was a loaf of sourdough in its bag by the bread drawer and he sliced off about a third of it, cut it down the middle, poured some olive oil on to one of the cut sides, and placed it next to the sizzling steak.

While everything cooked on one side, he put on a pot of coffee, then turned the bread and the meat, laid the eggs on the toasted side, broke the yolks, turned off the pan, and went in to shower.

The day, when he hit the street outside, was impossibly bright, warm, and fragrant. He felt hopeful and motivated, a far cry from how he'd woken up, when he couldn't figure out a move and then – unable to focus – hadn't been able to locate his car for ten minutes.

But running on automatic, he knew that whatever else he did he had to go to Erin's first, to check in and see Vincent and Rebecca, make sure they were getting along all right at their grandmother's. And that visit had provided him with a bonus as well as the usual territorial disputes.

Last night Ed and Erin had taken them to the Planetarium and they were telling him about all they had learned, and the cool way the night sky came up. Vincent didn't believe it was an optical illusion. He was sure it was the *real* night sky. 'It was. It was exactly the sky, Dad. They just opened the roof and there was the moon and the stars and everything.' Shooting a glare at Rebecca the literalist, daring her to contradict him.

But Hardy cut them off. 'I've seen it, too, Vin. It *is* the exact sky. I love that, too.' A warning eye at his girl – don't say anything. Let him have this one.

Finally he got to her. 'So, Beck, what'd you see?'

His daughter, always ready to show off a fact, no longer cared about the truth of the night sky. Her father had finessed Vincent and given her the floor and that was all that mattered. 'Well, the main thing was about, what's that moon, Vin?'

'I don't know, but around Jup—'

'Yeah, that's it. Around Jupiter, one of the moons has an atmosphere and water and everything you need for life.'

'What about heat?'

'Inside, Dad. Molten core and volcanoes. Just like a mile under the ocean here on earth. Where's the heat there? Inside. See?'

'Great. I bet it could happen.'

'Definitely. They even showed what could grow as if we were there. Some of them—'

'You know what I thought was the best thing?' Vincent had to get a word in.

'The Beck's not done, Vin. One more—'

'She'll *never* get done. She'll keep going till you have to go.'

Hardy thought of a new name for his 'don't have that child' book – *The Endless Referee*. But he sighed. 'Beck? Are you almost done?'

But she must have been truly happy to have her dad there, or else wanted nothing more than to please him, which did happen. She hesitated only a second before smiling. 'He can go.'

'OK, Vin, what did you think was the best thing?'

The boy was so thrilled with his good fortune – interrupting his sister and it worked! – that for a moment Hardy thought he'd forgotten what he was going to say. This happened all the time, and invariably made Vincent cry. But it was, suddenly, a morning for miracles. The fact had come back to him. 'How you can see a star when you can't see it?'

It must have been obvious that Hardy didn't understand.

Vincent tried it another way. 'When it's too dim, when you can't see it otherwise.'

'What is?'

'A star, or a planet, or anything in the sky. If it's really dim, the way you see it is you don't look right at it. You look to the side. We did it. It really works.'

So when Hardy left, his next stop wasn't Frannie or Abe or his reporter friend Jeff Elliot to catch up on the Beaumont case.

At his son's suggestion, he wasn't going to look directly at it for a while. He still had clients and phone messages and paperwork so he went to his office to attend to those.

And sure enough, somewhere in the middle of that, he remembered that Phil Canetta had stood behind him with his spiral pocket filing system, and he'd written down all the names on Ron's answering machine.

He had told Hardy he worked out of Central Station, so he looked up the number and made the call.

The Central Station, close to the border of Chinatown and North Beach, was where Hardy wanted to open his restaurant when he retired. Not that there weren't dozens of other fantastic dining establishments within a couple of blocks – Firenze by Night, Amelio's, Rose Pistola, the North Beach Restaurant, Caffe Sport, the Gold Spike – but the smells of coffee, breads, licorice, sesame, roasted duck, cheeses, fish, and sausages kept tourists in a near constant feeding frenzy.

Even the locals, such as Hardy, weren't immune. After his breakfast, he wasn't at all hungry, but as soon as he stepped out of his car and caught a whiff of it all, danged if he didn't think he could go for a little smackerel of something. It was a wonder, he thought, that the cops out of Central weren't the most overweight in the city.

Plus parking. The five-story public parking structure was directly across the street and would never under any conditions be approved by today's city planners because, after all, what kind of political statement could a *parking structure* make? Its only purpose would be functional, and the shakers in the city hadn't cared about that issue in years and years.

Hardy was walking out of its utilitarian perfection now, trying to figure whom he could bribe to condemn the station building so he and maybe David Freeman could open some hip new spot there. Somebody had done it recently with Mel Belli's old building and you couldn't get inside the place now. Freeman, another old lawyer, might react to the precedent, and certainly he'd know whom to bribe.

Canetta cut a completely different figure in his uniform. With the three stripes on his arm, his handcuffs, bullet belt, gun, and nightstick, he was definitely a cop through and through. He appeared more substantial than he'd been the other night – heavier, older, thicker in the chest.

Hardy had arrived at what might be considered early lunchtime, and Canetta obviously wanted to get away from the station if he was going to talk about any of this.

They stopped at Molinari's Deli so Canetta could get a sandwich – mortadella and Swiss with the waxy sharp pepperoncini Hardy loved and usually couldn't resist, although today he did. He bought a large Pellegrino water instead.

They walked up Columbus to Washington Square. A few minutes of small talk – an update on Frannie – brought them to an unoccupied bench directly across from the twin spires of Sts Peter and Paul. Coit Tower presided over the row of buildings to their right. In front of them, a bare-chested man with gray hair in a long pony tail was trying to train an Irish setter to fetch a frisbee.

Canetta unwrapped his sandwich and Hardy started talking. Somebody had been in the penthouse and at least erased the tape. Perhaps they'd taken something as well.

Canetta let a few seconds pass, looked sideways at Hardy, fiddled with his sandwich wrapper. 'That was me.'

Hardy tried not to show his surprise. 'You went back? After we left last night?'

A bite of sandwich. A long time chewing. Then a nod. 'I already had who'd called, right? Wrote 'em all down.' He patted his back pocket, where he kept his notebook. Then he went on, explaining, 'My answering machine at home, it only takes nine messages. I figured his might be the same. And if somebody else called him, I didn't want the machine full up.'

'Makes sense,' Hardy said, although that wasn't what he thought. But it was a done deed. And in any event, Canetta was going on. 'You know, they always say it's the husband.'

Hardy nodded. 'I used to hear that a lot when I was a cop. Now I'm not so sure it's true.'

'You were a cop?' Canetta looked him over with new eyes.

'It's been a few years, but just after 'Nam, before I went to

142

law school, I walked a beat. Glitsky was my partner, matter of fact.'

A moment's reflection while this settled. Then a question. 'So the head of homicide's your old buddy, and you're coming to me?'

'I'm the one whose wife's in jail. Glitsky's got two guys on the investigation, but it's three weeks old now and they're don't have a thing.'

'And you think you can help them?'

'No. I think I can help me.'

Canetta liked that and smiled. 'Little slow for you are they, huh? The suits?'

And there it was again, the animosity between the street police and the inspectors. Hardy had picked up a trace of it the first night and, not looking directly at it, it had seemed he might be able to get something out of it.

But he had to play the hand close. 'The way I see it is this. They're holding my wife because of something she knows about Ron, right?'

'OK.'

'Because Ron's their suspect?'

Another nod.

'So if I can give them somebody else, anybody but Ron, the heat's off Frannie. They'll let her go, since what she knows isn't part of a murder.'

He could see that the idea appealed to Canetta. The strategic considerations were provocative enough, but suddenly there was something more – the chance to show up the inspectors downtown. If Canetta was any part of the solution to a homicide, he'd get a hell of a lot of print and even more prestige. 'I told you the other night and I'll say it again, I think it's Bree's work. And you're saying you'd start with the phone messages?'

Hardy nodded. 'Ron had calls from both of Bree's camps. So I'm asking myself why they'd call *Ron*. What was in those files one of them talked about?'

'You're saying that was why she was killed.' His sandwich now forgotten, Canetta was already digging for his notebook.

'Not exactly. I'm saying if it wasn't Ron – and for my own reasons I'd prefer it wasn't – then this is the next rock to look under.'

'Valens and Jim Pierce?'

'Yeah. What?'

Canetta's eyes had narrowed. He was staring out across the park. 'Nothing really, except I know Pierce a little – that freelance security work I told you about.'

'And?'

A shrug. 'I don't think I should talk to him about any of this. He knows I'm not in homicide and he'd bust my sorry ass.'

This made sense, and Hardy agreed easily enough. 'But how about some of these others? You still in? This Marie, for example. Who's she?'

Canetta answered with a guarded enthusiasm. Clearly, he still wanted to be part of this, but he wasn't going to show how much. 'The insurance guy would probably be the easiest one to get a hold of,' he said. 'Bill Tilton. If he's local, he's probably listed.'

Hardy had his own notebook out now, and was copying the names. He planned to see Ron later today and get many of these answers, but Canetta could be useful – a badge in his service. 'OK, we've got one other person with a last name, this woman Sasaka, with the mystery appointment.'

A thought struck Canetta. 'Ron knew a lot of women, didn't he?'

Hardy didn't want to pursue that. Ron wasn't going to be his focus. Tapping his fingers on his pad, making a show of thinking, he finally looked up. 'What was the security work where you met Bree?'

'Hotel stuff. Bunch of suits down from Sacramento, lobbyists, politicians, one time the Vice President, secret service yada yada.'

'So what was your assignment? Did you guard individual people?'

'No, nothing like that.' Canetta obviously didn't like the work. 'Stand at the doors, take your hardware, be a presence. You know, these guys, they like to make a show. How important they all are.'

'But even at these meetings, Bree was somebody?'

He nodded somberly. 'Oh yeah. She stood out. I mean, first was the looks thing, especially in this bunch of geeks and wonks. But then she'd always give some talk and bring down the house. She had this . . . sincere quality, a lot of . . . passion, I guess.' Canetta was stumbling over himself, trying to make Hardy see. 'Like she really believed in things. I mean, she *got* to people – you know what I'm saying.'

At least, Hardy was thinking, she got to Canetta. But now the cop, his eyes far away again, seemed to be considering something. He was half-swallowing, and his next words nearly decked Hardy. 'Couple of other times, you know, I talked to her.'

He kept his voice neutral, but it was an effort. 'You mean personally?'

Canetta still wasn't completely committed to revealing this, but after a beat he nodded. 'Coincidences, really, the way it started. I was doing traffic duty a day or two after one of these shows.' A pause, deciding to keep talking. 'I don't know, three, four months ago. It's early evening, I pull her over for speeding about a block from her place. It's obvious she's had a couple.'

'She was drunk?'

'Maybe.' A quick exhale, letting some of the tension go. Hardy suddenly understanding a little about why Canetta didn't want to talk to him at the station house. He was already involved here. 'I'm alone in the cruiser. I recognize her of course. I don't cite her. She's not like out of her mind, blowing maybe a one is my guess. Long story short, she gets in and I drive her home.'

She got in his cruiser? Hardy wanted to ask if anything else had gone on. In his line of work, it wasn't uncommon to hear about some cop pulling over a pretty woman because the tread on her back tires was worn down, so he could meet her, be charming and find out if she was available.

Much more seriously, if less common, was that it wasn't unknown for a cop to get a woman's address off her driver's license and start stalking. Hardy was sure it was because he'd established his credentials as an ex-cop, a member of the club, that Canetta was telling him that he'd broken every rule in the book with Bree.

Still, it was unsettling.

And it wasn't over. 'So anyway, little while later, I'm passing the building and she's standing out on the sidewalk. I stop and ask her does she need a lift someplace, but no, she's waiting for somebody to come pick her up. We talk a minute.'

'What about?'

A shrug. 'She just thanked me for not writing her up. Said she didn't usually drink too much. She'd just been under a lot of pressure recently. Job stuff. I tell her I heard her talk a couple of times. It seems to me she's doing some real good with her work, making a real difference. But she shakes her head. 'It's all a mess,' she says, then like stops, not wanting to say anything else. Says she's sorry. I ask her for what, and she says like everything.'

A silence.

'Did you tell any of this to Griffin?'

'Who?'

'Carl Griffin, the inspector who got the case.'

A sideways glance. 'He didn't ask me. I'm just a station cop – what could I know?' The sergeant had gotten himself hunched over, elbows on knees, during the telling. Now, suddenly, he sat back up as though surprised at where they were. He remembered his sandwich and took a bite, his jaw working furiously.

Hardy killed a minute with his water. 'You married, Phil?'

'Eleven years,' he said evenly. 'We got a son just turned

146

twelve. Sometimes you think if things were different, if you could have a choice . . .'

Hardy clearly heard what he didn't say – you meet someone like Bree and you wish you wish you wish, but the option isn't there anymore.

'But you'd meet with her, with Bree?'

'Nothing that arranged. I'd pass by the same time of day and she got so she'd be there sometimes. We'd say hi, how's it goin', like that. Tell the truth, the feeling I got was she wanted to be reassured that I was there, like her protector.' He took in a ton of air and let it out slowly. 'And then she gets killed on my watch.'

15

Jim Pierce lived in a three-story Italianate structure set behind a wraparound high, white stucco wall. The property was in what realtors would call a serious neighborhood, on North Point, a block from the Palace of Fine Arts. On this lovely Saturday in the early afternoon, the tourists and even what appeared to be some locals were out in droves, enjoying the Marina district, escorting hordes of children through the Exploratorium, eating gourmet picnic items and feeding the ducks in the lake with the leftovers.

All of which Hardy got to see in his seven-block walk back to North Point from the parking space he finally located after circling the lake four times. As he went, Hardy found himself considering the possibility that the ducks were inadvertently being fed bits of duck from Chinatown – the odd smear of duck pâté, maybe some seared duck cracklings, or breast slices from someone's salad – and that this cannibalistic feeding would someday give rise to the dreaded Mad Duck Disease, which wouldn't be discovered yet for another twenty years, by which time it would be too late. Today's trendy duck eaters would be dropping like flies.

He'd let his mind wander as a defense to the sense of intimidation he'd felt when he'd first identified the house from the address Canetta had provided. But now he was here, before the imposing, black, solid metal gate, and there was nothing to do but push the button. A pleasant, contralto, cultured female voice answered. 'Yes. Who is it?'

Hardy told her. Said he was afraid it was about Bree Beaumont again. He was sorry. Keeping his role vague, since he really didn't have one.

She hesitated, then asked him to please wait. For a moment, he thought he might have gotten lucky, and he put his hand on the knob, waiting for the click as it unlocked. Instead, an impatient male voice rasped through the speaker. 'Who the hell is this? I've already talked to you people half-a-dozen times. I've talked to the grand jury. When are you going to let me have a little peace? I swear to God, I'm trying to cooperate, but I'm tempted to ask for a warrant this time. This is getting a little ridiculous.'

But the gate clicked, and Hardy pushed it open.

For all the imposing nature of his house, and even with the impatient tone in his voice, Jim Pierce came across as a nice guy. He opened the front door before Hardy was halfway up the walk. 'Do they change investigators downtown every five minutes nowadays? No wonder you people aren't getting anywhere.' Hardy squinted in the bright sunlight. Pierce wore a white polo shirt with a colorful logo over the left breast, a pair of well-worn but pressed khakis, tassled loafers with no socks. 'I'm just watching the game. Notre Dame, USC? The Irish are eating them for lunch. You like football?'

'I used to like Notre Dame back when Parsegian coached,' Hardy said. He was on the porch stairs and Pierce was already a step into the dark interior of the house. 'You ought to know I'm not with the police.'

Pierce stopped and turned back. 'I thought Carrie said it was about Bree . . . oh, never mind.' It was his turn to squint. Hardy stayed outside, framed in the doorway. 'So what can I do for you? What's this about?'

Hardy introduced himself as a lawyer doing some work for Bree's husband, Ron. 'You called him last week.'

A flash of surprise. 'I did?'

'Yes, sir, I believe so.'

The expression held as – apparently – he tried to remember. 'All right, then, I must have. Did I say what it was about?'

'You asked him to call you back. Something about Bree's

effects. Did you ever hear back from him?'

Pierce didn't have to think about it. 'No.'

'Can I ask you what you wanted?'

The nice-guy image was fading slightly. Pierce was getting tired of fielding questions about Bree. 'One of my duties involves community relations,' he said. 'I think she took a lot of boilerplate with her when she left – form letters, standard language PR materials, disks. It would be helpful to have it back.'

'So why didn't you ask her for it when she was alive?'

'I did. She wasn't very well disposed toward the company after she left. I thought Ron might be a little more ... malleable.' By degrees, Pierce had moved back to the doorway, and now stood perhaps two feet from Hardy, his hand back on the door, by all signs ready to say goodbye.

But something stopped him. 'Now how about if I ask you one?'

'Sure.'

'As a lawyer, what are you doing for Ron? The police don't have suspicions of him, do they?'

'They're eliminating suspects right now and he's one of them. Maybe I can find something to get them off him.'

'So you don't think he killed Bree?'

Something in his tone set off bells. Hardy cocked his head. 'You do?'

'No. I didn't say that.'

'That's funny. That's what it sounded like.'

'No.' He sighed again, this time the weariness unmistakable. 'Lord, where will this end? I don't know who killed Bree. I'm still having a hard time believing anyone could kill her, that someone purposely ended her life.'

Hardy suddenly noticed the pallor under Pierce's ruddy cheeks – lack of sleep, time spent indoors. The darkened house. He put it together that, like Canetta, Pierce was in a kind of mourning. Another guy laid out by Bree's death.

The woman certainly had cut a swath.

'If you had to guess, Mr Pierce, why was she killed?'

A blank look, his mind no longer on Hardy. 'I don't know.'

'I realize that you can't talk about what you told the grand jury . . .'

Suddenly Pierce seemed to realize they were still in the doorway. 'I'm sorry. Where are my manners, keeping you standing out here? Come on in.'

Hardy stood a minute inside, his eyes adjusting. Now that he'd asked him in, Pierce seemed uncertain what to do next. He motioned to a large bowl on a table next to the door. 'Help yourself to some candy, if you'd like. Almond Roca. The best.'

Hardy thanked him and took a couple, unpeeling the gold wrapper on one of them as Pierce led him back through the foyer. It wasn't just the Almond Roca – 'the best' seemed to be the underlying theme of the place. Formal living areas, one-of-a-kind furniture, ten-foot ceilings. They bypassed the winding staircase. The television droned in a small room and Pierce poked his head in. 'Halftime,' he said, and kept walking.

The last door on the right opened into a modern kitchen, where a woman sat at the island counter. Facing away from them, reading a magazine, she half turned as they entered.

'Excuse us, Carrie. Mr Hardy, my wife.' Then, explaining. 'He's not with the police after all. Mr Beaumont's attorney.'

She got off her stool and stood, extending a cool, firm hand. A nod of the regal head, holding on to Hardy's hand an instant longer than was customary. Mrs Pierce was no child, no recent trophy wife – she appeared to be just to either side of forty – but Hardy decided immediately that she was not just very attractive, but almost disturbingly beautiful. Widely set, startling blue eyes dominated the face of a northern Italian goddess. He estimated she was wearing two thousand dollars' worth of tailored casual wear that emphasized the slim waist. Her dark hair was pulled back in a severe style that highlighted the sculpted bones of her face. Simple designer gold earrings dangled from what seemed to be designer earlobes and a wide gold necklace graced a flawless expanse of finely pored, honey-toned skin over the rise of a deep and dangerous cleavage. 'Have they charged Mr Beaumont?' she asked in her cultured voice, a pretty frown clouding her perfect brow.

'Not yet.' Hardy hoped he wasn't stammering. 'I'm trying to keep that from happening. I was just asking your husband why he thought Bree Beaumont was killed.'

'Or why he's a suspect?' Carrie Pierce said it matter-of-factly. *He was Bree's mentor from the beginning, that's why*. They worked closely together and of course people talked. People tend to be jealous, not to believe that men and women who work together can be friends without . . .' A brief look of distaste. 'I mean, the world doesn't really turn around sex, after all.'

Hardy thought it was good coloration for Carrie Pierce to believe that. He doubted that any man had ever looked at her and not thought about sex. But if she wanted to retain a sense of her value as a person outside of that context, she'd better believe that there was more.

'The point is,' Pierce said, 'that evidently someone – one of my colleagues perhaps – had told the police that I'd been furious at Bree for leaving Caloco, especially so abruptly.'

'And were you?'

Pierce looked at his wife, then nodded. 'Pretty mad, yes. Betrayed, hurt, all of it. But that was personal.'

'But her leaving? Changing sides in these gas additive wars I keep hearing about. That was business.'

Pierce wore a look of amused toleration. 'And you think that the big bad oil companies got together and, because she'd had a philosophical change of heart, we decided to kill her?'

Hardy had to smile himself. 'Actually, hearing it out loud it doesn't sound too plausible.'

'It's completely absurd,' Carrie said. 'Regardless of what you may hear on the radio, murder isn't really one of Caloco's business tools. Or any of the seven sisters.'

'Seven sisters?'

Pierce explained. 'That's what they call us, the spin-offs of

Standard Oil after antitrust broke up the mother company. But none of the sisters would have any reason to kill Bree or anybody else. Frankly we don't need to.'

Hardy said it mildly. 'Even for three billion dollars?'

Pierce had on his tolerant face, the one Hardy supposed he used for the public. 'And what is that figure, three billion dollars? Where does that come from?'

'That's the number I've been hearing. Isn't that the yearly income from this gas additive everyone's fighting about?'

'MTBE?'

'That's the one.'

Pierce nodded. 'That sounds about right. Three billion.' He pulled out a stool, sat on it and indicated Hardy take one, too. Which he did. Carrie excused herself and moved over to the main counter to pour more coffee.

Hardy tried not to follow her movements, but it was not easy. He tore his eyes away, back to Pierce. 'So my point is that that's a lot of money. And if Bree led the charge against this stuff . . .'

But Pierce was shaking his head. 'No.' He lifted his hand, ticking off the points on his fingers. 'First, Bree didn't have anything like that kind of power. She wrote our drafts, she was a great and persuasive spokesperson, but Jesus Christ himself could come down and say MTBE was the devil and it wouldn't just go away. The stuff has cleaned up the air unbelievably. It works, Mr Hardy. The EPA loves it. Hell, it *mandates* it – that's a long way from being outlawed. It's not going away because one woman says it might have side effects, which, PS, is nowhere near proved. Second, and this is always a tough one to sell, but three billion really isn't all that much money.'

Hardy had to reply. 'Three *billion*? We're talking three *billion* dollars.'

Pierce nodded. 'It's all relative. It's mixed into gas at eleven per cent. And basically the stuff's only used in California, and only for half the year at that. So you do the math. Three billion represents about ten per cent of half of

153

California's gasoline bill. It's a drop in the bucket.'

'You're telling me you wouldn't miss three billion dollars?'

'Somebody in some department might notice, but long-term? That's exactly what I'm saying. It's nothing.'

Carrie came back over with an urn of coffee, china cups and saucers, sugar, and cream on a silver platter. 'It's the hardest part of Jim's job, Mr Hardy. Making people see that this isn't all about money. They think because we make a profit that we must be evil. But Jim hired Bree to do good, to find out how to make a better product, better for the world. No one seems to understand that. And that cost billions, too, to re-tool the refineries—'

Pierce reached over and patted her hand. 'What Carrie's saying is that it's a complicated issue. It's true that we've spent billions developing MTBE and for a while everyone was thrilled with it. It seemed to be doing the job. Now some questions have come up and we're looking into them. But the point is that we're committed to clean fuels and if it turns out that we have to develop some new refining tool, we'll do that, even if it costs billions, which it will because everything costs billions. That's the price of admission in this league.'

He took a sip of his coffee. 'But the other point, Mr Hardy, is that Bree getting a case of the doubts is no reason on God's earth for any oil company to do anything, much less have her killed. And that's essentially what I told the police.'

Hardy picked up his own cup and took a drink. Most of what Pierce said made logical sense if he accepted the premise that three billion dollars wasn't a lot of money, but that remained a bit of a leap. 'I once figured out how long it would take to count to a billion,' he said. 'If you did nothing else. One number every half second, twelve hours a day. You want to guess?'

Pierce shrugged. 'I don't have any idea. A week?'

Hardy shook his head. 'Thirty-two years, give or take a few months.'

Pierce chuckled. 'Get out of here.'

'It's a really big number, a billion,' Hardy said.

'Can that be right?' Carrie asked.

Hardy nodded. 'It's right. But my point is, it might be why people seem to have a hard time thinking three billion isn't a lot of money. Why Bree might have been killed for it.'

'She was one person, Mr Hardy,' Pierce said.

'So was Hitler. If he'd been killed, it might have avoided World War Two.' He shrugged. 'Look, I'm not saying I don't believe you. I'm trying to get a handle on what I keep hearing on the radio, that the oil companies had a motive to kill her.'

Pierce remained unruffled, as though he'd heard it all before, which he probably had. 'You're welcome to look, Mr Hardy, but it will waste a lot of your time.' He sipped coffee. Hardy had the impression he was stalling for a moment. Then he seemed to reach some decision, and sighed. 'You know the source of all this radio nonsense, don't you?'

'No. I thought it was kind of a groundswell . . .'

Pierce was shaking his head. 'Not at all. It's a well-funded group of eco-terrorists. Don't laugh, that's what they call themselves. Eco-terrorists.'

'And?'

'And they all seem to be working to get Damon Kerry elected since he's the standard bearer against MTBE.'

'All right.' Hardy didn't see where this was going.

'Well, at the time she left us, Bree was very much under the spell of Damon Kerry, too. Perhaps more, although I shouldn't say that after all I've had to endure on that score.' He glanced at his wife, whose lovely face again betrayed her distaste at this subject.

Pierce turned back to Hardy. 'What I'm saying is that at least these are the kind of people who admit to resorting to violence, or the need for it. Maybe somehow Bree crossed them, joined the camp and was going to renege, something like that.'

'You're not saying Kerry—'

'No no no, not personally. But somebody behind him.

Possibly. Really I don't know. I don't like to point a finger at anybody, but . . .' He trailed off.

Hardy remembered Canetta's comments about Al Valens, who had also left a message for Ron Beaumont. A question presented itself. 'You said this group – these terrorists – are well-funded. Where do they get their money?'

Carrie nearly blurted it out. 'That's easy. SKO.'

Pierce snapped at her. 'We don't know that, not for sure.'

'Of course we do.'

Husband and wife glared at each other.

'Who?' Hardy asked.

Making a show of reluctance, Pierce let out a long breath. 'Spader Krutch Ohio.'

'The farming conglomerate?' Hardy asked.

Pierce nodded. 'Corn. Ethanol, the other additive. It's a huge company, as you say, heavily subsidized by the government. They've got a stake in seeing MTBE outlawed.'

'So they could make the three billion dollars?' Hardy asked.

Carrie's color was up. 'They would kill for it.'

Pierce shook his head from side to side. 'I doubt that. But there is, I believe, very little doubt that they are the source of these funds.'

Hardy digested this information for a moment. 'Have you told the police about this?'

'What exactly is there to tell?' Pierce stood up. He'd given Hardy several minutes – nearly a halftime's worth – and now the interview was over. 'They asked me about my suspicions. I told them I'd heard about these economic motives and frankly, gave them short shrift. Poor Bree wasn't assassinated, she was murdered.'

Hardy realized that this, from an oil company's senior vice president, was self-serving. But that didn't mean it wasn't true. Still, he thought, three *billion* dollars.

They had all begun moving back toward the front door. Carrie laid a hand on his arm, guiding him through the dimness. 'If there is anything more you need,' she said. 'Jim and I want to help, but we don't really know anything more than we've told you.'

They'd arrived in the foyer and Pierce went for the door. 'Now that we've opened this can of worms, Mr Hardy, if you're convinced it isn't Beaumont, you might look into Kerry's campaign after all. The funding, maybe the eco-terrorist thing. There could be something there.' He sounded skeptical, though.

Hardy stopped, blinking in the sudden sunlight let in by the open door. It was the second time that Pierce had inadvertently alluded to Ron's involvement in the murder. 'But personally, you still think it's Beaumont, don't you?'

A temporizing smile. 'I believe these things tend to be personal, let's say that. If Bree had just started an affair with one of Kerry's people and Ron found out . . .' He trailed off. 'Well, that's motive, anyway.'

Hardy wanted to say, 'So's three billion dollars,' but instead he merely thanked the couple for their time, handed them his card, and turned back for the long walk to his parking space.

16

Sergeant Canetta's sandwich from Molinari's had given Hardy the idea. For all his peregrinations of the morning, there hadn't been a minute when Frannie wasn't somewhere in his consciousness. Now, heading downtown for another visit to the jail, it occurred to him that perhaps every instant she spent locked up didn't have to be hell.

Since it often worked for him, he reasoned that some good food might improve things temporarily for Frannie to the point where it was only as bad as purgatory – same conditions as hell, but you really knew it would end someday.

So he stopped and bought a spread of delectables from David's Delicatessen – lox, bagels, cream cheese, chopped chicken liver, pastrami, onion rolls, pickles, even three bottles of creme soda, which was her favorite drink in the world that wasn't made from grapes.

Only to be harshly rebuffed when he arrived at the jail. Was he crazy? The desk sergeant wanted to know. Didn't Hardy know better by now? Visitors weren't allowed to bring *anything* for the inmates into the jail – any piece of cake might have a razor blade or weapon in it, any drink some dissolved drugs.

So reluctantly, Hardy left the bag at the desk. The best of intentions . . .

One step into the room, Frannie turned from the guard and saw him sitting at the table, smiling at her. He spread out his arms. 'Sorry it's just me,' he said. 'I bought all your favorite food in the whole world, I really did, but they wouldn't let me bring any of it inside.' With a helpless expression he repeated that he was sorry.

She dissolved into tears. Just standing there in her orange

jumpsuit, hands at her sides, looking at him and crying.

Nat Glitsky didn't like being interrupted when he was at temple.

Lots of times when he'd been younger, he'd been less than diligent at keeping the Sabbath, but now in his eighth decade he'd come to believe that the Ten Commandments had gotten everything exactly right if you wanted to have a world full of healthy and productive people. People should pay attention to the wisdom in all ten of them, he believed. They really should. Keeping the Sabbath, taking a day off, kept you sane.

But nowadays even religious people mostly only acknowledged nine. Keeping holy the Lord's day was not only forgotten, it had been completely subverted, even reversed. Woe betide the lazy bum who took a whole day off every single week to reflect and try to gain some perspective on his life and work and the world around him. There wasn't time for that. There was only work. It was wrong.

Nat's working days were over, and all he wished now was that he'd kept the Sabbath sacred more often back when he'd get overwhelmed with childraising or working or the pressures of his marriage. It might not have changed his life much, but at least it would have planted the seed in his son Abraham, who was always crushed under his workload, and who now was sitting – fidgeting really – next to him.

And that was what adhering to the commandments was all about, too. It was generational. It fostered the long view that human nature never changed. Only individual humans did. But not so often as you'd think.

Nat finished his prayer and hit his son on the thigh. OK, they could get up and go outside now.

On the steps of the synagogue, they both stopped, squinting into the bright sunlight. 'I love the boy, Abraham, you know that. It's nothing to do with that. It's you.'

Abe drew in a deep breath. 'What's me? I didn't plan this,

you know, having to go downtown on Rita's day off. They need me down there.'

Nat rolled his eyes, dismissing that excuse. 'They always need you down there. Your son needs you out here. Suppose I just say no, I've got to go back to temple – then what?'

'I don't know. I guess I go get Orel and bring him down with me.'

'Among the criminals? There's a fine solution. Better I should take him back here.'

'Except he's got his soccer practice.'

'Oh yes, right. Much more important than temple on the Sabbath.'

'Well, he's there, Dad, and I told him you'd be picking him up. If you're not, fine, but I've got to know right now – all right?'

Suddenly, the serenity of the temple vanished, and a rare flash of anger took its place. Nat's voice took on a hard edge. 'Everything's *now* with you, Abraham. You want to ask yourself why that is, maybe?'

Abe raised his own voice. 'No. I don't need to ask myself that, Dad. You want to know why? It's because everything is a crisis. Everything has to be done five minutes ago, and so Saturday rolls around and all the stuff that needed to be done on Friday . . .' Abe reined in his own escalating temper. 'I don't know,' he said. 'I don't know. I don't mean to yell at you.'

Nat reached up and put a hand on his son's shoulder. Abe had his mother Emma's height and, of course, her color. He towered over his Jewish old man, who now shrugged. 'I been yelled at before, Abraham. It's not the yelling I'm worried about. It's your boy. It's time passing and then it's gone and you never saw it.'

Glitsky had told his father he'd be getting home in time for dinner with him and Orel.

Nevertheless, the discussion nagged at him as he drove

down to the Hall of Justice. It was still on his mind when he walked through the doorway into the long hall that led to the DA's office, airport for Flying Assholes Airways.

What did they really need him for now anyway? On Saturday afternoon?

The politicos thought they could just snap a finger and he'd have to come a-runnin'. And he was proving that they were right, because here he was. He should have just said no, he had other plans, he couldn't come down and discuss Ron Beaumont. But it was too late now.

Scott Randall was in Sharron Pratt's office with her lord-ship, the DA's investigator Peter Struler, Chief of Police Dan Rigby and Abe's predecessor as head of homicide, Captain Frank Batiste, who was now an assistant chief. And my, weren't things heating up? Four of the five of them – everyone but Batiste – were already in a friendly discussion about something that abruptly halted as Glitsky's shadow crossed the room's lintel.

'Ah, Lieutenant Glitsky.' Pratt was sitting on her desk and actually clapped her hands as though in delighted surprise that Abe had dropped in.

Batiste, Glitsky noticed, had found a convenient neutral corner and was memorizing the stains on the ceiling tiles. He was a good guy and his body language was telling Abe a lot. This wasn't his party, which meant that he'd been called down by the chief to neutralize Abe and make sure that homicide accepted the message, whatever it was.

Rigby and Randall sat on either end of the low couch looking at some papers spread on the table in front of them.

'Ah, Ms Pratt.' Unable to stop himself, Glitsky silently brought his own hands together. Sometimes imitation wasn't the sincerest form of flattery. Sometimes it meant that you saw through pretense and were telling the pretender that she was full of shit.

He stopped in the doorway and went into his best at ease. He nodded at the men, but no smile. 'Hey, guys.'

There was an awkward moment during which some glances were exchanged, Rigby evidently waiting for a signal that it was time to begin. He cleared his throat. 'About this Beaumont thing, Abe. And now the newspaper stories about this woman in jail.'

Glitsky nodded. 'Frannie. Her name's Frannie Hardy.'

'Yes, of course it is. Frannie.' The chief looked over at Pratt, got some secret message, cleared his throat, and spoke again. 'We've just about decided to put out an all points on Ron, the husband, and we wanted to run it by you first, to get your input.'

'We wanted to be sure we kept you in the loop, Abe,' Pratt added.

Glitsky did a quick take at Batiste and the two conducted a millisecond's worth of non-verbal communication of their own. Then the lieutenant folded his arms and leaned his bulk against the door jamb. 'I really appreciate your concern, Sharron, thank you. And this all points bulletin? It would be in light of new evidence that Investigator Struler's come up with – would that be it?'

Scott Randall spoke up. 'We want him for questioning, that's all. We want to talk to him.'

'You don't need me to talk to him.' Glitsky couldn't have been more laid back. 'You don't need me for an APB. But I'm curious about what you plan to do if you find him after this all points manhunt.' He looked at Struler, then Randall. Across the room, Batiste brought a hand up to his mouth and pulled on it to keep the corners down.

'What do you mean?' Struler asked. 'We bring him in and—'

'You arrest him, you mean?'

Cornered, Struler looked to Randall, then Pratt. He nodded. 'Sure.'

'With no evidence? No chance to even get past a prelim and go to trial, much less win? You want a lawsuit for false arrest, or what?'

Chief Rigby cleared his throat again, getting into the middle of it. 'Come on, Abe, it's not like there's *no* evidence.'

Glitsky turned to him. 'It isn't? I haven't seen any if there is.'

'The man's disappeared,' Randall said.

Glitsky shrugged. 'So? What's new?'

'The murder was at his house,' Pratt added. 'There's no sign of anyone else. She may have been having an affair and told him she was leaving. Process of elimination leaves Ron.'

Glitsky withered her with a look of disbelief and wondered, not for the first time, if the City and County's top attorney had passed the bar or ever won a case in court. It didn't seem possible. 'You want to take that to a jury and get beyond reasonable doubt, Sharron, you've got my sympathy.'

Rigby, a political animal himself, tried to smooth the waters. 'The point is, Abe, that in the real world we've got to move along on this.'

But Pratt couldn't keep herself out of it. 'I've had calls from a lot of citizens plus we're getting some very bad response to this woman being in jail.' Pratt had made something of a career out of ignoring the rules of law. Now she seemed to be having a hard time reconciling herself to the fact that her political problems weren't going to go away even if she broke more of them. 'I got a call from the mayor this morning, do you realize that?'

Again, Glitsky shrugged. 'Talk to Judge Braun about that.'

'The mayor has talked to her.'

'And?' Although they wouldn't be here if Glitsky didn't know the answer. Braun wasn't budging.

Randall butted in with the crux of his theory. 'If we get Beaumont in custody, Abe,' he said, 'we can shift public opinion away from Frannie and on to Ron. He'll be the bad guy for putting her in this position.'

Now Glitsky had it all on the table. These people were really from Mars. 'If memory serves,' he said, 'it was you who put her in this position, wasn't it, Scott?'

163

But the young attorney waved that off. 'I was perfectly justified and Judge Braun was also well within her rights. It's just that we're starting to get a lot of political flack—'

'And want to sacrifice Ron Beaumont. Same as yesterday.' Glitsky's eyes raked the room. 'This is not how it works, guys.' A shake of his head. He turned to Rigby and asked the direct question. 'Chief, what do you want me to do?'

Rigby was by now sitting on the front two inches of the couch. He looked up balefully. 'What have you got, Abe?'

'We've got Griffin's notes – basically nothing. I've got a better one for you.' He turned back to Pratt. 'Sharron, who, specifically, has been pressuring you to go get Beaumont?'

Again, some unspoken message seemed to pass among the airport staff – Struler, Pratt, Randall. Glitsky was getting a little tired of the secret handshake stupidity, but experience had told him that if he let it run its course, it might lead him somewhere.

Pratt slid off the desk and went around it, where she opened a drawer, then closed it. 'Well, naturally, Caloco would like to see the case closed. They're taking a lot of flack in the media, as you may know.'

'And are they one of your contributors?' From Pratt's reaction, Glitsky could tell that the question had hit a mark. He hadn't done twenty-five years of interrogations for nothing after all.

But Pratt didn't blow. Her eyes narrowed slightly. Her game face appeared. 'They contributed to my opponent as well, sergeant.'

'And as long as whoever gets elected does them a favor whenever they ask, they keep the money coming, is that it? So what's the favor here? Find a likely scapegoat and hang him out to dry?'

'Sergeant, you're out of line,' Rigby barked.

But finally, Batiste took a few steps toward the group. He'd spent many years in homicide and suddenly had picked up a bad smell. 'With all respect, sir, Abe's asked a good question.

If Caloco's trying to influence the investigation, it increases the odds that they might somehow be involved.'

'That's ridiculous,' Pratt exploded.

Randall was up now, supporting his boss. 'Completely ridiculous. You can't make that kind of baseless charge, captain. Caloco's been the soul of cooperation . . .'

'I haven't made any kind of charge,' Batiste retorted. 'I'm saying the lieutenant, here, has the right to ask the question. Do you have anything on Caloco?'

'There's nothing on them. They came to us and gave us a case of documents,' Struler said hotly. 'And we got Ron implicated.'

For a long moment, nothing moved in the room. Finally, Scott Randall whispered 'shit' under his breath. Even Rigby the politician – there to steamroll Glitsky into official compliance – frowned. Into the well of silence, Batiste dropped a little echoing pebble. 'What documents?'

Glitsky picked it up. 'I haven't seen any documents.'

'They weren't any part of the original investigation.' Pratt was hustling to put her finger in the dike, but the water was spraying all around her. 'Caloco came to us, voluntarily.'

'With what, exactly? And when?' Glitsky, suddenly, was glad he'd come in on this lovely Saturday afternoon. But he had to give it to Pratt, she didn't break.

Boosting herself on to the desk again, she gave a little apologetic smile. 'Ms Beaumont had been a valued employee and a couple of weeks after she was killed, when no suspect had turned up, Caloco called my office and offered all the files they had related to her.'

'And naturally,' Glitsky said, his voice thick with sarcasm, 'because they related to a murder, you informed my detail immediately so we could evaluate all the information.'

'You'd already dumped the case,' Randall said.

For another moment, Glitsky stood in the doorway. He had straightened up from his slouch long ago. This was not just petty politics, but a serious breach of legal ethics. Formal obstruction of justice out of the DA's office. Glitsky was having trouble accepting it.

But he knew what he was going to do with it. 'I'll expect that box and all its contents on my desk within the hour.'

Glitsky hadn't received the box from the DA by the time Dismas Hardy appeared at his office minutes after leaving his wife at the jail. 'Working on the sabbath?' he said from the doorway.

Glitsky, slumped over bunches of paper, gave him the evil eye. 'Don't start. Really.'

'OK. Meanwhile, while I'm not starting.' He tossed a bag on to the desk in front of him. 'I figured I was here, I'd see if you were and give you the leftovers.'

'Today's my day for leftovers.' He pulled the bag over to him. 'What is this?' Glitsky's face didn't exactly light up – Hardy thought that would be impossible – but Hardy was gratified by the expression. 'Is this lox? Tell me this is lox.'

'Your favorite. There'd be more except the desk sergeant at the jail ate the first two pounds.'

Glitsky had ripped the bag open and was spreading out the contents on the brown paper. 'You got this into the jail?'

'Technically, the answer to that would be no, though they do love me down there, I can tell. But no food inside, so they held it at the desk while I visited Frannie. Can I come in?'

'Since when do you ask?'

Hardy shrugged, moving forward. 'New policy. Ask first. I'm trying it out.' He sat on the wooden chair across from Glitsky's desk. 'While you're eating,' he said, 'I've got to tell you about these three leprechauns.'

Glitsky rolled his eyes. Hardy's jokes were a constant torture. 'You ever wonder why it's always three?' But his mouth was full and he was chewing happily.

'So they're all standing outside the *Guinness Book of World Records* building and the first one says he's got the smallest hands in the world and he's going to show them to the Guinness

166

people and get in the book. A couple of minutes later, he comes out, all thrilled—'

'OK.' Glitsky was between bites. 'Second guy's the feet, third guy's the dick. What's the punch line?'

Hardy was used to this, Glitsky's perennial cut to the chase. 'Third leprechaun comes out and he looks depressed and his friends ask him what's the matter – does he have the smallest dick in the world or what?'

'I can't wait.' Another bite of lox and bagel.

'Guy shakes his head, looks at his friends and says, "Who the hell is Abe Glitsky?"'

With the expected reaction – that is, none – Glitsky sat back. 'I had a good time recently. Want to hear about it?' He outlined the events from his recent meeting with Pratt and the rest of them, and the withholding of Caloco's documents.

By the time he'd finished, Hardy was sitting back in a kind of shock. 'You're telling me Dan Rigby was in on this, too? Do you realize you could have a good shot at taking down Pratt's office? In fact, I know a local lawyer who'd be happy to help you. Get yourself promoted to chief.'

Glitsky made a face. 'I don't want to be chief. Sometimes I don't even want to be head of homicide. I just want to be a cop again. Catch bad guys.'

'You might be doing that here. What do you think's going to turn up in the box?'

'Whatever's in there.' He'd find out soon enough. 'Can you believe the arrogance, though? It never occurred to any of them that they didn't have every right to that evidence. It came to their office so it was theirs and whatever they should legally do be damned.'

'You better watch out,' Hardy said, 'You're starting to sound like a lawyer.' He pushed back his chair a couple of inches. 'So that's what brought you down here today?'

Glitsky nodded. 'More or less.'

'And here I thought it might have been your two inspectors – checking into Carl Griffin's investigation as your best friend had suggested – had stumbled on to something.'

'Well, since you mention it.' Glitsky bunched the brown paper bag and tossed it into his wastebasket. The papers he'd been studying before Hardy's arrival didn't appear to be in any order, but he started picking through them as though he'd arranged them in some way. 'Here's copies of some notes from Griffin's notebook. He was working the building where Bree lived. No sign he'd gotten anywhere with witnesses, but it was Carl and he didn't write any follow-up' – he glanced up at Hardy and shrugged – 'so who knows?'

Glitsky picked up another stapled group of pages. 'Crime scene. Zip. No glass anywhere to match what was in her scalp.'

'Which was what?'

A flip of a page. 'The theory is that it was from a leaded crystal wine or champagne glass. The Beaumonts didn't have anything to match on hand.'

Hardy was into Griffin's notes. 'Here's Jim Pierce again. Damon Kerry. Al Valens. How'd Griffin get these guys?'

'The grieving husband, your friend Ron. Wanted to help find whoever killed her.'

'And he thought one of these guys . . . ?'

But Glitsky was shaking his head. 'He just gave Carl a bunch of names, Diz. People Bree had hung out with.' A pause. 'Why did you say Jim Pierce *again*?'

'What?'

'You said "Here's Jim Pierce again." '

Hardy smiled. 'That wasn't me. It must have been somebody else.' Then, relenting. 'It'd be neat if the odd slip of the tongue got by you once in a while. Anyway, I just visited him – Pierce – and his wife a couple of hours ago. You'll be gratified to know that your inspectors had already been there.'

A nod. 'Rattling his cage is all. He's got a decent alibi.'

'Just decent?'

'Driving to work. Left home around eight, at the Embarcadero office forty minutes later.'

'Forty minutes? I just did it in fifteen.'

'This is Saturday afternoon. Try it on a weekday morning, rush hour. Coleman and Batavia did it last night and it took 'em an hour. And he was *at his desk* forty minutes later.' Glitsky shrugged. 'OK, anything's possible as we know, but nobody's put him anywhere near her place. He told my guys he hadn't seen her in four months. They're checking, but so far they hear the same thing. No contact.'

'What about Damon Kerry?'

This time, Glitsky's mouth tightened. 'He's running for governor, Diz. I just don't think so.'

'I don't either, but was he around at least?'

Glitsky nodded. 'He was in town, shooting TV spots.'

'Seeing her?'

'Sometimes. Often.'

'Were they sleeping together?'

This almost brought a true smile, which for Glitsky was a rarity. 'What a quaint way to put it. Let's just say that for a married woman, she spent a lot of time with him, but it's not like Kerry's such a hot item that reporters are on him around the clock. His people quote resent the implication. She was a technical adviser on environmental matters. That's the story.'

'On the payroll?'

'No. Another committed volunteer, which is what makes this country great.' He held up a hand. 'I know, but Griffin never got to him and here four days before the election, without any physical evidence, you don't just send two inspectors down to grill him.'

'Why not? I would.'

Glitsky liked that. 'I'm sure you would, which is why you don't work for the city anymore. No, what you do is what we've done – ask him to come down and give a statement and of course he's promised full cooperation. As soon as he's got a free minute, which ought to be by Christmas, he's going to give it top priority.'

A weary sigh. 'You know, Diz, you and I might have our

good reasons for hoping it isn't Ron, but it still might be. Really. He looks a lot better than Kerry, or Pierce for that matter, and that's even before what's in the mystery box.'

Hardy didn't want Glitsky thinking this way. He was shaking his head. 'I don't think so. I like it that Kerry's in election mode, he's stressed to the max and this lady hits him with something that'll derail his campaign. He's got no time to think so he does the first thing that occurs to him and she winds up dead. Oops. Makes perfect sense to me.'

'He's at her house?'

'Could have been. Do we know? You find his prints?'

'Prints, please.' Fingerprints were useful when they could be cross-checked against those of known criminals, but if someone hadn't ever committed a crime, their prints would not be in the database. 'We got prints from the door to the balcony and some dishes in the sink. Ron's prints and the kids, which we didn't need to run 'cause we knew who they were. Then we've got a dozen, fifteen more, unidentified. Could be other kids, family friends, anybody. But no known criminals.'

'Maybe Damon Kerry, though.'

'We may never know and even if he was, so what?'

'It puts him at the scene.'

Glitsky rolled his eyes, his patience with amateur detective work growing thin. 'Why wouldn't he be at the scene at some point in the last few months? He knew her. So he went to her house? So what?

'Listen,' he continued, 'I'll tell you what. *You* get to Kerry, borrow his shoes, and find some lead crystal residue on them. Then find somebody who can put him at Bree's place or better yet, can prove they were doing each other, or stopped doing each other, or anything . . .' His voice wore down, his eyes came up. 'The more I think about it, Diz, and I hate to say it—'

Hardy held up a hand. 'Then don't.'

17

The Pulgas Water Temple sits in a peaceful and picturesque location among low rolling hills about twenty miles south of San Francisco. A semi-circle of high white Ionian columns rises behind a reflecting pool and forms an elegant structure that commemorates the completion of one of the most famous (or infamous) engineering feats in California history, the Hetch-Hetchy Project. This marvel of architecture and city planning captured the plentiful water and snowmelt of the Sierra Nevada mountain range at Yosemite and delivered it, mostly underground over nearly two hundred miles, into a shallow valley that had once been an Indian prayer grounds.

This once-holy spot is now the Crystal Springs reservoir, the source of San Francisco's drinking water and, in fact, one of the principle reasons that naturally dry San Francisco is a major metropolitan center and not a quaint tourist destination with nice views and bad weather.

The sculpted grounds of the Temple is a popular picnic destination and this bright, warm afternoon held a typical Indian summer scene – family blankets with food and drink spread on the grass, boats in the reflecting pool, dogs and kids and couples and a handful of bicyclists and solitary readers. Occasionally a Sheriff's patrol car from San Mateo County would cruise the lot, but there was no regular security presence at the site. There had never been any need of one.

The parking lot was nearly filled and the nondescript Chevy Camaro that pulled off the main road and into it had to park at the far northern end, nearly three hundred yards from the Temple.

The two middle-aged men got out of the front seat and the

two women from the rear. All of the eventual witnesses agreed that the group was dressed too warmly for the day, the women with scarves over their heads, the men with hats pulled low, but as they got out of the car, they attracted no attention. Without exchanging a word, they congregated at the trunk, then two men and one of the women began walking toward the Temple with a large picnic basket. The other woman got back into the car in the driver's seat and rolled down the window.

From where they had parked, the three carriers hadn't been able to hear a thing except the twittering of the birds and the casual noise of the picnickers, but as they got closer, a low roar gradually became audible, then undeniable.

'Either of you guys ever jump in here when you were a kid?' the first man asked. He didn't want an answer, was babbling out of nervousness, and neither of his two companions said a word. In any case, his story was drowned out in the sound of the water pouring out of the input pipes into the temple, but he kept right on talking. 'When I was growing up, this was *the* thing to prove your manhood, let me tell you. I knew a guy broke a leg and almost drowned, but I rode it halfway down to the lake.'

He was referring to what had once been a popular rite of passage for teenagers on San Francisco's peninsula. For years, males with testosterone poisoning would come down here with other guys or their girlfriends, mostly at dusk, and jump over the low wall of the temple down fifteen feet into the churning, ice-cold water, which surged at thousands of gallons per second into a circular, tiled pool. The flow would pick these kids up – or occasionally push them down and not let go – and shoot them out a fifty-foot submerged tunnel, then to the canal that led to the reservoir.

Now, in response to the occasional drowning, the state had installed a wide-meshed steel grate to cover the pool and jumping in was no longer an option.

As the three conspirators got to the low wall, the woman – she was by all accounts the leader – looked back and made sure that their car had pulled out of its space and was now idling, ready to take them out of here. There was a young couple on the platform with them, the boy's arm around his girl, both of them mesmerized by the rushing water, unlikely to move away in the next five minutes.

A solo man, mid-fifties, in shorts and hiking boots, was climbing the low steps to the temple even as she waited, and behind him a family of four were getting up from their blanket, looking like they were walking this way.

The shorts and boots man caught her eyes for an instant, and she too quickly – stupidly – looked away. Guilt, guilt, guilt. He kept looking at her. She'd caught his attention, a critical mistake. He seemed to notice the picnic basket on the ground at her feet. His brow darkened, perhaps at the basket's unlikely presence there, perhaps at the somewhat odd trio in scarves and pulled-down hats, jackets, and heavy pants.

She cast another quick glance to the family behind them. Yes, they were coming here, too, up to the temple. Their car was in place now, waiting. She couldn't wait any longer, even if it had to get a little ugly. They'd planned for this contingency. They were ready.

She nodded to her two partners, jerked her head indicating the middle-aged solo hiker. In their planning meetings, they had decided that if fate handed them a situation like this, they would take full advantage of it. This would increase the profile of what they were doing. The public outcry was always vastly more satisfying if people got hurt or dead. That possibility made the game that much more meaningful. It also gave it a greater edge of excitement.

One of her men lifted the picnic basket to the edge of the railing while the other strolled casually over behind the man, who was now – apparently – transfixed by the show beneath them, the crashing water and noise and simple *power* of the spectacle. But then he looked up again and saw the picnic basket in its even more unlikely place. He started to raise a hand, began to speak so she could hear. 'Hey, what's . . .?'

It was time to move. Another nod and both men went into action. Her partner, who had once jumped into this temple to prove his manhood, caught the solo hiker from behind and flipped him over the edge as if he were a sack of flour. At the same time, her other partner had opened the top of the basket and taken out one of the five-gallon buckets, dumping it whole on to the grate while she did the same with the other one.

And then they were running, the basket left behind, the teenage lovebirds left flat-footed, unable to decide whether to help the older hiker or chase the bad guys.

They skirted the approaching family on a dead run, piled into their waiting Camaro, and sped with squealing tires from the parking lot.

Hardy heard about it on the radio on the way to his office after his talk with Glitsky. The emergency news report was warning citizens of San Francisco to avoid using their tap water until the actual substance that had been dumped into Crystal Springs could be positively determined.

'. . . although the labeling on the buckets recovered at the Pulgas Water Temple led authorities to suspect that it is the gasoline additive MTBE . . .'

Suddenly Hardy reached forward and turned up the volume. He'd never heard of the stuff before this week and now suddenly it was everywhere. The announcer was continuing. 'A group identifying itself as the Clean Earth Alliance has faxed a communiqué to this station and other local news media claiming responsibility for the poisoning.

'Damon Kerry, the candidate for governor who has been running on a platform to outlaw the use of MTBE as a gasoline additive in California, is in San Francisco today. In a just-concluded press conference at the St Francis Hotel, he responded to critics who have accused him of some kind of complicity in this attack. He had this to say about this latest escalation in what has been called the gasoline additive wars.'

Hardy had arrived at the entrance to the parking lot

underneath his building, but he waited out in the street, not wanting to lose any of the transmission. An angry-sounding voice came over his speakers. 'The people who have tried to poison San Francisco's water supply are terrorists. They say that the purpose of this poisoning is to call the bluff of the oil companies who contend that MTBE is not a significant health hazard in drinking water. They say that this vile act will dramatize their position. But I say that what they have done is unconscionable and criminal. No one associated with my campaign has anything but contempt for these people and their actions.'

The emergency bulletin switched back to the station's DJ, again cautioning citizens about the hazards of drinking the water, and giving some more details about the attack itself, the man who'd been pushed over into the temple and who was now in critical condition with a broken back, and the spotty descriptions of the terrorists.

Hardy heard it all in a kind of trance, then looked at his watch, slammed his car back into gear and pulled out on to Sutter Street. Whatever he'd been planning to do in his office could wait. He wasn't a dozen blocks from the St Francis and that's where he was going.

Al Valens was in charge in the lobby. He was short, energetic, well dressed and powerfully built. Hardy stood on the sidelines for a moment inside the revolving doors of the hotel's famous clock lobby, taking the lay of the land.

Valens was smiling, frowning, slapping backs, nodding sagely – whatever the minute demanded. Reporters, the curious, and the usual press of clueless tourists were still milling about. Cameras and lighting equipment were being packed up and put away. 'Hey,' he heard the short man say to a small knot of reporters, 'You heard Mr Kerry say it, and now you're going to hear Al Valens say it. We had nothing to do with this. Nothing. This is awful. These people are cretins.'

Valens threw a worried glance up the stairs to the Compass

Rose Bar. Hardy and Frannie had met there a hundred times. He knew where Kerry was hiding.

There was, of course, still some security around him – four uniformed hotel guards, a plain-clothed bodyguard, and a man in a tuxedo whom Hardy recognized as the room's *maitre d'*. Kerry himself was in an area cordoned off behind a velvet rope. He sat forward, alone, on a low couch. Occasionally, he would reach for the glass of water that rested next to an iced pitcher on the table in front of him.

The name and face of Damon Kerry had been familiar in San Francisco for the better part of the past twenty years. He'd made his début as a city supervisor. There he served two fairly distinguished terms that gave the lie to the initial impression that he was a spoiled rich kid whose daddy had bought him the office as a toy. Kerry was always a Greenpeace, Save the Whales for Jesus kind of guy – in San Francisco that always flew politically – but he also actually put in time cleaning up oily bays and beaches, serving in soup kitchens, *doing* things.

When he moved up as an assemblyman in Sacramento, he continued with his activism – especially in environmental areas – and his San Francisco constituency never abandoned him. He was their boy, liberal to the bone, sincere and electable, but always before in a low-key way. He was about to be forced to leave office under California's term limit laws, and this – some said more than any personal ambition for higher office – got him rolling on the MTBE bandwagon and into statewide exposure. Also, of course, Al Valens got involved.

Kerry was one of the perennially and effortlessly young-looking, and Hardy wanted to hate him for it. He was in his mid-forties, but he passed for less. There wasn't a line marring the ruddy, healthy skin of his face. He was trim in a dark-blue suit, neither small nor over-imposing. Sitting on the couch, he was the boy next door grown up and made good. An open face, appealing without being too handsome. Clear blue eyes, a strong nose, one perfectly chipped tooth. On looks alone, on the vibe he projected, you wanted to like the guy.

But it was a passive scene up the stairs here in the bar. All the action was in the lobby below them. Hardy thought he could take some advantage.

Walking confidently over, he nodded easily at the bodyguard, and put a bright tone to his voice, a decent volume. 'Is that Damon Kerry?'

The nearest hotel guard did his job, moving into Hardy's way. 'Hey, no interviews. He's done that. You missed it, too bad.'

It wasn't Hardy's intention to threaten or bluff. He stepped a little to one side, holding up a hand as though apologizing. 'I'm not a reporter.' His voice went up another notch as he faced Kerry behind the velvet rope. 'I'm Ron Beaumont's attorney. Bree Beaumont's husband?'

'I don't care if you're the Queen of England. I said no interviews and you're not—'

But Kerry's head had jerked up and now he was on his feet. 'No, no, it's all right.' The politician's smile, hand outstretched. 'It's all right,' he repeated to the security troops. 'I'll talk to this man.' Then, to Hardy, up at the rope. 'Hi. Damon Kerry. What can I do for you?'

'I don't know for sure. I'm trying to clear my client before they decide to arrest him. When I heard you were down here, I thought I'd take a chance, see if you'd talk to me. Maybe it's my lucky day.'

Kerry threw a look over Hardy's shoulder, perhaps expecting Valens to come and take him away from all this. But help wasn't on the way and he came back to Hardy, and offered another weak smile. 'What did you want to talk to me about?'

Hardy was tempted to get sarcastic – tell him he'd seen him on television and wanted to know who did his hair. There was only one topic that Hardy could be here about, and Kerry had to know it, which was the reason he'd gotten this far. He motioned to the rope separating them, to the couch Kerry had just left. 'Maybe back there?'

Reassuring his guards for the third time that it was OK, Kerry moved the rope aside and let Hardy come through, then followed him to the couch where they both sat. Kerry put on an interested face and they spent a minute on the familiar topic of Hardy's first name – how Dismas had been the good thief on Calvary and was the patron saint of murderers.

'But what I'm here for,' Hardy concluded, 'is maybe you can give me a better take on Bree. People say you two were close and I wondered if she ever mentioned any enemies, or that she was afraid for her life?'

Kerry reached for his water glass and took a quick drink. 'Honestly, no. Her death alone was a big enough shock, but when I heard that someone had killed her . . .' He shook his head. 'I thought it was impossible. Nobody could have hated her, not personally. She was the sweetest person alive.'

'So you think it was related to . . . what? This gas stuff?'

Another shake of the head. 'I don't know. A burglary, maybe. She was at the wrong place at the wrong time.' He lapsed into a short silence. When he spoke again, Hardy had an impression of greater directness. 'I can't imagine, really, although after what happened today, I sometimes feel I'm at a loss to explain anything anymore. I mean who would poison *drinking* water? What twisted logic makes these people do anything? If they could do that . . .' He trailed off. 'How about her husband? Your client? Doesn't he have any thoughts on this? Didn't I read that he's disappeared?'

'He just knows it wasn't him. I don't think it was either. What do you think?'

Kerry looked out beyond his security perimeter, then back to Hardy. 'I don't suppose he'd be under suspicion if there wasn't some evidence, would he?'

'It happens all the time. Do you know Ron?'

'No. We've never met, not personally.'

Hardy frowned.

'What?'

178

'Nothing. I guess I'd just assumed you'd been to their place socially.'

'No. Bree was a consultant and friend – a good friend, even – but she kept her family separate. I never even met her children. Still, you understand I'm not saying anything accusatory about her husband. I'm sure he's devastated by this as well.'

Hardy leaned forward, his elbows on his knees. 'He really didn't kill her.'

The intensity seemed to startle Kerry. 'All right.'

'But somebody did, Mr Kerry. Please, I have to get a take on who she was, out in the real world, not with her husband and family. You say she had no enemies, she was the sweetest person on earth, but I know Caloco wasn't happy with her, for example. Maybe somebody else wasn't either. Somebody killed her. I've got to see who she was. Can you help me at all here?'

Kerry's reaction was surprising. Notably, he didn't look up for the saving arrival of the cavalry. Instead, his eyes turned inward for a beat, and then he sat back on the couch, Hardy thinking man-oh-man, here's another one.

He didn't come up with it immediately – Hardy had obviously caught him off guard by moving away from specific questions. Kerry had probably been expecting the kinds of questions Hardy had been expecting to ask about motives and opportunities.

But now it was clear that whatever Kerry said, he wanted to get it right. At length he came back forward, hands clasped in front of him, but easily this time, far more relaxed than he'd been. He met Hardy's eyes for the first time. 'She was the ugly duckling.'

This seemed to contradict everything Hardy had heard about Bree to this moment – her beauty, charm, brains, persuasiveness. His face must have showed his confusion, because Kerry jumped in to explain. 'What I mean by that is if you want to know who she was, you've got to start with that.'

'With what, exactly?'

Kerry drew in a breath, thought for a moment. 'The fact that while she was growing up, she was a nerd, a brain at a time when you didn't want to be smart if you were a girl. Well, she was a *really* smart girl, with glasses and goofy hair and no style at all and this kind of absent-minded "what's going on around me" feeling . . .' He trailed off.

'You knew her as a child?' Hardy asked.

A really genuine smile. 'No, no, I don't mean that. I only met her – knew her – for a few months, but we got to know each other pretty well.' A pause that Hardy elected not to interrupt. Kerry was talking, which was what he wanted. He'd start again. And after a sigh, he did.

'Anyway, that's where she came from. She wasn't very popular. She had no friends, no social interests. Just studying and chemistry.'

'But she was so pretty. She must have had dates? In high school?'

'No,' Kerry said. 'Guys didn't think she was pretty, if you can believe that. She told me she didn't have *one* date. She went to school dances with her brother, it was that bad.' He wanted Hardy to understand. 'You know those movies where this really plain girl takes off her glasses at the end and suddenly she's the prettiest girl in town? Well, that was Bree, except that her movie didn't end until she was in her mid-twenties and by then she was so used to being plain and ignored by men that she just couldn't accept any other view of herself. Plus, her brains still made her threatening as hell to a lot of guys.'

Plus, Hardy was thinking, she was married, which meant she wasn't in the market. Or did it?

But Kerry, obviously still in thrall to her memory, was going on. 'The thing about her, and maybe it seems funny or contradictory or something because she was so smart, but the self-image stuff I think really slowed her down in how fast she grew up . . . I'm trying to think of the right word. She was just very naïve, I'd say, insulated. Almost unaware of anything in life, anything except her studies, which translated into her job. I mean, until . . .' Now Kerry really was at a loss.

'Until you?' Hardy prompted.

Kerry lifted his shoulders, an admission. 'It was starting to happen before we met. She was ready for it.'

'For what?'

'The change, the conversion. Well, it wasn't really that.'

'OK. What was it?' Hardy became fleetingly aware of a buzz out in the room, a rush of convivial laughter from a gaggle of young couples pulling tables together. Afternoon drinks after shopping in a different world than that inhabited by Hardy and Frannie. He came back to the candidate for governor, with whom he seemed to be having a genuine communication. It was almost surreal, but he was going to keep it going if he could. 'What was the big conversion all about then?'

'It was her whole life, really.' He fixed Hardy with a thoughtful expression. 'This may sound presumptuous . . .' Again, he stopped and Hardy waited. 'It wasn't so much that she grew up all at once as the fact that she realized she *had* grown up. She was a beautiful swan. She could fly.'

'OK.' This didn't make all the sense in the world to Hardy, but he'd sort it out later. 'But this conversion was public, right, on some radio show? And had to do with you?'

A shrug. 'I don't know how much of it had to do with me. But the debate we had seemed to mark a shift. She realized we had the same goals and we'd been set up to be on different sides. Actually, she'd been set up. She got bitter about her employers and I can't say I blame her.'

'Jim Pierce?' It was a guess, but from Kerry's reaction, a good one.

Kerry nodded. 'He was the one who first recognized her for what she could do, I mean politically. He groomed her into a mouthpiece, but as I say she was naïve. She bought his line because she bought him. He was Big Oil, but he cared about

181

the world just like she did. Ha. But he was her father figure at the same time. He loved her when she was still the ugly duckling and that carried a lot of emotional weight.'

'He loved her? You just said he loved her.'

'I don't know about that. What he did do was keep her nose to the grindstone, reward her handsomely for doing what he wanted, pat her on the head when she did good, and tell her not to worry about other things she might be hearing or thinking. She wanted to please him and she didn't look up.' He hesitated. 'I was really just the catalyst, I think. It would have happened without me eventually. She was ripe for it. She'd grown up.'

'And started seeing you.'

This suddenly brought Kerry back to where he was, what he was in fact doing, which was talking to a lawyer about a murder case. His public persona – always open and charming – was especially unnerving to Hardy as it fell like a shroud between them. 'Not the way I think you mean, Mr Hardy. She was married, after all.'

'But you're not.'

Kerry favored him with the candidate smile, went back to his watch, and decided that if reinforcements weren't going to come and rescue him, he'd go to them. 'Well, no. Never been married. Never found the right girl.'

He slapped his knees and stood up. 'It's been very nice talking to you, but I've got to get my campaign manager back out on the trail. This water poisoning today.' He scowled. 'Terrible, just terrible.' Then the smile was back, the hand outstretched again. 'Don't forget to vote now. Take care.'

He walked over to his security retinue and Hardy sat back down on the couch, watching the party coalesce around Kerry as it began to drift down into the main lobby.

When they were good and gone, Hardy reached over and, using the cocktail napkin that the hotel had thoughtfully provided, lifted the water glass Kerry had been using. He poured the remaining water back into the pitcher and slipped the glass into the pocket of his nylon windbreaker. 'Take care yourself,' he thought.

But, feeling smug about the glass with fingerprints, he suddenly realized he'd forgotten the main question he'd wanted to ask the Kerry camp. He nearly jumped up from the couch and caught up the candidate and his entourage as they arrived at where Al Valens had just finished up with a reporter.

'Excuse me, Mr Kerry.'

The security detail moved to keep Hardy at his distance, but Kerry again told them it was OK. He was a candidate, it was election time, you talked to people.

'I had one last question, this time for Mr Valens if you don't mind. It won't take a minute.'

Kerry broke a seemingly genuine smile. 'OK, Colombo, sure. We've always got a minute. Al. This is Mr Hardy. He's Ron Beaumont's attorney.'

Valens cast a quick glance between Hardy and Kerry, then thrust his hand out. 'Nice to meet you. What's your question?'

'I was wondering why you called Ron Beaumont last week – something about Bree's files?'

The smile flickered briefly. 'I don't think that was me,' he said. He looked at Kerry. 'Did we call Ron?'

'Not that I remember.'

'You didn't call Ron Beaumont and leave a message last Wednesday, Thursday, something like that?'

Valens made a little show of thinking about it for a moment, looked again at Kerry, then shook his head. 'I think you must be mistaken. Isn't he out of town? I heard he was out of town?'

Hardy was sincerely contrite. 'I'm sorry. I must have been misinformed.' A broad smile. 'Mr Kerry, thanks again.'

Kerry waved him off. 'Don't worry about it. Any time.'

'Shit.' Valens' voice was unnaturally shrill in the telephone.

'He knows something. This guy Hardy. Who is he? What's that about?'

Baxter Thorne spoke to Valens in his calmest tones. 'Al, it's always better to tell the truth. Especially in front of Damon. Tell him you forgot. You've been consumed with these terrorist accusations against him today. Your head was spinning and you couldn't recall for a minute. In fact, you remember now that you did call Ron – here, this is good – to see about some memorial words he wanted to include about Bree if, no when, Damon gets elected. In his acceptance speech, that is if Ron wouldn't object, if it wouldn't be too painful. That's why you called.'

'But how did this guy Hardy know . . . ?'

Thorne was sweet reason. 'You left a message. He must have heard the message.'

'But how?'

'Well, he must have been there then, mustn't he? At Bree's place?'

'Looking for the report?'

'I don't know. Perhaps. Certainly looking for something. But you said he was Ron's attorney, right? It might not have had anything to do with our problem. Don't worry. I'll look into it. You've got a campaign to run.'

'All right, all right. But it worries me.'

'Don't worry about it, Al. It's nothing. And if it's not nothing, I'll take care of it.'

18

The evening remained clear and warm with no fog and Hardy felt he'd picked up a scent. People were evading and lying, and this juiced him up.

He wished he had a set of Al Valens' fingerprints as well as Damon Kerry's. He had no explanation for why Valens would lie about calling Ron. Still, he did have Damon Kerry's cleverly purloined water glass and he dropped it off on Abe Glitsky's desk with a cryptic note that it contained crucial evidence in the Bree Beaumont case and should be dusted and checked against prints that had been found in the penthouse.

Hardy added that if Glitsky didn't do this he'd be sorry, a statement Abe would enjoy. The note also mentioned that Kerry had denied ever having been there and this was a new development.

It was still early – Hardy had time before his scheduled seven o'clock meeting with Canetta at his office. He could zip down to see Ron and his well-behaved children, deliver his update, and make everybody feel better.

He'd also filled a page of legal pad with questions that Ron would be able to answer for him, mostly to do with the names Canetta had copied from Ron's answering machine.

Who was Marie? Kogee Sasaka? Tilton? What did all these people want? What about Valens and Kerry and Pierce? How well had Ron known them? Or had Bree known them?

Then, the harder questions: Did Ron think or know that Bree was having an affair? If so, with whom? What about the baby she'd been carrying? Had she and Ron planned it? What had her last morning been like? What, if anything, had she been worried about? How involved, if at all, had Ron been with her professional life? Did he know what she was working on now?

And, most importantly, what was Ron's explanation for the fact that of all the men Hardy had talked to – Pierce, Kerry, even Canetta – why was it that her own husband seemed the least affected by her death?

Driving south on the freeway, heading for the hotel where Ron and his children had holed up, Hardy almost let himself believe he was beginning to make some progress. He would get answers from Ron, and maybe learn more about MTBE and ethanol and today's reservoir poisoning which, he reasoned, had to be related to Bree's murder. He was really getting somewhere.

'Mr Brewster has checked out.'

'Checked out?' Hardy repeated it as though it were a foreign phrase he didn't understand.

The concierge was a pleasant-looking young woman with a brisk and efficient manner. 'Yes, sir.' She punched a few keys at her computer. 'Early this morning.'

'You're sure?' An apologetic smile. 'I'm sorry. It's just that I thought we had an appointment and I'm a little surprised.'

She punched a few more keyboard buttons and noticing his obvious concern softened visibly. 'Maybe you got the day wrong?'

Hardy nodded. 'Must have,' he said.

So it was still early and he had noplace to be for a couple of hours.

Ron Beaumont was beginning to remind him of several clients he'd had in the past – they tended to lie and, when not held in custody, to disappear. It made him mad and crazy, but at the same time this behavior was so predictable among suspects that it didn't necessarily force him to believe they were guilty of anything. They were just scared, confused, misguided. Except for those who were, in fact, guilty and on the run.

As he drove by Candlestick Point, Hardy was trying his hardest to stick with the rationalization that Ron had his children to protect. There was the further point that if Hardy had been able to locate him at his hotel, others with less benign intents – the DA's investigators, for example – might be just as successful. And Ron hadn't promised Hardy that he'd stick around for continued consultation.

Nothing had changed, he kept telling himself. He had until Tuesday to find who had killed Bree. And Frannie would remain locked up until then anyway.

By the time he took the 7th Street offramp by the Hall of Justice downtown, though, his pique had progressed into a fine fury. Ron Beaumont, the son of a bitch, had a million answers at his fingertips, and now Hardy was going to have to find them on his own, if he could. And meanwhile the clock kept ticking. He didn't have the heart anymore for this cat-and-mouse nonsense. And especially not from someone who'd put Frannie where she was.

Force of habit almost led him to park across from the jail where he would visit Frannie and check back in with Abe's office. At this time, late on a Saturday afternoon, there was actually a spot at the curb.

But he kept driving. He wasn't going to leave any messages now with Glitsky to accompany his note on Damon Kerry's fingerprints. The way he felt about Ron would spill over somehow and muddy the waters. He didn't want Glitsky even glancing in Ron's direction as a viable suspect if he could help it.

And Frannie? She was the reason he was doing any of this in the first place. And sure, he could go hold her hand again but it would use up two more precious hours. Frannie wanted him to save Ron and his kids and the price of that – for her – was going to be that her husband couldn't come and console her every time he was in the neighborhood.

Truth be told, Ron's disappearance had kicked up a renewed dust storm of anger at Frannie, too. And a smaller zephyr at his own gullibility, his continuing efforts in a cause in which he had at best a manufactured faith. He was doing all this for his wife, at her urging. He'd let her deal with the consequences. See how she liked them apples.

But he had to admit that there were developments in this case that didn't depend on Ron Beaumont, that had piqued his interest on their own. The three men – Canetta, Pierce, and Kerry – who were in mourning over Bree's death. Today's MTBE poisoning. Al Valens lying. And always – three billion dollars.

Hardy was on automatic, some non-rational process having determined that he should go to his office. He still had two hours until Canetta was due to show up to trade information. The odds were in favor of David Freeman being around, working on Saturday. Hardy could bounce his discoveries and hunches off his landlord, a practice that was nearly always instructive.

If Freeman wasn't there, he'd pore over the copies of Griffin's notes that Glitsky had given him and see if some new detail caught his attention. It was a backup plan, but at least it was some plan.

And then suddenly the open curb at 5th near Mission called to him. One legal parking space downtown on a weekday qualified as a miracle, but seeing an entire *side* of 5th Street nearly empty was nearly the beatific vision. Fresh snow or a morning beach without footprints – you just ached to walk on it. He pulled over and came to a stop directly across from the *Chronicle* building.

It was a sign.

Jeff Elliot was the *Chronicle* columnist who wrote the 'Citytalk' column on the political life of the city.

When Hardy had first met him, he'd been a young, personable, fresh-faced kid from the Midwest who walked with the aid of crutches due to his ongoing battle with multiple sclerosis. Now, although still technically young – Hardy doubted if Jeff had yet turned thirty-five – the baby-faced boy sported a graying, well-trimmed beard. His chest had thickened and his eyes had grown perennially tired. Here in his office just off the city room, the old crutches rested by the door, almost never used anymore. Now, Jeff got around in a wheelchair.

But he was still personable, at least to Hardy, who over the years had been the conduit of a lot of good information and the subject of one or two columns. He and his wife had even been to parties at Hardy's house.

Jeff had undoubtedly come downtown today after the water poisoning. Barring an assassination of the President or an eight-point earthquake, this was going to be tomorrow's headline and there were political elements all over it.

But now that Hardy had stuck his head in his door, first things first. Jeff swung away from his computer and motioned him in. 'Big D,' he said. '*¿Qué pasa?*' Then he remembered and grew suddenly serious. 'How's Frannie holding up?'

Hardy made a face. What could he say?

Jeff shook his head in disgust. 'I'd sue Braun, Pratt, Randall, the whole lot of 'em. Or kill them. Maybe both.'

'No options are out of the question.'

'So you got my call at home?'

'No. I've been out all day.'

This surprised Jeff. 'Well, the message was that I was going to give this Frannie thing a couple of graphs on Monday, maybe get somebody's attention. I thought you could give me a good quote.'

Hardy smiled thinly. 'Nothing you could print in a family newspaper.'

Jeff looked a question. 'So you didn't get the message and yet you're here?'

'I saw a free parking place at the curb. Hell, the whole street. What could I do? I said to myself, "Self," I said, "why don't you have a little off-the-record chat with your good friend Jeff Elliot?" '

This brought a smile. Long ago, Hardy had neglected to

189

preface some remarks to Jeff that they were off the record. It hadn't worked out too well, and since then Hardy had made it a point to include the words 'off the record' in every discussion he ever had with Jeff, even purely social ones.

Jeff smiled. 'I was waiting for that.'

'Plus,' Hardy continued, 'I thought it was possible you might know something I don't.'

'Probably. I'm good on the Middle Ages and Victorian England.'

'Dang.' Hardy snapped his fingers. 'Neither of those. I was thinking more about Frannie, Bree or Ron Beaumont, this MTBE business.' Hardy thought a minute. 'Damon Kerry. Al Valens.'

Jeff cracked a grin. 'You done? I think you left out my wife and a couple of senators.'

Hardy spread his palms in a frustrated gesture. 'I can't seem to get much of it to hang together.'

The columnist swung his wheelchair around to face Hardy. 'In return for which I get the exclusive of the big secret Frannie's gone to jail about?'

'Nope, but you might get Bree's killer before anybody else.'

'Are you close to that? Everybody's saying it's the husband. Ron, is it?'

A shake of the head. 'Abe Glitsky, whom you may remember is head of homicide, is definitely not saying it. And Abe be the man on this stuff.'

'He's not on Ron?'

Pause. 'It's not Ron.'

He'd *almost* said that Glitsky was affirmatively saying it wasn't Ron, which wasn't true. But if that's what Jeff Elliot heard, he wouldn't correct the impression.

'So who's your guess? You got one?'

In his chair, Hardy drew a deep breath. He'd gathered a lot of information. But in spite of feeling as though he'd gotten somewhere in his investigation, he realized that he couldn't precisely define where that was. When he asked Elliot to tell him about Damon Kerry, it surprised him almost as much as it did Jeff. Where had that question come from?

Jeff was shaking his head. 'That's got to be a big negatory, Diz.'

'Maybe. But I'd sure like to know more than I do about the two of them, Bree and the good candidate.'

For a response, Jeff sat all the way back in his wheelchair behind his desk. He pulled at his mustache, scratched his beard, and brushed at the front of his shirt.

'No hurry,' Hardy prodded, shooting Jeff a hopeful grin. 'It's only Frannie doing hard time for keeping a promise.'

Finally, the reporter sighed. 'You know, the connections,' he said. 'You don't put them together.' But Jeff wasn't quite ready to spill anything, not yet. The impish smile from his youth fleetingly appeared as he came forward, his hands together on the desk. 'You know that off-the-record thing we do? This is one of those, private and personal.'

'Done. Understood.' Hardy was beginning to feel a little like a Catholic priest in a confessional. A couple more days like the last few and he'd know every secret in the world and wouldn't be able to tell any of them. But if that was the price for knowledge, he had to pay it.

Eve's bad trade. He could only hope it wouldn't turn out as badly for him as it had for her.

Jeff underscored it. 'So this is personal, your ears only. If it doesn't directly help Frannie, it stays here.'

'Deal.' Hardy got up and they shook hands over the desk. 'So what connections?' he asked.

'What you just said. Frannie in jail. Kerry in another file in the brainpan – the election, the water poisoning today, all that. I didn't put them together.' His eyes shone with interest. 'But they are together, aren't they? They're all Bree.'

'That's my guess.'

Jeff fidgeted in his chair, came to his decision, and nodded. 'Have I mentioned the off-the-record thing?'

Hardy was dying to learn what Jeff knew, but it never

191

helped to show it. He broke an easy smile. 'Once or twice.'

He waited.

'The thing about Kerry is that he's really a good guy, especially for a politician. I've been with him more than a few times, in press rooms, after the odd banquet, off the record – much like you and me right now, and he's decent. Plus he plays straight with us.'

'Us?'

'Reporters, media, like that.'

'OK.' And . . . ?

'OK, so a guy like that, sometimes a guy like me finds out a fact and kind of unofficially decides it doesn't have to be in the public interest.'

Hardy's eyebrows went up. 'Excuse me. I thought I just heard you say that the media could show some restraint.'

Jeff acknowledged the point with a wry face. 'I'm talking personal here. Me. It's not something I brag about, but it happens. Sometimes.' At Hardy's skeptical look, he spread his palms wide. 'OK, rarely. But the point is, Kerry's not married, he can date anybody he wants. As our President has pointed out, it's his private life. It's not news.'

'But Bree was married.'

'And maybe they didn't do anything let's say carnal. Maybe she just hung around a lot and it was purely the campaign and business.'

Hardy leaned forward. 'But you know otherwise?'

'Did I catch them *in flagrante*? No. But I know. My opinion is they were in love with each other.'

This took a minute to digest, although Hardy had come to suspect it.

But Jeff was going on. 'She only lived a half-dozen blocks from him, both of 'em up on Broadway, you know.'

'No, I didn't know about him. I knew she did.'

'Well, Kerry, too. His place is that little thirty-room shack just up from Baker. You'd remember it if you saw it, and you have.' Jeff seemed almost relieved to be able to let his secret out. If he'd promised not to print it, telling somebody who in turn couldn't tell was next best. 'Anyway, couple of months ago I was pushing Damon for an interview – as I said, we go back a ways, too – and he said meet him at his place after hours, he'd dig up something for me. He was coming in from Chico or someplace, and was going to be alone, which meant without Valens. Except when I got there, who opens the door but Bree Beaumont.'

'Dressed?'

Jeff chuckled. 'You've got a dirty mind. Let's go with casually attired. Casually and very, very attractively.' He paused, remembering, then blew out a rush of air. 'Very. Low green silk blouse, linen pants, barefoot. I distinctly remember she forgot her underwear on top. Believe me, it was the kind of thing you noticed, especially on her, even if you weren't a trained reporter like me, alive to every detail.'

Hardy wanted to keep him going. 'I keep hearing how pretty she was.'

'A couple of miles beyond pretty, Diz. In any event,' he continued, 'here's a bottle of champagne in a bucket on the coffee table, and otherwise the house is empty. So ask me, do I feel like I'm intruding? *Moi?*'

'So what was it?'

'Evidently she was planning to surprise him with a little welcome homecoming after the road trip. So he shows about ten minutes after I arrive, opens the door and it's like, uh, "Hi, Bree, fancy you being here. Now, how 'bout them gas additives?" Call me a genius, but I saw right through it.'

'You're a genius.'

Jeff nodded. 'Somebody has to be. So anyway, they were together, and I knew it, and they knew I knew it. And I told them I'd keep a lid on it.'

'I'm just curious, but why would you do that?'

He shook his head as though mystified himself. 'I don't know, Diz. I like the guy. I like his politics. It meant a lot to them.' He met Hardy's eyes. 'Bottom line is I just decided. It

193

shames me to say it, but I might even do the same for you.'

'You don't have to,' Hardy replied. 'I wasn't sleeping with Bree. But after she was killed, weren't you tempted to talk to the police?'

'Why? Nobody's saying Damon's a suspect.'

Hardy looked a question. 'At the least, Jeff, she's murdered and you know he's her lover. That's got to be relevant to the homicide investigation. Maybe even crucial.'

'It's also relevant to Damon's campaign, maybe even crucial. He didn't kill her, Diz. There is no way. Plus, I want to see him get elected, and I sure as hell don't have to tell the cops what I know. Maybe if some inspector had come and made some connection, asked me directly . . . I don't know, I might have been tempted. But nobody did. Nobody has.'

'But as *you* say, Jeff, it is all connected. It's got to be.' For emphasis, Hardy patted the desk between them. 'So today's bonus question is who did the water? What's the Clean Earth Alliance?'

Jeff shifted again in his wheelchair, brought a hand to his tired eyes and rubbed them. Glancing at his watch, he looked up suddenly to see that outside a sepia dusk had settled. 'When am I going to learn not to work on weekends? Why did I come in here on a Saturday?'

Hardy leaned forward. Jeff knew something else and was wrestling with how much to reveal. Hardy kept it low affect. 'You were going to write some graphs on Frannie.'

Which brought it all back home. Jeff sat still a moment, then wheeled himself around to a low file cabinet. Back at the desk, he laid open the thick file folder and began turning pages. 'The Yosemite Militia. The *Valdez* Avengers. Earth Now.' He looked up. 'And today's Clean Air Alliance. Get the picture?'

'They're all related?'

'Let's say I'd bet their headquarters is some cabin in Montana.'

'So who runs them?'

'Well, this is a matter of some debate.' Jeff pulled pages and ran down a synopsis of damage these groups had done, most of it in the realm of nuisance – vandalisms and graffiti – but in two cases something much more serious.

The *Valdez* Avengers had claimed responsibility for a pipe bomb explosion at an Exxon Gas Station in Tacoma, Washington, that had killed four people and injured twelve. Jeff looked up from the page. 'They didn't want people to invest in Exxon. That daring raid killed a little girl, six years old. Boy, that showed her.'

More recently, at the huge refinery in Richmond, just across the Bay, three guards had been severely beaten in a thus-far unclaimed attack. The refinery's statement was that nothing had been taken, and that the rest of their security team had driven off the five assailants, although they'd been unable to capture them. 'But you want my opinion,' Jeff concluded, 'that's when these clowns got their hands on the MTBE.'

'But couldn't they just as well have gone to the gas station and pumped it out at a buck twenty-nine a gallon?'

'Sure, but what's the fun in that? Diz, these people are thugs. They get their rocks off shaking things up, making the Big Statement. Like today.'

Hardy leaned back, crossed a leg. 'And you've got all this stuff in one folder.'

'Right. Like Bree and Frannie and Damon, it's all connected somehow. And now this stuff,' he motioned down to his pile of paper, 'it's part of that, too.'

'So who's behind it? I had a Caloco guy today tell me that SKO funded this kind of activity.'

But this didn't fit Jeff's world view. 'No, I'd be surprised at that. SKO's big. These independent bozos seem to hate big.'

Hardy pointed at the folders. 'You got any stories about attacks on ethanol producers or distributors?'

Jeff didn't have to look. 'No, now that you mention it. And that's a good point.'

'Maybe these groups don't know who's bankrolling them. Maybe SKO's got a front.'

Jeff nodded. 'But that means . . .' He stopped, the idea germinating. 'Why would they . . . ?'

'I've been using this mantra all day,' Hardy said. 'You ought to try it.'

'What's that?'

'Three billion dollars. Say it a few times. It'll grow on you.'

19

David Freeman was not asleep and he wasn't reading anything. But he was completely still, his feet propped up on the table in his Solarium, which was the nickname for the conference room just off the main lobby in his building. He wasn't wearing shoes, and one of his Argyle socks had a hole in the toe. His cigar spiked the room with its rich odor and left the air with a blue tint, although there was no sign that Freeman was drawing on it, or even was aware of it, stuck there in the front of his face.

Hardy tapped once on the open door.

Not a muscle moved. Freeman sighed. 'I was just thinking about you. How you doing?'

'I've been better.' Hardy pulled a chair and dropped himself into it. For a long moment, neither man said anything. Eventually, Hardy started. 'I just called home for my messages. Did you know it's Hallowe'en?'

'What is?'

'Tonight. It's Hallowe'en.'

For the first time, Freeman favored him with a glance, went back to his cigar, and blew a long plume. 'You forgot. Your kids are upset.'

It sounded like a chortle, but there wasn't any humor in it. None at all. 'What the hell am I . . . ?' He laid a hand on the table with exaggerated calm, drumming his fingertips. Da-da-dum, da-da-dum. 'I've got a meeting here in ten minutes, David. It's possibly even an important meeting, having to do with my wife being in jail, trying to get her out. Maybe I'm wrong, but this seems like something I ought to spend some of my time on.'

Another moment. Freeman had nothing to say, which was just as well. Hardy needed to vent.

'So we got a killer I'm trying to find without any help from the police. We got the city's water supply on hold for a couple of weeks. We got their mother rotting over downtown – have I mentioned that? And all these are somehow related and I've got no idea how. And do you know what the real problem is? I mean, the really big god damn most important thing wrong with the world right now tonight?' The drumming had picked up in tempo. 'You want to know?'

Humoring him, Freeman nodded imperceptibly. 'Sure.'

'All right, I'll tell you. It's that I am such a shitty father and care so little about my children that I forgot the most important holiday in their young and precious lives. It never hit my radar all day. Can you imagine? What else could I possibly have been thinking about?'

Freeman nodded again. 'It's the Nineties. Guy like you, you can't *not* be an insensitive cretin. Nothing to do but ignore it.'

Freeman was right. There wasn't any point bitching about Hardy's priorities. They were what they were.

He was that nineties' pariah, the linear, logical, fact-burdened, classically trained human. Even worse, some wiring flaw had predestined him to be more oriented toward justice than mercy. The rest of his San Francisco world was sensitive and child-centered and politically correct and of course the children's fun on Hallowe'en was much more important than any work Hardy might ever have to do.

He would just have to get over it.

In some countries, say Kosovo or Rwanda, Hardy was pretty sure many fathers didn't take time out every day to play with their children. Their goal – and he felt the same about his own – was simple survival. He wondered if kids in these countries considered their fathers insensitive.

The soul-wrenching truth of it was that Hardy cared more about his wife and children than about any *job*. Than about anything, for that matter. But this – today, what he was doing, was not some job. This was real life – his and Frannie's and the kids' real lives in a real crisis. Just like Ron Beaumont's kids and their lives.

And yet somehow both of his kids had assumed he'd zip on back to the Avenues and take them out trick or treating. It frustrated him beyond his ability to articulate. Young they might be, but could they really be unaware of the gravity of this situation? Of how much he treasured them? Of the *reason* behind every breath he took? Could they be that blind?

If they were, where had he failed them?

The old man swung his legs down to the ground, put his elbows on the table. 'What did you mean? You know they're related but don't know how? This water poisoning and Frannie? Is that what you're saying?'

Hardy was accustomed to Freeman's brain – it tended to take leaps in any direction that looked promising – but even so, it took him a second. And the segue, though abrupt, was just as well. It put him back on his work, on what he had to do, and the feeling part of it be damned.

When he'd made everything safe and secure again, it would have been worth it, and they could either understand why he'd done it and the way he'd done it or not. But either way, it would be done.

He nodded at Freeman. 'And while we're on it, possibly the election this Tuesday.'

Out in the lobby, they heard a harsh buzzing sound. 'That would be Canetta,' he said. 'My appointment. You want to stick around, I won't kick you out.'

'Are you kidding me? You couldn't if you tried.'

'Bill Tilton was, in fact, listed.'

They had gotten settled back in the smoky, dim room. Introductions made. Freeman brought up to speed. The land-lord's presence, Hardy sensed, only grudgingly accepted by Canetta. But the sergeant had information and he wanted to show off what he'd found. 'This isn't so tough,' the sergeant said. 'I could do this.'

'Sounds like you already did, Phil.' Hardy would give Canetta all the strokes he needed to keep him pumped up.

But Canetta seemed to be motivated on his own. 'He's an agent with Farmer's Fund Life Insurance. I called from the station so when he called back he'd know I was legitimately the police.'

'Smart,' Hardy said. He raised his eyes to Freeman, silently telling him to shut up. 'And he did call back?'

'Wasn't even an hour. So I asked him direct. Told him this was a murder investigation and we needed his cooperation. What'd he call Ron about? He said the company was a little sticky with the payout on Bree, her being murdered and all. On the side, Tilton tells me the claims guy doesn't want to send a check – we're talking two big ones – until it's pretty damn clear Ron didn't kill her. So I kept him yakking and he said it's the first time he's had this situation and it's made things ugly around his office. Now, this next, you're going to like this.'

Hardy waited, then realized Canetta needed some response. 'I give up.'

Another second of suspense, then a smile. 'His secretary quit over it. Marie couldn't believe Tilton could be such a shit to Ron, who was the nicest—'

'Marie?' Suddenly Hardy heard it.

Canetta smiled. 'That's what *I* said. And Tilton goes, "Yeah, Marie Dempsey." '

'The Marie from the phone messages?'

'As it turns out.' Canetta was almost beaming with child-like pride. 'Marie is, was, his – Tilton's – secretary.'

Hardy nodded in satisfaction. This was good. Two names to cross off. Insurance business. 'You know, Phil, you really can do this. You want I'll put in a plug to Glitsky.'

'Naw. Fuck Glitsky and the suits. I don't want to join 'em, but I wouldn't mind beating 'em.' Suddenly Canetta pointed to Freeman, who'd been uncharacteristically silent, to his cigar. 'By any chance, you got another one of those things?'

Freeman nodded, said sure, got up and disappeared back into the dark lobby.

'You sure he's cool?' Canetta asked.

Cool was about the last word Hardy would ever use to describe Freeman, but he knew what Canetta meant. 'He's the smartest guy you'll ever meet, Phil.'

Canetta threw a glance over his shoulder. 'Maybe the ugliest, too.'

Hardy, keeping his voice low, had to grin. 'Well, all of us can't have everything. But you can trust him, that I guarantee. You don't have to kiss him.'

A shudder traveled the whole length of Canetta's body. 'I'll try to restrain myself. I bet I can.'

'Can what?' Another of Freeman's many talents was his ability to appear out of nowhere. He had a handful of cigars, a bottle of red wine and glasses, all of which he kept a supply of in his office. He laid the cigars on the table. 'Help yourself, sergeant. I should have offered sooner. What did I miss?' He put down the glasses, and started to pour all around.

But Hardy had a hand out. 'None for me, David. I'm working.' And Canetta took the same road.

Freeman shrugged. He was working, too, but it was Saturday night. He could have a glass of wine – hell, a bottle of wine – and his brain would still hum along nicely, thank you, maybe even a little better than it was now. So would Hardy's and Canetta's, but David had learned long ago that you couldn't tell anything to baby boomers. They were working. Working was serious. They couldn't mix any fun in or they might – what? die? Christ, no wonder they all burned out.

But he sipped his wine and listened as Canetta went back to what he'd found. At least he'd lit his cigar, Freeman was thinking, although that, too, of course, would kill him. The sergeant was reading from his spiral notebook. 'Kogee Sasaka

201

has a massage place. Hands On. That's the name. I checked with some guys at the station. Legitimate. No busts, no complaints. She gives massages, if you can believe it. Anyway, that was the appointment she called Ron about.'

Canetta flicked at his pages. 'That was it. Tilton, Marie, and Kogee, wasn't it? And you did Pierce, right?'

'And Valens, as it turned out.' Hardy filled him in on the hotel interviews, ending with Valens' interesting fib about having called Ron.

'But Valens did call him.'

Hardy agreed. 'Unless someone was doing a pretty damn fine impersonation.'

'So why'd he lie about it?'

The question hung while Freeman swallowed his wine. Finally, he spoke up. 'That's where you push,' he said simply. 'Was the call about anything, or did he just leave his name?'

'No. Some report,' Hardy said. 'Bree's copy of something she was working on.'

'That she was working on *and* that Ron knew about,' Canetta said. 'I still think that's part of this. He realized it was important or valuable and he came back and got it.'

Hardy didn't want the sergeant going off with a hard-on for Ron Beaumont. 'I think Ron's going to be hard to find, Phil,' he said.

'If he came back,' Canetta countered, 'then he's still close by, am I right?'

'If he came back.'

'That's all I'm saying. If. And if I find him . . .'

'You'll let me know. First. Before you do anything.'

A nod. 'Absolutely.'

Canetta was gone. He told Freeman and Hardy that he thought he might see if Valens could be found tonight, and get this lie he'd told Hardy straightened out. Canetta knew the city's hotels like the back of his hand – Saturday night like this three days before the election, Kerry probably had five different appearances in various banquet rooms downtown. Shouldn't be too hard to catch up with the candidate. And his campaign manager would be with him, easy to talk to. This homicide stuff – a child could do it.

Meanwhile, the two attorneys had written down the names of every person in the investigation and now they had a bunch of yellow pages from legal pads strewn around the table with the by-now familiar names – Valens and Kerry, Pierce, Ron Beaumont. Even Frannie and Carl Griffin. The plan – Freeman's, with his love of context, as he called it – was to fill in connections under each name and see if they could connect the dots.

'OK,' Hardy said, 'you don't know anything about this. Where do you start?'

Freeman didn't hesitate. 'Griffin.'

A smile flitted at the edges of Hardy's mouth.

'What's funny?'

'Only that it never fails. I would have picked him last.'

Freeman chomped on his cigar, long since extinguished. 'He was the first horse at the trough, *n'est-ce pas*? That alone.'

This, Hardy thought, was why Freeman was so valuable. His input always triangulated the evidence, bringing different targets into sharper focus. 'OK, but Glitsky tells me he wasn't working Beaumont the morning he got killed . . .'

'It wasn't his case, or he wasn't working it.'

'No, he drew the case, but he had some others, too. He was in the field on one of them.'

'How did Glitsky know that?'

'Griffin told him before he went out the morning he got it.'

'He *told* him.' Freeman snorted the word.

'Why would he lie?'

The old man squinted across the table. 'Because you have been working all day and you're tired and stressed out, I'll just pretend you didn't ask that. Now, do we know what the other cases were?'

It continued like that around the daisy chain. Details about

Griffin's death – time, location – that might not jibe with the other cases he'd been assigned. Valens' lie about Bree's report. Hardy felt a little uneasy as Freeman, on his own, put Bree together with Damon Kerry. Also with Jim Pierce. 'Assume the worst, Diz. Life won't disappoint you so much. Bree slept around, maybe a lot with different guys. It gives us more to work with.'

Hardy wanted to avoid assuming the worst about women and their secret affairs. It was too close.

Forcing his attention back, Hardy listened as Freeman asked about Jim Pierce. 'Assuming he was sleeping with Bree, too.'

But having met the stunning Carrie Pierce during the day, this was difficult terrain for Hardy to negotiate. 'His wife is a world-class beauty, David. I can't see it.'

Freeman took the soggy cigar from his lips. 'You know, Diz, Jackie Kennedy wasn't exactly chopped liver. You know the basic difference between men and women around sex?'

'Equipment?'

'No, wise guy. Men want as many women as they can get. Women want the best man they can get. A fundamental truth.'

Hardy nodded. 'I'll write it down when I get home. But there's one other name we've left out here that I thought you'd enjoy.'

'Who's that?'

'Canetta.'

Hardy succeeded in surprising Freeman so rarely that when he did so, as now, he derived a disproportionate pleasure from it. Now the old man's eyes narrowed with interest. 'So how are you playing him?'

'I'm thinking he might tell me a lie. I'm thinking he's too involved too soon.'

A satisfied nod. 'You know, just when I think you're getting soft . . .'

'It's a long shot,' Hardy admitted. 'But he walked a beat near her place, he provided security at some functions for both Pierce and Bree, he let her off on a DUI . . .'

Freeman's bushy eyebrows shot up. 'That's real.'

'Real enough. They also had several curbside conversations.'

'Several?' A beat. 'All of them curbside?'

'That's what he says. But he wants me to believe he was truly infatuated with her. And maybe he was. I don't know.'

'And so you put him to work to find her killer.'

'Or to lead me away from looking at him.'

Freeman leaned back, pulled the cigar from his mouth, looked it over critically, and popped it back in. 'Sweet,' he said. 'You need me here, you know I'm in.'

Hardy nodded. 'I appreciate it, David. But let's remember that whoever this is, the guy's serious.'

A dismissive wave. 'Serious, schmerious. I've told you a thousand times, I'm bulletproof.'

'I've told you a thousand times, I hate when you say that.'

Freeman grunted. 'Doesn't mean it isn't true.'

S he was out again.

Jim Pierce couldn't face another society event, this one with adults wearing masks and other madness he didn't even want to consider. Hallowe'en. He'd begged off, as he had nine times out of ten for the past half-dozen years, fed up to the teeth with these cock and tail parties whose function was to make sure that his friends knew he was their friend, and they would tell by the size of the check.

Friends? He was too rich. He trusted no one. He hadn't a friend in the world.

The last one of these parties he'd attended – it had been a year before – had pretty much sealed his decision that he wouldn't be part of that scene anymore. This one, even for San Francisco, had been revolting.

The financial and political élite of the city were in a big, open warehouse in the South of Market area. There was often some artsy-fartsy performance supposedly related to the fundraising entity at these affairs, and that night after everyone had had a few, the main event began.

A naked couple appeared suddenly on a black-lit stage. Awful, drum-pounding noise made conversation impossible. The woman began carving some kind of devil worship symbols *into the man's back*.

Pierce had been twenty feet away, trying to talk to the district attorney and the mayor before the drums took over. What they were witnessing wasn't being done with mirrors. The blood flowed. And that was a mere preamble.

The woman had a bottle of Jack Daniel's bourbon from which she drank. Then she poured it over the man's new cuts and he screamed and screamed, writhing – but to the obscene beat – in real pain. The strobe lighting went red.

The drums increased. The man spread his legs and leaned over and – Pierce had trouble believing it still, though he had seen it with his own eyes – the woman shoved the neck of the Jack Daniel's bottle . . .

Thank God Carrie hadn't gone to that one – it might have given her a heart attack. But he'd gone, and that was enough. He was through.

The television droned in the small room under the stairwell. ESPN Sports Center. Twenty-four hours' coverage. Weekends he'd catch a good percentage of it, though it mostly repeated every half hour, the same stuff and the occasional update. But it kept him up on sports, something he needed for his image – a regular guy at work.

Well, not a regular guy. One of the bosses, actually, but at least one of the accessible ones. He hit the mute button and stood up, unsteady on his feet.

He'd promised Carrie he'd get himself something to eat. She'd be home in less than an hour now, and all he'd done was drink – couple of Scotches and a bottle of Pinot Grigio. He'd better eat if he didn't want to endure another round of the third degree.

Carrie had been going on and on lately – why wasn't he eating? He ought to take better care of himself. This drinking every night wasn't doing him any good either. What the heck was the matter with him? Maybe he should see a therapist. How come he wasn't working out anymore?

How about a back rub, he wanted to say. A Lewinsky maybe. Ha! Never. Not even when they'd first started out and every single time had been such a precious meaningful gift of her beautiful self, back when she at least pretended she liked it. Not often, but if everything was perfect and he was *romantic*, whatever that meant. Then he might get lucky. Lucky with his wife. Somehow the concept seemed a little skewed.

In the bathroom, there he was in the mirror. He'd aged ten

years in five weeks, he thought, although nobody else seemed to have noticed. He moved closer, slapped hard at his cheeks, but couldn't feel them. Tugged a few times half-heartedly at his penis. Nothing.

They each had their own private boxes – Carrie's jewelry safe in the floor of her upstairs closet, and Jim's business safe, in his office where Carrie never went.

He went to it now. Behind the desk he lifted the corner of the Persian rug and pushed down on the two parquet tiles while he simultaneously held the button under the top right drawer. This freed the other six tiles so that he could pull them up.

In another minute he was sitting in his big chair at the big desk. He held the gun – butt and barrel – in both of his hands. After a minute, he turned the cylinder to make it click once, then spun it.

He brought it up to his face. Oil and cordite and something else. The potential to bring instant death. Could you actually smell that?

Closing his eyes, he was just going to feel it there with his senses – smelling, the cold metal, the power of it. A wave of dizziness then.

He leaned into it. With exaggerated slowness, he brought it up and around until no part of the weapon touched him except the end of the barrel, tight up against the center of his forehead.

Abe Glitsky was not having his best evening.

Of all holidays, Hallowe'en was his least favorite. But beyond that, as a cop, he sensed in his bones that this Hallowe'en – tonight – was shaping up to be a disaster. It had the big triple whammy going against it – a beautiful, almost balmy night; a Saturday; and, as an extra added bonus, a full moon.

Scientists might debate whether a full moon had an effect on human behavior, but no policeman ever wondered about it at all. It was an immutable fact, and when the moon was full and the night happened to be Hallowe'en, watch out.

Glitsky had listened to all the news reports about the Pulgas water poisoning, and still was more than half convinced that it had simply been a Hallowe'en trick. That's the way Hallowe'en was – goofy little pranks involving razor blades and Ex-Lax and strychnine and now, in an exciting wrinkle for the new millenium, gasoline poisoning of the water supply.

So, although he would never be truly prepared for what the night might bring, Glitsky was in ready mode. He knew that every lunatic in the city was going to be in the streets tonight. Before morning he was going to be called on a couple of deaths.

It put him on edge.

That and his son Orel being out among the crazies. And Rita having gone for the weekend. And his judgmental (and right) father snoring on the living-room couch. And the irregular staccato of firecrackers, sometimes sounding enough like gunfire to fool even a veteran lieutenant of homicide.

As soon as Orel had gone into the night without a costume – which made Glitsky wonder why he was going out at all, but you picked your fights – he'd blown out the candle in the front window's jack-o'-lantern. Also in the front of the house, he had turned out all the lights, as well as unscrewed the bulb on the stairs to the front door of their duplex. He didn't want little streams of kids in horror outfits ringing his doorbell all evening.

Now he sat at the kitchen table with a large bag of frosted cookies, a cooling pot of tea, and the box of documents that Sharron Pratt had finally delivered up to his office. His mood was not improving as he read, and got positively ugly when the doorbell, as he knew it would, rang.

He'd let it go. They'd get the message – no candy here – and go away.

They didn't. The bell rang again.

They were going to wake up his father, that's what all this ringing was going to do, if it hadn't already. He pushed away from the table so violently that his chair crashed to the ground behind him. Uncharacteristically, he swore aloud.

Between the chair falling and the swearing, one of them succeeded in waking his father. 'Abraham. All right in there?'

'Just getting the door.'

'So much noise.'

Tell me about it, Abe thought, striding to the blasted door. Whoever it was, he was going to give them an earful. He almost hoped whoever it was would try some cute stuff – break an egg against the door, leave a burning bag of dog-doo for him to stomp out, or any one of the ever-popular Hallowe'en standbys – so he'd have an excuse to chase them down and haul them in downtown.

God, he hated this night.

He flicked on the lights inside the entryway and jerked open the door.

Dismas Hardy was standing there. 'Trick or treat,' he said. 'I think your porch light must be out.'

'. . . so I thought since nobody's home at my house, there's no reason to go there. And it's well known you're the saddest, most pathetic bachelor slash widower on the planet. You had to be home, right? I mean, where else could you be?'

Hardy was rummaging in Glitsky's cupboard, pulling out the occasional food item, giving it the once over, either replacing it on the shelf or putting it on the counter next to the sink. 'Anyway, I figure the two of us could hang out here, solve Bree Beaumont, eat some canned food, drink too much. Just have ourselves a good, old-fashioned guys' night out, except we'd be in. Sound good?'

Nat Glitsky had gone back to sleep on the front-room couch and his snores carried into the kitchen. Abe had pulled one of the chairs around and straddled it backwards. 'I don't have any alcohol in the house.'

Hardy pointed a finger, jumped all over him. 'See? That's exactly what I mean. Sad, pathetic, negative.'

'Yeah, well, I don't drink, as you may have noticed over the past twenty years.'

Hardy was still rummaging. He noticed several California lottery tickets stuck to the front of the refrigerator with magnets. He pulled them off and held them up. 'You realize that the lottery is the tax for people who aren't good at math, don't you? Did you win?'

'Probably,' Glitsky said. 'I usually do. Couple of grand or so every week. I'll check tomorrow's paper and let you know.'

Hardy shook his head and went back to the cupboards. 'OK, but while we're on this, let me just say that I am appalled to find Spam in your larder.'

This finally got a rise out of Abe. 'I love Spam. It's the great unsung food of our time. And PS, *you* like canned corned beef hash.'

'That's because hash has flavor.'

'Spam does, too. In fact, it has *more*.'

'Yeah, but it's a bad flavor.'

Glitsky shrugged. 'It's the number-one snack food in Hawaii.'

'*There's* a strong recommendation. You're talking the same Hawaii where they actually eat poi? You ever eat poi? I wonder how they feel about Spam in Alaska, where they eat blubber?'

But Glitsky wasn't to be denied. 'They make it with seaweed and rice. It's a sushi dish, called spam musabi or something.'

Hardy turned around in his best announcer's voice. 'Ladies and gentlemen, in tonight's entry on "Bad Food Ideas," we're hearing that perennial favorite Spam and – are you ready for this? – *seaweed* linked as a gourmet treat. We're waiting for your calls to vote on whether this is, as it appears to be, a . . . Bad Food Idea.' He focused on Glitsky. 'Are you out of your mind?'

'I didn't make it up.' He got off his chair, though, and crossed the small room in a couple of steps. 'Come to think of it, though, I could eat something. What did you pull down?'

Hardy had selected two large Spaghettios with franks, an extra-large Chef Boyardee Ravioli. He was going to mix them, and was opening the cans. 'You got anything green in the refrigerator that's supposed to be?'

Glitsky went to check.

But now the dishes were in the sink and there wasn't much good-natured anything going down in the kitchen.

Hardy had gotten the short version of the immensely relevant Caloco document from Glitsky and now was leafing through it on his own. It was a 'Separated Employee's Audited Statement' and it did not make pretty reading.

While Bree worked for Caloco, it seemed she had a Platinum-Plus company Visa card with a credit limit of a hundred thousand dollars. When she quit the company, they had of course closed that account. But an auditor's review of Bree's records – routine after a certain level employee's termination or resignation – had subsequently revealed the existence of a second name authorized to sign on the account – Ron Beaumont.

Ron didn't work for Caloco and so this was unusual, but if it had stopped there, that would have probably been the end of it. According to the audit, Ron had never used the card and so the presence of his name on the account made no obvious financial difference to Caloco.

(Hardy couldn't help but recall the object lesson in Caloco's corporate culture that he'd learned earlier in the day when Jim Pierce, straight-faced, told him that some clerk in some department might notice a missing three billion dollars, but the corporate entity would never miss it. If three billion was a drop in Caloco's bucket, a mere hundred grand was a molecule – invisible to the naked eye.)

But the audit had turned up something else that was very disturbing. The electronic superhighway created its own version of a paper trail, and Bree Beaumont's card was linked going forward as the security instrument to another, Mellon

212

Bank, Visa account. That account, with a credit limit of a hundred and fifty thousand dollars, did show a regular history of purchases in San Francisco, all of them paid every month. The monthly accounts were sent to a Ronald Brewster at a post-office box. And nobody at Caloco had ever heard of Ron Brewster.

Hardy got to here and his stomach went hollow. He looked up. 'Didn't Caloco try to close the second account, the Brewster account?'

Glitsky had been sitting quietly, arms crossed, waiting for this. He shook his head. 'That's page three. The Mellon account had only used the Caloco account for security to open it. Far as Mellon was concerned, Ron *Brewster* was a great client with a five-year history of regular payments. No way are they closing the account. Plus the Mellon account, it's not using any of Caloco's money. So Ron's got himself a hundred-and-fifty-thousand-dollar line of credit.' Glitsky leaned forward, elbows on the table. 'You'll also notice that the Mellon account doesn't include Bree as a signatory, only Ron. And guess what? Ron Brewster's signature looks a whole lot like Ron Beaumont's writing. We're dealing with a white-collar whiz kid here, Diz, on the run with a phony ID.'

Even for Hardy, familiar with the purported excuse for Ron's duplicity, it was difficult to remain neutral in the face of this. And he figured it would be impossible for Glitsky.

Which proved to be true. 'I'm going to throw Coleman and Batavia on to him first thing in the morning.'

'They working Sunday?'

'They are now.' A look. 'Are you telling me this doesn't make you sit up around Ron?'

'No,' Hardy agreed, 'I'll admit it makes him look a little weak.'

If Glitsky had a smile, he was wearing it now. 'A little weak, that's good. Weaker than a signed murder confession at any rate, but not by much. And that's not all. Check out page five.'

Hardy turned the pages quickly, glancing over the information, and as he scanned, Glitsky kept up the color commentary. 'That electronic linkage Caloco can access finds four other accounts connected to the Mellon Visa.' Hardy read the names. Ron Black. Ron Blake. Ron Burns. Ron Blanda. 'Guy's got a million dollars in credit. Five phony identities. You gotta believe he's got passports for all five.'

No argument there. 'It wouldn't surprise me at all. And you know how I hate to say this, but—'

Now Glitsky was smiling. 'But that doesn't make him a murderer. But I'll tell you something. It doesn't make him a boy scout either.'

Hardy had to agree. 'No. But why would any of this make him want to kill his wife? You got a theory on that?'

Clearly, this was still unsettled water for Glitsky. The scar through his lips went white as he thought about it. 'She must have been ignorant of the accounts. When she found out he was using them on her collateral from Caloco, she busted him for it, they fought, and it got out of hand.'

'So it was just a fight?' Hardy wasn't grinding any ax, but he did have a point to make. 'That's not murder one. It's not usually murder anything. At the most it's manslaughter, maybe even self-defense, which is no crime at all.'

'I don't care what the lawyers call it. It gets me the guy who killed Bree.'

'Maybe.' In the longish silence Hardy was aware of Abe's father's regular breathing in the living room. 'Maybe,' he repeated. 'But what about the guy who killed Carl Griffin?'

This brought Glitsky up short. 'What guy is that?'

'You're homicide. You tell me.'

'Are you telling me they're related, Bree and Carl?'

Low-key, Hardy shrugged. 'Are you telling me they're not? Seems likely they could be, unless you've got a suspect with Carl.' It was a question.

Glitsky took a moment before answering. 'We've got nothing on Carl. I've told you this. He was going out to the

214

Western Addition to talk to one of his snitches, who apparently got some kind of drop on him.'

'And what?' Hardy ladled on the sarcasm. 'He asked the snitch to hold his gun a minute while they talked, and it went off accidentally? Is that what happened?'

'Must have been,' Glitsky replied sardonically. But Hardy had something and Glitsky, perhaps for the first time, was seeing it. 'He was sitting in his car, Diz. Even Carl wasn't that dumb.'

'OK. So what do you think happened? You remember where the car was found?'

A nod. 'A little cul-de-sac called Raycliff Terrace, just off Divisadero.'

Well, Hardy was thinking, strike that idea. Divisadero ran right through the heart of the Western Addition, so Griffin was where he was supposed to have been. But, being thorough, he asked his next question anyway. 'What's the cross street?'

Glitsky didn't know offhand and in a minute they had a map spread out on the table between them. A loud silence ensued. Raycliff Terrace was off Divisadero all right, and on the map it looked close enough to the ghetto, but to anyone who knew the city at all, it was so far economically from the low-income housing units of the Western Addition that it may as well have been in Beverly Hills.

The cross street was Pacific, the eponymous artery of Pacific Heights, one of San Francisco's most aristocratic neighborhoods. And, more tellingly, one block from Broadway.

Hardy spent an instant leaning over, making sure. With a kind of pang about his own incompetence, he realized that this had been David Freeman's idea – his comment that Griffin had been the first horse at the trough. Was the old fart ever wrong?

Hardy straightened up and walked over to the refrigerator, where he pulled a magnetized pen off the door. Back at the map, he marked an X. Then another one. After a moment's reflection, a final thought struck him, and he scratched out a third one. 'Bree Beaumont,' he said, putting the tip of the pen on the first mark, two blocks from Raycliff Terrace. 'Broadway and Steiner. Damon Kerry, Broadway and Baker.' Three blocks west of Bree, one block from Raycliff. He put the pen on the third X. 'Jim Pierce. Divisadero and North Point.' Eleven blocks north. Griffin had been killed surrounded by the players in the Beaumont case. Which, to Hardy, argued that he wasn't killed in a drug sting gone wrong. His death was related to Bree's.

Frowning, Glitsky was silent. Finally he put a finger on Hardy's first mark. 'Ron Beaumont, too.'

Hardy had to admit this unwelcome fact. But it wasn't his point and in a minute he was fairly sure it wouldn't be Glitsky's. 'Can you see Griffin coming up here with his snitch, Abe? I can't. You see the snitch letting himself get driven this far out of the 'hood?'

Glitsky shook his head. 'You're right. It didn't happen. Not up here.'

Hardy ran with it. 'It was somebody Griffin wasn't afraid of, maybe even trusted.'

'Enough to let him hold his piece? It's hard to imagine.' He had his fist balled over the Xs and he lifted it an inch, then brought it down with a great deal of force. 'Damn,' he said. He slammed the fist down again. 'God *damn* it, Carl.'

From Glitsky, this was a violent explosion. He raised his eyes, the whites shot now with red. 'Anybody else I'd say no chance. Carl? I've got to say maybe.' He ran his palm over the entire top of his head. 'Lord, Diz, how is it nobody saw this?'

But that wasn't what Glitsky really wanted to know, so Hardy thought he'd spare him. Hardy had his own problems with this new information – there was another X, Hardy knew, that he hadn't put on the map.

Phil Canetta had his own weapon. Griffin wouldn't have had to voluntarily pass over his gun – the situation that Glitsky had found so untenable. Canetta could have simply hopped into the passenger seat of Griffin's car, pulled his own piece,

216

and moved things along right smartly from there. Relieved Carl of his gun, and had him drive to a secluded and quiet dead-end street. Made him dead.

But then, the more he thought about it, if any of his other suspects owned a weapon, they could just as easily have done the same thing.

The good news was that he had gotten Glitsky thinking, and not exclusively about Ron. It wasn't a certainty, of course, and nowhere near proven, but suddenly now to Hardy the overwhelming probability was that Griffin's murder was in fact linked to Bree's.

'When was he killed?' Hardy asked. 'Carl.'

Glitsky was still getting used to it, and Hardy couldn't blame him. If this was what had happened, the proximity of Griffin's murder scene to the homes of the suspects in Bree's murder was an egregious oversight for homicide to have missed. Glitsky was back sitting down at the table. He cupped his hands in front of his mouth and blew on them. 'It was a Monday. Somebody reported the body mid-afternoon, say two thirty. Forensics had him dead an hour, an hour and a half.'

'So. Lunchtime.'

Glitsky made a face. 'He hadn't eaten. Except some chocolate.'

Abe's son Orel was just getting back from trick or treating, if that's what he'd been doing, as Hardy was at the door on his way out. Glitsky had been on the phone for the past twenty minutes leaving messages with his inspectors to make it to the hall the next day, and with the crime scene unit to make sure that Griffin's car got another careful going-over in light of what might be these new developments. If Hardy knew Abe, and he did, all of this was going to go on awhile, with the coroner, the various labs, and so on. He didn't feel any great need to hang around. It was after ten by now and he was exhausted.

But he couldn't go home yet – he really had to go by Erin's

and at least kiss the kids goodnight. So now he was in the Cochrans' living room and his own son Vincent was asleep with his head on Hardy's lap. Rebecca was curled up on his other side, still awake – Hardy was going to do an experiment someday and see how many days his daughter could go without any sleep, but for now he was contented enough with her quiet form snuggled next to him. At least she'd know he'd come by on Hallowe'en after all.

Both the kids had gone out in Erin's sheets as ghosts. The elaborate costumes Frannie had made for both of them – Cinderella for the Beck and Piglet for Vincent – were lost to the insanity of the past couple of days.

But at least they'd had their holiday night. Their respective caches of candy were already sorted in piles on the rug. The wonderful Erin had made it all work, and for this Hardy was more than grateful.

She'd also mixed a shaker of manhattans – it had been a long day for everybody, and they'd spent the last twenty minutes having a nightcap and catching up on Hardy's progress, ending with the potentially blockbusting discovery about Carl Griffin's death.

But Erin had a clear focus on her priorities – this might be a fascinating turn of events, but if it wasn't about Frannie and getting everyone's life back to normal, she wasn't interested. 'This policeman was before anything happened that involved Frannie, wasn't it, Dismas?'

'By a couple of weeks.'

'Well, then, how can they keep her—' A glance at the Beck, who was hanging on every word. 'How can they keep her where she is?'

Hardy saw her point, but it wasn't any help. 'She's in for fighting with a judge, Erin. That's all it comes down to. My guess is whatever happens with the investigation, they'll let her go Tuesday morning.' He said it easily but harbored an uneasy fear that it might turn out not to be true. With Ron's disappearance, all bets might be off.

'She's OK, though, isn't she, Daddy?' See? The Beck might be quiet, but she never sleeps.

Arm around her, he patted his girl. 'She's fine, Beck. In fact, maybe I can see . . . do you want to talk to her?'

'Oh, Daddy, so much!'

Gently, he moved Vincent's head off him on to the couch. The long shot had just occurred to him, but the idea might work. 'Let's give it a try.'

He got the jail's number and called the desk, gently reminding the deputy about the deli lunch he'd provided for them that day – sure, the guy had heard about it. What could he do for Mr Hardy?

He could let his wife in Adseg use the phone and call out to talk for a minute to her kids. And after a brief hesitation, the deputy said he'd see what he could do.

Five minutes later, the phone rang at the Cochrans'. Hardy was nervous as he picked it up. 'Frannie?'

Hearing her voice, he realized he should have gone to see her again tonight when he'd passed right by on the way to Jeff Elliot's. Twenty times a day wouldn't be too much. He should forget all this *faux* police work. Glitsky was on it now and it would move along on its own. 'How are you holding up?'

He heard her take in a breath, and knew she was summoning her strength to answer. 'Pretty good,' she said with a cheer so false it made him sick.

The Beck was unable to restrain herself, in her excitement pulling at his leg, the cord, whatever was near by. He figured it wouldn't be a good time to reprimand her for it. 'Listen, I've got somebody here who wants to talk to you.'

'OK, but come back, please.'

Hardy handed the phone to the Beck and stood there listening to the details of the past two days, the questions she'd had to endure at school, when was Mom coming home, what were they doing to her down at the jail – all his precious daughter's thoughts and worries that Hardy hadn't been able to take time for.

Vincent woke up and was groggily leaning against him, sucking his thumb although he'd stopped doing that six months before. 'Is that Mommy? I need to talk to Mommy.' Too sleepy to cry, but leaning in that direction.

So the kids both got to talk. Then Erin – was there anything Frannie needed her to do tomorrow, for school on Monday? She shouldn't worry, Grandma was on the job.

There wasn't any criticism of Hardy stated or implied, but he knew. He knew. He was good at some things, and at others hopeless. And now he felt keenly that the father role, the one that perplexed and frustrated him so often if not always lately, had become a victim to his need to figure things out, to keep busy, to win.

The priority was wrong – he felt it in every bone.

But what else could he do? He could give lip service to David Freeman's input, to Glitsky's machine, but he knew and cared more about this investigation than Freeman and Glitsky combined. Like it or not, he was the prime mover. Lives – and not just his family's – now depended upon him and what he did next.

Finally, his turn came again as Erin corraled both of the kids back to bedrooms, to bedtime.

He told Frannie that he loved her, but he couldn't leave it at that. He might hate himself for it, but he had to find out more. 'I've got to ask you, have you heard from Ron today?'

'No. How could I? They'd don't let anybody call me here.'

'No, I know that.'

'Well, then.'

Hardy told her. Ron had disappeared from his hotel.

He listened to her breathing for a minute. 'Why would he do that? I thought – didn't you say? – he asked you to help him. What does this mean?'

'I don't know. I was hoping maybe you could tell me.'

'No, unless he just got scared for the kids again.'

'But why wouldn't he have left some message with me?'

'I don't know that either. Maybe he will.'

'Maybe,' Hardy said flatly. 'I hope so.'

A silence hummed on the line. 'Dismas?'

'I'm here.'

'I've told you everything I know. Really. I don't know where he is, what he's doing.'

If he didn't completely believe it, he felt at least he had to accept it. 'OK.'

Another silence preceded the tremulous voice. 'Tell me you believe me, Dismas. Please. I need you to believe me.'

'Of course,' he said with deliberate ambiguity. 'I'll see you tomorrow, OK? Bright and early.'

'That would be good,' she said. Then, 'Dismas?'

'Yes.'

He waited.

'I love you,' she said.

His knuckles were white on the phone. He knew he was being imprecise. 'Me, too.'

He finished two solid manhattans with Erin and Ed and they talked about the water poisoning and the poor middle-aged hiker from the water temple who had finally died from his injuries. Erin got Hardy a blanket and a pillow and told him he should stay here on the couch and have breakfast with his children in the morning. They were missing him, if he couldn't tell.

He was asleep in ten seconds.

21

Valens had left Damon Kerry up at his mansion an hour ago and back at his hotel he paced as though he were caged. His suite at the Clift was bigger than some apartments he'd lived in and the wraparound view of San Francisco was expansive, but none of that mattered.

It was now near midnight of what had been the longest and one of the most difficult days of his life. The only thing that made it even remotely worthwhile was today's latest poll that put Damon essentially dead even for Tuesday's election. Technically he was still two points back, but with the pollster's margin for error, the campaign was neck and neck.

Finally, the buzz came and he walked over, looked through the peephole, and pulled open the door.

Thorne cast a last quick look behind him at the hallway, then stepped into the room. 'This is just not smart, Al,' he said in his softest tone as he pushed the door closed, twisted the deadbolt, and connected the chain. Turning, he faced Valens, his expression betraying nothing – a bland smile, rheumy eyes. 'This isn't a good idea. We must not be seen together.'

Valens barely noticed the rebuke. He was too wound up. 'It's midnight, Baxter. Nobody's looking, trust me. It's just this . . .' He spread his arms, the enormity of it. '. . . today.'

Thorne nodded understandingly. 'The election's in three days. This always happens. It's nothing unusual. It might even get worse.'

'I'm not talking about the election. Christ, the election is the good news. I'm talking about a dead man at the bottom of the Pulgas Water Temple and this attorney Hardy going to Bree's place and . . .'

'Wait, wait.' Thorne held up a palm. 'Why don't we sit down? Do you have anything to drink? You could use a cocktail. In fact, a cocktail might be just the thing.' He crossed the room to the bar, motioning for Valens to sit on one of the suite's brocaded sofas. 'This is really a remarkable room.' He admired the view for a moment, then turned, asking as if it were an afterthought, 'What does the dead man at the water temple have to do with us?'

The question was an instruction and a threat and it caught Valens flat-footed, no doubt as Thorne had intended. He went back to pulling soft-drink and single-serving liquor bottles from the bar area. 'But speaking of cocktails, in the light of all the frenzy around this unfortunate MTBE poisoning, it occurred to me that the candidate could make an extremely dramatic presentation in the next day or two that might put him over the top to stay.'

He'd arranged the bottles and some glasses on a little tray and brought it over to Valens, placing it on the coffee table, then sitting on the couch kitty-corner. He reached for his inside pocket and extracted a flask.

'What's in that?' Valens asked.

Thorne loved a surprise. For an answer, he smiled and unscrewed the cap, then poured a half inch of the clear liquid into one of the glasses. Picking it up, he smelled it, then passed it across the table. 'You tell me.'

A sniff. 'It's alcohol.'

Another smile, this one beaming. 'Yes it is. Absolutely right. It's ethanol, straight up.' Thorne popped the top on a bottle of orange soda and reached over pouring it into the glass. 'Bottoms up, Al. Really.'

'You want me to drink this?'

'I think that's the idea. Go on, it won't hurt you.'

But Valens couldn't seem to force himself to move. After a second or two, Thorne said, 'Oh, for heaven's sake,' took the glass and drained it in a couple of swallows. 'Since when have you been so timid, Al? Did you think I was going to poison you?'

'No, of course not. I just . . .' He met his employer's eyes. 'I don't know, Baxter. I'm just fucking worn down.'

Thorne gave him an avuncular pat on the knee. 'A couple more days and it's over. You hang in there and it will all have been worth it. Now' – back to business – 'what do you think about my idea?'

'I'm not sure exactly what it is. Make ethanol cocktails?'

Suddenly Thorne's face showed some animation. 'Actually, that might be even better. That's just an inspired idea, Al. Really. Reporters will always take a free drink, won't they?'

Valens felt some of his own tension break. 'That's been my experience.'

'Exactly. You see, I was thinking of having Damon drink some ethanol – as I just did – at a press briefing. Think of the contrast . . .' Thorne was getting wound up, although his voice never changed its inflection. 'A few gallons of MTBE finds its way into the water supply and the whole city is shut down, the poisoned water smelling and tasting like turpentine.' He paused briefly and held up his flask. 'While the other additive, the *natural* additive, ethanol, is so safe you can drink it. In fact, people have been drinking it for ever. I love it,' he said. 'This could be very strong.'

But Valens wasn't so sure. 'If Damon will go for it.'

Thorne's face clouded. 'Why wouldn't he?'

'Because he's careful, Baxter. He's not an idiot. He's never specifically endorsed ethanol. He's just opposed to MTBE.'

'Which if my logic hasn't failed me leaves only ethanol.'

'True.' Valens hated Thorne's attempts to micro-manage – he'd done a damn fine job with the campaign, and controlling the candidate, to date. He turned to reason. 'But our strategy, you remember, has always been to let the voters make that leap, which they're doing by themselves. This other is a little . . . *overt*, don't you think?'

'Sometimes you need overt.' The voice was eider down; the tone was cold steel.

Here was Thorne's defensiveness, which he'd seen often

enough before. It was a signal to Valens that he'd better walk softly, because the truth was that Thorne frightened him badly. He wasn't fooling Valens that he wasn't behind this water poisoning.

Sometimes, though, such as today, people died.

'I agree,' Valens said. 'Sometimes overt is good. So how about I ask Damon, and get his take on it? If he'll go, we go.'

'All right,' Thorne said mildly, 'since that's our only option anyway.' He was pouring a couple of the airline portions of vodka into his glass. He added an ice cube, topped it off with more orange soda, slid back more comfortably in his chair, and took a long drink. 'Now, about this Hardy fellow. I've done some research. It turns out he may be a bit of a problem.'

This was not what Valens needed just now. He came forward to the first two inches of the couch. 'How's that?'

In his low-key way, Thorne outlined what he'd discovered about Frannie, the grand jury, Ron Beaumont, a little of Hardy's history, and that he was a meddling lawyer who wasn't always loath to get his hands dirty.

'We can only assume,' he concluded, 'since he buttonholed Kerry, that he's made the leap – no pun – from Bree's death to gasoline additives, which is not good news for us. I do wish we could locate Ron.' A sigh. 'We should have acted more quickly, I'm afraid. I blame myself, really. I should have just hacked into her system and deleted the damn thing instead of—'

But Valens was shaking his head. He didn't want to get into another discussion with Thorne about the 'instead of.' 'No,' he interrupted, 'she would still have had the hard copy and probably a backup disk. That's what I was trying to get her to give me, to hold her off until after the election.'

'Come on in, Al. Thanks for coming by.'

He took in the incredible penthouse at a glance as he came through the door. He'd never been here before and the grandness of it surprised him, although maybe it shouldn't have –

everything about Bree Beaumont made an impression. He was, he believed, largely immune to the attractive power of her physical presence but he wasn't fool enough to deny its existence.

She was Damon's girlfriend and as such a campaign factor to control, so he tried not to think of her as a woman. He didn't care that she was a woman. She was butting into his campaign and his business and he didn't like her, period.

But this was the first time he'd ever been alone with her. As she led him through the ornate living room and back to the sitting area near the balcony, he was subliminally aware of the tasteful decorating, the fancy art, the panorama out the windows.

There was a better view close up, however. He couldn't keep his eyes off Bree's perfect ass, which she'd poured into a pair of designer jeans. He'd never before seen her in jeans. Or in a T-shirt with nothing under it. Or barefoot. Her blond hair cascaded halfway down her back. He thought he could encircle her waist with both his hands.

Somehow all of this made him vibrate with a dull anger – that she could walk around like this, around him, and that the vastness between them was so great that it was literally unthinkable for him to have any reaction to her. She was so far above him that he did not exist. This did more than simply piss him off.

She was making small talk as she led him back. 'Sorry I'm such a mess,' she said. 'I've been working all afternoon on the computer and lost track of the time.' He was half listening and all the way still looking when she suddenly turned – did she catch where his eyes were? – and motioned to one of the low, upholstered chairs. 'Anyway, just to thank you again for coming. I wouldn't have bothered you but I don't know what to do. I wanted your advice before I burden Damon with anything else.'

'I'll do what I can,' Valens said lamely. He was a few inches under six feet – about Bree's height – and weighed in at near

*two hundred pounds. Brown hair, heavy shadow, under-
starched white shirt and rack suit. His tongue wouldn't work.
'I appreciate your thinking of me.'*

*Perhaps sensing his reaction to her, she stood a moment,
awkwardly, then motioned to one of the chairs. 'Do you want
to have a seat? Can I get you something to drink? I've got
anything really.'*

'Yeah, I'll take a beer, thanks.'

*He watched her again, then forced himself to look out over
the balcony to the city beyond. In a heartbeat, she was back
with a bottle of some foreign beer, a chilled Pilsner glass, and
a plastic bottle of Evian.*

*Valens thanked her politely. 'This is a nice place,' he said,
pouring.*

*She was unscrewing the cap on the water bottle and she
stopped, her face turning wistful. 'Yes. Though I'm afraid it
looks like we're going to have to let it go pretty soon. But I
shouldn't complain – it's been very nice, more than we ever
thought we'd . . .' She stopped. 'The upkeep's just too much.
And anyway, Ron and I – my husband? – well, you know.'*

'He's not around, is he?'

*She shook her head. 'No. He and the kids went . . . well, it
doesn't matter. They're out now.'*

*Valens took a deep draught, then tried to ask it gently. It
wouldn't do him any good to show anything. 'So is this about
him?'*

*The question seemed to surprise her. 'No. Nothing about
that really.'*

He waited.

*She looked out over his shoulder, absently bringing the
water bottle to her lips. 'I've been doing a lot of soul-searching
lately, Al. And also a lot of research.'*

'OK.'

*She brushed some hair away from her face. 'You know, ever
since Damon got me to start questioning my assumptions on
my work on the petroleum side, looking in different directions*

as he'd say, it's really been . . . I guess you'd say an education.'

Valens nodded.

'Which is funny, given that I'm considered an expert on all of these issues.'

A shrug and an attempt to smile. 'Well, you saw the light, that's all.'

But she shook her head. 'I don't know what I saw really. I think, other than just being so hurt that I'd been misled by people I trusted and mad at myself for being so stupid – I mean. Al, I am not stupid – anything else, OK, just not stupid.'

'No,' Valens said, trying to keep it light, 'we could go with not stupid.'

But the levity went by her. Impatiently, she brushed her hair away again. 'But even more, other than that, Damon got me back to why I started doing all this . . . my work, I mean . . . in the first place.'

'Which was?'

She stopped. 'This will sound stupid.'

Valens shook his head. 'No, we've agreed we're not going with stupid. So why'd you start working in the first place?'

'I wanted to do good.' She let out a breath in a whoosh. 'OK, there. I've said it.'

'OK.' Big deal, he thought. 'So you wanted to do good?'

'And I did, too. I did what I set out to do, with MTBE. Do you know how great that stuff works cleaning up the air, Al? It cuts toxic emissions down to almost nothing. You go out to Pasadena now in August and you can see the mountains. Or even out there.' She pointed to the window. 'You can see it! It has made the world cleaner, do you realize that? Do you see what an incredible achievement that was?'

Now she was all wound up and had to stand to walk off some of it. Over to the balcony doors, pulling them open, letting in a blast of cool air. It seemed to calm her after a moment, and she turned around to face him again.

'Anyway, in spite of its bad press now, the point is that it really worked, and I was part of it, a big part of it. The EPA

loved it, everybody loved it. Can you understand how invested I was in it? How when the complaints started to appear, I didn't want to look? I couldn't look.'

'Anybody could understand that,' Al said, although he wasn't sure that he could. 'That was natural.'

'It was,' she agreed. 'It was so natural.' Sighing, she came back to the chair across from him and sat in it, their knees almost touching. 'Anyway,' she said, 'then I saw it, what I was doing, because of Damon.'

'And you did right.'

'Well, as far as it went.'

Valens cocked his head. 'What do you mean?'

'I mean I guess I was angry. I'd been made to look like a fool and I didn't want it to happen again. I realized that Damon was starting to look like he was pushing for ethanol, even if he wasn't really doing it directly, and I wasn't positive he wanted to go in that direction, either.'

For Valens, this was the worst possible news. His candidate wasn't a scientist – he didn't need to know the details. All he needed to know was that MTBE polluted the groundwater and ethanol didn't. Therefore ethanol was better. But he couldn't show his concern. Instead, he stalled for a minute with his beer, then smiled. 'Well, Bree, as you say, he's never made ethanol part of his platform.'

'Except it's there. You know it is, Al.'

'And is that so bad?'

'Well, it's not a great fuel. It's expensive to make, it's not as efficient . . .'

He had to cut her off. 'But it's no danger in groundwater, and does make gas burn cleaner, right?'

Bree grimaced, hesitated.

'What? Tell me.'

'We don't need either of them. The whole additive industry is basically just one giant, greedy scam. The oil companies, as we know, are making billions on MTBE. But that's not all. Have you ever heard of SKO, the farming conglomerate?'

229

Valens felt his head go light. 'Of course.'

'Well, it's making zillions, too, in subsidies for ethanol. They can't make the stuff profitably, but somehow they've convinced the government that it's in the national interest that we keep making it.'

'Maybe it is. Maybe—'

But she cut him off. 'No. No, it's not, Al. Listen to this. Did you know that it takes more energy to produce ethanol than the stuff generates as a fuel?'

'I don't think so, Bree. How is that possible?'

'Tractor fuel, cost of shipment, storage, refining, like that.'

'Well . . .'

'Well nothing. And since it has less fuel energy than gas, it guarantees worse gas mileage, which affects everybody who drives. Plus,' she continued, having worked herself into a high dudgeon, 'do you realize that every dollar of SKO's ethanol profits costs the American taxpayer thirty dollars? And I'm leaving out all the science here. This is just the crappy business stuff. It's just awful.'

Valens had no response to any of this. He didn't know if any of it was true or not, and didn't care, but it was clear that she had come to believe it and might take her message to Damon. That was the issue. That's what he had to deflect.

He kept his voice under control. 'But Bree, almost all businesses—'

'But Damon isn't involved with almost all businesses. He's involved with this one. And this ethanol thing isn't even the worst of it.'

He waited, hardly daring to breathe. What could be worse than what she'd already come to? 'So what is?' he asked.

She leaned forward, and her zealot's eyes locked into his. 'We don't need either of them.'

'Either of what?'

'Either MTBE or ethanol, or any other gas additives for that matter. The EPA has mandated them, but the whole thing is a scam. The whole thing, do you realize that?' Her voice *went up several decibels with her outrage.*

'I . . . I'm afraid I don't understand,' he managed to stammer.

'No, no. I know you don't. How could you? Nobody does. Wait a minute.'

Suddenly she was up, nearly running, disappearing into a hallway across the kitchen area. In another moment, she reappeared carrying a large handful of papers. *'Look,'* she began without preamble. *'I don't expect you to understand the science,'* she said, *'but let me try to explain some of this.'*

He listened for what seemed an eternity as she went over the salient points of the report she'd been working on for the past month or six weeks. It contained a great deal of data – graphs, equations, analyses of comparisons in burn rates, emissions, efficiencies of gasoline – and gradually even Al Valens began to see what Bree had assembled.

Culled from patent applications, lawsuit transcripts, internal memos, executive summaries, and expert testimony of dozens of combustion engineers, Bree's report detailed a startling truth – that the oil companies had discovered a way to formulate gasoline so that it burned cleanly without the addition of oxygenates, without any additives at all. *'So you see, Al, it's what I was telling you. The whole additive question is a scam. Damon's got to be made aware of this. I've got to tell him.'*

When she finished, Valens gathered his thoughts. It wouldn't do to alienate Bree now. If she did go running to Damon with this, if she convinced him to start talking about it, it would be a disaster. He sighed histrionically. *'This is terrible,'* he said. *'Just awful. I wonder why it hasn't made the news in a big way?'*

But Bree knew the answer to that one. *'It's a bunch of individual papers, experiments, opinions. That's how we scientists work – on small problems, little tweaks here and there, which are fascinating and challenging in themselves.*

'Like with me and MTBE. At the beginning, in layman's terms, my job was to prove it made for cleaner air. And every

*way I tested it, it worked. And then somehow my job changed
and gradually I wasn't really a scientist anymore. I was a
spokesperson defending what I'd done, what Caloco believed
in, what I believed in. So I wasn't interested in groundwater,
in cleanup, even in this reformulated gas. My job, my life, was
MTBE. The rest of it wasn't my problem.' She looked at him
hopefully. 'Do you understand at all?'*

He nodded. 'Of course. Of course I do.'

*She squared the pages of her report, and sat back with it in
her lap. 'But I was wrong.'*

*'No. I don't think so. I think you trusted your employers.'
Valens reached across and touched her knee with his fingertips.
Quickly. Even through the jeans, it burned. 'Bree, you did the
right thing calling me about this. I want you to know that.'*

*She let out a long breath. 'I didn't know what else to do.
Part of me feels like I should tell Damon, but he has so much
on his mind already . . .'*

'Exactly.'

'But if I don't . . .'

*Valens interrupted with the answer she needed. 'If you don't,
he'll understand. In fact, after the election, he'll thank you for
it. The issue at this point in any campaign, much less a
squeaker like this one, Bree, is focus. If he loses focus, the
voters get confused, he's dead. And this stuff, you've got to
admit, it's a little complicated.'*

She broke a small smile. 'A little, I suppose.'

*'Don't suppose. Believe me on this one.' Now they were
more than allies – they were really pals. It was time to make
his pitch. 'Bree, that report, you got it on your computer too?'*

'Yes.'

*'You know, it's pretty volatile stuff. It gets in the wrong
hands, maybe your husband's . . .'*

'What?'

*'He could delete it maybe. Shred the hard copy. And then
where's all your hard work? If he connects it with you and
Damon . . .'*

'No,' she said, 'Ron would never do anything like that.' She hesitated. 'Ron accepts the situation.'

He shrugged. *It wouldn't do to push.* 'Well, it's your decision, but I could take all that stuff – your disks, everything. Keep them someplace safe till after the election.'

But she was firm. 'It's safe here. I don't want Damon to see it until I tell him, until we have time and I can explain it, and also why we decided not to tell him sooner.'

'After the election?' Valens wanted it nailed down, although what he really wanted was all copies of the report or, better yet, for Bree to disappear along with it.

'I think so,' she said. 'As we've decided.'

But as the door closed behind him, Al knew he hadn't pushed hard enough. He stood in the landing by the elevators, wondering whether he should knock again while she was still alone, and go in and take what he needed, personally and professionally.

Because if he knew Bree at all, and he did, she'd never be able to keep this to herself. She'd get cozy with Damon one night and just have to tell him, and then Damon would decide that the right thing to do would be to share it with the public.

And while it was one thing to be a White Knight crusading against an evil corporate polluter, it was quite another to be a paranoid left-wing fanatic who believed that the Environmental Protection Agency was part of the Great Government Gasoline Conspiracy. That, while possibly true, would not fly, and Valens knew it.

It would cost Damon the election. It would cost Al his potentially lucrative future relationship with SKO. It would infuriate the volatile and unpredictable Baxter Thorne.

No. It wouldn't do.

From his endless bag of tricks, Baxter Thorne had produced Dismas Hardy's telephone number and suggested that Valens call with an amendment to his earlier lie about not having called Ron.

When Hardy wasn't home, Valens left a message, then came over to the couches again, where Thorne was on his fourth little bottle of liquor after his opening shot of pure ethanol. 'That ought to help,' Thorne remarked, his voice firmly under control. 'But I don't like him meddling in our affairs. He really doesn't belong in this picture, does he? I don't know where he's come from.'

Valens found that he was afraid to reply. There was a glaze in Thorne's eyes – maybe not all from the alcohol – that scared him.

Thorne leaned back, crossed one leg over the other, and took another long pull at his glass. 'He's got you telling a fib. He may know something of the report if he's been to Bree's.' A silence settled which Valens took to be ominous. 'And if that's the case, he may decide to share it with Damon, or the press.'

A long moment passed. Suddenly, Thorne put his glass down, slapped his knees, and stood up. 'Well, Al, thanks for the cocktails.' He headed for the door. 'It seems to me Mr Hardy has a little too much free time on his hands. I think perhaps a . . . distraction would be good for him just at this time. You say he isn't home right now?'

'He wasn't when I called.'

'Yes, that's right, that's right.' Thorne checked the peephole, opened the door an inch, turned to face Valens, apparently came to some decision, then pulled the door all the way open and left without another word.

PART THREE

22

In San Francisco, there is summer, which is windy, harsh and damp, although it rarely rains. And then there is Indian summer, from late August into mid-October, when the days are warm, the skies cloudless, the breezes kind. For the rest of the year, it's all fog and low clouds near the coast, clearing inland by afternoon, highs in the low sixties and winds from the west at fifteen to twenty.

When Hardy woke up on the Cochrans' couch at a little after six, it was obvious that Indian Summer was over and the rest of the year had kicked in. He sat up stiffly and took a minute getting his bearings – it had been a while since he'd slept on a couch in somebody else's living room. The dim outlines of morning bled through the Venetian blinds, but he somehow knew at once from the quality of the light that the fog had come in. Involuntarily, he sighed.

Ten minutes later he was on the road, lights on in the soup. It was going to be another long day and he needed some fresh clothes and a shower. Erin, of course, had already been up too, making coffee in the kitchen, and he told her he thought he'd go home, check his messages, clean up, and try to be back with them on Taraval before the kids awoke.

When he turned off Geary on to his block, though, he was struck immediately with a sense of foreboding – he'd lived on this street for most of three decades, and there was a familiarity to it that was deeper than anything rational. Something, this morning, was out of the ordinary. In the fog, he couldn't see down to the end, where his house was, but it definitely felt wrong. There was a blinking red glow up ahead. He slowed down even further, on alert, equally reluctant and compelled to keep going forward.

Then, gradually emerging from the murk, the definable shapes, images from some horrible dream. Three fire trucks were still parked in the street, hoses trailing from them in the gutters like bloated serpents. A couple of black and white police cruisers – the source of the red strobes – their bubbles on. A half-dozen men in uniform were standing on the sidewalk, on his lawn, milling in the wet morning street.

In a daze, trying to keep the rising sense of panic at bay, he parked carefully, pulling straight into the curb. Getting out, he was aware of the crackling sounds of radio static and perhaps, of smoldering wood.

He moved forward without any awareness of it, transfixed by the still-smoking ruin that had been his home for over twenty years. The white picket fence had been trampled to bits by the firemen and their equipment. What had been a small, carefully maintained lawn was a mess of mud and charred wood. The front porch wasn't there at all, and the ruined living room behind it yawned obscenely open in the gray dawn. His chair. The mantel over the fireplace. Their beautiful cherry dining set, destroyed.

He was on the property now.

'Sir?' A man in a white helmet was suddenly in the path, cutting him off. 'I'm sorry, but you can't . . .'

'I live here,' Hardy said. 'This is my house.'

Miraculously, much of the house had been saved. Some late Hallowe'en revelers on their way home had seen the flames within minutes after the blaze had begun around four a.m. and called the fire department on their cell phone. As a result, the back half of Hardy's home – kitchen, bedrooms and baths – had remained relatively unscathed, although the cleanup was going to take weeks, and the burned smell might never go away.

The incident commander – the man in the white helmet – had given him permission to survey the damage, but he was to be accompanied at all times by Captain Flores. They were talking about evidence and preservation of the scene and it struck Hardy that he was, at least for now, an arson suspect.

Flores and Hardy stood in the center of the kitchen and Hardy was trying to answer the captain's questions. But his mind kept jumping. He noticed his black cast-iron frying pan on the stove where he'd left it. Looking down the now-gaping open hallway, he noticed that his front door was still on its hinges, perhaps salvagable. He would plane it and paint it again.

Their footfalls crunched over the glass and debris. 'No. There couldn't have been any fire left burning in the fireplace,' Hardy was telling Flores. 'I hadn't been home since yesterday morning. We haven't lit a fire in there in months.'

'Well, pretty obviously that's where it started, up front. You got any gas pipes in there? Do you smoke?'

'No and no.'

Captain Flores was a sweet-faced young man with a drooping mustache. He followed Hardy back into the burned-out front area of the house and they stood in what used to be the dining room – the dusty rose drywall now mostly gone. The roof was open above them and water still dripped randomly. Hardy let out some air. 'What do you do with this?' he asked.

Flores saw similar scenes every day, but that didn't make it any easier. 'Do you have insurance?'

'Yeah, but that's not what I meant.'

'I know.'

Hardy turned to him. 'Somebody did this, didn't they?'

The captain shrugged. He might have some suspicions but he wasn't going to share them with a civilian. 'That's always a thought. It's why we've got arson investigators.' He indicated a couple of guys poking around by what used to be the porch. 'At this point it's a little early to make that determination. But if you know something I don't, I'll pass it along.'

Hardy had his hands deep in his pockets. 'I don't know anything,' he said, referring to a lot more than the fire.

Flores scraped a toe along the burned hardwood floor and sighed. 'You're not going to want to hear this, but this might be somebody's idea of a Hallowe'en prank.' He paused. 'It's happened before.'

Hardy gave it a moment, shook his head. 'I don't think so.'

If anything, the morning fog had grown heavier.

One of the first things Hardy did after the incident commander stopped him was ask if he could get a patch through to Glitsky's home on the patrol car radio. Next was his brother-in-law Moses McGuire.

Now the lieutenant sat on the hood of his car, feet resting on the front bumper, leaning forward with his elbows on his knees, his head down. Even with all his years in homicides, at terrible crime scenes, here Glitsky almost couldn't bear to look.

Hardy had been silent, withdrawn with shock and rage, when Abe had arrived. Gradually, Glitsky had gotten him away from the arson people, from the house itself, where the effects of the fire weren't so pervasive. Now he was coming out of it, beginning to pace. 'I'll tell you one thing – they think they're warning me off? They think I'm going away now? They should have killed me instead.'

'Who's that?'

'Whoever did this, Abe.'

'Somebody did this to get at you?'

Hardy nodded. 'It's a warning. It has to be this Beaumont thing.' Hardy stopped in front of him. 'You think it's not?'

Glitsky was silent.

Hardy raised his voice. 'Well what the hell do you think this was, Abe? Spontaneous combustion?'

Glitsky met Hardy's eyes. 'I don't think it's a great time to get in an argument with you, how about that?' He slid off the car, and put a hand on his friend's shoulder.

Hardy could only manage a nod. Glitsky gave his shoulder a last squeeze, moved off a few steps, then turned and with an almost visible effort, forced himself to look at the house. 'If you need me, I'll be downtown. I'm going to work.'

Flores was at his elbow, and Hardy was back in the house, in the little enclosed area behind the kitchen where he kept his safe. Flores didn't want to let him back in – they might trample over more evidence. The captain made it very clear that until they were done with their investigation, this was the fire department's house, no longer his. But the arrival of Glitsky – a highly ranked city cop who was obviously a personal friend – had given Hardy some credibility, and Flores cut him a little slack. They could go up through the back door, and Hardy could get what he needed, although he had to show Flores his license to carry, and even then, when Flores saw what he wanted, he could tell he was pushing it.

But this time he felt no twinge of the reluctance he'd felt the last time he'd gone for his guns. There was also an old badge from his days as an assistant DA. He didn't think too hard before grabbing it. Then, tucking his Police Special into his belt, he pulled his jacket down over it and walked back into the desolation in the front-yard area.

Moses had finally arrived a few minutes after Glitsky's departure, and now was standing at the front side of the house by the chimney, which was still standing. Moses had picked up something and held it out as Hardy and Flores mushed through the mud. 'Start your new collection,' Moses said somberly.

It was one of the exquisitely fragile Venetian glass elephants that had grazed, cavorted, and trumpeted on their mantel over the past decade, which Moses had rearranged with nearly every visit. Until last night there had been fifteen of them – Hardy had just recently acquired the latest one for their anniversary. And now against impossible odds at least one had survived, perhaps blasted out into the yard by the force of water.

Hardy took it and turned it in his hand, then handed it back to Moses, asking his brother-in-law to hold on to it for him.

241

After ten more minutes of surveying damage, he excused himself. Moses didn't have to open the Shamrock for another four hours. He agreed that Hardy needed to go down to the jail and break the news to Frannie. Then to the kids. Moses would stay here with Flores and take care of the first round of details. He was glad to be able to help.

But Hardy wasn't going to the jail. He pulled over at the first gas station he came to and called Phil Canetta's home number.

A tired, worried woman's voice answered. 'Hello. Phil?'

Hardy told Mrs Canetta who he was, that he was working with her husband. Could he get in touch with him this morning? It was important.

'I don't know where Phil is. He went out after dinner and never came home. He always calls,' she said. 'If you do talk to him . . .'

Hardy promised that he'd have Phil call her, then hung up, frowning. This was unexpected and unpleasant. Canetta had left Freeman's office, gone somewhere, presumably on this investigation, and hadn't come home?

The wind gusted around the phone booth and he hunched himself further into his jacket. He dropped another quarter and punched some buttons.

'This better be good.'

'Jeff, it's Dismas Hardy. Sorry to wake you, but I need to know where Al Valens stays when he's in town.'

'You need that, huh? How about I need some more sleep? What time is it anyway?'

'Early, but I've got a hot item for you. Swing by my house sometime this morning.'

'After I get up.'

'Fine. That'll be good enough. Valens, though?'

Jeff thought a moment. 'I think the Clift. What do you got? Is this about Beaumont?'

'Good guess,' Hardy said, 'though what isn't lately?'

'You're right, everything.' The reporter sounded truly

242

exhausted. 'What time is it?' he asked for a second time.

'I don't know, Jeff. What's the matter – you get home late last night?'

'As a matter of fact, after you left I hung for a while, talked to a colleague about this very stuff, finally went home and had dinner, couldn't sleep, and decided I had to pay a call on Damon.'

'At his home?'

'I'm a sympathetic reporter, remember. He's a night owl. He'd see me. He has before.'

'So when was this?'

'Late, a little after midnight. I felt like I'd never get any sleep if I didn't get an answer or two on all this stuff.'

'And?'

'And he wasn't home.'

'Until when?'

'I left at one and he still hadn't come in.'

'And yet you got to sleep after all.'

'Not enough. I'll catch him today after—' Jeff sighed. 'This thing with you – you ought to be able to tell me about it now over the phone, don't you think?'

But Hardy didn't want to do that, knowing there was a lot more power in the physical reality. 'Come by the house,' he said. 'You'll be intrigued, I promise.'

It was against the rules, but the clerk was persuaded by the badge to give Mr Hardy of the DA's office the room number of Mr Valens. He took the elevator to the fifteenth floor and walked the long hallway back to the suite at the end.

Hardy heard some muttering, 'All right, all right, just a second,' and prepared himself to move. It took all of his restraint not to draw the gun. When Valens cracked the door, he put his shoulder against it and kept coming.

'What the . . .' Valens was wearing slacks and shoes, but still was wrapped in one of the hotel's white bathrobes, and now he clutched it in front of him.

243

Hardy quickly closed the door behind them. 'Sorry to be so pushy, but we have to talk.'

'Who the hell . . .?'

'Dismas Hardy. Maybe you remember. We met briefly yesterday with Mr Kerry. You said you'd never called Ron Beaumont. Is any of this coming back to you?'

Valens was backing away, but got stopped by a chair. He nearly fell, then righted himself. 'Sure. Mr Hardy. I remember.' He grabbed at the robe, which had fallen open. He was getting his bearings back, tying the sash, but still obviously wary of the crazy man who'd crashed his door. 'I called you just last night at your home to correct that. I had forgotten that I did in fact call Ron. With the press of yesterday's events it temporarily slipped my mind. Didn't you get that message?'

'No, I didn't. You know why? Because my answering machine went up in flames this morning with the rest of my house.'

The fiddling with the robe stopped. 'Are you saying your house caught fire?'

'Not all by itself. Somebody helped it.'

Valens drew a deep breath and spoke very carefully, still clearly unnerved by Hardy's entrance, his continued presence. 'I'm very sorry to hear that.'

'Yeah, well, I'm in a little bit of a bad mood about it myself.'

Valens sat against the back of the chair. He stole a glance at his watch, at the door.

'Are you expecting somebody?'

A nervous shrug. 'Damon's got a breakfast meeting in an hour. I'm scheduled to pick him up.'

But Hardy shook his head. 'Not until we clear up a few things between us. Bree Beaumont, the fire, like that.'

Valens straightened up, put on a face. 'But I really don't understand. What do those things have to do with me?'

Suddenly, Hardy's adrenalin seemed to kick itself up another notch. He pulled the gun from his belt, took a step

244

toward Valens and pointed it at him. 'What do they have to do with you? I'll tell you. I'm investigating Bree Beaumont and you lied to me yesterday. I'm getting close. The fire was somebody warning me to stay away and the only person I can think of who's got any reason is you. How about that? Is that clearer?'

Valens spread his hands. Patent terror. 'I didn't set your house on fire, Mr Hardy. I was in this room all night. I'm in the last days of a political campaign that I've been waging for nearly a year. Bree Beaumont is not in my life. Damon Kerry is. I didn't lie to you.' Another empty gesture. 'You don't need that gun. What you're calling a lie was a simple mistake. I forgot something, that was all.'

But Hardy's blood was way up, his voice dripping sarcasm. 'Oh yes, you *forgot*. You called the husband of a murdered woman who'd worked on your campaign, and it clean slipped your mind.' He snapped at him, raised the gun. 'You *forgot* that? I don't believe you.'

'It was only for an instant. By the time I realized I'd made a mistake, you were gone. So I called you last night.'

'You called me last night? Although your focus, as you say, isn't on Bree Beaumont, you're telling me that in the final hours of this campaign, you called me at home, at night, to correct this insignificant detail?'

Valens swallowed.

'Which, in any event, you know you can't prove because my answering machine is a pile of ashes. Is that what you're telling me?'

Valens shrugged. 'No, but I—'

'And while we're at it here, Mr Valens, maybe you can tell me how you got my home number, which is unlisted.' And here Hardy realized that one of the roundhouses he was throwing had finally scored. Valens cast his eyes around the room as though hoping to find an answer. None was forthcoming, and Hardy pressed at him. 'Was it one of your campaign workers, maybe? The same guys who came by my house?'

'No!'

'No? What? Was it different guys?'

'No. You're twisting what I'm saying. I don't have any guys. I didn't do any of this.'

'You didn't call me? That's your new story.'

'No, I did do that. I admitted that.'

He had moved up to within a foot of Valens. Sweat had broken on the man's face. It was all Hardy could do to not push him backwards over the chair and physically beat the truth out of him.

Hardy was in a genuine rage. He actually trembled with anger. 'If you don't say something I want to hear in the next five seconds, I'm going to shoot you in the face.' He cocked the gun. 'Give me one reason. Right now.'

'What do you want?'

'I want why you called Ron and why you didn't tell me.'

Valens didn't waste any time making something up. Backing away, he blurted it out. 'Bree's got some files that could hurt Damon's campaign. Some reports, changing her position again.'

'Back to MTBE?'

'No, still against that.'

'Then what was the change?'

'She got religion. She'd decided that all additives were unnecessary. Ethanol, too.'

'And that hurts Damon Kerry?'

'It could if it got out, if Damon went that way.' Valens held up a hand. 'Look, I can't . . . that gun . . .'

'It won't go off by itself.' But Hardy uncocked it. 'Bree hurting Damon Kerry,' he said, getting back to where they were.

Valens drew a shaky breath. 'Damon gets a lot of lift from talk radio because his message is so clear. Bree didn't understand that most people aren't scientists.'

'So you're saying Bree didn't tell him this earlier?' Hardy lowered the gun slightly. 'Why not? I thought she was his consultant on this stuff.'

'She thought it might adversely affect the campaign, as I just told you.' Lowered or not, Valens couldn't take his eyes off the weapon. 'Then when she died . . .'

'Was killed.'

'OK, was killed. Well, frankly, after that I wanted to get my hands on that report so I could get rid of it.'

'So Kerry wouldn't ever see it?'

Valens hesitated. 'That's right.'

'Because you didn't want Kerry to know what Bree thought?'

A nod. 'She was turning into a zealot. She was dangerous.'

'And had to be eliminated?'

Valens didn't approve of the word. 'She had to be managed.'

'And you did that? How?'

'By convincing her to wait until after the election before she told Damon. He wouldn't do anybody any good if he didn't first get elected, and I made her understand that. She agreed to wait. It was only after she . . . was killed, that I realized Ron might inadvertently let the report leak, not knowing what it was, not seeing its importance. So I called him to ask if he'd give it to me.' He pointed at the gun. 'You know, you don't need that thing. I'm telling the truth. The call to Ron was straightforward, really.'

Hardy's shoulders sagged. The rush of adrenalin had worn him out and he realized that Valens was right. He stuffed the gun back into his belt and backed up to the desk, sitting on the corner of it. 'It couldn't have been that straightforward,' he said. 'You lied to me about it.'

'If you remember, Kerry was there with us. I wanted to keep it from him until after the election.'

Hardy shook his head. 'You weren't ever going to show it to him, were you?'

'Maybe not,' Valens replied. 'Maybe someday. But Bree's conclusions weren't really the issue – it was that she was the source of them and she had such an influence on Damon. I mean, everybody in the industry knows you can formulate gas

247

with low emissions. You don't need additives. So what? Except if Bree gets messianic and Kerry makes it his new war cry . . .'

'Then he looks like a fool, or a pawn, for having supported ethanol for so long.'

Valens nodded. 'That's the simple answer, but it's close enough. If he sees the report and knows it's from Bree, he moves on it now, he makes it a campaign issue. That's who Damon is. So he confuses his voters, he looks like he's waffling, all of the above. I couldn't let it happen.'

'How about if I say that sounds like a reason to kill her? How about if she changed her mind and was going to tell him and you had to stop her?'

Valens had a good answer to that. 'Then I wouldn't have had to call Ron to get my hands on the report last week, would I? I would have searched the house and just taken it after I killed her.' He glanced furtively at his watch, spoke now as if asking permission. 'Look, I do have this breakfast with Damon. And I really did leave a message last night that I'd made a mistake – it wasn't a lie – and I did call Ron.

'As to why I remembered to call you, it was what you said. I knew it wasn't insignificant at all, a call to a murdered woman's husband. You were an attorney. It wasn't brain surgery figuring you wouldn't go away if you thought I was lying.'

Hardy hated that it had gotten to here, to some sort of belief in the basic truth of what Valens was telling him. But there was one last question. 'So how'd you get my phone number?'

A nervous smile. 'I called the office and asked if somebody could find it. When I got back here, I had a message.'

'Just like that?'

Valens shrugged. 'I say I want something, somebody usually finds out a way to make sure I get it. I don't ask how. That's how politics works.'

'Or doesn't,' Hardy said.

23

'She's checked out to . . .' The jail's uniformed desk sergeant squinted at the log. 'Glitsky, homicide, next door.'

Hardy wondered about this new development as he walked in the bitter fog around the corner to the main entrance of the Hall. Frannie was signed out to Glitsky? How did that happen and what did it mean?

He'd stowed the gun in the trunk of his car so he wouldn't have to confront the Hall's metal detector. It remained a miserable morning. Hardy checked the time, surprised at how early it still was for all that had gone on. He wasn't entirely certain he'd done the right thing by letting Valens go about his campaign business, but he couldn't imagine that the man was going to disappear, at least not until the election. If some real evidence of wrongdoing by Valens turned up before then, Hardy would bring it to Abe's attention, but in the meanwhile, he had more important things on his mind.

His house, his wife, his life.

The Hall's familiar lobby – on weekdays a perennial throbbing and vulgar mass of disgruntled humanity – was empty this early, and his footfalls echoed. Knowing he'd have no patience with the elevator, he took the inside stairway to the fourth floor, then walked down the long hall to the homicide detail – an open room with fifteen back-to-back desks and several square columns poking about, floor to ceiling, seemingly at random.

There wasn't a body to be seen in homicide itself, although through the grimy, wired-glass windows, he could look across through the fog to the jail, where spectral shapes moved in the outer corridors.

The door to the lieutenant's office was open. No one was inside, but Hardy noticed that Kerry's water glass that he picked up yesterday was gone – a good sign. He knocked anyway. 'Anybody here?'

'Yo!' Glitsky appeared in the doorway of one of the interrogation rooms.

Before he could say anything, Frannie appeared behind him. They met in an embrace in the middle of the room.

'I had to tell her,' he heard Abe say. 'I didn't know how long you'd be hung up back there and she had to know.'

The words barely registered. He was lost in holding her.

But Glitsky was still talking, explaining. 'I'm on my way driving down here, I realize we bring witnesses over from the jail every day to talk to them. So I just went and signed her out into my custody. It's Sunday, nobody's here to question why I got her. It seemed like a good idea.'

'It's a great idea.' Frannie said. 'Plus Erin's bringing the kids down.'

'And I'm going out for some food,' Glitsky said. He was already putting on his jacket. 'It'll be a party.' He pointed a finger at Hardy. 'While I'm gone, I'm leaving you in charge. Don't let her escape.'

They were alone together in the homicide detail's interrogation room, kitty-corner at the table. The fog was pressing tight up against the windows, the wind gusting audibly.

It wasn't exactly warm inside either.

First was the house, Hardy's assessment of how bad it was, what they were going to have to do about living in the next weeks, the somber details. It hit Frannie especially hard that, even after her expected release from jail on Tuesday morning, she wouldn't be able to go back to her old life. 'This is all because of me, isn't it?'

It was difficult for Hardy to tell her it wasn't. He couldn't imagine that anything relating to Bree Beaumont's death would have had any effect on their lives if Frannie had not become involved with Ron, hadn't promised to keep his secrets.

'You did what you had to do,' he told her equivocally. 'But at least I've got somebody scared and that's always instructive.'

'It's more than just that.'

'Maybe,' he admitted.

'Do you think something else could happen? To you?'

In truth, Hardy thought if he kept pushing, which he fully intended to do, that something else surely *would* happen. That's even what he wanted – without an act there couldn't be a mistake upon which he could capitalize.

And this, of course, was not without risk, even serious risk. But, answering her, he simply shook his head. 'If I get any closer, I'll give it to Abe. Let the pros run with it.'

Frannie tightened her grip on his arm. 'You can do that now, Dismas.'

'No,' he said pointedly. 'Not if I want to protect Saint Ron's kids . . .'

'I wish you'd stop calling him that.'

Hardy figured he'd earned the right to call Ron Beaumont anything he wanted. He waved the objection off. 'The point is, if I want to protect his kids, that's why I'm doing all this, isn't it? That's what I'm supposed to believe.'

'What do you mean, "supposed to believe"?'

He tried to control it, but he heard his voice take on a harder edge. 'I find who killed Bree by Tuesday and everybody's life goes back to normal, right? Except ours now. Now ours is a mess.' He'd gotten her to tears and he didn't care. 'And you want to know the real laugh riot here, Frannie? I'm not even sure Ron didn't do this to us.'

'That's crazy,' she said. 'He would have had no reason to do that.'

He firmly grabbed his wife by the shoulders and turned her to him. 'Listen to me. How about if he thought I was there alone, sleeping? The house burns down with me in it. Then he's got you. Did that ever occur to you?'

'No! That's not it.'

'So where is the son of a bitch?'

'I don't know, Dismas, I don't know.' She took his hands and held them in front of her. 'But Ron and I . . . there's nothing like that.'

Hardy hesitated. Although he was well into it, mention of Ron Beaumont was still personally fraught with peril for him. Still, he had to go ahead. 'You know, Fran, I've really been trying to keep Abe from looking at him officially. But it's beginning to look as if whoever killed Bree also killed Abe's inspector half a mile from Ron's house.'

'That doesn't mean . . .'

He squeezed her hand. 'And just so you know, Ron apparently had a few different identities.'

'What do you mean, identities?'

Hardy outlined Glitsky's discovery of the previous night, which now seemed about a year and half ago.

When he was through, Frannie took a while to answer. 'He must have thought he might have to run again someday to save the kids.'

'I'm sure that's what he'd like everybody to believe, and maybe it's true, but he's getting a hell of a lot of play out of saving his kids.'

'That's because that's what he's doing, Dismas! I believe that. You did too when you met him, remember that? He didn't start any of this any more than I did.'

Hardy clucked. 'I know. He's just a poor victim.'

'God, you can be mean,' she snapped.

'Sometimes it's useful,' he replied. 'I'd just like you to consider the possibility that this guy is the great pretender.'

'No.'

'For two or three different reasons – insurance, credit cards, you name it – he kills Bree and sets you up as his alibi. When the cops start to get close to him, he cons me into muddying the waters digging up other suspects, giving himself a few more days to disappear. I don't see much wrong with that picture.'

But she was shaking her head. 'It's not him. Listen to yourself, Dismas. He didn't give himself more time to disappear and also stick around to burn down our house so he could have me. You can't have it both ways. You think he had something going on with me, don't you? That's what this is all about, isn't it? The real one you don't believe is me.'

'You've never denied it, goddam it! How about that?'

'You never asked!'

Hardy spun around and walked to the window, the fog. An eternity passed before he sensed any movement. He was afraid to turn. She came up and hugged him from behind. 'He's just a dad from the kids' school, we got to be friends, this happened. That's all.'

She continued talking quietly into his back. 'I know you hate the whole victim mentality, Dismas. I don't like it either. But sometimes people are in situations they didn't create. Like us, now, too. We've just got to keep trying to do what's right, don't you think?'

'I don't know what right is anymore.'

'Yes you do.'

'All I know is I want to hurt whoever did this.'

'No, you want to hurt anybody right now. It doesn't have to be who did all this. Maybe you're so hurt . . .'

'And what if it's Ron after all? If we've both been conned.'

'Is that the worst that can happen? That somebody took advantage of your good heart.'

'I don't have a good heart.'

'Yes you do. And you're risking it here and afraid somebody's going to smash it and make you look like a fool in the bargain. But either way it's over on Tuesday, isn't it? If you don't find whoever really did it.'

Hardy turned around to her. 'And I've helped him escape.'

'Except if he's run away, then he didn't burn our house, and vice versa. Think about it, Dismas. It's not him.' She brought a hand up to his face and rubbed it against his cheek. 'More than anything, I just don't want you to be hurt. Or us to be hurt.' Her eyes pleaded with him. 'Do you think you could stand to kiss me please?'

Frannie, Erin, Ed, and the kids were finishing their lunch – Chinese takeout was all Glitsky had been able to forage on a Sunday morning.

The opening minutes had been brutal, the kids' emotions over finally seeing their mother again, then the double-whammy as they heard the news of the fire. By the time they were an hour into it, though, Hardy realized that it was as normal a family meal as you could have in a homicide interrogation room. Vincent was sitting on Frannie's lap, Rebecca was non-stop chatter about school stuff. They were all making plans about logistics, moving ahead, solving problems.

Eventually, Hardy got up and wandered out over to Glitsky's office. Over the course of the morning, he'd been tangentially aware of activity in the main room, the odd homicide inspector moseying on in for Sunday duty, maybe to write up some reports.

Hardy stopped in Glitsky's doorway. The lieutenant was at his desk, hunched over paperwork. He knocked and Glitsky looked up, and waved him in. 'Budgets,' he said, and threw his pencil down on the desk. 'Utilization percentage. Field efficiency ratios. Unit integration coefficient. I've been filling out these things for five years and I still don't know what a unit integration coefficient is.'

'Give it an eighty-seven,' Hardy said. 'That's usually good for a coefficient.' He sat down across from the desk. 'I wanted to thank you for bringing her up here,' he said.

Glitsky nodded. 'I'm sorry I couldn't have done it sooner. But with the crowds passing through here every other day of the week, somebody'd leak it to Sharron Pratt, who tells Marian Braun, who goes ballistic and takes it to Rigby. Then I'm fired and I hate it when that happens.'

'Well, you did it today,' Hardy said sincerely. 'And I wanted to thank you.'

'Thanks accepted.' Glitsky leaned back, hooking his hands

behind his head. 'In other news, you'll be delighted to hear that I've put Batavia and Coleman on alibis for the time of Griffin's death.' A short pause. 'Also for early this morning. Maybe eliminate somebody.'

'Maybe find somebody.'

'Maybe that too. Also, I put in some calls – if Ron Beaumont used one of his credit cards, we know where he is.'

'Or was.'

'Close enough. Anyway, last thing is I took your glass to the lab, but nobody was on. It might be a day or two.'

'Utilization coefficient difficulties?' Hardy asked.

Glitsky shook his head in mock disgust. 'I can't teach you anything. It's not utilization coefficient, it's unit integration coefficient, but yeah, that's probably it. Anyway, meanwhile I thought it was time I got a look at the crime scene myself. When the party's over in there, I thought you might like to come along.' He looked at his watch, made a gesture of apology, and lowered his voice. 'Speaking of which . . .'

He still had the key to the penthouse, but Hardy couldn't very well pull it out with Glitsky next to him. So they had to ring the building superintendent, David Glenn.

Glenn was in his early forties, handsome in a no-nonsense way. He wore a tonsure of buzz-cut blond hair around a lot of clean scalp. His body was trim and well defined in shorts and a Gold's Gym T-shirt and he projected an easy and friendly can-do competence.

'You guys getting any closer?' he inquired as the elevator brought them up.

'Any day now,' Glitsky replied.

This seemed to satisfy Glenn somehow. 'So it's not Ron, after all?'

'I didn't say that,' Glitsky replied.

'Yeah, I read it was, but if you're still looking . . .'

Glitsky was firm. 'That's where it is, Mr Glenn. We're still looking. It might be Ron when we stop.'

'No, I don't think so. I hope not.'

'Why not?' Hardy put in.

Glenn shook his head. 'Ah, you know.'

'Nope.' Hardy said, playing cop. 'Why don't you tell us?'

'Well, most tenants here, I couldn't pick 'em out of a lineup. They park down below underneath, ride the elevator to their places, I never see 'em. Ron, I got to know a little, that's all.'

The elevator door opened and they were on the small landing in front of the Beaumonts' door, although the view today through the one window was a gray blanket. Glenn stepped out with them, pulled a key from the ring he was carrying, and fitted it to the door. 'You get a take on people, that's all.'

'And Ron . . . ?'

The key worked, but Glenn just stood there a minute, thinking about the question. 'The guy's a miracle with his kids. I suppose that's it.'

'A miracle?' Glitsky asked. Hardy didn't ask because he knew what was coming.

Glenn shrugged. 'You guys got kids?'

Hardy answered. 'A handful between us.'

'All right, then you know. I'm divorced myself, but I got a couple, and even the good ones try the patience of a saint, am I right?' He waited, then answered himself. 'I'm right. But Ron? Every day out to school, every day pick 'em up. Weekends with soccer and horses and who knows what else, and I've never seen him lose his patience with them. I mean, me, I get mine twice a month and I'm biting their heads off. Couple of times, me and Ron would take all of them to the park or something, and I'm pulling my hair—' A smile, acknowledging the baldness. 'Ron's just cool. Always.'

'What about with his wife?' Glitsky asked. 'The word is they were having problems.'

A nod. 'Maybe. Maybe disagreeing, who doesn't? But I don't see Ron fighting. He'd walk away.'

'Did Bree walk all over him, Mr Glenn?' Hardy asked.

The superintendent hesitated. 'I didn't know her so well. She worked long hours. I'd almost never see her. Sometimes in the elevator . . .' He stopped again.

Glitsky. 'What?'

Glenn shrugged. 'I got the impression she was like an absent-minded genius – you know what I mean? Real inside herself with all this brilliant stuff, and then like she'd forget what floor she lived on. Sometimes she'd be just sitting in the lobby, like she was trying to decide what floor to get off on.' He shook his head. 'Too smart, really. Unconnected.'

Hardy had a hunch. 'To the kids, too?'

'I don't know. I don't know I ever saw her go out with them. She kind of had a life of her own, I think.'

Glitsky pushed it. 'And yet you got the impression that she and Ron were happy together?'

'I don't know happy. But times you'd see them together, they were . . . comfortable, I guess.' He shrugged. 'A family, you know. Comfortable.'

'Phil Canetta?' Glitsky's face betrayed no trace of recognition. 'Can't say it rings a bell.'

'The guy you sent over from Central Station the first time I came here,' Hardy explained.

But Glitsky was still shaking his head, perplexed. 'I called the desk, that was all. Said they might want to dispatch a body to make sure you didn't hurt yourself, or more likely that you didn't hurt Ron Beaumont if he turned out to be home. Did this guy Canetta say he'd talked to me?'

Hardy hesitated. Even though Glitsky was his friend, this was not a casual moment. 'Not really. I just assumed it.'

'And you were both *inside* here?' Glitsky didn't like this one bit. 'How did that special moment come about?'

'The door was open.'

'Open?'

Hardy made a face. 'Picky, picky. You're too literal some-times. Anybody ever tell you that?'

If Hardy thought this was going to side-track Glitsky, he was mistaken. 'Was the door open?'

A shrug. 'It wasn't locked. I knocked, tried the knob, it turned. I walked in.'

'You walked in? Had Canetta arrived yet?'

'No. That was later. But if you're wondering, I had plenty of time to plant evidence or steal anything I wanted, neither of which I did. You're just going to have to believe me. Now how about if we talk about something else?'

Glitsky sighed heavily. 'Someday, you pull stuff like this, I'm not going to be able to help you – you know that?'

Hardy kept a straight face. 'It's a constant worry. But you wanted to come here today, and here we are inside, legally and all with your warrant. What did you want to see?'

They'd already looked out over the balcony and now stood in the middle of the open kitchen, where Glitsky had been casually opening drawers, the cupboards, the refrigerator. 'The usual,' he said distractedly. 'Everything.'

They began in the back, in the children's bedroom. The room was just as Hardy had last seen it.

Across the hall, they moved to the master bedroom. Two steps in, Glitsky stopped so abruptly that Hardy nearly walked into him. 'What?' he asked.

'You tell me.'

Hardy cast his gaze around the room. It was nearly a perfect square and quite large, perhaps twenty feet on a side. To his left, a door was open to a blue-tiled bathroom. Next along the wall were three paneled sliding doors, a long closet. On the back wall, a couple of high windows presided over a king bed neatly made up with blankets, no comforter or bedspread, with a reading table on Hardy's right side. A darkwood chest of drawers with several pictures of Ron, Ron with the kids, Bree with the kids. None of Ron and Bree.

Along the right wall, some hunting prints hung over an exercise area – a stationary bike and some barbells. Then another doorway, leading to another bathroom, was slightly ajar. Finally, coming back around to where they stood, there was a comfortable-looking stuffed leather chair with matching ottoman, another reading lamp, and a Bombay & Company lion's claw table which seemed to double as a writing desk, with its brass lamp, large green blotter, and ship in a bottle.

'I like it,' Hardy said. 'I could use a room like this.'

'You don't feel it?'

Hardy took another second or two. 'I don't feel anything, Abe, except that this is a great room. I want a room like this.'

'That's my point,' Glitsky said. 'Every guy wants a room like this. You know why? This is a guy's room.'

He crossed to the closet and pulled aside one of the paneled doors. Hardy was a step behind him and found himself looking at several suits, coats, shirts, a tie rack. On the floor were a dozen or more pairs of shoes, neatly arranged – dress, tennis, sandals, slippers. Glitsky nodded as though he'd found what he expected.

He walked to the other end of the closet and slid that door back. It was far less crowded. Glitsky started flicking the few hanging items aside. 'Two dresses, three skirts, and four sweaters,' he said, then went into a squat, reached around on the floor, arranging. 'Three and a half pairs of women's shoes, not to mention three more dresses on the floor. How in the world did even Carl miss this?'

'Maybe he found something else that caught his attention and got him killed first.'

Glitsky stood slowly, grimacing, a hand on his back. 'How do you get this old?'

'Stubbornly refuse to die?'

Glitsky broke a small smile. 'Words to live by. Bathroom?'

'No, thanks, I just went.'

The smile vanished as mysteriously as it had come. 'Hopeless,' Abe said, and pushed open the bathroom door. Compared to the spaciousness of the master bedroom, it wasn't much more than a utilitarian closet – six by eight feet with a double-hung window over a blue tiled sink, a towel rack with one orange towel, a toilet with the seat up. Significantly, Hardy thought, there was no tub, only a glassed-in shower.

Hardy reached around and opened the medicine cabinet, which was nearly empty – bottles of Tylenol, Nyquil, some Band-Aids, razor blades. 'Lots of couples have different bathrooms.'

'Happy ones don't have different bedrooms, though,' Glitsky replied. 'I've done research. It's a true fact.'

Glitsky was moving again, and Hardy tagged along. They passed back through Ron's room and stopped at the dresser, which Glitsky opened with the same basic results – a few articles of women's underclothes in two of the drawers. But four of the drawers out of six were packed, even overpacked, with Ron's clothes – jeans, junk, polo shirts and T-shirts, sweaters, socks and underwear. When Glitsky closed the last drawer, he straightened up. 'You know,' he said, 'you could take a million pictures of this room, and I bet the scene guys did, and you wouldn't see any evidence of a crime.'

'I don't either. So they lived in different rooms, so what?'

'This, to you, isn't some evidence of marital conflict?'

Hardy shrugged. 'It doesn't mean he killed her. Besides, Frannie said they were having troubles.'

'Don't remind me. It does make me wonder, though,' he said, 'just how she got pregnant.'

Immersed in paper at the desk in Bree's office, Glitsky was going through the hard copy file, folder by folder – propaganda by the armload on what Hardy thought must be every imaginable side of the additive issue. Legislative reports, news clippings, executive summaries from various think tanks, media alerts. MTBE, ethanol, reformulated gasoline. It ran the gamut from copies of faxed pages to four-color advertising pieces, from page fragments to small booklets.

'Fascinating stuff,' Glitsky said. He was going fast, to Hardy's eye ignoring everything that wasn't personal in Bree's personal files, laying a slush pile of Bree's professional work on the desk to his right, behind him. Hardy made some noise that might have sounded like asking for permission, got a grunt in reply, so grabbed a handful and walked out into the hallway, where he folded it all up and tucked it inside his jacket.

He then returned to Bree's room.

Further evidence that Ron and Bree had lived separate lives, all right. Her bed was smaller, a double. It had a bright floral comforter and flounced pillows that matched. Even now, a month after her death, a woman's scent of perfume and powder hung subtly in the air. Her bathroom was done in light salmon tones and was three times the size of Ron's, with an oversized tub and make-up table, as much a woman's bathroom as Ron's was a man's.

Back in the bedroom, Hardy stood at the bookshelves – floor-to-ceiling built-ins that covered half the back wall. Possibly it shouldn't have surprised him after what he'd heard about Bree the ugly duckling from Damon Kerry, but the entire bottom shelf was filled with paperback romance novels. Next up was a half shelf of paperback commercial fiction, then a couple of shelves of hardbound literary fiction – almost entirely by modern women writers. Toni Morrison, Joyce Carol Oates, Barbara Kingsolver, Laurie Colwin, Amy Tan – a scientist with good literary taste, Hardy thought. Then a surprise – what looked to be a full set of Tony Hillerman. So Chee and Leaphorn had been in her consciousness, too. Maybe helping to spark the idealism that had driven her so strongly in her last months.

On the top shelf, though, at the end of the large section on travel books, next to a new copy of *What To Expect When You're Expecting*, was the one Hardy thought he recognized and knew he wanted. He took the oversized book down and brought it over to the small reading chair next to the bed.

Her high school yearbook. Passages 81, from Lincoln High in Evanston, Illinois.

There were the usual autographs: 'To the smartest girl in

the world.' 'Chemistry would have beat me without you.' 'Who needs boys when you've got brains?' 'Lab rats rule!'

And then, from one of her teachers, the one Hardy needed: 'To Bree Brunetta, my best student ever!'

He quickly turned through the seniors and found her – Bree Brunetta. Without the maiden name, he never would have been able to find, much less recognize, the ravishing Bree Beaumont from the uninspired and formal cap-and-gown photograph.

Bree Brunetta, at seventeen, had been slightly overweight with dark unkempt hair, bangs down over her eyes, braces, clunky glasses. The ugly duckling indeed, Hardy thought. There was a recent picture of Bree with the kids next to the bed and he looked at the smiling face with the shining blond hair, the cheekbones, the perfect mouth – it was hard to reconcile the two images.

He flipped through the rest of the book quickly. Bree had been an active and seemingly well-rounded student, a member of the Debating Society, the Science Club, the Chess Club. She played clarinet in the band and was the 'features' editor of the student newspaper. She was voted the Smartest Girl.

Hardy happened to notice one other detail, one of those cruel high-school moments that scar a kid for life. Bree was voted 'least likely to get a date with Scott lePine,' the Most popular Guy, Best-looking Guy, and Most Likely to Succeed. Whichever kids dreamed up that category must have thought it was hysterical. Hardy guessed Bree wouldn't have thought so.

There were some letters on three-ring binder paper folded over in the back, and he was just opening one when he heard Glitsky's steps coming quickly down the hallway. He folded the letters back and put them with the literature into his inside pocket as well. Then he closed the book as Glitsky appeared at the door to Bree's room. His eyes had a haunted look. 'I just got beeped. I've got to go,' he said.

'You mind if I stay behind a few minutes?' Hardy asked.

'Sure, no sweat. Just lock up when you leave.' Glitsky shook his head. 'Get real, Diz. We're out of here. We're not arguing about it, either, OK? Or making one of our clever remarks.' He let out a long breath. 'Somebody just shot another cop.'

24

The two-man arson team was still at his house when Hardy drove up. He parked semi-legally and came up on to where the lawn had been before stopping to get their attention. They were huddled over an area near what had been the front bay window. 'How you guys doing?'

They both looked over at him with no interest, then held a quiet conference before one of them straightened up, and jumped down on to the porch's foundation. 'Your friend said to tell you he went to work. Otherwise, we're going to be here a while.'

'You got any idea what a while is?'

A flat glare. 'Hours, not minutes.'

This was pulling teeth, but Hardy needed to get some information. 'You finding anything?' At this, the arson investigator spread his hands in a futile gesture, and Hardy cut him off. 'You can't tell me anything, can you? I might have done it, right? Set fire to my own house.'

'People do it all the time.'

Hardy knew this was true. The man was doing his job, actually protecting Hardy's interests. 'OK,' he managed to say mildly. 'I was wondering, though, if I could go into the back and get a few things – clothes, toiletries, like that? Check my phone messages.'

In spite of what he'd told Valens, Hardy didn't think the answering machine in the kitchen had been destroyed. Driving over here, it had occurred to him that it might be instructive to see what the tape held.

But to this inspector, whether or not Hardy had friends on the police force, he was a righteous suspect. He remained all business. 'No, sir. I'm afraid not. There's no electricity in any case. I don't know if the captain made it clear to you, but this house is fire department property until we clear it to you.'

There was nothing to be gained from antagonizing the man, although maintaining his demeanor took a serious coefficient of his resources. He forced a patient smile. 'No, I understand that. But I'd like to be able to make some plans. Can you give me any estimate how long that will be?'

Maybe Hardy had worn the inspector down, but it seemed for an instant as if there was a tiny thaw. 'Safest guess will be tomorrow morning sometime.' He paused. 'Maybe about the time your reporter friend runs his column.'

No, Hardy realized. It wasn't a thaw after all. It was a way to tell him that Jeff Elliot had been by, another unwelcome interruption to their task. Jeff had probably bothered them to distraction. 'If we get done by dark, we'll get it boarded up for the night. Somebody'll be here tomorrow to let you back in . . . if we're ready.' It was a dismissal.

There wasn't anything he could do.

On his private stool, right up by the front window, behind the bar at the Little Shamrock, Moses McGuire was nursing his Sunday Macallan on his private stool. He allowed none of the other bartenders either to drink or to sit, even for an instant, when they were working. His belief was that professional bartenders got paid to stand while they waited on customers – it showed respect. If they wanted to sit, he invited them to come around to the bar side and take a short break at some risk to their job security, but if they were behind the rail, they stood. And on either side of it, during their hours of employ, they were dry.

McGuire himself, though, as the owner, could do any damn thing he wanted. When he and Hardy argued about the unfairness of how he applied his rules, he would explode. 'I'm a noble publican, not some goddammed wage-slave bartender.' And since McGuire owned three-quarters of the place, his word was the law.

He'd carefully drawn Hardy a tap Guinness and brought it to the bar after the foam had settled out to a perfect head. Now Hardy was down an inch or two into it. The time was a bit after two and the fog wasn't going to burn off – not today, maybe not until Christmas. The trees at the edge of Golden Gate Park, no more than a hundred feet away directly across Lincoln Boulevard, were barely visible.

Three other customers quietly took up space in the oldest bar in San Francisco. On a couch in the dark far back, an obviously smitten young couple was possibly engaging in some kind of discreet sex. They had ordered Old Fashioneds – the most frou-frou drink that the purist McGuire allowed at the Shamrock. In the tiny side alcove, a lone, silent mid-thirties dart player with a shaved head and a camouflage jacket was working on his game, drinking Bushmills Irish, Bass Ale, and a raw egg for protein out of a pint glass.

A year before, Moses had picked up some recently released recordings done in the thirties – Stephane Grappelli on violin and Django Reinhardt on guitar just swinging their brains out with the Quintet of the Hot Club de France – and whenever things were slow as they were today, he'd run them on the juke box.

McGuire twirled his glass around on the condensation ring that had formed on the bar. 'You're welcome to come stay with us, you know. The lot of you.'

'Thanks, Mose, but Erin's already got the kids. She's got a bigger place.'

He twirled his glass some more. 'And when is Frannie out?'

This was treacherous territory. Hardy couldn't tell Moses that Ron had released Frannie from her promise without revealing that he'd talked to him. And that would, in turn, lead to the minefield of secrets, none of which Hardy could disclose.

And some of which he still, after everything, didn't know if he believed.

So he sipped Guinness, taking a minute. 'My bet is that Sharron Pratt lets her go Tuesday morning. She's taking too much political flack.'

'Why Tuesday?'

Hardy explained a little about the difference between the judge's contempt ruling and the grand jury contempt citation. Two different animals with similar names. Fortunately, this seemed to satisfy Moses. But he twirled his glass a few more times and Hardy knew him well enough – he might have bought the latest explanation, but there was more he needed to talk about. 'So what are you thinking?' Hardy prompted.

'How to say it.'

'Just say it, that's all.'

Moses drank Scotch, put the glass down, and looked his brother-in-law in the eye. 'OK. How's it all turn to shit so fast?'

Hardy found some humor in the felicitous phrase that McGuire had been struggling to conjure. The pickin's were so slim in the rest of his life that he actually chuckled.

McGuire's countenance took on a familiar dark tone – the Irish temper had always flared with the slightest friction. 'It wasn't a joke.'

Hardy realized he must be on his third Macallan after all, not his second. Well, he thought, it had been stressful couple of days for him, too.

'I didn't think it was a joke, Mose. It's so true I wanted to cry, so I laughed. You hear what I'm saying?'

Moses sipped, nodded, an apology. 'I mean, one day she's taking the kids to school and baking cookies, and next day, bam!' – he slapped the bar with his palm – 'all of a sudden next day she's in jail and her house is burned down. How does shit like this happen?'

What could Hardy say? That Frannie had taken a series of little steps, secret steps? That it wasn't really anything at all like 'all of a sudden?'

And it wasn't only Frannie, either. Hardy had taken them,

too, the tiny incremental steps away from intimacy. More, he'd *felt* the shift in the bedrock of their marriage, the first cracks in the faultline. They'd allowed things to change with the pressures of raising the children – the communication eroded, their respective daily lives on different planets.

This is where it had gone wrong, what had led them to here, but he wasn't going to air all that now. He lifted his glass and killed another inch of Guinness. 'I don't know, Mose. I don't know.'

McGuire leaned over the bar. Whispered. 'Tell me she isn't sleeping with him.'

'She says no.' Hardy made eye contact. 'She wouldn't do that.'

'She wouldn't,' he agreed quickly, but the relief showed. Her brother, at least, believed it. 'She'd tell you first, before anything happened, even if she was only thinking about it. That's who she is.'

'OK.' Talking about it wasn't going to make it better or worse. It was just going to invite other people to participate in the discussion, and Hardy wasn't doing that, even with Moses. He and Frannie might have their serious differences, but they were as one in a way that made them aliens in the modern world – they believed that their private lives were private.

'But your house . . . ?' Moses asked. 'This morning you were saying it was part of this, too.'

'Part of who killed Bree, Mose. Not part of me and Frannie.'

'And you're close to finding that? Who did that?'

'If I am I don't know it, but somebody must think so. I've got to believe hitting my house was a warning to back off.'

Moses sipped his Scotch, then put it down carefully. 'Unless whoever it was thought you were home, in which case it wasn't just a warning.'

Hardy considered for a beat. 'No. I doubt that. I'm not that much of a threat.' He shook his head, the idea rattling around. 'I don't think so,' he repeated, more to himself than to Moses.

'Well you don't have to think it for it to be true. If I were you, I'd put it in the mix.'

'What, exactly?'

'That somebody's trying to kill you.'

On that cheery note, the front door banged open and a mixed six-pack of humanity flowed in, talking football, calling for beer. Moses shrugged at Hardy, gave them a welcome, and headed down the rail for the taps.

It was a signal for Hardy that he didn't want to waste any more time philosophizing with his brother-in-law. Moses was right – there was far too much he didn't know. He was vulnerable and couldn't allow himself the luxury of letting his guard down.

So with neither plan nor destination, Hardy left two-thirds of his Guinness. He'd parked around the corner on 10th Avenue and pushed himself through the fog, hunched against the wind. Getting in behind the wheel, he hesitated before turning the key, then broke a thin smile as the engine turned over. See? No bomb. Flicking the heater up to high, he pulled out, got to the corner, and turned right. He had no idea where he was going.

All he knew was that the Little Shamrock wasn't anywhere he needed to be just now. He needed to work. Time was running out. He couldn't go back to his house – the fire department owned it. There were still his children, and Frannie. But he'd already seen them today. That would have to be enough.

Where the hell was Ron Beaumont? Or Phil Canetta?

What did he have? What could he work with?

The only thing that came remotely to mind was his paper-work, the lawyer's constant companion and last refuge. At his office he had his copies of pages from Carl Griffin's file, the notes he'd taken last night with Canetta, the propaganda he'd liberated from Bree's office, and the letters from her high school yearbook. At some point, he reasoned, some part of all of that might intersect.

David Freeman believed that lawyers should work around

the clock. He had had full bathrooms installed on each of the three floors of his building so that his associates would not be able to use the lame excuse after an all-nighter that they had to go home to freshen up and get ready for court.

In twenty-five minutes, Hardy was in his office – showered, shaved, and changed into the shirt that he'd stashed in his file cabinet a couple of months before.

When he got seated at his desk, he retrieved the four messages he'd received since last night, hoping against hope that one of them would turn out to be from Canetta, or even Ron Beaumont. If Al Valens had left a message Hardy hadn't been able to get back at his home, then maybe either or both of the men he *wanted* to talk to had tried as well, or called here at his office afterwards.

But no such luck.

Three of the calls were from clients in various stages of feeling abandoned and the last was Jeff Elliot. When Hardy called him back, he was himself on fire over the blaze at Hardy's house, although he did pay a fleeting moment's lip service to sympathy for Hardy's loss. 'Is there anything I can do to help you, Diz? You got a place to stay?'

'Yeah, we're covered, Jeff. Thanks, though.'

But back to the scoop. 'And you think it was arson?'

'I'd bet a lot on it. In fact, I wouldn't rule out that it's the MTBE people, the *Valdez* Avengers, all those jerks.'

'If that's true,' Jeff said, his enthusiasm overflowing, 'it's a giant break in that story.'

'That's my goal,' Hardy said drily. 'Sacrifice my home for a good story. Maybe you'll win the Pulitzer and I'll be happy for you. We can have a party in my new house.'

Elliot apologized. 'I didn't mean it like that, Diz.' He paused. 'But don't you want to get whoever did this, take 'em down?'

'You don't know.'

'I bet I do. All I'm saying is here, maybe we've got a real connection.'

'Between who?'

'That's what I think I have, Diz. Do you want to hear it?'

'Talk,' Hardy said.

'OK. After you left yesterday, I went with what you said – the guy from Caloco—'

'Jim Pierce.'

'Yeah, all right, Pierce. He'd told you that SKO funded these cretins, right?'

'Right.'

'Well, what if that were true? Where was the connection? So I started poking through among all the crap I showed you yesterday – that thick file of paper – and realized that a lot of the pro-ethanol stuff comes from this organization named the Fuels Management Consortium, FMC for short. It's here in town. Familiar?'

'No, but this stuff wasn't my major until a couple of days ago. I thought FMC made tanks and stuff, big equipment.'

'Same letters, different company.'

'OK. Go on.'

'Well, FMC produces pro-ethanol, anti-MTBE press releases. Tons of them. Sometimes the source of them is a little hard, like impossible, to recognize because they get picked up by intermediaries – syndicated as hard news stories in the dailies, also in industry publications, the *Health Industry Newsletter*, *Environmental Health Monthly*, like that. So I never put it together that it might be one source.'

'And then you did?'

'Right. Plus every time some more MTBE leaks into another well, we get the update before the ink's dry on the EPA report.'

'I'm listening.'

'OK, so a few months ago, we – the *Chronicle* – we decided to do a big spread on the dangers of MTBE. I mean, this was a four-day, front-page feature. Lots of scary stuff – cancer clusters, birth defects, the usual. Even a lay person such as yourself might remember it.'

'Vaguely.'

'Well, Kerry had just taken the primary and suddenly this was news, and we ran it. Anyway, the reporter who wrote the article, as it happens, is a friend of mine named Sherry Weir. She shows up in the office last night on this water temple poisoning as I'm thinking about our discussion, yours and mine. She tells me that FMC was the prime source for her feature – it's an impressive propaganda factory.

'So yesterday, when Sherry hears about the Pulgas Temple, her first stop on the way to the office is the FMC offices in the Embarcadero Buildings. OK, she knows it's Saturday after-noon, they're probably closed up, but it's a shot. And what does she find?'

'An armed nuclear weapon?'

'She finds that nobody's there, all right, but out in the hallway for pickup is the day's press releases, bound and labeled for distribution, all about the water poisoning, dooms-day in San Francisco, sidebars on the dangers of MTBE pollution, like that. Anyway, she pulls a few off the top of the pile and brings them back for her article.' A beat. 'Get it?'

'I'm not sure.'

Jeff's voice went down to an excited whisper, but it rang with triumph. 'They *had to be* written and printed up before it happened.'

Hardy took a moment to let it sink in. If this were true, it appeared to link some of the eco-terrorist activity with FMC, but not necessarily to SKO, and certainly not to Valens or Kerry. How could it help him?

But Jeff thought he had the answer to that, too. 'Because FMC is run by this joker named Baxter Thorne . . .'

'Who works for SKO,' Hardy guessed.

'You're too smart, except not so fast, Red Rider. Back when she interviewed him, Sherry couldn't get Thorne to admit who paid him. He calls himself a public affairs consultant. According to him, he represents all kinds of environmental groups and other clients, but says his contracts demand confidentiality. She asks him specifically about some of these activist groups and he admits he's given them some advice.'

'Advice. That's a nice word.'

'I thought so, too. But even nicer is this. I call this buddy of mine, a colleague in Cincinnati, at the *Sentinel*—'

'You've been a busy boy, Jeff.'

'This could in fact be my Pulitzer, Diz. You'd be busy, too. Turns out that Baxter Thorne is not unknown in Cincinnati. It wasn't exactly common knowledge, but my buddy knew – for years Thorne was the dirty tricks guy for Ellis Jackson.'

'Who is . . . ?'

'You're going to love this – Jackson is the CEO of Spader Krutch Ohio.'

Hardy felt a little tingle along the back of his neck and knew it wasn't the cold outside leaking through his office window.

Jeff was going on. 'So we've possibly got SKO paying for dirty tricks in San Francisco. We've got somebody who might put MTBE in the water, might kill Bree Beaumont . . .'

'Might burn my house down,' Hardy added evenly.

'That, too,' Jeff agreed. 'But what we don't have and we do need is how, if we're on the right track, Baxter Thorne came to be worried about you.'

'Somebody told him.'

'I'm with you. But who?'

Hardy wracked his brain, trying to keep himself from the knee-jerk reaction for the second time today that it had to be Valens. But it might go higher – Hardy couldn't rule out that a directive could have come from Damon Kerry himself, although Jeff Elliot wasn't going to accept that.

But why stop with Kerry? The connection between SKO and him might even be Phil Canetta – cops who worked freelance security at conventions had also been known to provide muscle, to help with dirty tricks. Had Canetta ever done that kind of work with SKO, he wondered. Or with Baxter Thorne?

'I really don't have any ideas, Jeff,' he said, 'other than I'd like a few private moments with this Thorne fellow.'

'Did you talk to Al Valens this morning, by the way?' Jeff asked. 'At the Clift? Since you woke me up for it.'

'Didn't I tell you all about that?'

He heard Jeff sigh. 'No. I think you left it out.'

And suddenly, the morning's information clicked with what he had just learned from Jeff. Bree's report. She had changed her mind about ethanol and Valens had tried – successfully he said – to keep her from talking to Kerry about it. Who would this silence benefit even more than Kerry himself? SKO. And SKO's operative in San Francisco Baxter Thorne.

What if Valens' efforts to keep Bree quiet hadn't worked after all? What if someone needed to shut her up?

Valens again, once removed.

Maybe.

But Hardy didn't want to lead Jeff Elliot there. He had his own agenda and he figured he'd sure as hell earned the right to pursue it now. 'I thought he'd told me a lie,' Hardy said mildly, 'and I wanted to talk to him about it.'

'And had he?'

'It was more a misunderstanding. It got straightened out.' Deflection time. 'You ever catch up with Kerry?'

'Today's agenda,' Jeff promised, 'if I get to it.'

'What would stop you?'

'One of the problems doing a daily column,' Jeff said, 'is you've got to write it. Kerry's going to be impossible until Tuesday. Tomorrow I'm going for Thorne.'

'How are you going to get to him?'

Hardy would bet Jeff's eyes weren't tired now – he was on a scent. 'A little classic bait and switch. I've put in a call to FMC that I'd like an interview on the Pulgas story, which he'll want to talk about. Once I'm in the door, I'll ask different questions.' He changed his tone. 'I think we're very close, Diz, really.'

'I hope so,' Hardy said, 'but do me one favor, would you?'

'What's that?'

'Don't go alone.'

After they hung up, Hardy immediately put in a call to Glitsky's pager. Jeff Elliot might hate him for it, but from Hardy's perspective, this was now a police matter, and that's where it was going.

In fact, even without Bree Beaumont, the case could be made that the arson at Hardy's house, if it had been started by the same people who dumped the MTBE, was related to a San Francisco homicide, and therefore in Glitsky's domain. Even though the Pulgas Water Temple was in San Mateo County, it was city property and Glitsky could assert at least dual jurisdiction – he had authority to investigate the death of the middle-aged hiker who'd been killed there yesterday.

And now, with the new information Hardy could supply from his talk with Jeff Elliot, that investigation might lead him to Baxter Thorne, and perhaps all the way back to Bree.

Waiting for Glitsky's call, he got up from the desk, stretched, and came around front to throw a round of darts. But he didn't retrieve any of them. Instead, he walked to the window and looked down on to Sutter Street, then returned to his chair and pulled his collections of paper up closer to him.

Now that he knew he was looking for something specific – evidence of any relationship between FMC and Bree – he thought he might have a better chance of seeing it.

But the telephone rang.

'Yo.'

'Get a carphone, some kind of beeper, something, would you? I've been calling all over town trying to run you down.'

'I've been here at my office. And I called you, remember?'

'Yeah, well, I couldn't imagine you'd be working on a Sunday so I didn't think of there.'

Hardy ignored the bad attitude. Abe had gone to a murder scene and had spent the last several hours there. It was understandable that he was in a surly mood. 'OK, so now we're talking. You interested in what I called about? You will be.'

'Not as much as why I want to talk to you.'

Glitsky's tone wasn't getting any better.

'What?' Hardy asked.

'The cop who got shot.'

It suddenly hit him. If Glitsky needed to reach him on that matter, there could only be one reason. His stomach went hollow in a rush. 'Phil Canetta.'

His friend's voice was grim. 'You heard it here first.'

'Where are you?'

Glitsky told him.

25

Hardy was in the Muir Loop, just inside the Presidio. He'd driven through the urban forest many times before, and in his memory it was serene and lovely, a two-lane road overhung with boughs, winding through an expansive eucalyptus glade.

But today in the late afternoon it seemed that menace dripped from every branch. With the dense fog, visibility was no greater than fifty feet. He crept along at fifteen miles per hour, squinting into the nothingness. There were no curbs on the street here, no street lights, and twice he felt his tires leave the asphalt.

At last Hardy got a glimpse of some parked vehicles and slowed down even more. With the fog, the scene was etched in stark relief – the outlines of three squad cars, a couple of vans, some news trucks by now, the unmarked cars of inspectors. He pulled in behind the line of them, zipped up his jacket, and tried to pick Glitsky out of the milling group of spectral figures.

The lieutenant was at the back door of one of the vans, and as he got closer, Hardy recognized Glitsky's companion – John Strout, the lanky, drawling coroner for the city and county. He was nearly on them before Glitsky noticed.

'John, you know Dismas Hardy.'

'Sure do.' Strout had worked with Hardy before and testified at several of his trials. That Hardy was now a defense attorney made it odd that he was at this crime scene, at this stage, but Strout had been around the block many times, and very little surprised him. 'How you doin', Diz?' He extended his hand and Hardy took it.

'I've been better,' Hardy admitted. 'It's been a long day.'

Strout was his usual laconic self. 'Wish I could say the same for our victim here. His day only lasted a couple of hours. I reckon, given the choice, I'd go for long.'

'Yeah, well,' Glitsky jerked a thumb. 'Hardy's house caught fire this morning.'

'Not by itself,' Hardy said sharply.

Strout caught something between the two men. 'There some connection with that and this?'

Glitsky gave Hardy a shut-up look and said he wouldn't rule it out, there was some possibility, but they had a ways to go on this one first, on Phil Canetta. He didn't want to jump to conclusions.

Hardy got Glitsky's message – the relationship between Canetta's murder and Bree's, to say nothing of Hardy's house – wasn't going to be part of the public debate. Not yet. It was not even immediately clear that Glitsky was overtly, officially pursuing the Griffin parallels.

'So what did go down here?' Hardy asked.

Strout took his boot off the van's bumper, looked across the street, said, 'Reckon they're close enough,' and headed out. Hardy and Glitsky followed.

The car had all four of its doors open. Strout walked around off the fringe of the road to the driver's door, but Glitsky touched Hardy's arm and the two of them stayed in the street, on the passenger side. They could see inside clearly enough in any event, and just as clearly, Glitsky wanted a private ear.

But the first sight of Canetta was more bad news. He was dressed as he'd been at Freeman's last night, the last time Hardy had seen him. There was no way now that Hardy could pretend that his relationship to Canetta wasn't relevant to Glitsky's investigation, and that in turn was going to have to lead to further revelations, none of them even remotely unpleasant.

The body was slumped against the back of the seat, canted slightly to its left. Strout spoke in the professorial drawl he adopted when reciting undisputed facts on the witness stand. Today, though, Hardy found the impersonal tone unsettling.

'You can see if you lift that right arm' – he was doing it – '– rigor's let up enough now – that the second bullet . . .'

'The second bullet?' Hardy asked quietly.

Glitsky nodded grimly. 'He wasn't shot here. First one was in the chest. He was facing the shooter.'

Hardy heard Strout over their conversation. '. . . probably fragmented into some ribs and ripped the heart into pieces . . .'

He shut that out and went back to Abe. 'So you're saying he was carried into the car and driven here?'

'And pushed over to make it look like he drove out on his own. I'm not just saying it. That's what happened.'

'But why would somebody . . .?'

'Because this is what Griffin looked like and they got away with that. Turned out, I'd say it was a bad idea.'

Hardy agreed. 'It connects them.'

A nod. 'Not only that, my guess is Canetta was shot with Griffin's gun.'

Strout continued. '. . . time of death, but he's loosened up enough, it had to be ten hours ago, maybe longer.'

'So who found him?'

'Couple of joggers.'

'And Strout's saying . . . ?'

'You just heard. Late night, early morning. The second shot's in a closed car, pea soup outside. Nobody heard a thing.'

Before Hardy could ask, Glitsky expanded on it. 'I know what you're going to say, but don't. This damn sure could've been Ron. We'll get to that.' He held up a hand, stopping Hardy's reply. 'But because I like to be thorough, I also put Batavia and Coleman out on alibis for all of your own personal heroes – Pierce, Valens, even Kerry. We're talking between two and six a.m., but guess what?'

'They weren't all home in bed.'

Glitsky's mouth turned up, but it wasn't a smile. 'Insight like that is what keeps us friends. Maybe they were, but we haven't been able to reach any of them. Pierce wasn't around today. His wife said he was out on his boat from early this morning. Also, we've got Kerry's schedule but he's not sticking to it – he and Valens didn't make his first banquet. Two days from the election, he's in flex mode, I guess. Valens—'

Hardy had to cut in. 'Valens was at Kerry's until nearly midnight. After that, Kerry left home.'

'How do you know that?'

'Jeff Elliot.'

'Where did he go?'

'Only the shadow knows. But he lives like five blocks from here. And while we're on it, Pierce isn't much further and all of it's downhill.'

Glitsky was silent for a couple of seconds. 'I see you've done your homework. How do you know all this, hell, *any* of it?'

'I'm motivated. I talked to Valens this morning . . .'

'When was that? I was with you half the morning.'

'Must have been the other half.' He knew Glitsky wouldn't let it go, so he continued. 'It had to do with my house.'

'Valens had something to do with your house?'

Strout finished his monologue and straightened up, looking over the car's roof. 'This boy's been sittin' here in the cold long enough, Abe. You needin' anything else here?'

Glitsky shifted his attention to the coroner. 'Not me, John,' he replied. 'If crime scene's done, you can tag him and bag him.'

Strout took a last look into the car, at the body of Phil Canetta, and clucked sympathetically. Again he straightened up. 'Scene calls. I hate 'em, y'know that? They ain't medicine out here, are they? It ain't just a stripped body with something to tell you.'

There wasn't anything to say to that. Everybody there felt the same thing to a greater or lesser degree.

Glitsky gave Strout a gentle slap on the shoulders as he

passed. Then he walked a few paces back to where the head of his crime scene unit was huddling with a couple of his team. Hardy heard him say, 'If there's enough lead left, get ballistics to check it against the slug that went through Griffin. I'm betting it's the same gun.'

A short discussion ensued, after which Glitsky returned to Hardy. 'Valens. This morning. Jeff Elliot. Bet you thought I'd get side-tracked, didn't you?'

'Never crossed my mind,' Hardy said. 'I know we've got to talk, but maybe someplace else.'

Hands in his pockets, the lieutenant took in the gloom around them. The body was on the coroner's gurney and the tow truck started its mechanical cranking, getting ready to lift Canetta's car and take it to the police lot.

Hunching his shoulders, Glitsky gave a last shudder against the cold. 'Good call,' he said.

In one of his brothers' old rooms down the hall that led off the back of the kitchen, Orel Glitsky was sprawled on the floor, watching television and doing homework. Rita was with him, reading, her Spanish radio station playing softly on the end table next to where she sat on the sofa.

Hardy at his heels, Glitsky checked in with his household – letting them know that he was home now, sorry he'd been out most of the day, glad to see everybody was doing fine. Rita looked up from her book and told him she'd heated up some tortilla pie for a snack and it was probably still warm in the oven. Glitsky got Orel's attention finally, and asked his son how his day had gone. He got a nod, though his boy's eyes never left the TV. 'OK.'

'What time did your grandfather go home?'

A shrug. 'I don't know.'

'A little after twelve,' Rita said. 'When I got here.'

No one was trying to hide any displeasure about Glitsky's working on a Sunday after having dumped Orel on his grandfather the day before.

'So . . . anything neat happen today? You guys do anything fun?'

Rita just looked at him.

'Orel?'

The boy shrugged. 'Not much.'

Glitsky stood a moment longer in the doorway, then sighed heavily and headed back down the hallway. 'So glad I asked,' he muttered.

It was only a few steps to the kitchen, where they closed the door behind them against the competing sounds. Glitsky pulled around a chair and straddled it backwards. 'They think I want to be gone working all weekend? They think going to murder scenes is my idea of a good time?'

Hardy let him stew, since there was no answer anyway. Sometimes people had to work – a bitch, but there it was. His kids hadn't understood that he couldn't go trick or treating last night. Now it was Abe's turn to deal with it.

He grabbed a kitchen towel, opened the oven, and pulled out the flat pan that held the remains of the pie. Hardy grabbed plates from a cupboard, put them down on the table, and started serving himself.

'What I don't understand,' he said, 'is how they can sit there and read and study and listen to music and watch TV all at once. I can't think with all that other noise going on.'

Glitsky turned his chair around the normal way, and pulled the pan over. 'That's because you're over forty. Nowadays they teach that stuff in school. Multi-tasking. Makes you a better person, more productive.' He spooned out some food on to his plate and pushed it around a little. 'It's just one of the reasons the world is so much better now than it was when we were kids.' He forked a bite and popped it. 'So. You want to just start or would you prefer that I ask questions?'

Dark slammed down like a trap door.

An hour later, Hardy was in the tramped-down mud behind his house. Out here closer to the ocean, a fine drizzle had started to condense out of the fog. In the brisk, chill wind, he was impressed by how much the moisture added to the already substantial pleasures of the evening.

Up the backyard stairway, still outside, he turned his key in the back door and, somewhat to his surprise, it opened. He fully expected that the fire department's security team would have provided their own locks for the various entrances, but though they'd tightly boarded up the front and posted the property with 'No Trespassing' signs, that seemed to be the extent of it.

So he was inside. From the lower shelf on his workbench, he grabbed a flashlight and passed on into his kitchen. He didn't need the flashlight yet – the distances and angles were all second nature. He checked around – there was no dial tone on the wall telephone, no light in the refrigerator when he pulled it open. The neatly folded, heavy brown-paper shopping bags were where they always were, in the drawer at the bottom of the pantry. He grabbed one off the top.

In his bedroom, he risked a short beam. His tropical fish – seventeen of them, a collection that he'd nurtured through various permutations over twenty years – were all belly up on the surface of his aquarium.

A muscle worked in his jaw. He turned off the flashlight and crossed the room. The answering machine was on a small reading table. He unplugged it from the wall, disconnected the telephone jack, and placed it in the bottom of the paper bag on a corner of the bed. Next was his dresser – he threw in underwear and a couple of sweaters on top of the answering machine. In his closet, he gathered up a heavy jacket, a business suit, and some shirts, all of them smelling of smoke. A complete change of clothes for his wife, too. For when he got her out.

Something in him wished he didn't need to do it, but he knew he had to. Leaving everything on the bed, he walked back up through the kitchen into the burnt-out front of the house and stood in the middle of what used to be his dining room.

He'd once represented a plaintiff who had suffered severe burns in an industrial accident. He remembered preparing the expert he was going to put on, who'd defined the various degrees of burn – first, a sunburn; second, a blister; or the worst, third-degree burns, causing irreparable loss of skin and terrible disfigurement. Any serious percentage of third-degree burns over the body was most often fatal.

But what he felt now seemed even worse – a fourth-degree burn to the core of him, one that charred the edges of his soul.

After a time he moved again – back through the kitchen, to the bedroom for the things he'd left there. He picked up the bag by its paper handles, the clothes by their hangers. At his workbench, he carefully replaced the flashlight, then let himself back out into the awful, awful night.

Hardy left his bag of clothes in the car, but brought the answering machine up to his office, where he plugged it in and found that Al Valens was, at least, not lying all the time. He was the first message – just what he'd said.

The second one stunned him.

No name, but immediately recognizable. 'I'm sorry to have moved out of the hotel. I hope I haven't caused you too much inconvenience.'

Hardy almost laughed out loud – not too much inconvenience indeed.

'The only answer is that I've got to be very cautious. I know you will understand. If you could get to me so easily, so could the police. They might have been following you the next time you came down. I don't know. The point is, I felt like I had to relocate. But I wanted you to know I'm still near by and appreciate what you're doing, but very nervous about you coming to me. I hope you're having some luck. Thanks.'

'Sure, no problem,' Hardy said, then punched at the answering machine's button, sat back in his chair and tried to gather some thoughts.

But it was all a jumble. Just today his house had been

burned, Canetta had been killed. He'd been running since first light and had one day left to discover any useful truth. He glanced up at his dart board on the wall around his desk. He didn't remember throwing them, but his three custom-made darts were stuck haphazardly around the board.

He forced himself up, around the desk, and flicked on the bright room overheads. The darts were his worry beads, and he pulled them from the board, walked back to the tape line he'd marked on the floor at eight feet, turned and threw the first one. Triple twenty – a good start.

He threw the second dart, then the third. Walked to the board, pulled them down, and returned to his mark.

If Ron hadn't left town, what did that mean?

The kind reading was to take him at his word. He was cautious, nervous, paranoid, all of these things certainly understandable. He wanted to be near by in case – as did not appear very likely now – Hardy succeeded in exposing Bree's killer. If that happened, he and his children could return to their lives. And from what had already happened to the other principles in this drama, Ron was right to be worried.

But as Hardy threw his darts, a more sinister interpretation kept wanting to surface, and he had a difficult time keeping it down. Ron was still near by. Close enough to set fire to Hardy's house. Close enough to kill Canetta.

If he'd only left a phone number on Hardy's machine. Surely there was no danger in that. Then he could answer some of the questions that were fogging Hardy's consciousness.

What was the truth, for example, about Ron and Bree's marriage? The separate bedrooms, the infidelity? Ron might be a 'miracle' of a father, but he wasn't the same as a husband. This was not the happy couple they pretended to be. At the very least, Bree was having an affair with Damon Kerry. And she had become pregnant, apparently by him. Although Hardy felt he couldn't rule out Canetta, or even Pierce.

And if the father was anyone but Ron, this was a motive for murder. For Ron to kill.

Beyond that, if Bree were habitually unfaithful, might that mean . . . with Ron . . .

Hardy tried to shut out the thought, but finally it couldn't be dismissed any longer. Of course it could mean Frannie. Although, finally, today, she had told him no, it hadn't been like that. Or had she? Like what, exactly? He hadn't cross-examined her. He hadn't had the heart.

And why would he be fool enough to believe her in any event?

Freeman's words from last night's conversation echoed and picked at him – Hardy and Glitsky believing that Carl Griffin had gone to interview a snitch *because he had said so*. When in fact that's not what he'd done. In fact, Griffin had lied.

To his boss. And for a lot less reason than Frannie had.

Nothing but the truth was a noble courtroom concept, but Hardy knew from a lifetime of trials that even there it was systematically abused. And in life it was much worse.

But he stopped himself before going too far down this road. Frannie wasn't just another random person. She was the mother of his children, the wife he'd promised to love, honor, and respect. And if those three did not include trust, a basic belief not only in her honesty but in who she was, he was lost anyway.

Frannie had told him clearly. She had been attracted to Ron but had remained faithful to him. Ron was a good friend, but that's all she'd let it be. Hardy really had no choice but to believe her, to take it on faith. She was telling him the truth.

And that was the only truth he could let himself act on. To do less would betray both of them.

26

It was Sunday night and Glitsky hadn't spent enough time at home this weekend. He had a feeling he wasn't going to anytime soon, either.

In his job, once in a very great while he called in a favor. Three years before, Glitsky had spoken up in defense of Paul Ghattas on one of the dozens of EEO lawsuits that were forever being filed among and between workers in the Hall of Justice. Ghattas, a lab tech whose first language was Tagalog, had made a comment to one of his female co-workers that she had interpreted as sexual harassment. The two had been discussing the location of a stab wound, and Ghattas had fumbled with language for a moment, then used the word tit, rather than breast.

Glitsky had been in the lab at the time, waiting for results on another case, and had been the only witness, hearing the whole thing, including Ghattas' abject apology afterward.

The woman had screamed, 'Don't you piss on my leg and tell me it's raining,' and run out of the room.

Before Ghattas' comment, the lab setting had been professional and neutral. But the woman had been offended to the point of being unable to continue coming to work for the following ten days. Then she'd filed her suit which, it turned out, had not been her first. She wanted Paul Ghattas – a ten-year veteran and father of four – dismissed. She wanted full pay for days missed. She wanted disability for the six months she estimated it would take her to get over the emotional trauma she'd had to endure.

Glitsky had worked with Ghattas many times. The man's English was poor, but he was a competent workhorse in the

287

lab. So, realizing even at the time that he was wading into troubled waters, Glitsky had stood up for him at the hearing, where – against all odds in an environment where to be accused was to be guilty – Ghattas was exonerated.

So Paul was happy to accompany Abe to the Hall at seven this Sunday night. Glitsky left him downstairs at the lab, then went up to his office. Checking Damon Kerry's fingerprints against all the others found at Bree's apartment was going to take Ghattas some time and Glitsky had a slew of his own work now to move on.

The litany of information that Hardy had recited earlier in the evening had been deeply disturbing, mostly because Glitsky hadn't known any of it. And as head of homicide, to say nothing of being Hardy's best friend, he should have. Batavia and Coleman weren't brain dead by any means, and yet somehow between them they'd missed getting any kind of a toehold in this case.

He was half tempted to arrest Hardy for what he'd withheld from him just on general principles, for not mentioning diddly squat about what he'd found, what he had been doing. Like, he had been working with Canetta. He'd made the connection to Griffin. He'd talked with Valens this morning when neither of Glitsky's inspectors could locate the campaign manager. Now he had Baxter Thorne, who had possibly been at least the brains behind dumping the MTBE into the Crystal Springs Reservoir and, more relevantly, had killed a man in Glitsky's jurisdiction in the process.

But for all Hardy did know, Glitsky realized, he had a blind spot, and that was Ron Beaumont. It was a common truth in homicide that the spouse did it, and in spite of all the activity surrounding Bree's oil interests, Ron still looked pretty good to Glitsky. He had fled the scene, using multiple identities. Judging from the bedrooms in the penthouse, he and Bree hadn't been intimate recently, and since she was pregnant, this provided a pretty solid motive.

Glitsky hated to give the DA the satisfaction, but he could

no longer ignore Ron as a suspect. In fact, from his perspective, the best suspect.

Abruptly, he sat up in his chair, coming to the unpleasant realization that his friend was still holding out on him – otherwise Ron would be on Hardy's own short list, too. He would have to be. Therefore, Hardy knew something more and he wasn't telling. He hadn't told Glitsky even as he had pretended to bare his soul a couple of hours before, when they'd planned to meet again down here when Hardy got his belongings together.

Now Glitsky was in a slow burn, thinking that by God, friend or no friend he should arrest the duplicitous bastard when he got back down here after all. He started punching Hardy's office number into his desk phone, give him an earful if he was still there, but he heard footsteps out in the hallway and stopped, replacing the receiver.

A minute later, Inspector Leon Timms, the crime scene specialist from Canetta's murder, was in his doorway. 'You asked me to put a rush on the ballistics check, Abe. Can you believe it? There's somebody in at the lab.'

'Paul Ghattas,' Abe replied. 'I dragged him down from his house. Fingerprints.'

'Fingerprints?' In spite of their exalted presence in books and movies, Timms knew that in real life, fingerprints were rarely a factor in police work. But he merely shrugged – if the lieutenant wanted to check prints, he was welcome to. 'He ran the ballistics for me. The guy's a one-man shop down there.'

This was good to hear about a man whose job he had saved, but Glitsky had his sights elsewhere. 'So what did he find?'

Timms nodded. 'Same shooter. Griffin's gun. For sure.'

When Hardy arrived, he was happy but not surprised to learn that Glitsky's surmise about Griffin's gun was correct. He wasn't as happy when his friend got up, closed the door to his office, and asked him what he knew about Ron Beaumont that he wasn't telling.

'What do you mean?' But that effort at deflection went about as far as Hardy had imagined it would – nowhere.

Glitsky was propped on the corner of his own desk, hovering a foot or two over where Hardy sat in his hard chair, pressed back against the office wall. As Glitsky intended, this posture made Hardy uncomfortable. 'What do I mean?' he repeated with an edge. 'Let's see if I can explain it. You know the whereabouts and most of the life history of everybody who's even remotely involved in the death of Bree Beaumont. You discover that Carl Griffin's death is probably connected, too. And today Canetta makes that pretty much a certainty. We've got four or five suspects and no righteous alibis for any of them, but you don't appear to have any suspicion at all about the one I feel the best about. If you're keeping score here, that would be Ron.' Glitsky had his arms folded, his game face on, and it wasn't any kind of an act. The eyes were unyielding. He wasn't going to be breaking out the peanuts in his desk drawer for a little philosophical chat.

Hardy sucked air and held it in, then let it out in a rush. 'You won't like it.'

'I didn't expect I would.' Glitsky waited through another pause.

'I'm in this for his kids.'

The eyes, so lately flat, narrowed. Glitsky's nose flared and the scar in his lips went white. He took a breath or two and when he finally spoke, it was in a terrifyingly controlled voice. 'You've *seen* him? You're representing him?'

Hardy knew that any attempt to finesse this would only infuriate Abe more. 'I've seen him once. Friday night, before things had gotten anywhere near here.'

'So where was this?'

'The Airport Hilton.'

'So he was leaving town? Has he left?'

'No. Neither. He was ready to if he had to. That was all.'

'That was all. That's nice. And then somehow you decided it wasn't important to let me know about any of this?'

'No. I never made that decision. You were specifically *not* looking for Ron at that point.'

'Well, I am now. Where is he?'

'I don't know.'

'My ass.'

Hardy shrugged. 'I'm not lying to you. I haven't ever lied to you, Abe. I've omitted what you didn't need to know.'

'Well thank you so much.' Glitsky made a face of disgust, his voice now rising in indignation. 'How about if that's not your decision to make? How about if it's my job to do this, not some hobby I can pick up and lay down when the mood strikes me? *That ever occur to you, Diz? You ever think about any of this?*'

But Hardy wasn't about to go begging for mercy or forgiveness. He'd done what he felt he'd had to do. He believed it was defensible. 'Look. Ron called me last night. The answering machine is still in my office with the message on it. You can come listen to it anytime you want. I don't know where he is or how to reach him and it pisses me off just a bit myself.'

'But it's not your *job*, Diz.'

'Don't kid yourself, Abe. It's a hell of a lot more than my job. First it's my wife, then my house; next it's maybe me, my life. If I had even the smallest suspicion any of this was Ron, you think I'd gamble all of that? You don't think I'd give him up to you? Hell, I'd lead the parade.'

'Not if he was your client.'

Hardy lowered his own voice. 'He's not it, Abe. You've known that all along. You go after him, you're barking up the wrong tree.'

'Yeah, but that's what *I* do, bark up trees. Things fall out, I pick 'em up, and maybe it points me to another one.'

'Maybe it doesn't.' Hardy came forward in his chair. 'There isn't time, Abe.'

291

Glitsky glared, very little of the fury gone. After a couple of seconds, he stood up, walked back to the door, opened it, and left the room.

He was standing at the back windows of the homicide detail, arms folded, looking out through the black fog to the jail across the way.

Hardy came out of Abe's office and walked up behind his friend. 'I'll tell you everything I can,' he said to his back, 'but there's some things I can't.'

Glitsky didn't turn.

'Ron has a situation that makes it awkward for him to get formally involved with the law or the courts. If he gets in the system, his kids suffer. That's why Frannie couldn't give him up. It's what she couldn't talk about. You heard what the supe in his building said, Abe. The guy's a good father. Like you and me, right.'

Still no answer, but Hardy noticed that Glitsky's shoulders rose and fell. He was listening.

'I know, I know. Why didn't I tell you sooner? Why'd I do things with Canetta? I don't know. I didn't know. I was trying to figure it out. If it's any help, I paid my dues around it, wouldn't you say? And the bottom line is Ron didn't kill Bree.'

Finally, the lieutenant half turned. 'Except if he did,' he said.

'He didn't.'

Glitsky was a statue.

They both became aware of footfalls in the hallway, moving fast. Hardy turned just as an excited Asian man appeared in the doorway. He was slightly out of breath and tried to compose himself in the few steps over to them.

'One of last ones I try, Abe. Sorry. But it match up.'

'You got a match?'

'Yeah. Same as on glass, whoever that was.'

'From the prints in the penthouse?'

292

Ghattas nodded and nodded. 'Definite sure.'

Hardy spoke up. 'Kerry?'

Ghattas looked at him, then to Glitsky for permission. The lieutenant nodded. 'Looks like.'

'What is that?' Ghattas asked. '*The* Damon Kerry?'

Glitsky nodded. 'If you're sure about the glass, he was at Bree Beaumont's and said he wasn't.'

'Oh, definite sure.'

'Then it was Kerry.'

'Well, shit,' Ghattas responded. 'Very shit.'

'My thought exactly, Paul. Good work. And thanks for coming down tonight. It was a big help. You need a lift home?'

'No. I call my wife. Ten minutes, she's here.' He nodded and was gone.

Silence reigned again and Hardy waited. Glitsky chewed the inside of his cheek.

'You're probably remembering right now that it was me who picked up that glass,' Hardy said.

27

Jim Pierce sat in the pilot's seat on the flying bridge of his yacht, bundled against the weather. He was drinking rum neat from a metal cup and sucking on the butt of a Partagas cigar. The craft was plugged into the marina's power source, and he had the small television going, although he wasn't faced toward it – it was background noise, that was all. Laugh track. A brisk sea wind carried a load of wetness in through the open windshield.

He felt a movement in the boat, but didn't turn.

'Do you know what time it is?'

His wife was a vision as usual. Even more so now, as she was flushed from the cold and the slight exertion to get out to the boat. Her hair had gathered the fine drizzle and, backlit, turned it into a halo. 'I would guess around nine o'clock,' he said evenly.

'What were you waiting for out here?'

'You to come and get me? And look, now you have.'

'The police have been around again.'

'Well, when it rains, it pours. What did they want this time?'

'There's been another murder apparently. A policeman.'

'And they came to see me?'

'Apparently he was related somehow to Bree.'

Finally, he met his wife's eyes. 'Well, *I'm* not related to Bree.' He took a pull of his liquor.

'Don't get hostile with me, Jim. Please. Where have you been?'

He kept looking at her. 'Right here,' he said. 'I told you. Waiting for you to come and get me.'

'And you came down here last night?'

He nodded. 'You weren't home from your party. I got stir crazy. What did they want?'

She threw a glance behind her as if worried that someone would hear. Then back to him. 'They wanted to know where you were. I told them. Didn't they come by here?'

He pointed with his cigar in the direction of the water. 'I was out.'

'In this fog?'

He shrugged. 'Living dangerously. What difference does it make? So what did you do all day?'

'I was home until noon, waiting for you to get back. Then I had lunch with my mother and brother. Then there was the Library do – the Sponsors' Dinner?'

Jim Pierce slapped at his forehead in mock consternation. 'That was tonight? And I missed it?' He tossed her a dismissive look. 'See,' he said, 'you had a fine time without me.'

'Everyone wondered where you were. They said they missed you.'

'I'm sure they did. And I them.'

She had her arms crossed, and now leaned back against the railing. 'I don't know why you're so cruel, Jim. I don't know when that started.'

He took a beat, carefully lifted his metal cup, and took a slow sip. 'Oh, I think you can figure it out. You get rejected enough, it makes you bitter. Some people, they get bitter, they take it out by being cruel.'

'I never rejected you.'

A stab of staccato laughter. No, he thought, you just made it impossible to ask anymore. But he said, 'That's right. It was me.'

A long, dead silence.

One of the channel buoys at the mouth of the marina chimed deeply, followed almost immediately by the forlorn moan of a foghorn. Jim Pierce tossed his cigar butt into the bay and reached over to flick off the television.

His wife looked as though she were waiting for him to say something, so he obliged her. 'It doesn't matter,' he said. 'Nothing matters.'

'You can't do this!' Valens was actually near to screaming. He had pulled Damon Kerry out on to the roof of whatever goddam hotel they were in after his talk to whatever goddam group it was. 'You can't do this with two days to go! You're alienating people, don't you understand? And you can't do that and win.'

'I'm being myself,' Kerry said. 'I've never lost an election and I've been myself in each one.'

'Yeah, but Damon, you've never run for *governor* before! This is not a city supervisor job. This is high office, and that's why I'm on board, remember? I do this. I keep candidates from being themselves, especially with forty-eight hours to go. I'll tell you what – you want to be yourself, be yourself on Wednesday.' He paced off a few steps and swore succinctly.

Kerry came up behind him. 'I am not alienating my electorate. I'm trying to reach people, to tell the truth. People respond to that, to me.'

'No,' Valens said. He turned around, despising the law of politics that the tall guy always wins. Kerry had him by half a foot, and this close, Valens had to look up at him. But he was going to say his piece – uphill, downhill, sideways – and Kerry was going to have to hear. 'No no no. Listen to me carefully. You are not trying to reach people or tell the truth or be yourself or any of that. You are trying to get yourself elected. That's all you're trying to do right now. And we're running behind all day, missing meetings, you're deviating from the script . . .'

'There's no script. There's—'

'No, Damon. The script is all that's left at this point. Repeat, repeat, repeat. Smile, smile, smile. And keep moving, keep moving, don't miss an opportunity to repeat repeat repeat.'

'Except we missed a few this morning, didn't we, Al? And

why was that? Because you were late picking me up.'

'*You* overslept, Damon.'

'I depend on you, Al. I was exhausted and I'm getting sick. And what about you? The job of the campaign manager is get the candidate where he needs to be. That's what he does. He doesn't keep the candidate from being himself.' He put a couple of fingers up to his forehead. 'I really am getting sick,' he said. 'I've been sick for weeks.'

Valens was at the edge of the roof. Below him, he was aware of the gauzy glow of the city's lights through the fog. He'd been in similar situations in nearly every election with which he'd been involved – the schoolgirl squabbling during the last leg of a campaign.

Damon Kerry undoubtedly was feeling sick, and Valens didn't really blame him. The pace was grueling, the pressures unrelenting. Valens might be frustrated and worried in his own right, but for the sake of the election, it was time to calm the waters. 'Damon,' he said gently, 'we've got one more day and tomorrow starts early. Why don't we get you back home, to get a good night's rest if you can? We're close now. We can still pull this out.'

'It's not just the election.' Kerry was shaking his head. 'You don't know, Al.'

'Yes I do, Damon, I really do. And what I know is that it *is* just the election.'

But Kerry wasn't on that page. 'All I know is that if I hadn't started down this path, Bree would still be alive. If she hadn't . . .' He trailed off.

But they had covered this ground a hundred times, most often late at night when Kerry's defenses were down. Valens laid an avuncular hand up on his candidate's shoulder. 'She did, though.' He patted the shoulder gently to demonstrate his commiseration. 'Let's get you home, get some rest,' he said. 'It'll look better in the morning.'

Thorne was at the kitchen table in his apartment halfway up

Nob Hill, putting the finishing touches on a memorandum he'd print up tomorrow regarding the oil companies' ten point eight million dollars in contributions to the country's political campaigns this year. In the memo, he noted that Damon Kerry had not accepted one dime from this source. Thorne thought that if he got the news release distributed early enough in the day, it would certainly get into some of Tuesday's papers, perhaps before many people had gone to the polls, and might even make a few late-breaking news shows looking for a filler by tomorrow night.

Every little bit helped, he believed, especially in light of the continuing MTBE poisoning story which was gratifyingly ubiquitous. Kerry's opposition to big oil was going to play very well, possibly right up through election day.

He proofread his final copy, then placed the papers in his briefcase, opened a cold beer, and poured it into a chilled Pilsner glass. Then he went into his living room and turned on the television.

The late evening news didn't let him down. It led off with the continuing followup on the Pulgas Water Temple story. The Water District had taken samples in the city's drinking water and found levels of MTBE that were lower than the EPA standards, and so technically 'safe.' But the levels were still deemed 'detectable,' and residents were advised to 'use caution.'

Thorne smiled at the language, and at the hysterical reaction of the public that the media play nearly guaranteed. MTBE was bad stuff, all right – an aspirin's worth in an Olympic-sized swimming pool was toxic – but ten or fifteen gallons in a reservoir the size of Crystal Springs wasn't going to make anybody sick, not immediately anyway. Nevertheless, over thirty people had sought medical attention in emergency rooms all over the city after drinking the water yesterday and this morning.

On-the-street interviews indicated that nearly everyone tasted 'something funny' in the water, a turpentine taste.

Thorne had made a point of drinking a few glasses in the course of the day and had tasted nothing.

There was a nice clip of several dozen dead trout floating near the dump spot. The location of this school of fish – where the concentration of MTBE was several million times greater than it was at the pumping station for the city's water supply – was simple luck, but Thorne found it particularly pleasing. It gave the impression that the whole lake had been polluted.

Kerry got a couple of great sound bites calling for an immediate moratorium on MTBE use, and this was echoed by one of the state's senators and the mayor, God bless him, who had even gone further. 'There is no reason to tolerate even for one more moment this dangerous and insoluble toxin in our gasoline where there is an environmentally safe and effective substitute so readily available, and by this I mean ethanol.'

Kerry's opponent, by contrast, spoke from a location in Orange County and sounded to Thorne like an idiot. 'It is not MTBE that has caused this terrible crisis any more than it is guns that kill people. People kill people, and people – criminals – have poisoned the San Francisco water supply. Gasoline without any additives would have produced the same effect, and no one is talking about making gasoline illegal.'

Police had no clues as to the identity of the individuals or the location of the headquarters of the Clean Earth Alliance, who claimed responsibility for the act, although when found, they would be charged with the murder of 53-year-old . . .

Thorne hit the mute button, sat back, and enjoyed a sip of his beer. All in all, he had to consider this a resounding triumph. There was, of course, no Clean Earth Alliance. His operatives had scattered to the four winds. Life was good.

But his smile faded with the new image on the screen – the house – and he reached again for the remote, bringing up the sound. '. . . determined that the cause of the fire was arson.'

The serious male anchor nodded sagely. 'What makes this so interesting, Karen, is that this house was the home of

299

Frannie Hardy, wasn't it? The woman who is still in jail for refusing to testify regarding the husband of Bree Beaumont, the expert on gasoline additives who was murdered nearly a month ago.'

'That's right, Bill.' The camera closed in on Karen. 'It's hard to believe that there is no connection whatever between Bree Beaumont's murder, the MTBE poisoning at the Pulgas Temple, and the arson this morning.'

Thorne hit the mute again, his frown pronounced by now. Last night he had been both wired and a little drunk; he'd had perfect cover in the thick fog. He was also feeling godlike after the Pulgas thing had gone so well.

When would he learn? You might want it and love every minute of it, but you didn't do things yourself. You hired experts to take care of operations. That was the safe way. Otherwise it was you who got interrupted, who had to improvise, who perhaps left physical evidence at the scene.

He sat, scowling, ruminating over the possibility that he had personally exposed himself now, perhaps even gotten himself implicated with Bree Beaumont, and that had never been his intention. He tried to remember if he'd known that Hardy's wife was the blasted woman in jail. He just couldn't dredge it up – not that it mattered now.

And the last problem, maybe the biggest problem, with screwing things up yourself was then sometimes you had to fix them yourself.

28

Sunday night, and Glitsky sprung Frannie again for a couple of hours. It was going to be the last chance to get away with that before the work week began, and she considered any single second outside of her cell well worth the trouble.

They were all still pretending that Frannie was going to be free on Tuesday, but Hardy, at least, knew it might not be so simple.

If Scott Randall didn't cooperate, if Sharron Pratt didn't relent under the mounting criticism in the press, if Frannie discovered another reason why she couldn't reveal what Ron had told her – for example, if Ron simply reneged on releasing her from her promise – any of these could and would prolong the nightmare.

And in any event, Hardy was going to have to get a hearing scheduled to vacate the contempt charge. He was all but certain that this would not be a cake walk.

For two hours, Glitsky fielded calls from the dispatcher trying to get a fix on Damon Kerry's location, provided information on the day's events to the police beat reporter, and organized his utilization coefficients. Hardy and Frannie were together alone in the interrogation room off the homicide detail, the shades drawn and the door locked by a chair propped up under the doorknob.

Hardy made up an excuse so he could stop by his car and pick up the gun. He had no plans to go unarmed until this had passed. He knew Glitsky would disapprove – he might get himself in big trouble, hurt someone, and wind up on trial himself. But he took solace in the old saying, 'Better tried by twelve than carried by six.'

Then they took Glitsky's car and parked across the street from Kerry's house. The plan was to wait until the limo pulled away so they'd get the candidate alone. But the limo had barely stopped when a short, stocky form emerged and began crossing the street toward them.

'That's Valens,' Hardy said.

Glitsky moved, opening the driver's door, gun drawn. 'Stop right there,' he ordered, 'right now. Police.'

'Police? Jesus Christ! What are you doing here?'

Hardy opened his own door and got out, but let the car remain between him and the others. He felt for his gun, riding in the small of his back, hidden under his jacket.

'Hey.' Valens held his hands out in front of him. The fog had finally lifted somewhat, and the voices seemed to carry like the ping of crystal. 'I'm coming over to see who you are, OK? Two guys, dark car, middle of the night, get it?'

Glitsky was advancing toward the man. 'We get it. Are you Al Valens? Is that Damon Kerry's car?'

Valens nodded. 'Yeah. And he's in it, trying to sleep. He's the Governor of California in about two days, OK?'

'Sure,' Glitsky responded. 'But right now today I'm Lieutenant Abe Glitsky and I'm the head of homicide. I'd like to have a few words with Mr Kerry.'

'Not possible.' Valens shook his head emphatically. 'The man has been running all day. He's got twenty appearances tomorrow. He's not available.'

Glitsky allowed himself a tight smile. He spoke in a conversational tone. 'I'm not asking.' He started for the limo.

But Valens wasn't giving up that easily. He side-stepped into the lieutenant's path. 'You got a warrant? I want to see a warrant.'

Hardy was amazed. He had never seen Glitsky this patient, taking the time to politely answer someone who refused to get out of his way. 'I don't need a warrant to talk to him on the street, which is what I'm hoping to do.' Glitsky stopped, and tried another tack. 'Mr Valens, are you trying to tell me that Mr Kerry doesn't want to cooperate with a police investigation into the murder of one of his consultants? You might want to ask him about that.'

Valens thrust out his chin. 'Hey, don't pull that crap on me. We have already cooperated with you guys every time somebody came around to ask. We've answered questions 'til we're blue in the face. Now it's late at night and this is pure straight-up harassment. I want to know what Republican money is behind you on this.'

'Please move to one side,' Glitsky said.

Valens pointed a finger. 'This is a mistake, lieutenant, I'm telling you. In two days, Damon gets elected and I get your badge, you hear me?'

Glitsky stopped walking, glanced around to Hardy, and came back to the campaign manager. 'Here are Kerry's options. He can talk to me or refuse to.' Glitsky paused. 'Listen to me, Valens, the reason I'm here in the middle of the night is to save him embarrassment. Nobody knows. I don't want to make it public. But I will if I need to. Do you understand me?'

This, finally, broke some of Valens' bluster. 'So does he need a lawyer present? What's this about really?'

Glitsky brought his hand up and rubbed his eyes. 'He's always welcome to have a lawyer, but he's not under arrest at this time. If he decides to call his lawyer, we'll wait. If he doesn't want to talk to us at all, I wouldn't be at all surprised to read about it in the paper tomorrow, but that of course would be his decision.'

'You son of a bitch. Who is behind this?'

Glitsky moved up a step closer. 'That's a very ill-advised choice of words and I wouldn't continue in that vein if I were you. Now, as to who is behind this, *I'm* doing it alone. It's police work. There is no political motive. I'm investigating a murder.'

'That murder is almost a month old. What's the hurry tonight?'

'The hurry tonight is that there was another murder last night. A policeman.'

Valens narrowed his eyes. 'Connected to Bree?'

'That's one of the things I'd like to find out. You have to understand, Mr Valens, that when police officers get killed, other cops get a little testy. And I'm there now, so don't push me. I really am trying to maintain a low profile around this. If that weren't the case, I could have pulled together a pretty good crowd by now, don't you think?'

Glitsky let the simple truth of that sink in for a moment. 'Now, is Mr Kerry going to consent to an interview or not?'

Valens hesitated for a number of seconds. Then, with a last furious glare, he turned and walked back to the limo.

There was another lengthy outburst after they got inside the house when Valens recognized Hardy. He wasn't a policeman, so what the hell was he doing here? This was a man who had broken into Valens' hotel room that morning, and had threatened him with a gun.

'Did you file a report with the hotel? With the police? Do you now want to press charges?' Glitsky asked the questions mildly, but they put an end to that.

'I'll be recording this conversation, by the way.' Glitsky said it as casually as possible, allowing no opportunity for debate. He was positioning his portable recorder on the table and holding up a hand, forestalling any and all of Valens' continuing objections.

He gave the standard introduction, identified those present, and had Kerry acknowledge that he was speaking of his own free will, that he was not under arrest, and that he did not want to have a lawyer with him.

'But why is this man here?' Valens asked, indicating Hardy, not wanting to let that issue go.

'He'll facilitate the discussion,' Glitsky responded. 'And Mr Valens, *you* are here as a courtesy. Don't interrupt again.'

Valens had a legitimate gripe – there was no legal reason for

Hardy to be there, but the campaign manager held no cards. What was he going to do? Notify the media and let the public know that his candidate was a murder suspect? No, he and Kerry had to cooperate, and as long as Glitsky allowed it, they had no choice but to tolerate Hardy's presence.

But Glitsky did have a reason and it became apparent immediately. 'Mr Kerry,' he asked. 'I'm sure you remember talking to Mr Hardy yesterday in the lobby of the St Francis? A rather lengthy discussion about Bree Beaumont, wasn't it?'

'I believe it was the bar, but yes.'

The candidate had a damp washcloth on his forehead. He was nearly reclining on the couch, his stockinged feet up on the coffee table in front of him. Although it was anything but warm – either out in the night or here in the house – his skin had a sheen as though he were sweating slightly. Glitsky thought he might have a fever and, if so, that would be to the good.

'Well, the reason I brought Mr Hardy along, and the reason that we're here talking to you at all, frankly, has to do with that conversation.'

Kerry might be tired and feverish, but he shifted slightly, summoning some reserves of energy. 'All right,' he said.

Glitsky nodded. 'Do you remember telling him that you had never been to Bree Beaumont's apartment?'

'That was me!' Valens exploded, interrupting, pointing at Hardy again. 'That's what I called this guy about last night. I already told him all about that. I forgot, that's all. And still that's why he broke into my hotel . . .'

'Mr Valens, please.' Glitsky stilled him with a glare. 'Mr Kerry?'

Kerry had by now straightened up to a sitting position. He mopped his brow with the washcloth. 'Yes, I said that.'

'And you stand by that now? That you've never been inside Bree's place?'

Kerry crossed one leg over the other, and sighed deeply. 'I suppose you've got somebody who saw me there? Took my picture? Perhaps Mr Hardy here?'

'Damon, hold it!' Valens again.

But Kerry seemed almost amused. A wry expression crossed his face. 'It's all right, Al. It's all right. The lieutenant says he'll keep this low profile – isn't that true, lieutenant? So long as I didn't kill Bree. We have your word on that, on this tape.'

'If I can,' Glitsky responded.

'Yes, I went there.'

Glitsky and Hardy exchanged glances. 'Why did you tell Mr Hardy you hadn't?'

'What difference does that make, lieutenant? Is that a crime? He might have been a reporter, trying to get some dirt on me and Bree. He might have been with my opponent, trying to smear me, make it look like I was having an affair with a married mother of two.' He shrugged. 'He said he was Ron's attorney and it's my belief that Ron killed her. He was building a case. So I lied to him. The easiest thing was to lie.'

'You believe that Ron killed her?'

'Yes.'

'Why?'

A shrug. 'She was his major source of support financially. She was going to change that arrangement. When he found out, he lost it.'

'How do you know that?'

'She told me the first two. The last I surmise.' By now, Kerry had come forward on the couch. The signs of fatigue had vanished. Hunched over slightly, his elbows on his knees, the washcloth now bunched in his right hand, he struck Hardy as a man engaged in watching the last seconds of an extremely close football game. 'Frankly, I'm amazed it's taken you – the police – this long to get to him. Judging from this interview, you're still not there, are you?'

'He has an alibi for the time of the murder,' Glitsky replied calmly, his patented non-smile making a minor appearance. 'We're still laboring under the law of physics that you can't be in two places at once. But while we're on the topic, where were you on the morning she was killed?'

Kerry actually chuckled. 'This is ridiculous.'

'It's a simple question.'

'Yes it is, which doesn't make it any less ridiculous. You're implying that I am a suspect in this woman's murder?'

But Glitsky knew how to interrogate, and the first rule is you don't answer questions – you ask them. 'I'm asking where you were when she was killed. Again, a simple question.'

'All right. Here's the simple answer. I couldn't even tell you exactly the *day* Bree was killed, lieutenant. I'm in the middle of a thirty-million-dollar campaign for governor of the most populous state in the nation. I've had between ten and thirty appearances a day for the past six months or more.'

Glitsky nodded. 'You're on the record saying you were home, here, that morning. Alone. Do you remember that?'

'*I* said it,' Valens put in. 'I told your inspectors. Hell, I've told them half-a-dozen times. Damon needs to sleep once in a while. He'd been out late the night before. We'd been shooting commercials that had to air the next week. The day she died he had to fly to San Diego at noon, so he slept in.'

'Look.' Kerry's color had come up now. 'It was a horrible tragedy that Bree was killed, and it is my most fervent wish that it hadn't happened. Beyond that, I hope you find her killer. But I do wish that this city had a more competent police force, so that I would not have to be bothered with this grasping-at-straws stupidity on the penultimate day of my campaign.'

Valens took his cue and stood up. 'That's it. I'm calling the mayor. He'll put a stop to this.' He faced Glitsky directly. 'You won't have to wait for the election, lieutenant. You can lose your badge tonight.'

Hardy reached over to the tape recorder, snapped it off, and spoke before Glitsky could reply. 'Good idea, Valens. You go ahead. Then I'll call Jeff Elliot and we can see where that goes.'

'You know Jeff?' This was Kerry, all attention.

'We're buds,' Hardy said. 'He was here last night and you weren't. How about that?'

Glitsky raised his voice. 'That's enough!' He lifted the tape recorder and turned it on again, then whispered into the resulting silence. 'This is my interrogation. I will ask the questions. Mr Kerry, I need five more minutes of your time, and then I will walk out the door with Mr Hardy. You've admitted you were at Bree Beaumont's penthouse. What were you doing there?'

A disgusted shake of the head. 'Visiting her. She was one of my consultants and beyond that, we were friends.'

'Were you alone with her there?'

'Yes. Is that sinister?'

Glitsky abruptly changed his tack. 'What did you do after midnight last night?'

Kerry collapsed back on to the couch. He mopped his brow again with the washcloth. 'Last night? What does last night have to do with anything?'

'A policeman was killed about five blocks from here last night.'

Kerry cast a glance over at Valens. 'They'll stop at nothing,' he said. Then, back to Glitsky. 'And I killed him, too, I suppose. I'm not busy enough running for governor. I've got to premeditate several murders as well, among them a cop. I must have a low tolerance for boredom.' He sighed. 'Last night, I took a walk.'

'You took a walk?'

'That's right. Al left at around – when Al, eleven thirty? – and I was wound up. The MTBE poisoning. Bree. Even Mr Hardy here. I decided to walk off some of the tension.'

'Do you own a gun, Mr Kerry?'

'Sure,' he said. 'I've got a basement full of Uzis and semi-automatics. AK-47s are my favorites. When I'm not killing women and policemen, I like to dress up like a postal employee and spray up some McDonald's someplace.' He forced himself to his feet. 'This was a voluntary interview, as you noted. I would appreciate a copy of the transcript of that tape in *my* headquarters by tomorrow. And I assure you that I am going to speak to the mayor, and you can do any goddam thing you want about it, both of you.'

He was halfway across the room when Glitsky, a dog with a bone, spoke up after him. 'Do you own a gun, Mr Kerry? You didn't answer me.'

The candidate stopped and turned slowly. In measured tones, he answered. 'I have a Glock nine millimeter in my bedroom for protection. I did not shoot your colleague with it. You have my word.'

Glitsky smiled and pounced softly. 'How did you know he was shot?'

Kerry stood stock still. His eyes, for an instant stained with fear, darted to Valens. Then, recovering, he came back to Glitsky. 'From your questions about guns, that's a perfectly reasonable assumption. Now good night, lieutenant.'

Driving back downtown, for the first several blocks neither man said a word. At a red light on Geary, they stopped and Hardy half turned in the passenger's seat. 'Offhand,' he said, 'I wouldn't say that went too well.'

Glitsky looked over at him. 'I don't know. He has no alibi. He owns a gun. You notice he said "several murders"?'

'When?'

'Wait.' Glitsky fiddled with his tape recorder, rewound a minute, got to the spot. And here was Kerry's voice again: 'I'm not busy enough running for governor. I've got to premeditate several murders as well, among them a cop.' He flicked it off. 'Several,' he said, 'is not two. Two is a couple – Bree and Canetta. No one knows about Griffin being part of this.'

'But he didn't say "among them some cops," or "a couple of cops." '

'No, he didn't,' Abe admitted. 'I know he was being

sarcastic. But still ... it'll be instructive if he does call the mayor.' A pause. 'He's a lot quicker on his feet than I'd given him credit for. I might even vote for him.'

'Assuming he didn't kill anybody.'

'Even then.' Glitsky seemed amused. 'You never want to underestimate the value of brains in your elected officials.'

'I don't know,' Hardy said. 'Our President's got brains.'

'Yeah, but they're all south of his head.' The light changed and they moved.

'I'll tell you one thing,' Hardy commented. 'Kerry's got brass balls if he did any of this.'

'I think we just got a glimpse of them,' Abe said. 'The guy is no pansy. You get the impression he hasn't talked to any cops before, that it's all been Valens up to now?'

'A hundred per cent.'

'And here's a last bit of five-cent psychology. To my mind, Kerry's *exactly* the kind of guy that Griffin could have wound up handing his gun to. I could see him asking Carl for a ride in the cruiser. Wow, this is what it's like being a cop. You mind if I just hold your gun for a minute? And it's all loaded and everything?'

'Or,' Hardy countered, 'he packed along his Glock and forced him.'

'Or that, too.'

'Griffin just drops by his house? Knocks at the door?'

'I don't know. It's hard to see that.'

'Do we know where he was when Griffin got it?'

'It was the day of Bree's funeral. He was in town. Valens says he was sick over Bree's death. Canceled his appointments, but made the funeral.'

Another silence descended. After a few blocks, Hardy looked over at Glitsky again. 'Lord,' he said.

'It's interesting,' the lieutenant admitted.

The two cars were parked next to one another in the cavernous city garage under the Hall of Justice. There was a guard trying

310

to keep warm in a small booth by the back doorway, which was the main entrance. But otherwise, except for Glitsky and Hardy, the place was empty, which was not surprising after eleven o'clock on a Sunday night. Glitsky asked the guard to bring up the lights and in a moment the dark and grimy garage was lit up like a showroom.

Yellow crime-scene tape hung from traffic cones and this segregated the immediate area where Griffin's and Canetta's cars had been parked from the contiguous body shop and parking spaces for the city-issue vehicles.

All doors and the trunks of both cars were open. Under the car on the right, a dark blue Lumina, someone in the crime scene unit had written block letters in chalk: CANETTA. The car over GRIFFIN was a gray, mid-sized Chevrolet with minor body damage and a lot of years behind it.

But for the moment, their steps echoing as they navigated the garage, they were still on Kerry. 'So you think your badge is really in trouble?'

'For interrogating a righteous suspect?'

'They're going to claim it's political.'

Glitsky snorted. 'They don't support much of what I do, but I've got to believe they won't step on me for this. There's probable cause here in spades. In fact, I'm going to put somebody on a warrant for the Glock tomorrow. See if it's where he said it was, what it might tell us . . .' He indicated the cars before them. 'Maybe that Glock has spent some time in one of these, and picked up something for its troubles.'

They'd come up to Canetta's car, on their left. Glitsky pulled some latex gloves from his jacket pocket, handed a couple to Hardy, pulled his on, and stood over the yawning trunk.

'What are we looking for?' Hardy came up beside him.

'There shouldn't be anything,' Glitsky responded. 'The theory is it's all bagged and labeled at the lab, or if they're done boxed up in the locker.' And in fact, the trunk looked pretty well cleaned out. Still, they checked the wheel wells, under the rug, under the speakers – everywhere.

Hardy went up the passenger side, Glitsky the driver's. The front seat had been removed, although there was still fresh evidence of the blood Canetta had spilled on the rug. The visors had nothing stuck under or in them. The glove compartment was empty. In the back, it was the same story.

Glitsky wasn't saying a word and though Hardy still wasn't sure why they were doing this, he was along for the duration. Over at Griffin's car, as with Canetta's, they started at the trunk. There was a little more evidence that Carl had lived and worked in his vehicle – beverage stains, tobacco burns – but it had evidently been sanitized by a team of professionals.

At least, until they came to the back doors. The back seat and the rug in front of it contained the usual, by now, stains and odors, and Hardy was about to stand up when Glitsky made a sign. 'Last one,' he said. And they lifted the back seat up.

Hardy whistled.

Glitsky looked for a moment, his expression fixed. 'Don't touch,' he said. 'Let's go.'

They crossed back to the guard's booth, and Glitsky picked up the telephone and punched in some numbers. 'Get me operations,' he told the dispatcher. 'Is Leon Timms on call? Good. Page him. Yes, ma'am, right now. Have him call me.'

Glitsky gave his number and they waited two minutes or less. The phone rang.

'Leon, Abe. I'm down here at the garage and just had occasion to lift the back seat of Carl Griffin's car. Yeah. Uh huh. Well, they missed this. Uh huh. I know. I am, too.'

He rolled his eyes at Hardy. 'Well, listen, the point is that we're behind the curve on this investigation, you might have noticed. Right. Leon, listen up. Just so we're clear, I expect all that waste paper, Kleenex, French fries, sugar cones, condoms, coins, bullets, shoelaces, boxtops, coupons, lottery tickets – everything – to be checked out, bagged, and catalogued, and up at the lab by the morning. Starting now. Uh huh. That's right, it is. I know. I don't care.'

Hardy had no confidence that he'd be able to stay awake on the ride across town to Erin's. Freeman's building was closer, and there were still things to do there.

Now, on his couch back in his office, he fought to keep his eyes open. He had his legal pad beside him and had drafted the motion he'd submit to the court – to Marian Braun in fact – on vacating Frannie's contempt citation. He checked his watch – nearly one o'clock.

He read another line, nearly dozed, and started awake.

There on the low table in front of him, weighted down by his gun, was every scrap of paper he'd accumulated over the past four days. He was going to read them thoroughly when he finished his motion. He started to fade again.

The gun. He'd berated himself recently for allowing himself to fall asleep with the gun in plain view next to him, and this time he wasn't going to do that.

His legs didn't want to answer him, his shoulder throbbed, and his mouth was dust, but he made himself walk to his desk, open the drawer, put the gun in, and lock it.

It seemed a long uphill mile all the way over to the light switch by the door and then back to the couch, but he finally made it, pulled his jacket over him, and fell to the side, asleep before he knew what had hit him.

29

It was nominally a breakfast meeting in the mayor's private suite at City Hall, but none of the participants, except one, seemed to have much of an appetite. The plate of sweet rolls sat unmolested in the center of the long, rectangular table.

By ten minutes past seven the mayor himself – Richard Washington – hadn't made his appearance. But everyone else had assembled and gotten their coffee poured by seven a.m., the hour his honor had appointed for this emergency session.

It was the first time Scott Randall had ever been inside the mayor's offices and typically, although by a wide margin the youngest person in the room, he was unimpressed. Someday, he thought it was entirely possible he might wind up here himself. He'd do the walls a different color – something that said power a little more distinctly, though still subtly. Maroon, perhaps.

He stood off by himself beside the vast sideboard under an ornately framed mirror at the far end of the room. He was on his second Danish – he'd wolfed the first – and now sipped at his coffee as he surveyed the other guests. Sharron Pratt, his boss, was in an intense discussion with Dan Rigby, the chief of police, and Peter Struler – Randall's own DA investigator.

The attendance of Marian Braun was a surprise to Randall – Superior Court judges often liked to pretend they were above the political fray. But she had obviously come at the mayor's bidding, although she was fastidiously ignoring everyone, and obviously unhappy. Pencil in hand, ostentatiously making notes on some thick document in a three-ring black binder, she'd already been sitting at the table when Randall had arrived.

The mayor's major domo was unfortunately named Richard,

too. Scott Randall suppressed a smile recalling that the common name led to the inevitable sobriquets of 'Big Dick' and 'Little Dick' for the mayor and his assistant. Little Dick was chatting with a couple of staff members that Randall recognized, although their names escaped him.

Finally – Randall checked his watch: seven thirteen – Mayor Washington burst into the room. Purposeful, overworked, impatient, he was talking at high volume to a middle-aged woman who trailed behind him scribbling non-stop in a steno pad. Washington wore a camel's hair coat over his suit. He was reasonably tall and nearly burly. Broken nose, veins in the face, a lot of unkempt gray hair. Walking fast as he came through the door, he kept coming until he got to his seat at the head of the table, when he stopped almost as though surprised at where he'd come to rest.

'All right.' He nearly bellowed, eyes all over the room. 'Everybody here? Let's get going.'

Little Dick had appeared behind him and helped him out of the overcoat, an automatic operation the mayor did not acknowledge in any way. By the time Washington was down in his chair, the woman had poured and flavored his coffee – three sugars and cream, Randall noticed – and had disappeared.

The mayor slurped from the cup, swallowed, and waited an instant for one of the staffers to stop fidgeting in her seat. After another moment, Marian Braun looked up, put her pencil down, and closed her binder.

Washington nodded at her and looked around the table, coming to rest on the young man near the far end. 'You're Randall,' he said, pointing a thick finger.

'Yes, sir.'

'How old are you, son?'

Randall bridled slightly at the condescension, but what could he do? 'Thirty-three, sir.'

'You married? Children?'

'No. Neither.'

Washington had him on the hot seat and seemed content to let him cook a minute. He slurped some more coffee. 'Somebody pass those rolls down here, will you? Thanks.' He randomly grabbed from the pile, took a bite, and chewed. 'You know why we're all here.' He wasn't asking.

Randall swallowed drily. 'The Frannie Hardy matter, I believe.'

'That's correct.'

At this formal corroboration of the reason that this meeting had been called, Marian Braun spoke up. 'Excuse me, Richard, but that being the case I can't be here. I can't discuss a case that's before my court.' She was already starting to get up.

But the mayor wasn't impressed. 'Why don't you stick around anyway, Marian, in case the second half of this conversation concerns the court budget for next year. Maybe that will be worthy of your attention.' He directed a fierce glare at her, and eventually, she yielded to it and settled herself back in her chair.

Richard Washington took another deep draught of coffee, and carefully replaced the cup in its china saucer. The silence was perfect.

The rage came from nowhere, which made it all the more effective. Suddenly the mayor slapped the flat of his palm on the table with enormous force. China rattled and some coffee spilled. Everyone jumped. 'Do you have any idea the amount of trouble you've caused with this, Mr Randall?' he exploded. 'Any idea?'

It took a split second even for the quick-witted Randall to recover. 'It was part of my investigation into—'

Washington interrupted again. 'You think we're all operating in a vacuum? Well, let me help you out . . .'

Pratt interrupted. 'With respect, sir . . .'

The mayor didn't seem any too happy with the DA, either. He faced her and snapped. 'What, Sharron?'

'The issue isn't that it's caused some political trouble. The issue is legal. Mr Randall did the right thing.'

Washington conjured with that for a moment. His voice with its normal inflection was almost more frightening. 'I absolutely reject that,' he said. 'What he did – what Marian did, too, for that matter – might not be illegal, but I wouldn't go so far as to say it was right.'

Pratt retained the serenity that only knowing that you are right can provide. 'The woman refused to cooperate with the grand jury, Richard. She was belligerent and disrespectful.'

'She was a housewife worried about picking up her children. That's what the media seems to have settled on, that's what Jeff Elliot wrote about yesterday. And now her house has been burned. Did any of you happen to notice that?'

'That's irrelevant,' Pratt responded. 'What's your point, Richard?'

'My point is that I'm taking a tremendous amount of flack for allowing this travesty to continue in my city. Mr Randall, in his inexperience, over-reacted. Folks, I want the woman released. Today.'

A collective gasp, then silence fell around the table.

'I can't do that, Richard.' Braun was firm. 'The first contempt citation expires tonight, and she has to serve that out. Mr Randall here can call her before the grand jury first thing tomorrow morning, at which point her continued incarceration will be up to her if she decides to talk or Mr Randall if she decides not to.'

The mayor made no effort to hide his sarcasm. 'Thank you, your honor, but I want it clear that holding innocent citizens in jail out of personal pique doesn't sit well with me.'

Randall finally found his voice again. 'The woman is not innocent, your honor. She knows something.'

'She knows something.' Washington nodded, his mouth twitching at the corners. 'I'm glad you brought that up, Mr Randall. Chief Rigby,' he whirled, 'has anyone been charged or indicted in the murder of Bree Beaumont to date?'

'No, sir.'

'So this Hardy woman knows something about somebody,

317

but we don't know what and we don't know if it's got anything to do with that murder?'

No one answered. Washington glared around the table. 'And yet she sits in jail.' He shook his mane of hair in disgust. 'I called this meeting to acquaint all of you with my very strong feelings about this matter. I'm going to air those feelings at this morning's press conference, and I wanted to do all of you the courtesy of a heads up. No one has more respect than I do, Marian – and you, too, Sharron – for the judicial process. But I'm hard pressed to believe that this woman knowingly holds the key to a murder. So this is mere pettiness.' He pointed again at Randall. 'And, son, for you, this is what we call overweening ambition. It's not an admirable quality. If you hadn't tried to end-run the police department, we wouldn't be here now. Chief Rigby?'

'Yes, sir.' From his expression, he knew what was coming. The chief of police was the pawn of the mayor, appointed by him, accountable to him. And Rigby had just found himself on the wrong side of the fence.

'Apparently you've been trying to make kissy-face with Ms Pratt so that her fear and loathing of the police would not too greatly interfere with the day-to-day workings of the department. I even applaud your intentions. But we've got a homicide department and it's not run by Mr Struler here, or by Ms Pratt. If you don't like Glitsky, get a new head of homicide. But the police department investigates murders and you back up your people. Clear?'

It was to Rigby. But Washington wasn't through yet. 'Sharron, Marian. You're both elected officials. I'm just a layman in matters of the law, but this comes across as serious arrogance and the public seems to have a bad reaction to that particular trait. You might want to think about that.'

Hardy opened his eyes and for the second time in as many days had to take a minute to figure out where he was.

Down a floor, in the lobby of the Freeman Building, he put

on a pot of coffee, then went in for a shower. In ten minutes, he was back in his office, dressed in his smoky clothes and drinking coffee from an oversized mug.

The fog remained. He put in a call to Erin, told her where he was, and spoke to the kids, who were polite and even solicitous. Was he all right? They missed him. He and Mom were coming to stay with them so they'd all be together at Grandma and Grandpa's in two days, right? They really, really, *really* missed him and Frannie.

He believed them.

After he hung up, he went back to the couch and sat. His brief from the night before was ready to submit for typing downstairs, and he left it with the early morning staff at word processing, then took the stairs two at a time back to the work that waited for him.

The xeroxed pages of Griffin's notebook.

Griffin had been working on a number of homicides at the time of his death. Snatches from each of them were scattered on each page – names, dates, addresses. Arrows for connections. Exclamation points. Phone numbers.

In his previous passes through the pages, whenever Hardy had run across a name that didn't appear elsewhere in some other file on Bree Beaumont, he'd assumed it was from one of the other cases. It was tedious and inexact, but he had to eliminate on some criterion, and this had seemed as reasonable as any.

This morning, though, he resolved to read it all through again. Things had changed. And if Damon Kerry had a connection to Baxter Thorne that Griffin had been aware of, he wanted to know about it. Hardy hadn't even heard of Thorne or FMC the last time he'd read the pages. Nor a lot else.

Carl had been shot on Monday, 5 October. Bree had died on the previous Tuesday, 29 September, so he started there. At least Carl tended to enter dates with some regularity.

It appeared that on day three of his investigation, 10 01,

he'd slogged through the usual opening gambit of talking to people who lived in the deceased building. Suddenly the name O. or D. Chinn (or something in a smeared scrawl very much like it) popped up at him.

Hardy had assumed this was an Asian witness from one of Griffin's other cases and hadn't considered it at all, but now, suddenly, he remembered the superintendent in Bree's building and consulted his own notes on his yellow pad. David Glenn. D. Chinn. Close enough.

But there wasn't much Hardy recognized written under it. There was either a B or an R, then 805. A time? 'NCD!!!'

Then, a new line. 'Herit., TTH. !!!' And a phone number.

Those damn three exclamation points – they clearly meant something significant, but Hardy for the life of him couldn't figure out what NCD was. TTH could only mean Tuesday Thursday, but what, in turn, was that about?

Hardy checked his watch. Still too early, before eight o'clock, but he went to his desk and called the number next to 'Herit. TTH !!!' anyway.

It was a woman's voice in a heavy Asian accent and Hardy nearly hung up, frustrated for even wasting this much time. This note must have referred to one of Griffin's other cases after all. But Hardy heard out the recording. 'Many thank you for calling Heritage Cleaning. Office hours are Monday to Friday, eight thirty to six. Please leave message and call back.'

'And the case breaks wide open,' Hardy muttered to himself as he hung up. 'Now we know where Griffin did his laundry.' He went back to the couch, to the notebook.

Still on 10 01, the inspector evidently spent part of the day talking to the crime scene and forensics people downtown. There were scribblings Hardy took to be about Strout, Timms, Glitsky. Then, further down, another maddening three exclamation points – 'fab. wash,' 'r. stains!!!'

He shook his head, nearly getting all the way to amused at the prosaic truth. More laundry.

By Friday, Griffin was checking alibis. Apparently he had

spoken to Pierce, JP, and perhaps his wife, CP. 'Time checks?' Evidently referring to Pierce's alibi.

The weekend intervened.

Then on Monday, more alibi checking, this time with Kerry. And here Hardy consulted his own notes for corroboration. 'SWA 1140, SD.' Southwest Airlines to San Diego around noon. That checked. But what had Kerry done before being picked up to go to the airport? Griffin's notes didn't give a clue.

A few lines down the page, and apparently still under Kerry, there was another number: 902. If it were a date, it was over a month out of synch, so Hardy assumed it must be a time. And if it *were* a time, it would comport very closely with the hour of Bree's death.

So what had Griffin discovered about Kerry's whereabouts at nine o'clock? And why so precisely?

It had to be a phone call, Hardy reasoned, but where were the phone records? He flipped quickly through the few pages, but was sure he would have noticed them sooner if they'd been there, and sure enough, they weren't.

He chewed on possibilities for a couple of minutes, then got up again, went to his desk, and picked up the phone.

'Glitsky, homicide.'

'Hardy, *bon vivant*, scholar, champion of the oppresse—'

'What?' Glitsky growled.

'I'm guessing Kerry called Bree or vice versa on the morning she was killed.'

'Great minds.'

'What do you mean?'

'Kerry's got both a residence and a cell phone. I checked already. I got a rush call in on both phone records this morning, to see if maybe he didn't sleep in late like he said he did. I'm waiting for the fax.'

'So what about Griffin? Did any phone records turn up under that back seat?'

'Not yet. I stopped by the garage again coming in. They'd

'barely got it cleaned out, much less catalogued.'

'But Griffin must have gotten the phone records, right? Don't you guys do that?'

'I would hope so,' Glitsky said, 'though I wouldn't bet the ranch on it.'

'So where are they?'

'They'd be with the stuff you have if he'd filed them.'

'Uh huh. See if you can guess whether they are.'

Glitsky sighed. 'His desk is cleaned out, Diz. It's all somewhere. Stuff related to his cases supposedly got forwarded to the new teams.'

'Maybe they were in one of the bags in the trunk, tagged already?'

'Then they'd be downstairs in the evidence lockup.' Another sigh. 'You think there's some possible phone connection to Kerry?'

'It'd be sweet if there was.' Hardy hesitated. 'I'm really starting to like the good candidate.'

'I told you last night, I might even vote for him.'

'That's not how I meant "like." '

'No,' Glitsky said. 'I know what you meant.'

After he hung up, Hardy went back to his couch and his notes. He had come now to the last full day of Griffin's life, and under Sunday found what he'd been hoping for: 'Box T., Embarc.2, 10/5, 830. Burn. or Bwn. $!! – ??'

He had earlier assumed that this might be a reference to a post-office box in one of the highrises along the Embarcadero. Now he saw it in a different light. It wasn't Box T. It was Bax T.

Baxter Thorne. As he read it now, Hardy realized that the note referred to an eight thirty a.m. meeting at Thorne's Embarcadero office.

Hardy stared at the cryptic note. Here, finally, was Thorne connected to Bree in Griffin's investigation. Had the inspector in fact gone to question Thorne on the morning of his death? Had they then taken a little drive?

322

Suddenly a detail kicked in. He bolted upright and checked his watch. It had at last gotten to eight o'clock, a little after. Jeff Elliot had told him he was setting a meeting with Thorne first thing this morning, and at it he planned to bait and switch him into a corner.

Half joking, Hardy had warned Jeff to make sure he didn't go alone. Now there was no joke about it.

He called Jeff's home and got no response. At the reporter's personal number at the *Chronicle*, he left a message, then checked the general switchboard. No. Mr Elliot hadn't come in yet. Would he care to leave a message?

In a flash, Hardy was grabbing his jacket. At the office door, he stopped still, then turned and went back to his desk.

In thirty seconds, armed, he was flying down the stairs, pausing for a second at the reception desk. 'Is David in yet?'

Phyllis replied in her usual icy fashion. 'Not as yet. I haven't heard from him at all this morning.'

'Is he at court?'

The gimlet eyes fixed on him. 'I wouldn't know, Mr Hardy. I haven't heard from him.'

'Oh, that's right.' Hardy thought it was kind of sad that someday he knew he was going to kill Phyllis. 'I think you said that.'

'Twice.'

'Right.' He couldn't help himself. 'So I guess he's not in?'

Although it was fifteen or twenty blocks from his office to the Embarcadero, there was no point in trying to drive. Between the morning traffic and parking when he arrived, it would take longer than walking.

So Hardy was breathing hard from the forced march. In spite of that, he was also chilled from the fog and painfully aware of a gnawing in his stomach – he hadn't eaten since mid-afternoon yesterday, those tasty few bites of lukewarm tortilla pie at Glitsky's.

The directory listed the Fuels Management Consortium on

323

the twenty-second floor and the elevator had him there in seconds. The office was anything but threatening. Lots of glass – they were floating in the clouds up here. Modern furniture, partitioned workstations, piped new-age music. The hum and bustle of a busy workplace.

'Can I help you?' The receptionist was a very young woman, perhaps even a teenager, with a warm smile.

Hardy returned it, fantasizing briefly about what it would be like to have a cheerful presence to greet people in place of Phyllis. 'Is Mr Thorne available?'

'I'm sorry, he's in a meeting right now. I can take your name, though. Did you have an appointment?'

'No, no appointment. Can you tell me, is he by any chance with Jeff Elliot? A *Chronicle* reporter?'

She looked down, biting her lip, clearly wanting to do the right thing, not knowing if she should give out this informa-tion. Hardy smiled at her, told her his name, and spelled it out. 'I'm a friend of Mr Elliot's. I'm sure he'd like to know I'm here.'

The streets on the walk over had been cold with the fog-laden wind, but Baxter Thorne's large, corner office was positively Arctic. The executive director of FMC wasn't a big man by any means, and seemed a shrunken, pugnacious, malevolent gnome behind the cluttered expanse of his desk.

In his wheelchair, Jeff Elliot simply turned his head when Hardy was announced. Thorne nodded at the nice receptionist and she withdrew silently, closing the door behind her. No pleasantries of any kind were exchanged.

From the feel of things, the bait had been taken and the switch had just begun. 'As a courtesy, Mr Elliot, although I'm beginning to wonder why I would want to extend one, I've admitted your acquaintance. Now what?'

'You don't know Mr Hardy?'

Thorne threw a glance Hardy's way, than came back to Elliot. 'I've never seen him in my life.' Hardy was taken aback by the voice – deep, quiet, cultured.

Elliot was shaking his head. 'That's not what I asked. I asked if you knew Mr Hardy.'

'Should I?'

'You seem unable to answer the question, Mr Thorne. I wonder why that is?'

Hardy, believing in his heart that Thorne was in some way behind the arson of his home, had to fight the urge to withdraw his weapon and end the cat and mouse right here. But he thought he'd let Jeff play the hand a while first. At the very least, he already seemed to have gotten under Thorne's skin.

The gnome cast a gaze out toward the side window, where the fog was swirling past. To Hardy, it felt for a moment as though they were in an airplane. The wind moaned – keened really – just at the threshold of sound.

Thorne looked back at Elliot. 'I don't know Mr Hardy.'

'Are you familiar with the name?'

'I don't know. It's common enough. I may have heard it.'

Elliot seemed to be watching for some giveaway reaction, but if there was one, Hardy didn't see it. 'His wife is in jail now for refusing to testify before the grand jury about the death of Bree Beaumont. Have you heard of her? Bree Beaumont?'

Thorne's face put his impatience on display. 'What is this? Twenty questions? Who do I know? You've asked me about press releases on the Pulgas water poisoning. I've told you that you may check with my staff. The releases were not ours. They were not prepared here.'

'One of my colleagues found them outside in the hallway on Saturday, bound for distribution.'

Thorne shrugged. 'So what? I didn't write them. I didn't put them there. Obviously, someone is trying to make us look bad, connected to these people, as they tried with Mr Kerry over the weekend. There's a pattern here, all right, but it's not of my making.' Disappointed in humanity, he shook his head.

'If this is your smoking gun, Mr Elliot . . . well, there's no story here.'

Spreading his hands, he assayed a cold smile. 'My clients are good people, Mr Elliot. They're not terrorists. They're concerned with exposing the endless lies that the oil companies have foisted upon an ignorant public, lies that polluted our air for years and now threaten—'

'How about Ellis Jackson? What's your relationship with him?'

Having established what he thought was a plausible deniability, Thorne softened slightly, the voice become nearly avuncular. 'What about him?'

'Is he your client?'

A sad shake of the head. 'I've told you I'm not at liberty to disclose the identities of my clients. I of course knew Ellis Jackson when I worked for SKO.' Another reasonable smile. 'The last time I checked, there was no crime in that. He's a great man. Now, if you're . . .'

'Not quite.' Hardy spoke up for the first time. 'You never answered Jeff's question about knowing Bree Beaumont. Did you talk with a Sergeant Griffin about her death?'

'Yes, I believe that was his name.'

'Then how could you not have heard of her?'

'I never said I hadn't heard of her. Of course I know who she was. She's been one of the most vocal and recognizable names in the field over the last decade. She was extremely courageous to change sides and go up against Goliath as she did.' He paused for emphasis, adding matter of factly, 'And of course they killed her for it.'

'The oil companies?'

'Can you doubt it?'

Hardy snorted in exasperation. 'I don't think so.'

But Thorne remained infuriatingly unruffled. 'I can't really tell you what to think, Mr Hardy. But if you think people, individuals, don't die over Big Oil, don't get killed, I recommend that you catch up on your research. Have you been following events in Nigeria recently? There are literally millions of other examples. And that's leaving out most of our wars from Kuwait going all the way back to World War Two. Oil and market share.'

The small, quiet, powerful man stood behind his desk. 'Now, really, I'm afraid that's all I have time for. I think you'll be able to find your way out. Oh, and Mr Elliot,' – a rictus smile – 'the libel laws in this state are quite severe, as I'm sure you know. It's one way my clients can combat an unscrupulous enemy. They have been quite aggressive in pursuing legal redress for unsubstantiated news stories.'

On the way out, Hardy pushing Jeff's wheelchair, the sweet young thing at the reception desk wished them a good morning, and gave Hardy a little wave.

30

Frannie sat on the table in the attorney's room at the jail, swinging her legs. She looked like a schoolgirl, the impression reinforced by the fact that she'd put her hair into pigtails. To Hardy, the jail's jumpsuit was still jarring to see on her. But after yesterday's two visits up in the homicide detail, he found the jail garb easier to accept. Soon, he told himself, it would all be behind them. Today was the last day. He prayed.

As soon as they got Ron's note out of the way. But like everything else, this wasn't going smoothly. 'What do you mean?' he asked. 'You're not sure you're going to be OK with this? With telling about Ron?'

Her face took on a stubborn set that Hardy didn't like to see. He forced himself to speak in a calm tone.

'Frannie, listen. By the time it gets to the grand jury again, if it does, it won't matter. He'll be gone, if he isn't already.'

'No.' She shook her head. 'I don't think so. He doesn't want to move the kids, start over someplace else. He'll wait. Just like he said he would.'

'But either way, he's released you from the confidence.' Hardy didn't want to push too hard trying to convince her, but he felt he had to nail this down. If it came to it, tomorrow Frannie would have to disclose Ron's secret.

It wasn't sitting at all well with her. But she nodded. 'I hate to give that creep Scott Randall the satisfaction. Besides, from all you've told me, it sounds like Ron isn't anywhere near the best suspect anymore.'

'No, I don't think he is,' Hardy admitted. 'But until they have another one dumped in their laps, they're going to pretend.'

'But really, it still comes down to me, doesn't it?'

'What do you mean?'

'I mean, you're close. Abe's close. Maybe it'll only be another day . . .' The legs had stopped swinging. Her hands were folded in front of her now, her eyes cast downward. 'What I'm saying is that if I still don't tell, maybe Ron gets some more breathing room.'

Hardy was sitting casually on one of the wooden chairs that surrounded the table. It was all he could do to remain in that posture. He felt the blood racing in his temples, and willed himself to keep his voice even. 'Ron doesn't want to you do that, Frannie. I can't imagine why *you'd* want to do that.'

She raised her agonized eyes. 'It's not a matter of wanting, Dismas. It's the last thing in the world I want to do. But I know what Max and Cassandra have already gone through, and as soon as I open my mouth, their world is over – don't you see that? If I can give you or Abe more time to save them . . .'

But Hardy was shaking his head. 'That's not what's going to happen, Frannie. What's going to happen is even if you don't talk on Tuesday, your friend Mr Randall is going to get his indictment on Ron.'

'But why? There's still no evidence, is there? More than there was last week?'

Hardy agreed. 'Very little. But that doesn't matter. There's probably enough for a grand jury. Ron's flight alone, if it comes to it. Phony credit cards, fake IDs, consciousness of guilt. And as soon as Ron is indicted, it's over for him and the kids. He'll be in the system and from there that's what will take over – the system. Regardless of what you do. That's the good news, Frannie. It's out of your hands.'

'So you're saying I have to tell.'

'I'm saying it wouldn't do any good not to.' Suddenly his temper flared. 'Jesus Christ, Frannie! It gets you out of here. What do you want?'

'What I want,' she yelled back at him, 'is to go to our home which isn't there anymore.' She angrily shook away the beginning of tears. 'And be able to hug our children.'

Hardy longed to reach for her, to tell her it was OK, that they were still all right. But he wasn't sure they were all right. He didn't miss the omission of himself as among those she wanted to hug. 'You can do that, Frannie,' he said evenly. 'At Erin's. We can all be there. Rebuild.' He added hesitantly. 'The house and us.'

She shook her head. 'No.'

His stomach clutched at him, but he had to ask. 'No what?'

'You say it, but I don't know if you really want to do that. What it might take.'

'And what is that?'

Now Frannie paused, took a deep breath, and let it out. 'Being each other's lives again.'

'But we are . . .'

Holding up a hand, she stopped him. 'Dismas. Remember when we were first together. Remember that? You were working just as hard then. You had your trials and your cases and your career. But mostly you had us, remember?

'And you'd come home as early as you could every day and I'd be on the front stoop with the Beck and Vincent, all of us waiting for you. And they'd come running to greet you, hugging your legs, so happy to have Daddy home again. And you so happy to see them, too. Remember that? And then you and I would go in and feed them and put them to bed and then go talk and laugh and wind up making love more often than not. Didn't that used to happen? I'm not making that up in my memory, am I?'

'No,' he said quietly. 'No, that's how it was.'

'So what happened?'

He had come around on the chair now, hunched over. Elbows on his knees, his hands together. His shoulders slumped. 'I don't know, Frannie. Everybody got too busy. Certainly nobody cared what time I came home. Nobody even says hi anymore when I walk in the house. You're doing so many kid things you're always exhausted, and if it's not about

330

kids, you're not interested. We don't have date night anymore. Where's any of our life together?' He looked up at her. 'Take your pick, Frannie. And OK, it was a lot me, all the things you say. But it was a two-way street.'

'And you say you really want to go back to that?'

He thought for a beat. 'No, maybe not to what we had a week ago,' he said. 'Something better than that, closer to what we used to have. But still with you and the kids.'

After a long, silent moment, she slid off the table and walked over to the door where the guard waited. For a second, Hardy was afraid she was simply going to ask to be escorted out. But she turned to face him. 'The best thing,' she said, 'would be if I didn't have to tell.'

Then she knocked for the guard.

Glitsky wasn't in his office. Nobody was in homicide at all, which seemed a bit strange at ten o'clock on a Monday morning. Hardy sat himself at one of the inspector's desks and opened his briefcase.

He thought he'd done pretty well with Griffin's notes this morning, and now he was going to pull out his own notes and take a minute to go over what he'd written about Canetta's findings. He stopped before he'd really begun.

He knew.

Marie Dempsey. Canetta had told him that he'd discovered she had been the secretary of the insurance guy, Tilton. That she'd actually been laid off in the wake of the claims adjuster's decision to hold off payment on Bree's life insurance until Ron had been cleared of any implication in the death.

So here was this woman without a job with the insurance company, calling Ron Beaumont twice – or was it three times? – in a two-day period. She wasn't calling him to walk him through processing his claim. It seemed weeks ago now, though in fact it was days, and Hardy had been concentrating on Frannie when he had heard those calls at the penthouse, but he remembered coming away with the impression that Marie was personal, not business.

He reached for the telephone on the desk and punched for information.

'This is Letitia. What city please?'

'Yes. In San Francisco. The phone number please of a Marie Dempsey.'

'How would you spell that, sir?'

He spelled it out, his patience all but eroded. Dempsey, after all, wasn't exactly Albuquerque, spelling-wise. But Letitia eventually got it. 'I don't show any Marie Dempsey, sir. Do you know what street she lives on?'

'No. How about just the initial?'

'M?'

Hardy ground his teeth. 'That would be the one, yes.'

'I show ten, no eleven M. Dempseys.'

'OK,' Hardy said. 'I'll take them all.'

'I'm sorry, sir. I'm only allowed to give out two numbers at a time.'

'Please, Letitia, this is important. There may be lives at stake. I'm not kidding. Could you please just give me the numbers?'

'I'm sorry, sir. I'm really not allowed to give out that information. Would you like to speak to a supervisor?'

'Can your supervisor read me the eleven numbers?'

'No, sir. I don't believe so. If you have access to a telephone directory, they should all be listed in there, though.'

'Yes, well, you see, I don't have a phone book handy, which is kind of why I called you.'

'Well,' Letitia said brightly, cheerfully, 'let me give you the first number. It's . . .'

Hardy wrote quickly, then found himself listening to a mechanical voice telling him that after he got his number, the phone company could dial his call direct for a charge of thirty-five cents. 'Press one if . . .'

He slammed the receiver down. Glitsky was in the doorway,

332

pointing at the telephone. 'That's city property,' he said. 'You break it, you buy it.'

'You got a phone book around here?' Hardy asked.

'I doubt it,' Glitsky said. 'They're harder to find than a cop when you need one. You want to guess how many homicides we got this weekend, Hallowe'en?'

'Including Canetta?'

'Sure, let's include him.'

'Three?'

'More.'

'Two hundred and sixteen?'

'Seven. Average is one point five a week. And we get seven in two days. I've got no inspectors left.'

Hardy nodded, looking around. 'And this would also explain your mysterious absence from your office all morning. I thought you might have gotten tired and decided to take some time off.'

'Nope.' Glitsky was terse. 'The first part's right, but that wasn't it.'

In his office, though, Glitsky did find a three-year-old phone book and it had seven M. Dempseys listed. The first one had the same number Hardy had written down from Letitia and he took that as a good sign.

He was copying and Glitsky was talking, shuffling through a pile of paper from his in-box. 'So if Kerry ever called the mayor as he said he would, I haven't heard about it, although as you've noticed, I haven't exactly been waiting by the phone.'

Hardy looked up. 'He's not going to call the mayor. That would only raise the profile around him. He just wants this – and by "this" I mean "you" – to go away.'

'You think I gave him the impression last night that I was going away? That he scared me off?'

'If you did, it was real subtle. What?'

Glitsky had stopped at a faxed page. He tsked a couple of times. 'Mr Kerry, Mr Kerry.' He held the page out to Hardy.

'AT&T Wireless for the morning of 29 September. Here's a conversation beginning at seven ten a.m., duration twenty-two minutes. Somebody called him.'

'The day he slept in?'

'That's what he said.'

'Maybe he only meant he slept in until seven and we just assumed he meant it was later.'

'That's probably it,' Glitsky replied sarcastically. He was shoving paper around on his desk again. 'You got Bree's number anywhere on you?'

As it happened, Hardy still had it in his briefcase. It was the number from which Kerry had received his call. 'Maybe I won't vote for him after all,' Glitsky said.

Hardy sat back, crossed his arms. 'So they have a fight first thing in the morning—'

Glitsky sat up straight, snapped his fingers, truly excited now. 'He's the father. She told him she was pregnant. She was going to blackmail him.'

All right, Hardy thought with relief. He never had to break his vow of silence to Jeff Elliot. Glitsky had come to it on his own. 'That's a reasonable guess,' he said mildly.

'He waited till he knew Ron had taken the kids to school, strolled over . . .'

But Hardy was shaking his head.

'Why not?' Glitsky asked.

'No. Not himself. He called Thorne. Thorne called one of his operatives.'

Glitsky glanced back down at the faxed page. 'Not from his cell phone anyway.'

'Damn,' Hardy said. 'Why is it never easy?'

'It's just one of the general rules. But why would Kerry calling Thorne make it easy?'

'This is one slick bastard, Abe.' Hardy explained about the leaflets that had been printed up before the MTBE dumping, and about Thorne's explanation for it.

Glitsky was enjoying the recitation. He was paying

attention, sitting back in his chair, his fingers templed at his lips. When Hardy finished, he spoke. 'So these terrorists who were trying to lay the blame on Thorne, they somehow assumed that Jeff Elliot's colleague would just happen to drop by on Saturday afternoon and find the flyers in the hallway?' Glitsky was almost smiling. 'Call me cynical, but that's a stretch.'

'We thought so, too. Jeff and I.' Hardy moved forward, put his hands on the desk between them, and spoke urgently. 'Abe, you connect Thorne to the MTBE gang and you win a prize.'

'Really. Gee, that never occurred to me.'

'I bet it did. But look, it gets better. Thorne wrote these leaflets, probably by himself at his apartment. So you get a warrant and have somebody search the place. You find a piece of paper, a computer file, and you solve a murder, maybe two or three.'

Glitsky cocked his head to one side, all interest. 'I'm listening. What's two or three?'

'He talked to Griffin the morning *he* got killed. Griffin.'

'Who did? Thorne?'

A nod.

'Are you sure of this?'

Hardy explained his reading of Griffin's notes – that the meeting with Thorne had been one of the last entries, 5 October, eight thirty a.m. 'It was that day, Abe, count on it. And you'll love this: Elliot thinks Thorne is bankrolling the good governor Damon Kerry through SKO. Somehow.'

'How?'

'Nobody knows, but if there's anything to it at all, it connects dirty tricks to Damon Kerry, who we liked so much last night and maybe even more this morning.'

Glitsky was still sitting back, contemplating. 'Thorne has erased any computer work, Diz. If not immediately, then for sure by now after talking with you and Elliot.'

'OK. Still, there might be hard copy in the garbage cans? Some dumpster behind the building.'

'I know, I know.' Glitsky had come forward and was shuffling more pages on his desk. He spoke almost to himself. 'But I've got no inspectors.'

Finally, he opened his desk and withdrew what Hardy recognized as a blank warrant form. He grabbed a pen from the middle drawer of his desk. 'OK,' he said, beginning to write. 'We've got the leaflets. We've got Griffin on his last day. So. Help me here. What else are we looking for?'

Hardy considered for a moment. 'The smoking gun connection to Kerry. Valens. Receipts, Thorne's phone records, anything.'

'I'm going to need some very serious physical evidence to get anywhere near Kerry. It's going to take more than a phone call he forgot.'

'Maybe get some DNA on him, and check it against Bree's baby?'

'That'll take six weeks if he's not elected, for ever if he is. And then, even if he is the father, nobody puts him at Bree's place that morning.' The scar between Abe's lips stood out. He shook his head in frustration. 'Even on a normal mortal, much less our popular politician, nothing remotely convictable.'

'Not even indictable,' Hardy agreed.

'OK, then.' Glitsky the strategist was back at it. 'We go for Thorne and squeeze from that direction. You talked to him. Can you think of anything else on him?'

'My house.'

The lieutenant met Hardy's gaze and nodded somberly. As a salve to his friend, he made a pretense of writing that down. 'I'll check with the fire department. What else?'

Hardy wracked his brain but after nearly a minute still came up empty. 'Nothing, Abe.' He sighed. 'Oh, except I did discover where Carl Griffin did his laundry.'

'Are you kidding?' Glitsky frowned. 'Carl never went to a laundry in his whole life.'

After Glitsky left to go try and get his warrant signed, Hardy copied down the remaining numbers for M. Dempsey, then sat

336

back pensively. Glitsky had closed the door when he'd gone, and now in the tiny cubicle, Hardy could work without distractions and he needed to concentrate.

It seemed that every answer he got raised another question. How wonderful, he'd thought, that Glitsky had found Bree's lengthy call to Kerry on the morning of her murder. But something about the information had nagged at him, and now here it was again. On his copied pages of Griffin's notes – the time 9:02. Or that had been his assumption, and it had led directly to Kerry's phone records and his lie. But the phone call hadn't been at 9:02. It had begun at seven ten.

So what was 902?

Then there was Heritage Cleaners, Griffin's laundry. Hardy pulled the phone on Glitsky's desk around and reached a woman who spoke English so poorly that he settled for what he hoped was the address of the place and politely thanked her, then hung up. He had no more strength this morning for disjointed conversations over that miracle of modern communication, the telephone. He would try to get time to stop by Heritage later in the day – when? when? – and maybe see what they did, why Griffin had put them in his notes.

It was all a mess.

He checked his watch. After eleven o'clock already.

And today was his last day to get it done. Frannie had told him that the best thing would be if she didn't have to tell, and the only way that would happen was if Hardy provided some answers before they questioned Frannie tomorrow again in front of the grand jury.

Suddenly, out of nowhere, with his mind vacant and receptive, he came to understand precisely what Frannie had meant by her last cryptic, challenging remark. Hardy had been telling her he'd listen to her. They'd work things out. He'd try to care more about what she did, what she cared about. So she'd heard him out and turned at the door, telling him OK, this is what is truly important to me.

Fish or cut bait.

31

'Your honor, if I may.'

Marian Braun looked up from her desk in her chambers. She wore wire-rimmed half-glasses under a barely controlled riot of gray hair and made no effort at all to conceal her displeasure at the interruption, or at the identity of the caller. 'You may not. I'm at lunch. I'll be back at my bench in forty-five minutes, counsellor. Talk to my clerk.'

Hardy didn't budge. He was taking a chance, but felt he had no choice. 'Your honor. Please. Time is short.'

Her scowl deepened. The mayor's outrageous effrontery and reprimand, the DA's arrogance and political posturing – all of this before she'd finished her morning coffee – still galled her deeply. To say nothing of the potential legal ramifications to which she'd exposed herself by allowing the mayor to bully her into staying for the duration of his meeting. She'd committed a serious ethical breach in this Frannie Hardy matter, and could only hope it wouldn't come back to bite her.

And now here was the damn woman's own husband, no doubt wanting more *ex parte* communication. Well, at least here was someone far beneath her on the pecking order. She could chew him up and spit him out with impunity and probably feel a little better after she did. If they were all trying to double-team her to subvert her ruling, she would pick them off one by one, starting with this meddling lawyer.

'Time *is* short, Mr Hardy. You're damn right. What do you want? And I'd better not hear one word of whining about the situation your wife put herself in.' She ostentatiously consulted her wristwatch. 'You have three minutes and I'm counting.'

Hardy wanted to strangle Marian Braun where she sat. At

the very least he longed to try to make her understand the staggering difficulties to which she had subjected his entire family. But neither of those served his purpose here this morning. This would remain impersonal, a legal matter, nothing more.

He moved forward rapidly, placed his briefcase on the chair before her desk, and opened it. 'I have here,' he said, 'a writ for a *habeas* hearing on my wife. I'd like you to grant an alternative writ for tomorrow morning.'

The frown remained, but Braun laughed harshly through it. 'Are you joking? What are you doing here with that? If you've got grounds to vacate the contempt, submit your motion in the normal fashion.'

'Your honor . . .'

The judge wasn't listening. 'And assuming you had grounds for this writ at all, do you expect the DA's office to answer by tomorrow morning? What do you hope to accomplish by this?'

'Quash the contempt charge before the grand jury.'

The judge drummed her pencil against the desktop. She observed him over the tops of her glasses. 'I admire your nerve, Mr Hardy, although I can't say the same for your wife's.'

Hardy nearly had to bite his tongue off, but he wasn't going to get drawn into a discussion about Frannie. 'I am specifically not addressing the judicial contempt, your honor. No one is arguing that. Only the grand jury citation.'

'Well, there's a rare and welcome display of good judgment.' She drew Hardy's piece of paper over to her, scanned it quickly, and repeated her initial response. 'You don't say she'll talk and you don't say why she doesn't have to. All you say is it would be nice to let her go. This belongs with the DA. They make this decision, not me.' She pushed the paper back over to him. He was dismissed.

But he didn't move. Braun glared up at him, and pushed the document another time. 'I'm going to lose my temper if you don't . . .'

'I don't trust the DA,' Hardy said. 'I can't take it there.'

Braun's eyes narrowed.

Hardy pressed on. 'It's been my experience that this particular administration will take a convenient position in their offices, and when it's on the record, suddenly it changes. In this case, they've abused the grand jury process—'

'That's a strong charge. How have they done that?'

'Your honor, with all respect, you know as well as I do. The grand jury is a prosecutor's tool. But it's not supposed to be a blunt instrument.'

'And that means?'

'It means Scott Randall's trying to make a high-profile case out of whole cloth and he's using my wife to do it. How many times did you see his name in the paper this weekend?'

'Not flatteringly.'

'What does he care? In six months it's all forgotten except the name recognition.' Hardy was surprised Braun had let him argue even this much – he must have struck a chord with her. She knew that this DA's administration had mostly a political, not a legal, agenda. As a judge, she'd no doubt run across her own examples of dishonesty and sleaze. Hardy played another variation on this theme.

'Your honor, we'd all like to believe the DA is going to do the right thing. But even if they were convinced this wasn't going anywhere with Ron Beaumont, there are folks down the Hall who would leave my wife in jail just to prove that they can.'

'Except my understanding is that Ron Beaumont is likely to be indicted.'

'If he is, there won't be enough evidence to bring him to trial.'

Braun had just about reached her limit. 'Well, that's the system, Mr Hardy. Get used to it.'

'The system's broken, your honor. If they're going to keep my wife in jail, at least make them do it out in the open.'

Braun put her elbows on her desk. 'You know, Mr Hardy, this morning I had the mayor himself try to circumvent the judicial process. I'm tired of people who want to keep making this stuff up as they go along.' She straightened up, pushing the paper away from her a last time. 'You got your pitch; take it to the DA. Your three minutes are up.'

Hardy had one last shot and he hadn't wanted to take it unless there was no alternative. But now he'd gotten to that. Still, it was a tremendous gamble. If it didn't succeed, the consequences would be devastating to his credibility, to his entire career. 'What if I can produce Beaumont at the hearing?'

Braun stared at him. 'I'd understood he'd fled.'

Hardy elected not to answer directly. 'Scott Randall doesn't have anything, your honor. He jailed my wife to save his own face. If he's got a case, let him make it in open court if he can.'

'You're telling me Ron Beaumont will testify at this *habeas* hearing tomorrow?'

Hardy nodded. His heart was stuck in his throat. 'If he's not in the courtroom, there's no hearing.'

He saw her wrestling with it. Braun had a temper, and he was personally enraged at what she'd done to Frannie. But like most Superior Court judges, she prided herself on her basic sense of fairness. Hardy counted on that now.

It was no secret that this particular DA administration systematically abused the grand jury process. Finally, because of Scott Randall's arrogance and grandstanding, Braun herself had just been squeezed and humiliatingly dressed down by the mayor.

She peered over her glasses, her mouth a grim pencil stroke. 'I want you to understand that if I wasn't so pissed off at your wife, I wouldn't give you this hearing. But I'm not supposed to let my personal feelings get in the way, and if I don't give you this hearing, I'm not going to be sure it wasn't personal.'

She pulled the writ over and scratched an angry signature at the bottom. As Hardy reached for it, she held it back one last second. 'If I take the bench tomorrow and Ron Beaumont isn't in the courtroom, you don't even get three minutes.'

Lou the Greek's had a kind of Chinese version of paella as the special. Chunks of octopus (perhaps *tire*), sausage, maybe chicken – it was hard to tell – and some red stuff, all mixed into the rice with soy sauce. Since every day the special was the only item on the menu, Hardy ordered it. A wave of hunger had hit him in Glitsky's office and he would gladly have ordered even some variant of spam musabi if it had been offered. It probably would have been better than the paella which, he had to admit, didn't quite sing.

But he ate most of it, sitting in one of the window booths which, at the underground Lou's, began at the level of the alley outside. As it was, he could have been eating tires for all he cared about the food.

Something far more compelling commanded his attention – the love letters of Jim Pierce to Bree Beaumont, the ones she'd saved in the back of her high-school yearbook. There were a dozen of them, all of them relatively short – half a page or a little more – and painfully, adolescently passionate. Hallmark poetry that made him wince: 'Never have/I touched or felt/Never/Even knew./Oh, the craving/Touching/Wanting/Only you.'

Three were on Caloco stationery. None were dated, although all of the paper had grown brittle, leading Hardy to conclude that the last of them had been written several years before.

So David Freeman had been right again, Hardy thought with awe when he put down the last letter. And why should that have been a surprise? Pierce might be married to a world-class beauty, as President Kennedy had been, but this was no guarantee that he wouldn't have affairs. Human nature, Freeman had said. Men want a lot; women want the best one.

Just as Hardy felt they were finally closing in on some kind of Kerry/Thorne connection to Bree's death, he didn't need this complication. He could understand Pierce's denials, especially in the presence of his wife. And judging from the age of these letters, the relationship might have ended years before, possibly before either of them were even married. But the discovery was unwelcome – he was trying to narrow his list of suspects, not expand it. And if Pierce and Bree had ever been lovers – now a foregone conclusion – it put the oilman back in the picture, at least tangentially.

'How was it today, Diz?'

Lou the Greek himself hovered over the table, breaking Hardy out of his reverie. He smiled, indicating his nearly cleaned plate. 'Maybe the best ever, Lou.'

The proprietor showed a lot of teeth under his thick gray mustache. 'People been saying that all morning. I'm thinking we might go regular with it.' He slid into the booth across the way. The dark eyes were not smiling anymore. 'Hey, I hear some things. You, your wife, the house? You OK?'

Hardy shrugged. 'Getting by, Lou, getting by.'

'You need anything, you let me know.' He brushed at his mustache, embarrassed. Lou hesitated another moment, then nodded. 'OK, then.' He extended his hand and Hardy took it. 'Good luck,' he said. 'And today's on me.'

Hardy thanked Lou and, struck by the unexpected kindness, watched him as he began to schmooze another table. It was one of the few personal interactions he'd ever had with the man in twenty-some years and he wasn't at all sure where it had come from.

Their common humanity?

The thought brought him up short. Unexpectedly, the urge to goodness was still in the world. It wasn't him alone, or Frannie alone. He came back to Ron Beaumont – if he was innocent, and Hardy was now willing to believe he was, he was living a nightmare as hellish as Hardy's own, or Frannie's.

And his wife was right – 'the best thing,' she'd said. The options were endless, but the best thing was if she didn't have to tell. And for that to happen, they were all depending on him. On his judgment and skill, yes. But more than those, really, at the base of it, on his humanity.

Turning back to Pierce's letters, he realized with surprise

that he wasn't going to go anywhere with them. At least not today. There was no time. For the moment, he knew all he needed about Pierce. He'd lied under duress. He had loved Bree. Maybe he'd even killed her – out of jealousy, rejection, his own despair.

But the trail to the truth did not lead through Pierce from where Hardy sat now. He had to choose his best course, and that led him back to Carl Griffin, who had died pursuing the same thing.

32

Heritage Cleaners ran its business out of an upstairs office overlooking a grimy, wet and – today – windswept alley in Chinatown. Hardy turned off Grant and into the narrow passageway. A thin trickle of some kind of effluent flowed down a narrow and shallow concrete trough that bisected the way. He passed several dumpsters rich with the odors of cabbage, rotten meat, and urine. The body of a small brown puppy lay pitiably against one of the buildings. Hardy couldn't help himself – he bent over, closer, to be sure it couldn't be saved. Then he gathered some newspaper, wrapped up the bundle, and placed it in one of the smelly dumpsters.

Checking the address, Hardy ascended the dark flight of stairs. If he were going to take his shirts to the cleaners, he thought this would be his last choice. But once inside, the office was a surprise. Though still a far cry from the modern antiseptic bustle of FMC's headquarters, Heritage was well lit, apparently organized, a couple of computers at some workstations.

And – the big surprise – it wasn't a laundry.

A frail-looking, elderly Chinese man sporting bifocals and a starched, white collarless shirt looked up and rose from one of the fours desks when the door opened. He spoke good if accented English. 'I am Mr Lee. How may we help you?'

Hardy handed him a business card. 'I am helping to investigate the death of a police officer and I wonder if I could have few minutes of your time.'

Mr Lee checked the card again. 'Are you with the police?'

'No.' At the man's frown, Hardy pressed ahead. 'But I

believe the officer may have come here and spoken to someone about a woman's death.'

The man did the math in his head. 'Two deaths now?'

'Actually, three or more.' He paused to let the fact sink in. 'I'm working with the police.' This wasn't precisely true, and Hardy was about to tell Mr Lee he could call Abe to smooth things over, but saw that he was nodding, accepting. 'The inspector was Carl Griffin.'

Again, a frown. Deeper this time. 'A big gentleman, wasn't he? Not too clean? He's dead?'

Hardy felt a spark of hope. 'Yes. He was killed a few weeks ago. I was hoping to find out what he questioned you about.'

The nodding continued, then Mr Lee motioned for Hardy to follow, and led him over to the desk he'd lately abandoned. The old man worked with the keyboard, nodded, and pointed at the screen. 'Twelve oh six Broadway,' he said. 'Our customers.'

'Do you clean the whole building?'

'No. There are, I believe twenty-three or four units, all individually owned. We contract through the superintendent for the public areas, and many residents are happy with our service.'

'And Bree Beaumont was one of them?'

'Yes.' Mr Lee shot a glance at Hardy, and ventured a personal comment. 'It was very sad about her.'

'Yes it was,' he said. Sadness was all over this case. He gave the sentiment a moment. 'So what is your schedule there, for cleaning? I gather you go on Tuesday and Thursday – is that correct?'

'Yes.'

'So you do each place twice a week?'

'No. Generally, we clean once. Half the units on one day, the other half on the other.'

'And which was Bree?'

'Thursday. Every Thursday.'

Hardy saw the reason for Griffin's earlier visit. If Heritage had come on Tuesday, possibly within an hour or two of Bree's death and before the crime scene unit had arrived, then trace evidence might be found among the cleaning supplies, in the vacuum cleaner bags and so on. But evidently this had not happened.

Still, he wanted to be certain. 'So you didn't go to her apartment on the day of her death?'

'No. That's what Sergeant Griffin asked us.'

'Did he ask if any of your staff saw anybody unusual in the hallways? Anything strange that they noticed?'

'Yes, of course.' Mr Lee was still seated, and now sat back, folding his arms patiently. 'But – have you been there? Yes? – then you know. It's really not that type of apartment building. There's only two units on each floor, except for the penthouse, where there is one.'

Hardy remembered. At Bree's twelfth floor, there was simply a landing with a window and a door. Residents weren't exactly out wandering in the halls, loitering about in the locked lobby. 'So there was really nothing to be found in any of your supplies. The crime scene had already been there by the time you came on Thursday?'

Mr Lee shook his head. 'I don't know that. But Inspector Griffin . . . just one minute.' Pulling open the drawer again, Lee pushed junk around for a minute, found that he wanted, extracted it, and handed it up to Hardy.

It was a crinkled piece of paper. Hardy's pulse quickened as he realized what it probably was – a sheet torn from Griffin's notebook. In the by now familiar scrawl, Hardy read: '10 01. Received from Heritage Cleaners. One Gold and Platinum Movado Men's watch, serial number 81–4–9880/8367685. Evid/case: 981113248. C. Griffin, SFPD Badge 1123.'

'Where did you get this?' Hardy asked. 'Where is the watch?'

Mr Lee shrugged eloquently. 'When the inspector came here, he said he still needed the watch. I should hold the receipt. If no one claimed it, eventually it might come to us.'

347

'But how did you get the receipt in the first place?'

'The inspector gave it to my supervisor in the building. They found the watch when cleaning.'

'And this was when your people found the watch? On the Thursday?'

Lee considered a moment. 'Yes. The date on the receipt is October first, see. A Thursday.'

'And no one has claimed it since? Reported it missing?'

'No,' Lee said. 'Not to my people.'

Hardy wasn't surprised to hear this. If the watch inadvertently got left behind, say snapping off during a struggle at the crime scene, it would be the height of folly to go back and try to get it. But stranger things had happened.

Of course, Hardy realized, it might also be Ron's watch. With the upheaval in his life since Bree's death, he simply might not have missed it. But Griffin would have just asked Ron about that. Wouldn't he?

Instead, he'd taken it as evidence, logged to the Beaumont case number. The problem was that by this time, Hardy knew the file backwards and forwards, and there wasn't any watch in the evidence lockup or anywhere else.

Hardy asked if he might have a copy of the receipt. When Mr Lee returned from making one, he handed Hardy the copy, then clucked sympathetically. 'I'm sorry I can't help more, but I haven't even heard about Sergeant Griffin's death until just now.' Mr Lee wasn't rushing him, but clearly he felt this investigation had little to do with him or his staff. It had taken enough of his time on a work day.

Hardy couldn't shake the feeling that there was more here. There had to be. He'd referred again to the notes before coming and Griffin had included his maddening exclamation points.

But now they were moving toward the exit. The words 'fabric wash' came to him, so he stopped at the door. 'Mr Lee, one last question. Do you do any clothes cleaning at all? Laundry work? Say one of your clients leaves a pile of clothes by a washing machine – would you dump it in for them? Or dry them?'

The proprietor considered this, then shook his head. 'We remove window drapery occasionally, or upholstery fabric, but no. Generally, we don't clean clothes.'

'And what about Bree's drapes or furniture? Did you remove either of those for dry cleaning? Were there any stains you needed to remove?'

'No. That would have been a special order, and I checked into that with Sergeant Griffin when he came here. And again, I am so sorry to hear about him.'

Scott Randall heard the rumor from one of the other assistant DAs, who in turn had heard it from one of the forensic guys who'd worked with Sergeant Leon Timms, unhappily cleaning and cataloguing through the night under the back seat of Griffin's car.

Although Glitsky had cautioned Timms and his staff not to discuss any possible relationship between the murders of Bree Beaumont, Carl Griffin, and Phil Canetta, by some inexplicable mystery of nature the word had leaked out.

Now Randall was at a hastily called late lunchtime strategy session with his boss and his investigator, Peter Struler. They had just taken their seats at Boulevard, an incredibly fine restaurant that was well off the beaten track of the rank and file of workers at the Hall of Justice.

Pratt, still smarting from her dressing down by the mayor, was inclined to dismiss the rumor, but Randall needed her support to move ahead, and he wasn't going to let it go. 'I think we have to assume it's true, Sharron. It sounds right. It *feels* true, doesn't it?'

Peter Struler was a fifteen-year, no-nonsense investigator and he spoke with a veteran's confidence. 'It's true,' he volunteered. 'Everybody assumed Griffin got hit on some dope sting, but he was doing Beaumont. Ballistics confirms the same gun whacked Canetta.'

349

Pratt's mouth hung open for a moment. 'Is that a fact? You know that for sure?'

Struler nodded. 'As soon as Scott told me what he'd heard, I moseyed on down to the lab, checked it out with some of the good guys. Same gun.'

'The same gun.' Pratt was trying to fit this information into her world view.

'The same gun that killed Griffin,' Randall explained again.

'But what was Canetta's connection to Beaumont?'

'Well, isn't that funny you should ask?' Randall tried to control an arrogant smirk and wasn't entirely successful. He leaned over the small table. 'You know the Frannie Hardy we took such grief about this morning? Poor little innocent thing.'

Pratt's eyes narrowed. 'Yes.'

'Well, our old friend, her husband the lawyer? He's up to his ears in this. Canetta was freelancing for him.'

'For him? What do you mean?'

Struler butt in harshly. 'Hardy was using Canetta's badge to get information he couldn't get on his own.'

'On what?'

Randall gestured expansively. 'All of this. Anything he could.'

'But why?'

'He'd probably tell you he wants to help his wife get out of jail, but that doesn't hold up. Despite the mayor, she doesn't get out until we let her go, and I'm not too inclined to go there.' Randall tossed a conspiratorial glance at Struler. 'I've got a theory on the real reason Hardy's involved, and Peter here doesn't think it's too bad.'

Pratt took a sip of her sparkling water, nodded attentively. 'Go on.'

'Hardy is Glitsky's best friend, right? You heard our good lieutenant in your office the other day, about what a true friend of his this Frannie is, what a great person. She took care of his kids when his wife died. Blah blah blah. Well, ask

350

Marian Braun what a sweetheart Mrs Hardy is.'

Pratt waved that away. 'So what's your theory, Scott?'

'All right, listen. We all agree Ron did this, right?'

Struler, if anything, was more certain than Randall. 'Absolutely.' He turned to Pratt and gave it to her one more time, so she would be clear on it. 'Straight insurance scam, ma'am. Bree was heavily insured. She was also Ron's support and had decided to throw him out on the street.'

'Why?' Pratt asked.

Struler continued. 'He had another girl on the . . .'

'Woman,' Pratt quickly corrected him. They were talking about multiple murder, but some things just couldn't be tolerated even for an instant.

The inspector made a quick face, fixed it, and moved on. 'Another woman on the side.'

'Not Frannie Hardy?'

'No, ma'am. We don't believe so. Anyway, I've got four witnesses from the building saying they'd seen Ron with another woman – same one – during the day when Bree was out working. They'd just walk out through the lobby holding hands, maybe sit on the bench out front.'

'So who is she?'

'That we don't know. Yet. We'll find her. Anyway, the point is, Bree found out about this.'

'How do you know that?'

'It's a reasonable conjecture,' Randall interjected, 'but maybe she didn't. Either way it doesn't matter. But you'll see, it fits.' He nodded back at Struler to continue.

'So what finally happened was Bree got herself another boyfriend, got knocked up, and was going to marry him.'

Scott Randall whispered. 'We're hearing it was Damon Kerry.' He exulted in his boss's stunned expression – there was nothing, he thought, like a good surprise. And he was going to have a couple more for Frannie Hardy tomorrow.

'Damon Kerry.' Pratt's eyes shone with excitement.

'That's the word on the street,' Struler said.

'It's really pretty smart the way they've figured it all,' Scott said.

'What? Who?'

'Hardy and Glitsky. Knowing Kerry would have to get involved . . .'

Pratt held up a hand. 'I'm afraid you're getting ahead of me. How is Kerry. . .?'

'Why do you think the mayor wants us to pull back on this, just at this time? Democratic mayor. Democratic – now – front runner for governor.'

'Yes, all right. But Damon . . .'

Scott Randall bulled on ahead. 'Kerry was having an affair with a married woman, Sharron. During his campaign. He got her pregnant out of wedlock.' He shook his head. 'No no no. It just can't come out.'

The DA still didn't see it. 'All right, but what about Lieutenant Glitsky? Where does he fit?'

This, to Scott Randall, was the easy part. 'Hardy,' he explained, 'is Ron Beaumont's attorney, right? Ron comes to him with this problem – he knows Bree's going to dump him. So if that happens, he's out two million dollars.'

'Two million?' The number was new to Pratt.

Randall smiled. 'It's a nice, round motive, isn't it?'

Struler interjected again. 'And Hardy's not exactly hauling big coin. He hasn't had a worthwhile trial in a couple of years. He's doing scratch defense work. Meanwhile, the wife has no job, he's got kids in private school. Money's an issue – count on it.'

'You want to go along that road a little further, Sharron,' Randall added. 'The smart bet says he set fire to his own house yesterday, to get some cash in.'

'So you're saying,' Pratt was getting into the idea now, 'that Hardy and Ron Beaumont conspired to kill his wife?'

Randall nodded, beaming. 'With Hardy's wife as the alibi.'

'So where does Glitsky fit in?'

Struler and Randall exchanged glances, and the inspector

took it. 'What does Glitsky make – seventy, seventy-five? He's the head of homicide and Hardy's pal, so they cut him in and it's a dead lock Ron's never arrested. Glitsky never moves on it. Period. End of story.'

Randall picked it up. 'Then they run a little squeeze on Kerry about the affair with Bree, which makes him go to the mayor, who in turn tells us to release Frannie for political reasons, yada yada – just make the whole thing go away.'

'That son of a bitch,' Pratt exclaimed.

'Exactly.' Randall's Martini arrived and he lifted the olive out of it and chewed contentedly. 'Every part of this fits, Sharron. And meanwhile, Beaumont's killed two other people, both cops who were getting the picture.'

Pratt liked the scenario, but she had to raise an objection. 'Except if Canetta was working with Hardy . . .'

But Scott had an answer for that, too. 'Canetta was supposed to be digging up dirt on Kerry and Pierce, the Caloco guy. Classic muddy-the-waters lawyer shit, pardon the French. Some other dude did it. Then Canetta ran across something, got wise, and tried to cut himself in.'

'And Ron had to kill him, too.' Struler sipped his beer.

'*And*, last but not least,' Randall said, 'then Glitsky lays down orders that nobody talks about Canetta or Griffin or anything else. He's, quote, pursuing his own investigation and PS, Ron Beaumont seems to have dropped off his radar.'

'Jesus Christ,' Pratt enthused, 'if this is true . . .'

'It's the case of the decade,' Randall concluded.

'It's true,' Struler repeated. 'It all fits.'

A silence descended briefly while the waiter brought their salads. Pratt played with hers for a moment, then put her fork down. 'OK, another objection. If this was so well planned, why did this Hardy woman let herself get thrown in jail?'

'Anytime you want,' Struler answered, 'I'd do four days for a million dollars.'

But Randall answered seriously. 'That was just a dumb

mistake like criminals make every day. She was nervous, and got pissy with Braun.'

That wasn't good enough for Pratt. 'But what about this secret she couldn't tell?'

'There's no secret,' Randall said matter-of-factly. 'She got over-confident and was extemporizing. She got too cute and talked herself into a corner, saying she knew Ron and Bree had problems, but didn't know what they were. It seemed an innocent enough question at the time. She didn't see where I wanted to go with it, and when she found out, it was too late.'

'So she . . .'

'My prediction is she'll back off on the secret tomorrow. Or make one up.'

Struler: 'She does that, it locks up this theory.'

Randall chewed happily. 'That's my plan,' he said.

'And meanwhile, the man Glitsky's protecting has become a multiple cop-killer.' Pratt was firm. 'Gentlemen,' she said, 'we've got to take these people down.'

From a freezing phone booth on Grant, checking back at his office for messages, Hardy learned that the fire department's arson team had called and more or less urgently wanted to chat with him. So had three of his clients.

Finally, he was surprised at the relief that washed over him when he heard that David Freeman had, at last, come in. Back on foot, from Chinatown he made it to Sutter Street, the Freeman Building where he worked, in under ten minutes.

His old, crusty – and still apparently bullet-proof – landlord was scribbling intently on a yellow legal pad at his desk when Hardy opened his door.

'I need a moment of your valuable time,' he said. He had scandalized Phyllis by overriding her 'He doesn't want to be disturbed,' by saying, 'Oh, OK. I'll leave him alone then.'

He never glanced back, walking directly past her station, over to Freeman's closed door, knocking, and pushing it open.

The old man's eyes betrayed him. He wasn't really as

annoyed as he sounded, although he did pull an hourly billing form over, make a note on it, and growl. 'Valuable doesn't begin to describe it. And I am on billable time here, Diz. You want input right now, it's going to cost you.'

'Everything does, sooner or later.' Hardy closed the door. Freeman's hair was doing its Einstein impression and the rest of him was decked in his usual sartorial splendor – dead cigar in his mouth, tie askew, wrinkled shirt unbuttoned, the coat of his shiny brown suit draped over his shoulders. 'Phil Canetta's been killed,' Hardy said soberly. 'You hear about that?'

The old man put his pencil down. 'I saw something in the paper this morning . . .'

Hardy was a couple of steps into the large corner office when the door opened again behind him – Phyllis. 'I'm sorry, Mr Freeman. I told Mr Hardy you didn't want to be . . . he brushed right past me and . . .'

Freeman held up a hand. 'It's OK, dear. Emergency.'

She spent another instant perfecting her expression of displeasure, though Hardy didn't think it needed much work at all. Then she made an appropriate noise of pique and backed back out.

'Dear?' Hardy said. 'You call her dear?'

'She is a dear,' Freeman said. 'Controls the riff-raff element. I couldn't survive without her.'

Hardy shook his head. 'You've got to get out more.' He'd made it to Freeman's desk, pulled around a chair, plopped his briefcase, and opened it. He picked up as though they'd been talking all morning. 'You were right about Griffin. That we ought to start with him.'

'I thought we were on Canetta.'

'Both.'

Freeman's eyebrows went up, another question, and Hardy sat down, telling him about the ballistics confirmation – both men shot with the same gun, the rest of what he knew. 'It looks like it wasn't more than a couple of hours after he left here,' he concluded.

'Where was he?'

'Just inside the Presidio.'

'I didn't read anything in the article about Griffin. Or Bree Beaumont either.'

'Glitsky wants it quiet for now. Damon Kerry is definitely involved, so there are, as they say, political ramifications.' Freeman didn't respond in any way, so Hardy went on, reciting the facts as he knew them.

By the time he finished, Freeman was sitting back in his chair, his hands linked over his comfortable middle, his neck tucked down into his ratty tie, his eyes closed. His chest rose and fell a couple of times. Slowly, he raised his head, and squinted across the desk. 'So where are you now?'

Hardy reached forward and lifted the stapled and marked-up copy of Griffin's notes from his briefcase. 'Griffin found something. I'm convinced it's right here.' He passed the pages over the desk. 'The yellow highlights.'

The bassett eyes came up, baleful humor. 'I guessed that.' After a moment's perusal, he flipped back a few pages, nodded, came back to where he was, and looked up again. 'So Griffin eliminated Ron?'

Hardy leaned forward himself. 'Where do you see that?'

Patiently, Freeman went over it. 'This first entry. R. at eight oh five, NCD, with the exclamation marks. "R" has got to be Ron, don't you think? Eight oh five is when he left for school with the kids, too early to have done it. NCD is "no can do." You got all this already, right?'

'Sure,' Hardy said, feeling like a fool. NCD, he thought. No can do. Just like WCB meant 'will call back.' But he'd never before run across the former. 'Sure,' he repeated. 'Ron was out.'

'OK.' Freeman nodded. 'I suppose the timing was right for him. Now what's this "Herit."?'

'I just came from there. It's the cleaning service that did Bree's place.' He leaned across the desk. 'Tuesday and Thursday as it indicates. They do Bree's on Thursday, so it was after

356

the crime scene had two days there. By the way, it's not there, but Griffin found a watch at the scene and tagged it into evidence.'

'When?'

'On Thursday. Heritage found it and gave it to Griffin.'

'And crime scene didn't on Tuesday?'

'I don't know,' Hardy said. 'I guess not. Glitsky would say they're overworked and underpaid. It's gone now in any event.'

Freeman was nodding distractedly, his eyes never leaving the page. 'Never mind, never mind. Here it is again. This fabric wash. "R. stains." Did Ron . . .? What was this? Semen?'

'I don't know. I don't think she and Ron were sleeping together.'

Now, Freeman did look up.

'They had separate bedrooms,' Hardy went on. 'Definitely Bree, and maybe Ron, too, were involved with other people. Sexually.'

'Charming,' Freeman replied. 'The modern couple. So you read the autopsy. Was there any evidence of rape that morning? Intercourse?'

'No.'

'Hmm. Rug stains?'

Hardy shook his head. 'Crime scene would have them.'

'Oh yes, those competent crime scene analysts.' Freeman thought another moment, then pointed to the briefcase. 'Do you have a copy of the police report in there?'

Hardy handed him another folder and sat while Freeman leafed through to the page he wanted. 'She was wearing a dark-blue cotton-blend skirt and pullover powder-blue sweater. Panty hose. Black shoes, half-inch heels. Ah, here we go.'

'What?'

'We've got what you'd expect – blood and dirt, but there's also a rust stain on the left hip and on the hem of the sweater. Rust.'

'When she went over the balcony,' Hardy said. 'It's an iron grillwork railing.'

'Well, there you go.' Freeman, pleased with himself, leaned back in his chair again.

'So why does it say "fab. wash"? That's got to mean forensics didn't find anything on the fabric, right? But they did find blood, dirt, rust . . .'

'Maybe it's some kind of detergent. Maybe it just means there was nothing on the drapes, or the rug, or the upholstery, all of which *was* true. Those fabrics were a wash.'

'Maybe.' It still troubled Hardy. Griffin's damned exclamation points were all over the place with the cleaners and this note, and he couldn't make them mean anything.

But Freeman, on his billable time, wasn't wasting any of it. To his satisfaction, he'd solved the mystery of what the 'R' stood for, so he was moving on, now down to the '902' phone call.

So Hardy brought him up to date about Bree's call to Kerry. When he finished, Freeman looked perplexed. 'But you say the call wasn't at nine oh two?'

'No. It was earlier – it began at ten after seven.'

'So what's this nine oh two?'

'I don't know. That's what I mean, David, about Griffin having it here, but I can't see it. I figured it was a time that would lead us to Kerry, and it did, but then the time was wrong.'

'So it's not a time.'

'No – look back. That's how he writes his times, everything. Eight oh five, eleven forty-five, now nine oh two.'

Freeman gave it another minute, then waved a hand. 'All right, let's pass on that and go on. What's "Bax T, . . . 830"?'

'The last person we know of to see Griffin alive. Maybe the very last.' Hardy went on to explain about Thorne and Elliot and Glitsky's probable warrant to look for printed materials. 'If Abe finds evidence on any of about four fronts, I think we can stop looking.'

Freeman drummed his fingers a couple of times. 'So why are we doing this, you and me?' Before Hardy could respond, the drumming stopped. 'Did Canetta by any chance work for this Thorne guy?'

'Not that I know of. Sometimes Jim Pierce.'

'In what capacity?'

'Security at hotel conventions, like that.'

'But not Thorne?'

'I don't know. I hadn't connected Thorne to any of this before yesterday, so I never asked.'

Freeman pressed it. 'Well, think about it. Wouldn't the ethanol producers have conventions here too? I mean, this is Convention City, USA. And all of them need security, right? If Canetta was in that loop, one of a hundred cops doing freelance . . .' A shrug. It was obvious. 'And you know for a fact that Thorne is involved with Kerry, too?'

'Through SKO, yeah, close enough.'

The old man cleaned an ear with his finger. 'OK, so what's this last thing – burn or brown and then a dollar sign?'

Hardy sat back. 'This, old master, is why I have come to you. Although wait a minute, let me see that.' He studied the scrawl for the tenth time. 'Bree's maiden name was Brunetta. This might say B-R-U-N. How's that?' He passed the pages back.

'Not impossible,' Freeman said. 'Maybe Thorne was black-mailing her about something in her past, when she was Brunetta. In any event, it looks like Griffin found some kind of money connection, and maybe called Thorne on it.'

Hardy recalled the box of Caloco documents in Glitsky's kitchen. Ron's – or had it in fact been Bree's? – talent for creating wealth, or at least substantial lines of credit. Had Thorne tried to get Bree under his control, and by extension under Valens' and Kerry's control, by threatening to expose her financial shenanigans? Or – even better – ruin her credibility and reputation with Kerry in the same way?

Hardy finally sat back. Freeman regarded him intently. 'You think Thorne did your house, too, don't you?'

It was Freeman's first mention of that incident and, perhaps as he'd intended, it caught Hardy slightly off guard.

'As you'd say, I don't think it's impossible.'

Freeman nodded sagely. 'And when you went to see him this morning, were you packing then, too? I know the expression is lawyers, guns, and money, but guns don't really belong.'

A sheepish grin flitted for a moment over Hardy's face. David was truly terrifying. He saw everything. 'I thought I might need some protection.'

But Freeman wasn't laughing. 'I don't think so. I think if he had given you an excuse, he'd have a bullet in him right now.'

Now, unbidden, the grin flickered again.

The old man pointed a finger. 'Listen to me, Diz. You've got every right to hate the man, but it's up to the law to punish him, not you. You've already put this where it belongs – in Glitsky's corner. Don't get yourself killed over it. Too many people have already. Two of them carried guns and knew how to use them. Does that tell you anything?'

Hardy nodded. 'They didn't shoot fast enough.'

Again, there wasn't any sign that Freeman thought this was funny. He checked his watch, looked down, and wrote something. 'Thirty minutes at two hundred an hour comes to a hundred bucks. I'll add it to the rent.'

Upstairs in his office, Hardy called the toll-free Movado number and gave the serial number of the watch to a helpful operator. All she could tell from the number was that the watch had been sold within the past five years in San Francisco, at the Jewelry Exchange. There was no record of the buyer's name.

33

The administrative offices of the main fire station on Golden Gate avenue did not bear much resemblance to the Hall of Justice. Here the expansive lobby was open to the public without the benefit of metal detectors and police guards in the doorways. The milling crowds of discontented lowlifes that were a common feature in and for blocks around the Hall were nowhere to be seen. Instead, the marble walls – inscribed with the names of the heroic dead of the department – seemed to shine with pride. Well-appointed business persons came into the building and walked purposefully to the elevators, in which they were whisked to their destinations.

So Hardy had no premonition of dread as he walked through the fifth-floor office labeled 'Arson Investigations.'

After leaving Freeman, he'd gone upstairs to his own office and returned phone calls for the better part of a half hour. He called Bill Tilton, the insurance agent, and pretended he was a potential employer of Marie Dempsey. She'd faxed him a resumé, he said, but he couldn't make out the phone number or address too clearly. Tilton, inadvertently breaking every confidentiality law in the book, gave him what he needed.

In the next call, a secretary with the arson unit told him that they wanted to talk to him at his very earliest convenience. If he would give them a time he could drop by the main offices this afternoon, the investigators would be there for him. He'd made an appointment for one thirty, assuming that the urgency was that they wanted to assign liability back to him.

His first sense that things were not right came as the secretary directed him not to one of the investigator's offices behind her, but to a small, empty office with a scarred metal table in the middle of it and four wooden chairs along one wall.

He'd been in enough of these, and immediately recognized this for what it was: an interrogation room.

He didn't have to wait long to find out. He hadn't even taken a seat. Walking to the one window, he looked down and out to the west. Visibility was a couple of blocks, and suddenly Hardy felt a chill of apprehension.

He turned quickly, intending to walk out and invite whoever wanted to talk to him down to his turf, to the Solarium. Freeman had counseled him to leave the police work to Glitsky, and it was good advice, but he knew more than Glitsky and he had a deadline. There was much he still had to do – he couldn't afford to be detained here. But as soon as he looked, he knew he wasn't going anywhere soon. Three men were standing in the doorway, in a pack.

'Mr Hardy?' 'How you doing?' 'Have a seat.' Friendly as undertakers.

The last one in closed the door.

Recognition kicked in. This was not the amiable Captain Flores, but the man who'd been so uncooperative and surly yesterday afternoon. He identified himself as Sergeant Wilkes, no first name. And, folder under his arm, he was running the show.

'This is my partner, Sergeant Lopez, and this,' he said, indicating a wiry young cowboy in a denim jacket, 'is Sergeant Predeaux.'

Predeaux, leaning one shoulder against the wall opposite them, broke an icy smile over the toothpick he was chewing. 'Rhymes with Pla-Dough,' he said.

'Sergeant Predeaux,' Wilkes added, 'is with the arson unit, too. He's one of our police members. Sergeant Lopez and I, we're with the fire department.'

'Good.' The antagonism was already thick in the room. Hardy, determined not to add to it if it could be helped, put on a face. 'So what did you find?'

Wilkes made a show of opening his folder. From Hardy's perspective as a lawyer, there wasn't much in it – a schematic of the house, a couple of pages of notes, and perhaps a formal report. Still, Wilkes took his time, going over it silently while everyone else waited. Finally, he decided the moment was right.

'We've got clear indications of accelerant, petroleum-based, probably gasoline, on the front porch. There is a lot of technical detail supporting our conclusion, but basically we have determined that this was in fact an arson occurrence. Both from the rate of burn and the initial call reporting the fire, we can pretty closely pinpoint the start of the blaze to about three thirty a.m. Sunday morning.'

This wasn't any surprise to Hardy, but the next line of inquiry, though no less surprising given the circumstances here, was unpleasant. Lopez shifted next to Wilkes, as though he'd been restraining himself. He spoke up. 'We understand you weren't sleeping in the house that night. Is that correct?'

Hardy shifted his eyes from one man to the other. He made it a point to nod and answer in even tones. 'That's right. Did I mention that to Captain Flores? I was with my children at my in-laws'.'

'And why was that?'

'Why was what?'

'Why were you at your in-laws'?'

'Because my children were there. It was Hallowe'en night,' Hardy said. 'They were staying with their grandparents and I wanted to be with them.'

'You're married, aren't you? Was your wife there?'

'Yes, I'm married,' he said evenly, 'and no, she wasn't there.'

'You having marital problems?' Lopez asked.

'Mr Hardy's wife is in jail,' Predeaux said, although it didn't seem to come as a shock to either of his colleagues.

Hardy paused. 'That's a long story.'

'We've got time.' Wilkes smiled insincerely.

Hardy returned it. 'I'm happy for you, but as it turns out, I don't.'

Predeaux moved a step forward. 'Did you make it a habit of staying with your in-laws?'

This, finally, was enough of a press that Hardy straightened up in his chair, sat back, and crossed his arms. 'I don't believe this.' He almost barked out a laugh, but stopped himself. 'You guys talk to my in-laws? They'll tell you I was there. I didn't burn down my own house, for Christ's sake.'

'Were they awake at three thirty?'

'Yeah,' Hardy replied crisply. 'We were all sitting up telling yarns around the campfire.'

'There's an interesting choice of words,' Wilkes said.

'Oh yeah,' Hardy replied. 'Very telling.' He came forward in his seat. 'Look, guys, I thought I was coming down here to get the lowdown on your progress, and maybe get my house turned back over to me so I could get to work rebuilding it.'

'You got insurance?' Wilkes asked.

He sighed wearily. 'Yes, sir. I've got insurance. Thank God.'

Predeaux piped in. 'Replacement value or loss value?'

Another aborted chuckle. 'You know, you may be surprised to learn that I haven't checked the policy lately. I don't have any idea.' He shook his head. 'This is ridiculous. If we're going to continue in this vein, I suggest we make another appointment and I'll bring a lawyer.'

'You think you need a lawyer?' Lopez asked.

Hardy assayed a cold smile. 'Here's a tip, sergeant. Everybody needs a lawyer.' He pushed his chair back and stood up, and squared off at Predeaux. 'Am I under arrest? Are you seriously thinking of charging me with this, 'cause if you are I could use the money the false arrest lawsuit will bring in.'

'Funny you should bring that up.' Predeaux pulled a chair around and straddled it backward. He transferred his toothpick to the other side of his mouth. 'You a little short on money?'

'Who isn't?' Hardy shot back. 'What's the matter with you people? I'm the one who got his house burned down. I've got at least two reliable witnesses who'll swear I wasn't anywhere near the place and guess what? I wasn't.'

'We're looking into it, as you say,' Predeaux responded.

'Well, good luck with that. Or with finding any evidence, which by the way, guys, is generally one of the traditional steps in a criminal investigation.'

'He's pretty confident, isn't he?' Lopez asked.

'Confident enough.' Hardy had had all he could take of this. They had no grounds and no evidence and he had other places to be. 'So Sergeant Predeaux, am I under arrest or not?' The other three men started holding a silent conversation. Hardy butted into it. 'Sergeant Wilkes, when do I get my house back?'

'That hasn't been determined.'

'Well,' Hardy snapped, 'when you get finished wasting your time and do determine it, you know where to reach me. Sergeant Predeaux,' he repeated, 'am I under arrest or not?' He stood by the door for a moment, waiting. 'I'm taking your silence as a "not." That makes this your lucky day.'

By the time he parked again in the Western Mission, he had gotten his anger under control to some degree. Although, considering the purpose of this visit, he didn't think he'd be able to squelch it entirely. He did, however, derive some pleasure from David Freeman's latest wisdom regarding his weapon.

Hardy, after some real consideration, decided to leave the Police Special in the trunk of his car for his visit to the fire department. This, he realized, turned out to have been a good idea. Driving out to the Mission, he imagined a scenario where Predeaux had, in fact, decided to place him under arrest. If Hardy had had his gun with him, he would have been sorely tempted to pull it out, get the drop on these three clowns and lock them in the room while he attempted to locate Ron Beaumont.

This, of course, would have ended his legal career and

365

maybe killed him in the bargain. It certainly would have curtailed his mobility in the next twenty-four hours, what with the manhunt and all. But, because of Freeman's little lecture, he hadn't brought the gun in. He'd have to remember to thank the old man.

Marie Dempsey's place was on Church Street about a block from Hans Spreckman's, an authentic bierstube which Hardy considered to be on a par with Schroeder's downtown, which in turn had a reputation as the best German restaurant in the city. The neighborhood had a certain friendly charm in spite of the overwhelming preponderance of pavement and stucco, and the lack of trees, lawns, and shrubbery. Maybe it was the scale of the buildings, or the trolley that passed on Church Street every half hour or so.

Today, though, a wet and heavy cloud still hugged the earth, and Hardy felt at one with it.

The address was the upper unit of a duplex in a square, gray two-story building with an internal stairway. From his experience at the Airport Hilton, Hardy thought there was little to no chance that Ron would open the door to a knock or a ring. This was the reason he'd finally opted not to try and call the various numbers he'd collected on the M. Dempseys of the city, but rather to discover the address on his own. He didn't want to give Ron any warning of his visit.

So he walked up the stairs and stood by the door and listened. A man's voice, singing quietly to himself, was barely discernible inside. There was definite movement, footsteps.

He pushed the doorbell, gave it very little time, then pushed it again. The footsteps had stopped. So had the concert. Whoever was in there was alone. He'd be very surprised if there were children. After another short wait, he knocked desultorily.

Walking back down a few of the steps, making his footfalls as heavy as he could, he then crept back up to the landing and waited. About two minutes later, the doorknob turned and

366

Hardy hit the door hard, leading with his shoulder. There was a satisfying bit of resistance and then he was inside, hovering over the man he'd knocked to the ground.

'Hi, Ron. How've you been?'

Struggling to get up. 'Mr Hardy.'

'Dismas, please. After all we've been through together, I think we're on first names by now.'

Ron was on his feet again and broke a nervous smile. 'All right, Dismas.' He let out a long breath. 'You may not believe this, but it's good to see you.'

Hardy was brusque. 'It's better to see you. Where are the kids?'

'They just went to the store for a minute.'

'With Marie?'

After a beat, Ron offered a resigned shrug, another attempt at an ingratiating smile. 'You're pretty good,' he conceded.

'I have my days,' Hardy admitted. Closing the door behind him, when he turned back again to Ron, this time he was glad he had it – he'd taken his gun out from his waistband, holding it so Ron could see.

'You don't need anything like that.'

'Maybe not,' Hardy said. 'But then again, maybe I do. So I figured I'd be prepared either way.'

The gun had Ron's attention, no doubt about it. He couldn't take his eyes off it. 'So what are you going to do now?'

'Not me, us.' They were in a small foyer. Hardy motioned over to the living room, visible behind them. 'Now we're going to wait for a little while and you'd better hope your kids come back with Marie in a reasonable amount of time. Or else you and I are going to take a ride downtown.'

'And do what?'

'And tell a DA named Scott Randall anything he wants to know.'

Ron took a seat on a low leather couch. Hardy, still pumped up, remained standing. 'My understanding,' Ron said, 'was that you were going to wait until tomorrow. Then Frannie was

367

free to tell anything, everything. And the children and I would be gone.'

He clipped out the words. 'Yep. That was it.'

'But?'

'But now she's not sure she can do it.'

'Why not? I've . . .'

Hardy raised his voice. 'It's not you, god damn it! It's not anything you forbid or allow. It's her.' He shook his head, reining in the emotion, and got his voice under control. 'The way she sees it, as soon as she tells them your situation, your kids suffer. They've got to move and start over.'

'But that's not Frannie's doing.'

It still galled Hardy to hear this man refer to his wife so familiarly, but there was nothing he could do about that now. He bore some of the responsibility for that himself. 'No,' he said, 'and as soon as they indict you, which is tomorrow, it's going to happen anyway.'

'So what's her problem with it?'

Hardy suddenly felt stupid holding the gun. Tucking it back into his belt, now invisible again under his jacket, he stepped across to a wingback chair and sat on the edge of it, across from Ron. 'She doesn't see it as a problem,' he said. 'She's willing to trade a few more hours in jail, to give me a few more hours . . .' He stopped.

'To find who killed Bree?'

Hardy leaned forward and eyed him coldly. 'Yes,' he said. 'To find who killed your sister.'

Ron didn't give it up right away. He put on a quizzical expression, as though he really didn't understand what Hardy had just said. 'You mean my wife. Bree.'

'I mean Bree all right,' Hardy replied. 'But she wasn't your wife. She was your sister.'

34

For the third time since they'd arrived, a cable car rattled by outside on Mason, shaking the floorboards of the apartment. The conductor had a heavy hand with the famous bells, too.

Ding ding ding ding ding!

Glitsky had always been under the impression that sounds were muffled by heavy fog, but this clanging, certainly, was an exception to it. He decided it must affect only the lower register.

The shaking under him increased and for an instant the lieutenant thought it might be a real earthquake. Thorne's work area was a desk in his living room, up against the front window overlooking the street. Glitsky had been going through a stack of computer printouts, and now pushed the ergonomic chair back a couple of inches, ready to bolt for a doorway if things began to fall around him. 'It's hard to believe that people pay real money to live with this experience.'

On the couch behind him, Jorge Batavia patiently lifted another page of printed matter from a suitcase he'd placed on the coffee table. He scanned it quickly, and set it on the pile of rejected paper next to him. 'It's new-age therapy,' he said. 'Every fifteen minutes you get to wonder if your building is going to fall down.' The sergeant put aside another page. 'You think you're going to die four times an hour, you squeeze what you can out of every minute. Your life experience is enriched.'

The shaking had stopped, punctuated by a last burst of clanging. 'Good theory.' Glitsky pulled forward again, and went back to his stack of paper.

There was also a computer on the table, but Glitsky didn't

dare even turn the thing on. He thought there was a reasonable likelihood that the thing was booby-trapped, so he had placed a call back to the Hall to have one of the cyber-specialists come down and unplug it, then bring it downtown for examination.

It wasn't as if he didn't have enough to look at. Thorne put out a prodigious amount of paper, and Glitsky and Batavia had been at his hard-copy files for almost an hour.

Batavia and Coleman had been checking in at homicide after Glitsky had returned to the office with his newly signed warrant. He had asked Batavia to accompany him on the search of Thorne's place while Coleman went to talk to Jim Pierce again about his activities on Saturday night.

While Glitsky and Hardy thought they might be closing in on Damon Kerry – perhaps through some agent of Baxter Thorne – Coleman and Batavia had moved Pierce up a notch or two on their possible suspect list. This was mostly because a review of the business calendar he'd provided for them had revealed another questionable alibi – a two-hour gap after Bree's funeral, during which he'd had lunch alone at a crowded Chinese counter restaurant. This was when someone had killed Griffin, and made it three out of three for Pierce's squishy alibis. That in turn piqued the inspectors' curiosity.

But Glitsky had developed a personal hard-on for Thorne. As Hardy had pointed out, even a tenuous connection to the weekend's water poisoning at Pulgas was going to make life very difficult for Mr Thorne. If they found any tie-in to Bree Beaumont, it would even be worse.

Between him and Batavia, they'd already done a thorough job on the kitchen, the waste baskets, and garbage cans. In the bedroom, there was nothing in or taped under any of the drawers of the dresser or night table, nothing tucked between the box spring and the mattress.

Glitsky went to the computer table while Batavia checked the bedroom closet and found shoes and hanging clothes and the suitcase filled with propaganda. Batavia brought the suitcase into the living room, but thus far, they'd found nothing at all – no longhand drafts or fragments of the damning press release, no final or proof copies, no printing or copying bills.

The rest of his records were similarly disappointing. His bills and check register revealed nothing unusual – phone, electric, rent, credit card payments. If he hired operatives, he kept no records of them here. There weren't any random keys. Apparently he didn't own a gun.

When Glitsky could free up another inspector or two, by Christmas, he intended to do a similar search on the offices of FMC, although he'd believed that his best hope on Thorne was an unexpected search of his apartment.

But maybe he was wrong.

After another few minutes, he heard Batavia move behind him. 'Well, that was a slice.' Glitsky turned around and saw the sergeant returning the large stack of pamphlets, letters, and other reading material back into the suitcase. 'All of these are older. Weeks, even months. Nothing on Pulgas.'

He closed the suitcase and stood up. 'I'll keep looking.'

Glitsky heard a key in the front door. He pushed the chair back and stood up as a short, well-dressed man appeared in the alcove. He wore a hat with a small feather in it, gloves, and a tweed overcoat. Behind him stood the building manager who'd let Abe into the apartment and then, apparently, called Thorne at his work.

The dapper man stared at Glitsky with a dead expression, then transferred it to Batavia as he entered the living room from wherever he'd been. His tone was completed uninflected. 'What is the meaning of this outrageous intrusion?'

'You're Mr Thorne I presume.' Glitsky had his search warrant in his pocket. He extracted it and held it out to the man, who glanced at it contemptuously, making no move to examine it. Glitsky shrugged and in a few words introduced himself and explained the basic situation. 'I'm afraid,' he concluded, 'that I'm going to have to ask you to leave the premises while we continue here.'

Thorne didn't even blink. 'No, sir. I refuse to do that. I've called my attorney and he'll be here shortly and put an end to this.' He was taking off his overcoat, hanging it on a peg in the alcove, planning to stay.

'He won't be able to do that, sir.' Glitsky held all the cards here, and he knew it. 'This is a legal search conducted pursuant to a murder investigation . . .'

'Baxter?' The manager interrupted, shifting from foot to foot in the still-open doorway. 'If everything's all right here, I've . . .'

'Sure, Daniel.' Thorne thanked him courteously and he backed out on to the porch, closing the door behind him. But the suspect hadn't lost the thread. He came back to Glitsky, asking quietly. 'Whose murder?'

'James Allen Browning of Pescadero.'

'I've never heard of him.'

'He was the victim of the Clean Earth Alliance attack on the Pulgas Water Temple the other day.'

'That again.' This time he allowed a tone of suppressed anger. He rolled his eyes.

'Again?' Glitsky asked.

Thorne ignored the question. 'And you think I had something to do with that? On what grounds?'

'Justifiable grounds, Mr Thorne,' Glitsky replied. 'A judge signed the warrant. That's all you need to know. Now I'm not letting you into this apartment until we're finished here. As a courtesy, we'll bring a chair over and I'll let you remain in that alcove. With your lawyer when he shows up. But nobody's touching anything here until we're done. Do you understand?'

The men were standing two feet apart. Thorne huffed, replying. 'Perfectly.'

Glitsky crossed the room, said a few words to Batavia, and went back to the desk. The cable car went by again as Batavia brought two chairs from around the kitchen table through the living room and into the alcove. Then he lifted Thorne's overcoat from its peg, as Glitsky had instructed him.

'Hey! What do you think . . . ?' For the first time, Thorne's voice rose.

Glitsky was up as if shot out of his chair, his own voice harsh with authority. 'You stay right where you are. Jorge, make sure he does. While you're at it, have him give you his wallet and check his identification.'

'I won't . . .'

'You damn well will,' Batavia said.

Glitsky took the overcoat from his sergeant and now held it up to his face. He'd smelled a strong odor as Thorne had removed the coat and hung it up. It hadn't been there when Glitsky and Jorge had entered the apartment and then, suddenly, with Thorne's arrival, there it was – gasoline.

Reaching into the pockets one by one, his hand closed around what felt like some kind of charm. Extracting it carefully, he instantly placed the piece. It was at least an exact replica, but Glitsky would bet it was an original, of one of the hand-blown Venetian glass elephants that he'd last seen dancing across the mantel over Hardy's living-room fireplace.

Sergeant Coleman was having trouble getting through to Jim Pierce, whose patience had all but run out. Coleman's had as well. He'd been kept waiting for nearly a half hour, and now, as he'd finally been admitted into the vice president's office, had been told by Pierce's secretary that the next meeting started in ten minutes.

Pierce was behind his desk. Distracted. No hand shake. Papers to be signed, decisions to make. He looked up at Coleman. The inspector, he said, could talk but he'd better talk fast. These continual interruptions were far beyond reasonable, getting near to the point of official harassment. If they continued, there were likely to be consequences.

The power play had its effect on the young inspector. The corner office was vast, ornate, intimidating. Windows and views, high enough to be over the fog. Coleman squirmed in the ultra-modern wooden chair – really more a stool with sides than anything a body would choose to sit in or on.

It crossed Coleman's mind that this might, in fact, be a special chair positioned in front of Pierce's desk for unwelcome visitors, to keep them from getting too comfortable. To make sure they wanted to leave soon.

Homicide inspectors are not a particularly reverent bunch. Most of them had seen everything at least twice, and Coleman was no exception. But sitting in Pierce's office, he found it next to impossible to imagine that the man who presided here would ever need to have recourse to murder. Coleman didn't really believe it, but he did at least want to nail down the facts, if for no other reason than that he wouldn't have to be in this position again.

'I realize you have cooperated up to now, sir, and we're grateful for that cooperation . . .'

'Well, this is a fine way to show it. What more could you possibly have to ask me that you haven't asked already?'

'We tried to reach you yesterday, sir, about Saturday night.'

'I know.' He reached for a fountain pen, signed something, put the pen back, blew on the signature, and moved the paper to one side. Then, immediately, he started reading the next one. He didn't look up. 'My wife told me you had come by. Again. About a police officer this time?'

'Sergeant Canetta, yes sir.'

'I do know that name. Where do I know . . .?'

'He had worked security for Caloco at several events.'

Finally, Pierce stopped fidgeting. 'That's it. He was the man who was killed?'

'Yes, sir.'

This seemed to affect Pierce somewhat. He sighed deeply and his mouth grew compressed, his brow furrowed. 'I'm sorry, inspector. I'm sorry for my rudeness earlier. I'm under some pressure here but that's every day and it's no excuse. I can understand how you feel when your colleagues are . . .' He straightened in his chair. 'All right. Go on. What do you need to know?'

'I'd like to know where you were on Saturday night.'

In spite of the apology, impatience thrummed under the surface. 'May I ask why that would be important? What did my wife tell you?'

Coleman said nothing.

And Pierce got the message, although it didn't make him any happier. He sighed again. 'I was home until early morning, perhaps dawn. Then I went down to my boat in the Marina.'

'But you were home during the night?'

'I just said that, yes.'

'Alone?'

Pierce nodded. 'Is that so strange, sergeant? My wife had gone out to a party that I didn't want to attend.'

'Did your wife see you when she got home?'

A short laugh. 'What did she tell you?' Then, ruefully. 'I doubt it. I spent the night in my study.' He met Pierce's eyes. 'We fought about the party, that I wasn't going. When it was over, I heard her come home, but wanted to see if she'd come to me and apologize. When she didn't . . . well, I got my back up.'

'So you slept in your study?'

'Not much. I was pretty mad and couldn't sleep most of the night. I watched some television.'

'Do you remember what?'

'I don't know, really. Some pay-per-view sports I guess. Mindless junk. Whatever was on. I dozed on and off.'

'Do you know offhand the company that provides your television service?' Coleman asked.

'No,' Pierce said. 'No idea, sorry. Do you know yours?'

'Do you mind if I check?'

'I don't know, I . . .' But then Pierce brightened slightly, although the smile didn't exactly light up the room. 'Oh, I see. Sure, of course. Whatever you need to do.'

Coleman, with relief, pushed himself out of the chair from hell. 'Thank you for your time, sir. I hope we won't have to bother you again.'

Pierce sat still for a long beat, then shook his head in disbelief. 'Before you go, inspector, maybe you can answer me one question?'

'If I can.'

'All right. Is there any reason on God's earth why I might have wanted to kill Sergeant Canetta? Since that's what I presume this has been all about. He did some security work for Caloco, OK. Where? What type of security work? And then what? I didn't even know the man. I doubt if I could pick him out of a crowd.' He paused and spread his hands, appealing to reason. 'I just don't understand. Is he related to me in some other way?'

Coleman heard him out. He really couldn't blame him for being angry and frustrated, but he wasn't going to give away anything that his boss had told him to withhold. 'It's a routine investigation,' he said. 'That's all it is. Thanks for your time.'

'That is a coincidence,' Baxter Thorne was telling Glitsky, 'but these little elephants are widely available. You can buy one at any quality gift store. It's my lucky charm. I've carried it with me for years.'

Another question, another simple answer. 'As I have already told you, Dismas Hardy was, I believe, the name of the gentleman who came by my office this morning and made some threatening remarks.' Glitsky still hadn't let Thorne enter the apartment proper. He sat on one of the chairs in the alcove and the lieutenant hovered above him. 'Beyond that, I can't say I know anything about him.'

Thorne was completely unruffled, going on again, answering Glitsky's next question in his maddeningly even voice. He even produced a reasonable facsimile of a heartfelt chuckle. 'I filled my tank, lieutenant, then I'm afraid I committed the cardinal sin of topping off. It got on my coat.'

Glitsky was coming around to a profound appreciation of just how slick this bastard might be when the telephone rang behind him. Batavia picked it up, listened for a moment, then held it out to Glitsky. 'It's for you. Vince.'

Glitsky told Thorne to stay where he was and crossed to the desk.

'Pierce is clean at last,' Coleman began and went on to explain what he'd learned at Caloco. Then he lowered his voice to a whisper. 'Can you still hear me?'

'Barely.'

'That'll have to be good enough. We got people here.'

'OK.'

'OK, so I'm writing up this Pierce thing at my desk and guess who drops by? He just left like five ago. Ranzetti.'

Glitsky frowned. Jerry Ranzetti was with the office of management and control, a department which used to go by the name of internal affairs. If Ranzetti had come to homicide, he was on the scent of a bad cop, and this wasn't good news for Glitsky. The homicide unit was small – thirteen men and one woman – and Abe felt he could personally vouch for the integrity of each one of them. 'I gather it wasn't a social call.'

'Well, he pretends. I pretend back. Then he says, oh yeah, maybe there is something, maybe I heard something about it, maybe I could tell him something.'

'Maybe,' Glitsky said. 'About who?'

Coleman paused and the voice when it picked up again was nearly inaudible. 'That's why I called, Abe. The guy he's sniffing around? It was you.'

35

'When did you know?' Ron asked.

'I had a pretty good idea by the time I saw your bedrooms, but I really didn't put it all together until I realized you must be having a sexual relationship with Marie. Bree's having an affair. You're having an affair. But somehow you were a happy couple, comfortable together? Contented? It didn't make sense. The only thing I don't understand is why you went to all the trouble? Why couldn't she just have remained Aunt Bree?'

'At the time, that option just seemed to leave us with a lot more to explain to everybody we met. Nobody questions a man and his children and his new wife. But a man, his sister, and the man's kids? That's different – it's a weird set-up, with a way better chance of striking somebody as funny, and we couldn't have that. You've got to understand – I'm wanted for kidnapping, maybe child pornography. This is serious shit. They are *on* me. We had to look exactly like a normal couple. Not mostly, exactly. And for a long time, we did.'

'Except for the affairs.'

Ron shook his head. 'OK, we had to keep the affairs secret. But since that's generally the nature of affairs with people who are really married, it's worked out all right.'

'So you and Marie. How long has that been going on?'

'A couple of years.'

'And she's OK with that? She didn't push you to get married?'

He sat back on the couch, crossing one leg over the other. 'No. To get divorced from Bree – we've had a few discussions about that, let me tell you. But that was before Bree died. Since then, I think she's waiting for an appropriate time to pass. My mourning period,' he added uncomfortably. 'So marriage hasn't come up yet.'

'Are you telling me she didn't know about Bree?'

'She still doesn't. Nobody does.'

Hardy sat back himself, giving that a minute to sink in. 'The kids?'

Ron Beaumont shook his head no. 'They were two and three when we moved out here. Maybe they'd heard of Bree as their aunt but they didn't remember. So after awhile, she was just Bree, their step-mom. A far better life than what they were used to.'

'So what about Dawn?'

This brought Ron's defenses up. Suddenly, he was all the way forward on the couch, by his body language ready to spring at this threat to his children, even if it was at a man with a gun. 'What about her?'

'That's my question.'

He stayed forward, tensed, his hands clenched in front of him. Hardy waited him out. Gradually, the words started to come. 'I had never met anyone like her, even remotely like her. I was a junior at Wisconsin. I met her in the library of all places – she was working on her master's thesis. Sociology.'

'So she was an academic, too?'

Ron laughed. 'No. Although she was smart, I suppose. No, I *know*. Very smart. Too smart.'

'What does that mean?'

He drew in a breath and blew it out heavily. 'She didn't feel anything, or – no, that's not precisely it – more like she decided what feelings were rationally defensible and the others she just didn't acknowledge. She wasn't going to live a pawn to her weaker emotions.'

'Which ones were those?'

'Oh, you know. The conventional ones that hold us all back, but especially women. At least according to Dawn. Love, need, compassion. Anything that stood in the way of her getting what she wanted.'

'Which was?'

A shrug. 'Pretty simple really. The usual. Money, power, excitement.'

Hardy almost laughed at the absurdity he was hearing. 'And she was getting all this as a sociology major?'

Ron shook his head. 'No. She started as a topless dancer. By the time I met her,' he paused, 'she called herself an actress.' He sighed. 'When I think back on it, what drew me to her was this sense of . . . I guess I'd have to call it danger.' He fell silent again.

'Go on,' Hardy prompted him. 'Do you mean physical danger?'

Another empty laugh. 'Yeah, I suppose, even that. Or at least it seemed that way to a sheltered kid from suburban Illinois. She was four years older than me and really nothing was off-limits physically.

'At the time, I thought I'd died and gone to heaven. I mean, here's this totally unconventional free spirit in an unbelievable body and she's in love with me and of course, we're both invincible, immortal. Nothing can touch us. We can mix and match with other couples, do every drug known to man, hang out in places I wouldn't go near today.'

He stopped, and seemed again almost to ask Hardy's permission to continue. 'I look back on that now and it seems impossible, like I was another person.'

'How long ago was all this?' Hardy asked. 'Twenty years?'

'Something like that.'

A nod. 'You *were* another person.'

This seemed to soothe Ron somewhat, and he went on. 'I think what I regret most is that both my parents died during this time, in the first phase when Dawn and I were together.'

'And how long was that, that phase?'

'Five years, maybe a little more.'

'Did they ever know what she did?'

'Oh no. She was a student, like me. But my dad, especially, saw through her, saw what she was. He tried to tell me, but I wasn't ready to hear anything critical from my hopelessly unhip father. I mean, he sold insurance for a living. He was in the Rotary Club, the Holy Name Society. What in the world could he tell me?'

'Only everything,' Hardy said seriously.

The comment made a connection. 'Exactly. But I was out on the sexual frontier and he didn't have a clue. I even thought he was jealous of me.' Again, that distinctive hollow laugh. 'So of course I gave up on them, not her. And then Dad died. And then two years later, Mom.' He looked down at his hands.

'So you were married five years?'

'Not yet. We were free. We didn't need the piece of paper.'

'So what did you do? Were you an actor, too?'

'No.' He thought for a moment. 'I still don't know why. Chicken, maybe. Screwing on film was too far for me to go. Like some part of me knew I'd outgrow all of that someday. I didn't want any record of it.'

'That wasn't dumb.'

'No. But it wasn't something I planned either. I can't take any credit for it, that I was this virtuous guy. It just happened.'

'So what did you do?'

The question seemed to embarrass him. 'Not much, to tell the truth. Dawn made sporadic but pretty decent money and I had majored in finance, so I managed it. We had enough to get by, and the main thing was we didn't want to be tied down to jobs. We had to live.'

'So what changed?'

'I guess I did.' Hardy didn't want to admit it, but there was a charming, self-effacing quality to Ron Beaumont. As everyone else who knew him said, he seemed to be a great guy. 'It wasn't any increase in wisdom,' he admitted candidly, 'just age. Maybe my conventional background started to catch up with me, I don't know, but I figured we'd done the bohemian thing, and it was time to move on. Frankly, the scene was getting old, not to mention us.

'So she got pregnant. *We* got pregnant. Then she decided to

381

have an abortion. We had a huge fight over it. She was going to do it anyway. And she did. And I moved out.' He sighed. 'Then I think for the first time she couldn't handle ... the emotions. She was thirty-one years old. The biological clock was ticking pretty good. The whole thing just tore her up. She was shocked that she couldn't rationalize some way to handle it, but she couldn't.'

'And you got back together?'

He nodded. 'We got married. I started working as a teller in a bank. We had Cassandra. A year later we had Max. She hated it.'

'What?'

'The whole thing. Babies. Crying, puking, diapers, no sleep. But mostly the boredom, being with them all day. She hated what I was doing, my job. She hated that we had no money. But you know the funny thing?'

'What's that?'

Hardy recognized serenity in the man's face. 'I loved it. I loved them. It was as though somebody just flicked a switch and suddenly I saw everything differently. It made sense. This was what we were here for. Certainly it was what I was here for.'

This was an incredibly difficult thing to hear. Ron was describing Hardy's own feelings at the birth of his first son Michael, who had died in infancy. That tragedy had plunged Hardy into a cold and dark void from which he thought he'd never escape.

But nearly a decade later, the births of Rebecca and Vincent had rekindled a flame that had burned brightly for several years. More recently, though, it had dimmed to where it now mostly felt to Hardy as if there was no light or heat, only ash covered by other stuff that didn't burn at all. He wondered if under it all, the last embers had truly died and if not, if there was a way to coax a new flame to life. When this was over, he promised himself, he was going to try.

'So what happened next?' Hardy asked.

'About what you'd expect up to a point,' Ron replied. 'Fights, more fights, still more fights. She wanted to go back to work and we fought about that.'

'Doing what she'd been doing?'

He shrugged. 'She said it was all she knew. I told her to learn something else, she was a mother now, think of the kids. Did she want them growing up in that environment?'

'And what did she say?'

'She said there was nothing wrong with that environment. It paid well and provided a valuable social service.' He rolled his eyes in frustration. 'I was being inconsistent. I was becoming too conservative. I was a hypocrite. You name it, I was it.'

'So she went back to it?'

'Not right away. Not for a while.'

'Why not?'

'I'd like to believe that it was my strength of will.' A dry chuckle. 'I didn't give in. But she really couldn't stand being at home, and I wasn't putting the kids in full-time daycare, so we switched. Big mistake on my part, as it turned out.'

'Why was that?'

'Because she was then the good working mother, and I was the nearly unemployable dad. The courts like mothers best anyway for custody, and when the dad doesn't have a real career . . .' He shrugged. 'He's dead meat.'

'So she went to work?' Hardy had to know what had happened.

Ron nodded. 'Some office job, which of course was incredibly boring and didn't pay anything like she was used to. She wanted out, but I kept wanting to make the family thing work.' He sighed. 'Anyway, we made it a couple more years with me not working – bad, bad mistake – but finally I had to get another job, too.' Ron's eyes grew hard. He was sitting on the front inch of the couch again, his hands clenched so hard the knuckles were white. 'Which is when,' he said, 'she started selling the kids.'

Marie and the children finally arrived back at the duplex which, truth to tell, was a great relief to Hardy. Belief in Ron Beaumont and his idealistic, over-the-top, melodramatic, perhaps heroic story had grown in him over the past days. To have it revealed now as false just when he'd come to accept it as the truth would have seemed a joke almost too cruel to endure.

They spent a few moments explaining Hardy's presence and involvement to a skeptical Marie. But Ron and the kids – Cassandra particularly – convinced her that Hardy was on their side. He could be trusted absolutely. He was Cassandra's hero. Clearly, she was thrilled to see him again, and so glad it was she who'd finally convinced him to help them. He told her he'd made a lot of progress. He'd give her a final report tomorrow. She loved that.

Otherwise, they were the well-mannered children they'd been at the hotel, although Hardy was delighted when Ron had to tell them to stop bickering over whose turn it was to get to choose the video. They were regular kids, after all. Much like his own. It continued to be a relief.

Marie – a handsome, physically confident yet soft-spoken woman in her late twenties – put on a brave front, but Ron's situation with the children here was precarious enough without the added bonus of a stranger. Even if that stranger was presented as their savior.

And, because life was never simple, Hardy got the strong impression, picking up on the household banter, that the near future of Ron and Marie as a couple was in doubt. If it turned out that Ron decided to relocate tomorrow with the children, it wasn't at all clear to Hardy that Marie would be joining them. Or that she even knew this was a contingency plan.

But after the kids had retired to the television, the two of them unpacked the bags with the practiced efficiency of a long-term couple. When they'd finished, Marie broke out a beer for each of the men.

Hardy stopped her. 'Oh, Marie? Excuse me. Have you all been here all weekend?'

Marie looked to Ron. 'Except just now, to go get groceries.'

'But yesterday? The day before?'

'What is this?' Ron asked. Hardy motioned for silence, then backed him off gently with a palm.

'Marie? Were all of you here all weekend?'

She met his gaze frankly. 'Yes. Ron got here midday Saturday and we all got settled. Then Sunday you remember was so bad, the weather. We just stayed inside and played games and watched videos.'

'What about Saturday night?'

'What about it? Did we go out? Why would we go out?'

'I don't know. I'm asking.'

'No.' She threw a quick glance at Ron, a small prideful smile. 'Definitely not.' The satisfied lover. 'Then last night Max had night terrors. We were up half the night.' She crossed her arms. 'Ron tells me tomorrow he'll be able to go home. We've kind of been making a game out of this. Is that what you wanted to know?'

'Exactly,' Hardy said.

Marie nodded, the worry back on her face. She spoke to Ron. 'If you need anything, just yell, all right?' She closed the door to the kitchen on her way out, telling Hardy it was nice to have met him.

He didn't completely believe her.

Although he did tend to believe what she'd said about Saturday night. And if Ron had been here with her, he hadn't been out shooting Phil Canetta.

But the questions had ruffled Ron's feathers. 'What was all that about?'

Hardy was matter-of-fact. 'That was about proving you didn't kill Bree, which is an issue to more people than you'd like to believe. By the way, do you now or have you ever owned a Movado watch? You know, the museum timepiece, little dot at twelve o'clock?'

Ron was getting sick to death of all the questions. 'By the way, isn't this getting a bit much?' Hardy didn't respond, waiting him out, wearing him down. 'No,' he answered finally.

'Did Inspector Griffin ever ask you the same thing? About a Movado watch?'

'No. Why?'

'No reason,' Hardy said. 'Now, the day of Bree's funeral – tell me about that.'

'Jesus Christ, I don't see . . .'

'Ron.' Hardy was firm. 'Humor me.'

Frustration showed in his face, but resolve must have shown more clearly in Hardy's. 'What do you want to know?'

'I want to know what you did, what the kids did, where you were.'

For Hardy, it was a fundamental recital. At eight o'clock, Ron and Father Bernardin had hosted a breakfast at the St Catherine's rectory for the pallbearers – four of the other soccer dads – and he'd of course kept the children out of school so that they could be with him. The funeral mass had been at ten. At around eleven fifteen, accompanied by Marie, the children, the priest, the pallbearers, and a couple of other acquaintances from Ron and Bree's limited social circle, he drove down to Colma, where she was buried.

Both Kerry and Pierce had been to the funeral. Neither had attended the burial.

There was a short graveside service, after which Ron took Marie, Bernardin, and the kids to lunch at the Cliff House. He dropped Max and Cassandra back at Merryvale at around two, about the time Carl Griffin's body was discovered.

There could no longer be any doubt. Ron hadn't shot Carl Griffin, which meant he hadn't used the same gun to eliminate Canetta. And finally, at long last, it was a near certainty he hadn't killed his sister. As he'd sworn all along, as Frannie had believed, as Hardy had hoped, Ron Beaumont was innocent.

It was a huge load off.

* * *

386

It was galling for Hardy to realize he could have known all this on Friday night, Saturday evening at the latest, if only Ron hadn't felt the need to bolt. But there was nowhere to go with that. Ron had in fact called him on Saturday, had tried to cooperate. He hadn't known what Hardy was going through. The only thing for Hardy to do now was get his remaining questions answered while he could.

He willed a neutral tone and began. 'All right, Ron, here we go again, OK? Tell me about Bree and Damon Kerry.'

'You've gotten to him, huh? I'm not surprised.' Ron sat back and tipped up his beer.

'Do you think he killed her?'

Ron had given this question a lot of thought, and he gave it some more now. 'The problem I've always had is pure logistics. How could he have done it?'

'That's not so hard. He comes by your place after you've taken the kids to school. They talked that morning, you know. Kerry and Bree.'

'I know.'

This was a surprise. 'Do you know what they talked about?'

'No. Not specifically. I think they just talked. They did all the time. But look, the man's running for governor. He doesn't just stroll down the street and kill somebody.'

'Maybe he drove, parked in the basement . . .'

Ron was shaking his head. 'And what if somebody sees him down there or in the elevator? And why?'

'She was pregnant.'

'No. They loved each other. They were talking about getting married. That's what Bree and I were having our problems about.' Ron spun his bottle nervously on the formica table. 'This wasn't my finest hour,' he said at last. 'I was upset enough with her when she started hitting the newspapers in connection with Kerry.'

'Why was that, though, exactly?'

'Because Bree isn't the most common name on earth. If Dawn ran across it . . .'

'How would she do that? Isn't she back in Wisconsin?'

'Why wouldn't she? She reads the paper. California news plays everywhere.'

'I thought she hated the kids.'

'When they were babies. After she saw how lucrative they could be . . .' He trailed off. 'Certainly she fought like hell for the custody judgment. She thought they were her property.'

'And after she got the judgment? After you' – Hardy still had trouble with it – 'took them? I'd think Bree would be the first place she'd look.'

'That's right. But it wasn't as though the court's judgment came as a surprise. Bree and I had months to prepare. When we got out here to California, I was Ron Beaumont, recently widowed. For over a year the kids and I lived in an apartment in Oakland, keeping a low profile.'

'What did you do? For a living, I mean.'

'What I do now. Computer-based financial work. I work from home.'

'So you stayed in Oakland until the investigators stopped coming around to Bree?'

'Right. Then we started "dating," and had a small, private wedding.'

'And no one knew you?'

'Not as Bree's brother, no. We'd lived completely separate lives since I went away to college. At that time, Bree was like fourteen. Then she came out here for grad school while I was living in Racine. None of her friends even knew of me, not that she had that many.' He shrugged. 'It was a perfect fit.'

'It was also a hell of a risk.'

Another shrug. 'High risk, high return. It was the best option. There was no way I was letting the kids go back to Dawn.' He struggled to try and make it clear. 'See, she really believed there wasn't anything wrong with what she wanted to do, what she did. Society's just too puritanical. Sex is natural. If some people are uptight, that's their problem.'

'Not kids, though. Nobody thinks it's OK with kids.'

Ron appeared at a loss. If Hardy didn't know this . . . 'Well, check it out. Somebody's taking ten million pictures a year.'

A short silence fell. Both men reached for their bottles.

'Anyway,' Ron continued, 'back to it. Say Dawn sees Bree in the paper, something clicks. Same name, same field. She checks into it even a little and finds out Beaumont used to be Brunetta, my name. I'm dead. The kids are dead.' He sighed. 'So, yeah, we had some words about it.'

'So what did she say? Bree?'

'It wasn't just saying,' Ron said. 'It's hard to explain, but it was like, all of a sudden, she just . . . became an adult.'

'The ugly duckling,' Hardy said.

'Right. I'm not saying she hadn't been an unbelievably generous sister – all for the sake of my kids. She never told me anything about her other men, though I knew she had them. It was kind of tacitly understood between us that none of them could ever be serious because her first duty was' – he motioned to the back of the duplex – 'to those guys in there. That's what she'd signed on for.'

'But why did she ever agree to do that? I mean, it was so unusual . . . ?'

'I think that was part of it. If I thought I'd been raised conventional, at least I broke out of that at about twenty. Bree was twenty-eight. She had her doctorate and her new job, but she'd really never experienced anything in the real world. So suddenly this gave her a purpose. She had no social life and she loved the kids. She was saving their lives. You know when you're young, you've got all the time in the world. You make lifetime decisions like it's picking a pair of shoes.'

Another silence. They both knew all about that.

'So what happened?' Hardy asked finally. 'Why did it start to unravel?'

Across the table, real anguish spilled over into Ron's face. 'The most natural thing in the world,' he said ruefully. 'She fell in love. She wanted her own life, her own family.' He hesitated, then went on. 'And I didn't want her to have it. I

389

didn't want to have to change. I was furious when I found out she'd gotten pregnant.'

'By Kerry.'

He nodded. 'She was going to tell him. I don't know if she ever did. It was another issue between us.'

'Wait a minute. You had your identity established, so why didn't you just pretend to get a divorce, then she marries Kerry?'

Ron was shaking his head. 'The next governor? I don't think so. Anybody but him, maybe, but if she's the new first lady of California, people are going to be pretty damn curious about her past. It would have come out.'

'So what did you suggest? What was your solution?'

'I don't know. I thought we could split up now, OK, then wait a year or two. Put some distance between me and her. If she would only have waited . . .'

'But she was already pregnant. She'd waited enough, hadn't she?'

To his credit, Ron wasn't proud of any of this. 'She really blew up at me. When was I going to let her live her life? How could I be so selfish after all she'd done for me and the kids?' He met Hardy's eyes. 'And, of course, she was right.'

They came, at last, to the nub.

Ron's initial reaction was a shocked disbelief that Hardy would even ask. Surely he could see that it was impossible? Ron couldn't do it. He got up, crossed the kitchen, went to the sink and threw some water on his face, wiping it dry with a dish towel. He stood for a moment leaning on his hands. Hardy spoke to his back. 'I'm afraid this isn't a negotiable invitation, Ron. You're going to be there.'

He turned around. 'How can you ask me to do this?'

'Because it's the only way.'

'It can't be. They'll arrest me. I can't let that happen. This is precisely what I've gone to all these lengths to avoid.'

'Ron, listen to me.' Hardy stood, his jaw set. 'This isn't the

390

grand jury. The deliberations aren't going to be secret. No prosecutor is going to be able to sandbag you. And besides, I need you to be there. For Frannie.'

'I don't understand why.'

'The simple answer is because there won't be a hearing if you're not sitting in the courtroom. I promised the judge.'

'But that . . .'

Hardy held out a hand, and snapped it out. 'Listen up, Ron. The real answer – and I really don't think it's going to get to that, but if it does – is you've got to be there to tell her she can talk.'

The conflict played in his face. 'But I wrote her that note that she . . .'

'I know what you wrote her,' Hardy snapped. 'That won't play, I told *you* that. She's got her own ideas on the timing of this thing, and nobody but you is going to change her mind.' He lowered his voice. 'You owe her this, Ron. You know you do. Hell, you owe it to me.'

Ron walked away again. The room was too small. At the window end, he stood staring out at the gray for nearly a minute, which seemed a very long time. Finally, he turned back. 'Do you know who killed Bree?'

'I know it wasn't you. I can prove it wasn't you.'

'I've always heard you couldn't prove a negative.'

Hardy had always heard that, too. But with Glitsky's corroboration, he could make a convincing argument that the same person had killed Griffin, Canetta, and Bree. Therefore . . .

'That may be true,' he said. 'But sometimes you get a good enough lawyer working on it, you can create the impression.'

But Ron kept up the challenge. 'And that would be you?'

Suddenly, Hardy had had enough. Marie and Ron and the kids might be playing all of this as some game that would end tomorrow, but it wasn't a game, and Hardy believed with all his heart that it wasn't going to end until he made it happen. His mouth turned up, though he'd gotten beyond smiling.

'That's right, my friend, that would be me.'

Ron stood by the window. Outside, Hardy could make out the little boxes on the hillside of Twin Peaks rising behind them. He was surprised to note that it was still light out. The fog had lifted to a low cover, smudged and dirty.

'Ron.'

Another long moment. 'I don't have any choice, do I?'

'I'm afraid not.'

He stared out the window in front of him, then turned and walked back to the kitchen table. He sat down heavily, spun his beer bottle again, and looked up at Hardy. 'I'll be there.'

Hardy studied him for a beat. 'You're sure?'

Ron bobbed his head distractedly. There was no more hesitation. He'd made up his mind. 'Yes, I'm sure.' He raised his eyes and offered a smile. Hardy had wedged him and then beaten him. He'd be there. Of course. He had to be. There was no other choice.

Hardy exhaled in apparent relief. 'OK, then. I'll pick you up here at eight fifteen? How does that sound?'

'All right,' Ron repeated. 'Eight fifteen. That's fine. I'll be ready.'

'Great.' Hardy again produced a victorious sigh. He extended his hand over the table. 'Sorry this has been so difficult,' he said, 'but it's going to work out, believe me. And thanks for all the cooperation today.'

Their discussion was over. Ron shook Hardy's hand again, keeping up the chatter. When they'd gotten to the front door, Hardy paused. 'Oh,' he said, 'one last small thing. Could I have a word alone with Cassandra for just a sec?'

Ron's visage clouded over. But Hardy, expecting the negative reaction, gave him a man-to-man smile, laying a hand on his arm. 'She's my pal, remember?' he said. 'She's the one who got me into this with all of you. It's only right we let her in on the plan, don't you think?'

They went just outside on the landing by the front door.

Ron and Marie and the kids were treating it as a game, and Hardy made it just another part of the game for Cassandra, their own personal secret. Her father had told her she could trust Mr Hardy, didn't he? If she wanted to double check with him, they could call him out here and ask, but then there was a chance that Max would hear.

The reason Hardy wanted to talk to her by herself, why they were alone out here on the landing was because her dad didn't want to have Max get all upset that she was the only one he was letting go to the sleepover at Rebecca Hardy's.

Her eyes were bright with excitement. 'Rebecca's having a sleepover? I love sleepovers.'

And Max would have been invited, too, except her dad had told Hardy he needed a good night's rest after last night's terrors. Vincent was going to be disappointed, but he'd understand.

No. She didn't have to go back in. Rebecca had extra toothbrushes. She could borrow some of her pajamas. It would be a blast.

But they had to hurry to get to Mr Hardy's car, OK? They needed to get away before Max found out. Otherwise she'd have to stay here and miss the sleepover.

He stopped five blocks away and put in a gallon or two while Cassandra waited in the car. Inside the station, never taking his eyes off her, he dropped a quarter into a pay phone.

Marie's voice was choked with tension, but he allowed her no time to speak, either. 'I'll be out front at eight fifteen as Ron and I discussed. Cassandra's fine.'

Erin Cochran was as mad as he'd ever seen her, and Hardy thought it likely that compared to her husband Ed, when he got home from work, her anger would appear mild as the driven snow. But his concern for people's feelings weren't in his mix anymore. He was running on instinct and adrenalin, and if the people he loved had a problem with that or with him, they'd have to get over it. He didn't have time.

'I borrowed her,' he said. 'Just for one night.'

'It's not funny, Dismas.'

'I don't think it's funny. I know it's pretty damn serious.' She had all but taken Hardy by the earlobe and dragged him inside from the backyard. The children, oblivious to any intrigue, were engrossed with a contraption they'd made up of an oversized cardboard container, ropes, some plastic lawn chairs, and a blanket. Erin threw an eye at them, making sure the adults hadn't drawn their attention. Then back to Hardy. 'I can't believe you're asking me and Ed to be part of this.'

'It was the only way, Erin.'

'I find that hard to believe. And if the police—'

'Ron won't call the police,' Hardy replied, cutting her off. 'He was going to run again and I need him tomorrow to get Frannie free.' Now he looked out at the children. 'Cassandra's my guarantee he shows up.'

'But you can't—'

'Erin!' He put his hands, not quite roughly, on her shoulders. The harshness he heard in his own voice surprised him. But that, too, couldn't be helped. 'Erin, listen to me! I did it. It's done. It's one more night.'

He brought his hands down. Erin's mouth trembled as she fought for control, couldn't speak.

'I've got to go,' he said.

394

36

Hunched over, he sat on the low upholstered chair by the balcony in the penthouse. The drapes were open and when he raised his head he could see off to his left the sunset bleeding a bruised orange into the purple sea. Suddenly, visibility had returned between the cloud cover and the earth. Up at the north end of the Bay, he thought he could even make out individual cars on the Richmond Bridge.

What had he done? What had he done?

The thought assailed him. Ron had agreed. He was going to do it. He would be at Marie's tomorrow morning so that Hardy could pick him up and they could go to the hearing. Hardy had convinced him that this was what he had to do. It was a done deal.

Except . . .

Hardy had no doubt at all. The conversion had been too swift and too unencumbered. Ron had made a decision, all right, but it wasn't to show up in court. Instead, Hardy would arrive at the appointed hour in the morning and Ron and his children would be gone with no trace.

He needed the leverage of his daughter. There hadn't been any other choice.

But if he were wrong.

His insides churned and his skin felt clammy. In front of him, his hands were clenched – the only way he could keep them from shaking.

Pushing himself up from the chair, he stood still, trying yet again to envision the struggle that must have occurred here. But nothing spoke to him. He crossed over to the French doors, unlocked them, pulled them open, and stepped outside.

It was all the same. The planters with their meager shrubbery. The small table and chairs, exactly as they'd been when he'd first come here. Three steps brought him across the slippery tiles of the balcony to the rough iron grillwork.

He tested its strength and found it solid. He wasn't tempted to lean his body into it, but again, hands on the rail, he was drawn to peer over and down to the enclosed rectangle of garden below. The sensation – the height itself – was mesmerizing. It held him there while seconds ticked until finally the vertigo straightened him up.

Backing away, he shuddered, wondering at the primeval power of the urge to fall – death's easy, frighteningly inviting availability with one instant of weakness.

Or assent.

It was unnerving.

The railing was wet from thirty hours wrapped in fog and he went to wipe his hands on his jacket. A foghorn boomed from down below and suddenly he stopped himself.

Rust stains. Fabric wash.

He turned his palms up. With the sun just down, the dusk had rapidly advanced, but there was still enough natural light to make out the faint striations.

For another long moment, he stood without moving. The switch for the light over the balcony was behind him and he turned around and flicked it. The rust wasn't dark on his hands, but it had come off the grillwork sufficiently to be easily identifiable.

Again he crossed to the railing, but this time he squatted so that the top of it was at his eye level. Where he'd stood, the condensation had of course been cleared; but beyond that he thought he could make out where his hands had taken the rust. Swiping the arm of his jacket strongly over the area, the smooth and rugged Gore-tex caught in a couple of places, and then when he pulled it away, the railing had left a line of rust on it.

But far more importantly, the metal itself reflected what

he'd done. The top thin layer of rust had wiped away. It was subtle, but unmistakable.

And it led to a similarly unmistakable and startling conclusion. If Bree's body had been dumped over this railing with sufficient friction to leave rust stains on her clothes, two things should have been immediately apparent to even an inept and overworked crime scene investigator. The first was there would have been a noticeable if not obvious spot on the railing where the rust had been disturbed.

And the second, Hardy thought, would have even been more telling. His own space-age jacket had caught a couple of times when he'd swiped at the railing. Bree had been wearing cotton and wool, the threads of which would have snagged all along on the rough ironwork of the railing.

His brain was spinning as he stood again and looked down over the lights coming on in the city below. He didn't have to go back and check any of his folders, the contents of his briefcase. He'd memorized most of that long ago anyway.

One of the most perplexing aspects of the crime scene investigation into Bree's death had been its inability to produce even a shred of physical evidence to tie any suspect to events in this room, on this balcony. And now Hardy understood why that had been.

Fabric wash.

No trace of fabric on the railing.

David Glenn, the building superintendent, remembered him and said he could come in, but they had to keep it short. Glenn had to keep working. His friends would be showing up any time for cards and Monday night football and if the food wasn't laid out, the shit hit the fan.

So they went to the clean, brightly lit kitchen where Glenn continued to arrange the cold cuts and cheeses, the breads and pickles and condiments. Hardy, who by now had pretty much given up on the idea that he'd ever eat regularly again, stood by the counter and tried not to notice the food.

'I don't know exactly,' Glenn was saying. Hardy had asked him how many people resided in the building, and if Glenn was familiar with all of them. 'There's only a couple of places – the Beaumonts and then the Mahmoutis on four – that have kids. Then mostly couples, three or four singles. Say forty, give or take, altogether.'

'Full-time tenants?'

'Well.' Glenn studied an olive and popped it into his mouth. 'Owners. I told you before. Some of these people I never see.'

'Never?'

Glenn considered. 'Almost, some of them. I could pass them on the street.'

'How can that be?'

'Easy, really. The place is designed for privacy. You got your parking space under the building. You take the elevator to your room. Some units, nobody's ever home. You ask me, nobody lives there, but we get the checks. Couple of them are companies. You know, hold the places for their executives when they're in town.' He must have seen Hardy eyeing the food. 'Hey, you hungry? You want a bite?'

'That's OK, thanks. Do you know who the companies are offhand?'

'Sure. There's just two of 'em. Standard Warehousing – I think they're out of Phoenix. And some Russians. Diamond merchants, they say. Talk about never here.'

'So, other than those, how many units don't have regular tenants?'

He chewed another olive. 'It's not something I give much thought to. Maybe two, I'd say, maybe three.'

'Is one of them nine oh two?'

He stopped chewing, stopped fussing with the food, and gave Hardy his full attention. 'Is this still about Bree?'

Hardy nodded. 'Would nine oh two have a balcony directly under hers?'

A slow nod. 'Yeah. All the twos are the back units. Rita Browning.'

398

'And who is she? Do you know her?'

'Not from Eve.' He shook his head. 'She's one of 'em.'

The last person Hardy wanted to see was Abe Glitsky.

And now, carrying a brown paper bag, here he was, being shown into the Solarium by one of Freeman's young associates. Aside from Hardy and Freeman, two other associates labored at the table drawing up subpoenas for the hearing in Braun's courtroom the next morning.

Freeman whistled happily, tonelessly, annoyingly, but none of the worker bees joined in. This was not volunteer overtime. Freeman had knocked on office doors, interrupting, recruiting. And they'd barely begun – after the subpoenas were prepared, they were going to serve them well into the night.

'We need to talk,' the lieutenant said.

Hardy gestured apologetically to the people working for him. 'Sorry,' he said. 'Five minutes.'

Glitsky wasn't so sure. He faced down the impatient stares and responded calmly. 'Maybe a little more.'

The frustrated comments of the young associates were not quite inaudible as they'd trudged up the stairs. Hardy closed his office door behind them, and turned on the lights.

Glitsky wasted no time. 'We're being set up.'

As he explained it, Hardy went over and sat down heavily on the couch. His papers and research materials were still spread all over the coffee table in front of him, but they seemed somehow unimportant anymore – old news, irrelevant.

Kind of like himself.

'From what I can gather,' Glitsky concluded, 'the DA's new theory is that we're running a coverup, protecting Ron Beaumont. You're his attorney, I'm your friend. We're all going to make a lot of money on Bree's insurance.'

'That'll be fun,' Hardy said grimly, 'when that happens.'

'I think so, too.' Glitsky wasn't smiling either. 'I hear you're pretty strapped for cash. I wouldn't even put it past you to burn down your house. How about that?'

'Just as a stop-gap measure before I collect on Bree.' It was a small relief to understand the grilling he'd taken with the fire inspectors that afternoon. Somebody had pointed in his direction as the arsonist, and now he knew who it was. 'This boy Scott Randall is a menace, Abe. You put him with Pratt and they start doing the tango together – watch out.'

'I'm watching. But they do have me thinking I've got to release the information about Griffin and Canetta being tied to Bree Beaumont.'

'Why is that?'

'To prove that . . .'

'You're trying to find who killed them? What do they have on you? What *could* they have on you?'

'I haven't arrested Beaumont.'

'You know where he is?'

'No.'

Hardy almost laughed. 'Well, there you go. That's a pretty good reason.'

'Yeah, but they're getting me on appearance. They cast Ron as the obvious suspect and I'm not looking for him. I'm covering for him.'

'You're looking at the facts instead. How about that? That's how it's supposed to work.'

'I know. I know.' Glitsky heaved a great sigh. 'You're right.'

'Not often enough,' Hardy said, 'but every once in a while and this is one of those times.' Although this was pure bravado.

In fact, the situation was worse than Glitsky suspected. Would anyone – Randall or Pratt or the internal affairs people – believe that Hardy had known of Ron Beaumont's whereabouts and hadn't told his friend the lieutenant? It was unlikely.

Further, if Hardy did tell Glitsky where Ron was now – and he had no intention on that score – what was his friend supposed to do? Become an accessory to the federal crime of kidnapping? Place Hardy under arrest? Or – even if Hardy

could somehow downplay what he'd done with Cassandra –
was Glitsky supposed to put Ron into the system, the very
result Hardy had struggled to avoid at such great cost?

He couldn't tell him. There was no way.

But by not telling him, he was leaving Glitsky vulnerable
to the charges that Randall and Pratt were asserting against
him, and that could cost him his job, his credibility, his honor.

'What?' Glitsky asked.

'Nothing. I don't know. Maybe an idea.' Hardy pretended
to search through the pages laid out on the table in front of
him. 'Here,' he said, 'right here. Bree's funeral.'

'What about it?'

Smoothly deceptive, hating himself for what he had to do,
he began to walk Glitsky through it. He said – it had just
occurred to him – that maybe Ron had an alibi for the time of
Griffin's death after all. Maybe the priest at – what church was
it now? St Catherine's? – maybe he'd been with Ron for most
of the day, or at least some reasonable portion of it, the
important times, taking care of the myriad details.

Abe remembered, didn't he? When his wife Flo had died,
he'd been at the synagogue from early morning until late in
the day. Had anybody ever checked with Ron what he'd done?
It was, after all, his sister's funeral.

'What do you mean, sister?'

Hardy felt the blood drain out of his face. 'Did I say
"sister"? I meant his wife. His wife's funeral. The point is, if
Ron's got an alibi for Griffin, he didn't kill Bree, did he? If
you got that, you rub it in Randall's face that you're not
covering up anything. Why doesn't he get out of your way and
let you do your damn job?'

Sitting on the corner of Hardy's desk, Glitsky made a swift
decision and pulled the phone over. 'Does it have the number
there? St Catherine's.'

It did, and when five minutes later he replaced the receiver,
the lieutenant was close to actually smiling, the scar between
his lips standing out white. 'Everything should be that easy,'

he said. 'Ron was with the priest all day. His kids. A couple of other people.'

'That's what it sounded like.' Hardy feigned satisfaction, leaned back in the couch, and broke his own smile. 'That's great.'

'It's at least good.' Glitsky didn't skip a beat. 'So that brings us,' he said, 'back to Baxter Thorne, who as you point out is one slick—'

He was interrupted by a knock on the door. Hardy got up to answer it. David Freeman stood in the hallway, hands in his pockets. 'Five minutes are up,' he said pointedly.

'One more,' Glitsky said.

Freeman looked at him, nodded, and came back to Hardy. 'If nobody's left down there when you make it back, don't blame me.'

'I'll be right there. Promise.'

Freeman shrugged – he'd tried – and started back down the stairs. Hardy turned back to Abe. 'You heard that,' he said.

'OK.' Glitsky handed the paper bag he'd been carrying over to Hardy. 'More stuff for your private collection. Photos from Griffin's car, the back seat, and what they'd tagged earlier. Only the so-called significant stuff is inventoried, but you can check the photos. Canetta. Couple of interview transcripts you might have missed.

'Also, Kerry does have a Glock. It's where he said it was and hasn't been fired since it was last cleaned – my guess is maybe a year, maybe never. Of course, he wouldn't have had to fire it if he pointed it convincingly enough.

'Finally, I know you're wanted down below, but here's the short version on Thorne. You're going to want to know, trust me.' When he finished with the damning but completely unprovable information on the gasoline and one of Hardy's elephants in Thorne's coat pocket, Hardy asked if they had found any evidence of his connection to SKO, to the MTBE dump, or any other terrorist acts.

The answer was no, but Glitsky was pulling another warrant

402

tomorrow, sending a couple of teams of search and cyber specialists back to the apartment and to the FMC offices. It was going to be the full press, with full phone-record followups and data searches for palimpsest disks, forensics teams.

'Where are you getting the staff?' Hardy asked. 'I thought you had seven new homicides, no troops.'

'I'm reassigning people,' he said simply. They started back toward the stairway. 'It's a new management tool I'm working on, called do what your boss asks and see if it improves your life.'

'I like it,' Hardy said.

'Me, too. I think it's going to work. And in case it doesn't,' he said, 'there's always the FBI.'

As it turned out, in the Solarium no one had gone home, although Hardy's return to the conference room didn't occasion the warmest reception he'd ever encountered. Still, the guys finished the work and left the office, spreading out to deliver the bad news to Kerry, Valens, Pierce, Thorne, David Glenn. Everyone Hardy could think of.

After much debate, Hardy and Freeman decided to serve both Randall and Pratt with subpoenas as well. They would have to appear in Judge Braun's court for Hardy's hearing, and wouldn't that just fry them?

He wasn't sure he would call all of these people as witnesses – or even most of them. But he wanted to keep his options open, and the turns in this case had surprised him often enough already. He was damned if he was going to be taken unawares in court.

This strategy, though, wasn't without some peril. The shotgun approach was an abuse of the subpoena power and might even earn Hardy a reprimand from the state bar, a contempt citation of his own, but he was beyond those considerations anymore. If his strategy failed, contempt would be the least of his problems.

And then, finally, at a little after nine, even Freeman packed up and went home, leaving him alone again up in his office, his pages spread out before him, his mind numbed by the gravity of his decisions, the impossibility of what he was considering.

If Ron's got an alibi for Griffin, he didn't kill Bree, did he?

Hardy's own words to Glitsky came back to torment him. He'd used them earlier to convince himself, believing them absolutely. It was so logical that it had to be true – Griffin was investigating Bree's death and Griffin had been killed. Same with Canetta. Therefore they were all, somehow, connected.

Except if they weren't.

Except if Carl Griffin, in the course of poking into lives as he did, had discovered an unpleasant truth about the last documented man to have seen him alive – Baxter Thorne. And except if Phil Canetta, stumbling upon the Thorne/Valens arrangement after he'd left Hardy and Freeman on Saturday night, had gone alone after the glory – to deliver a cop killer to all the suits downtown in homicide. And he'd underestimated his man.

Thorne.

A dangerous, decisive, quietly confident man of action, already armed with Griffin's gun, his adrenalin high from torching Hardy's house. Or had that been when he was feeling truly invincible, after he'd killed Canetta?

And that, of course, left Bree. And another killer entirely.

David Glenn's friends had begun to arrive. He said he wanted to help Hardy with 902, but he couldn't just let him in to a tenant's apartment. He could be fired for that. Why didn't Hardy just come back with the lieutenant, with a warrant, as he had before?

But again, agonizingly, Hardy couldn't come to Glitsky. And the reason was more personal, more compelling than anything else he was likely to encounter.

It was Frannie.

404

If Rita Browning – the invisible Rita Browning – was another of Ron Beaumont's credit card identities, if Griffin had discovered the Movado watch in 902 and not in Bree's apartment after all . . .

Hardy could not let Glitsky get to Ron. There could be no arrest, no police interrogation. Because if Ron continued to deny any involvement in the murder – and there was little doubt that is what he would of – then Frannie would always believe him. Worse, she would also believe that the system had betrayed Ron. Her friend Abe had betrayed her.

And her husband, too.

So if Ron had killed Bree after all, Glitsky wouldn't be any help – he couldn't be any part of it.

Ron would have to say it himself. In front of Frannie. In open court.

Hardy had to leave here, go see his children, make sure Cassandra was safe. Slumped, nearly reclining on the couch, he held his right hand over his eyes, shielding them from the overheads. His left hand fell on the photos Glitsky had left with him – extreme close-ups of the items under the back seat of Carl Griffin's car. Then there were the written forms – Canetta's autopsy report, *his* car. Interviews, interrogations.

Forcing himself up, he carried all the stuff over to his desk and went down the hall to throw some water in his face. When he returned, he had a moment of indecision – there was no chance that he could analyse any significant portion of all this material. What was the point of even starting?

But this, he knew, was the devil.

So he began, but after a quick scan knew that he wasn't equipped now to see anything in the photos of the junk, food wrappers, and French fries that had been under the back seat of Griffin's car. He'd try again in the morning, but expected nothing. Instead, he turned to the tapes, putting one of the micro-cassettes into his hand-held machine.

He listened to an understandably impatient but finally cooperative Jim Pierce talking in his office with Vince

Coleman – again. Next was Glitsky, Hardy, Kerry, and Valens from last night.

Hardy realized that this case – these cases? – must have gotten inside Glitsky as well. He'd put a rush on getting copies made of everything he'd delivered to Hardy, and then sat on his people to make sure it all got done.

Canetta's autopsy, especially. The morgue was backed up with bodies, but the coroner did his work on Canetta first. Hardy realized grimly, though, that this might not have been Glitsky's influence after all, but a final show of respect for a policeman killed in the line of duty.

He'd been at it for over an hour and the effects of the cold-water splash had long since worn off. And here before him now was the technical sheet from the autopsy of Phil Canetta. Entry wounds, exit wounds. A fresh wave of exhaustion rolled over him and he closed his eyes against it.

And against the other painful reality – if he hadn't recruited Canetta, the man would still be alive. The image floated up at him – Canetta enjoying the hell out of his mortadella sandwich just a couple of days before, his cigar on Saturday night at Freeman's. The sergeant had been very much alive – in tune with tastes, buffeted by the storms of love, hamstrung by his responsibilities. So much like Hardy, and now in a day gone to dirt.

Clothing. Powder burns. Next to the medical/chemical analysis of sugars, starches, and carbon compounds, someone from the coroner's office – maybe under Glitsky's questioning – had written down in the margin the layman's version of Canetta's stomach contents. Cop food. His last fast-food burger with a coffee and a candy bar – chocolate, beef, potato, almond, bread, pickle. Hardy passed over it, and went on to blood levels for alcohol, nicotine . . .

He closed his eyes and saw Canetta's face again on the bench in Washington Square, his eyes lit up with the memory of Bree Beaumont, the simple joy in his deli sandwich.

Enough enough enough.

He flipped desultorily through the rest of the pile, which seemed to go on and on. His office closed in around him, and he shut his eyes again, just for a second. Then, starting awake, realized that he must have dozed. Still, he couldn't quit. He didn't know yet . . .

Frannie, still in jail . . .

He turned another page, trying to will himself to focus. It was no use. He could barely make out even the letters, and those he saw formed words that had lost all meaning.

PART FOUR

37

Hardy tasted turpentine in the coffee. At the kitchen table – showered, shaved, and dressed – he added more sugar and turned a page of the morning paper.

It was six a.m. He had returned to the Cochrans' at a little after eleven. All three of the children and both adults had still been awake. There might have been giggling in the background, but the atmosphere in the house was as carefree as an operating room.

By two, after five increasingly firm visits from the adults, the kids stopped making noise. Hardy, on the couch in the living room, heard the clock chime the hour at least twice after that.

Now he rubbed at his eyes, trying to get the salt out of them. The sugar didn't improve the java and he set the mug down and massaged his right temple, which throbbed dully.

It was election day. The articles contained few surprises. The MTBE poisoning and resultant scare – as well as his opponent's lame-brained response to it – had given Damon Kerry a last-minute three-point boost in the polls and he was now truly the front-runner by a nose. The *Chronicle* recommended him.

Hardy was gratified to see that Baxter Thorne's libel threats didn't appear to hold much water with Jeff Elliot. The reporter's 'Citytalk' column didn't directly accuse Thorne of anything, but did manage to present a litany of facts in a way that led to some unflattering conclusions. The column promised an ongoing investigation.

Suddenly Vincent materialized at his elbow. His pajamas were a replica of Mark McGwire's Cardinals uniform. His step-cut hair was a shade darker than his sister's, but still in the general category of strawberry blond. His ears stuck out and the face, except for Frannie's nose, was Hardy's exactly. 'Do you have a headache? You're rubbing your head.'

Hardy drew him close, mussed the hair. 'Hey, guy. What are you doing up so early?'

'It's not early.'

'Well, it's not late, and you didn't get to sleep till almost two o'clock.'

'That wasn't me,' Vincent said. 'That was the girls. I went right to sleep after just a little whispering. Dad?'

'What?'

'I've got a question.'

Hardy longed for the day when Vincent would simply ask a question without announcing his intention to ask one, but he could only sigh now. 'Shoot,' he said.

'How come Max wasn't invited, too? How come it's always the Beck who gets her friends over and I get stuck with all the girls and then they don't want to play with me?'

'That was one question?' But Hardy pushed his chair back and pulled Vincent on to his lap. The sleepy boysmell still clung to his son and Hardy held him close for as long as he thought he could get away with it, maybe two seconds. 'I've been missing you, you know that?'

'I miss you, too,' Vincent said perfunctorily. 'But you're real busy lately,' he added, parroting the excuse Frannie had no doubt always supplied. 'We know that. But Mom, I *really* miss her. And you said she's coming back today. It's today, right?'

Hardy tried to ignore the stab that his son's answer had given him. 'That's the plan,' he said. Then slipped and added, 'I hope so.'

Vincent's face immediately clouded. 'But she might not? I thought you said it was today.'

'It is today. Don't worry.'

'Then why'd you say you hoped so?'

'Shh. Let's not wake up anybody else, OK.'

'But why'd you say that?'

'I don't know, Vin. I guess because I want it so bad, just like you do. It was just a figure of speech. She'll be home today.' He almost promised, but thought better of it. A promise, especially to his child, was sacred.

The boy's eyes brightened. 'Home? You mean like our real home? How can we do that if it was all burned up?'

Hardy rubbed his son's back and shook his head, framing his reply carefully. 'Home isn't just a house, Vin. It's where we're all together.'

'But so where are we going to live then?'

'I don't know for sure, bud. We'll find a place soon while we get our house fixed up again, and we can stay here with Grandma and Papa Ed in the meantime. You don't have to worry about that, OK?'

'OK.'

'Promise?'

Vincent shrugged. 'Sure.' If Dad said he didn't have to worry, that was the end of it. It was going to be all right.

Please God, Hardy prayed, don't let his trust in me be misplaced.

'So why couldn't Max come?' Vincent was back on his original track.

'You want to know the real reason? He didn't sleep enough the night before, so his dad thought it wouldn't be a good idea.'

Vincent considered this for a moment. 'His dad's nice,' he said simply.

Hardy could only nod dumbly. Just what he needed – another unsolicited testimonial on Ron Beaumont from his innocent, good-hearted son. 'That's what I hear,' he said. 'How do you know him?'

'School. He helps in class, sometimes with yard duty. He's nice,' he repeated. 'Is your head hurting?'

'It must be,' Hardy said. 'I keep rubbing it, don't I?'

Hardy had gotten into the habit of leaving the house before

413

the crazy rush of getting the kids ready for school kicked in. He'd given the alternative a try for several years, but the routine made him nuts. He'd get cranky and take that with him to work. It affected his performance, his job. And without that, where would they be?

For the last couple of years he'd wake up early, have his coffee and read the paper. He'd go in and kiss Frannie awake. Sometimes they'd talk – logistics. Then he'd shake the kids and be out the door.

So he'd missed the rite of passage, but sometime in the past few months, Vincent had learned how to make breakfast. French toast, pancakes – 'Just the mix, though. I don't do it from scratch' – scrambled eggs, oatmeal. 'You just tell me what and I'll do it.'

'You don't need any help?'

The look. 'Da-ad.'

He watched his boy adjust the flame under the pan, throw in some butter, expertly crack five eggs into a bowl and whip them up. Hardy tried to remember when he'd begun making his own breakfasts – he must have been about Vincent's age, but somehow he'd never assumed his younger child could be that competent. Not yet. Not for a long time. He was still a baby.

Vincent lowered the heat a fraction. 'I like them a little runny, but I can take mine off first if you want them cooked dry. That's how Mom and the Beck like 'em. Dry. But you know that. Mom says you always used to cook breakfast, so you'd know, wouldn't you?'

'Yeah,' Hardy said hoarsely. 'Sure.'

At the stove, Vincent turned at the tone. 'Hey,' he said softly. 'You OK, Dad?'

As the house started to wake up, Vincent went back to torment the girls and Hardy took his briefcase back to the dining room, where he could spread out a bit. He heard Erin in the kitchen, but she didn't come around the corner to wish him a good morning.

The photos were not so daunting this morning – the items from Griffin's back seat in sharp color focus – a Juicy Fruit gum wrapper. Two bullets. A ziploc bag, snack size, crumbs inside. Parking stub, Downtown Center Garage, dated 7/22/95 – three years ago! Assorted coins worth one dollar thirty-two. An Almond Joy, which Hardy bet would be pretty stale by now.

He forced himself to continue, but was getting convinced that there wasn't going to be anything here. It was a garbage can. He flipped the photos and the rest weren't any better – more stuff from the body of the car proper. Gilt paper with traces of chocolate – more candy. Several plastic lids from the tops of coffee cups and soft drinks. Sunflower-seed shells.

Glitsky had also thoughtfully provided a copy of the autopsy report on Griffin, as well as a final inventory of the personal belongings he carried on his body – a ring of keys, a Swiss Army knife, a half pack of Life Savers, two ballpoint pens, an empty ziploc bag.

It all looked like nothing to Hardy. Beyond that, he was reasonably confident that the lab had analysed every item listed here for fingerprints, oils, fluids, and whatever other tests they ran to find or eliminate suspects.

The following pages contained the same relative information from Phil Canetta and his vehicle and, aside from demonstrating that he was far more personally fastidious than Carl Griffin had been, provided nothing that Hardy could use.

Rebecca stuck her head out of the kitchen door, lit up in a smile. 'Oh, there you are. I'm so glad you're still here.' She crossed over and gave him a kiss on the cheek, snuggled up against him.

He kissed her back. 'I'm glad I'm still here too. Where's Cassandra?'

She remained plastered against him. 'She forgot to bring clothes, you know, but I told her she could borrow some of mine. She wanted to make sure that was OK.'

'I'm sure that would be fine.'

'Is she going to school? 'Cause she's missed the last few days, you know.' Rebecca lowered her voice. 'She's a little nervous, I think.'

'About what? Missing school?'

She shook her head. 'She's worried she's going to have to move. She said you were helping them, but she's still worried.'

'She told you about that?'

'Dad,' Rebecca said seriously. 'We tell each other everything. She is like my *best* friend.' She checked to see that they were still alone. 'She's all worried about something else, too. Do you know Marie?'

Hardy nodded. 'I met her yesterday. She seems like a nice lady.'

'Well, why's her dad with her when her mom only died like a month ago?'

'Maybe they're just friends.'

Rebecca's expression was startlingly adult. 'Dad. I'm sure. Cass thinks maybe her dad was already having an affair, before her mom died. She thinks that would be awful.'

'Well . . .'

She whispered urgently. 'You and Mom aren't with other people, too, are you?'

Hardy pulled her close to him. 'No, hon. We're only with each other. Promise. And we're going to stay that way.'

'Cross your heart?'

He made an X on his chest. 'Hope to die.' He gave her a pat. 'OK, now you'd better go tell her she can wear your clothes or you're all going to be late for school.'

'Oh!' She all but ran to deliver the news.

Hardy's eyes followed her out of the room. Then he glanced down at the pages on the table in front of him. Casually, he flipped through Canetta's autopsy. All the technical minutiae of violent death, as it had been with Griffin – state of rigor, body temperature, contents of stomach, angle of bullet entry. It was all too familiar and too ugly.

He picked up the pages and tossed them back into his

briefcase, and closed it over them. He stood, took a deep breath, and went into the kitchen to face the chill.

They all got to Merryvale a few minutes early, and Hardy went in, out of Cassandra's presence, to explain the situation to Theresa Wilson. Lying, he told her that he expected and had been instructed to tell her that both Beaumont children would be back in school tomorrow. Since she and Hardy had last talked, he'd been retained by Mr Beaumont and they'd been watching Cassandra while a few last-minute legal maneuvers were carried out.

Max was staying with some other friends out of town and should be back in school by the next day. Hardy was sorry for any inconvenience, grateful for her forebearance, but Ron had been afraid of the police jumping to the wrong conclusions – as they had with Hardy's own wife – and he hadn't wanted to subject his children to that trauma and upheaval.

'I understand,' Mrs Wilson told him from behind the doors of her office. 'I might have done the same thing myself. How is Frannie holding up, by the way? I read that she might be getting out of . . . her situation today.'

Hardy, going for the Academy Award for Best Actor, conveyed that he wasn't happy about what had taken place with his wife, but he was no longer worried. Everything was under control. 'I'm going down to pick her up right now,' he said.

'Well, then, you mustn't let me keep you. God speed.'

Hardy walked across the parking lot and stopped by the door to his car. Back toward the school, cars were still pulling up and letting out other children. The fog, he realized, had only made a token effort this morning, and now there was even a hint of sunshine in the sky. He made out a small knot of kids standing by a bicycle rack, his daughter was among them. And Cassandra Beaumont.

Hidden in plain sight.

38

An objective observer would have concluded that the two men standing on the curb of Church Street were business associates working out some tedious details in their latest deal. Both were close to the same age, in good physical shape, and conservatively dressed in business suits – one of them an Italian double-breasted with a deep olive tone, the other a Brooks Brothers charcoal with a microscopic maroon pin-stripe.

A closer look would uncover a different truth. Both of the strong, perhaps even handsome faces were landscapes of strain and fatigue. And the deal was not going well.

Listen:

'I want to see her.'

'Not until after you've testified.'

'How's this? I won't testify until I do.'

Pin-stripe smiled coldly. 'Maybe you're forgetting that I've still got her. It's pretty straightforward. You want to get your daughter back, I want my wife. We trade. That's the deal. That's the only deal.'

'You son of a bitch.'

'Maybe. But at least an honest son of a bitch.'

'What does that mean?'

'It means I haven't lied to you.'

'As though I have?'

'Do you think I'm an idiot? Are you telling me you wouldn't have packed them both up and been gone when I got here this morning?' A pause. 'That's what I thought, so don't shit me. I did what I had to do. Your daughter's safe.'

'Except for the trauma you've—'

'Not even that. She's not even going to know any of this happened. Not unless you force me.'

The Italian suit walked off a few steps and the other followed.

'I'm the only friend you've got. Don't you understand that by now? Nobody's going to touch you until you tell your story.'

He whirled around. 'And after that?'

'After that, if you're telling the truth, you've got nothing to worry about.'

'*If* I'm telling the truth? I am telling the truth.'

A long silence. Finally the man in pin-stripes stepped off the curb, around to the driver's side door of a late model Honda. 'Get in the car.'

With over an hour to kill before Marian Braun's courtroom was called into session, Hardy didn't want to push his luck by entering the Hall of Justice. If he and his prisoner should run across Scott Randall or Peter Struler, he considered it a dead certainty that somehow they would get Ron into custody. Hardy would be powerless to stop them if they initiated the booking process under whatever guise.

Lou the Greek's was dark and private enough. Few if any of the morning drinkers were going to look up and recognize anybody. Most of them had personal, more desperate agendas of their own for being there at that hour and one of them – David Freeman – was working. He was on the first stool at the end of the bar, just as he and Hardy had decided the night before.

A couple of steaming mugs of coffee rested untouched on the table between Ron and Hardy.

'Rita Browning? Where did you get that?' Ron was shaking his head, apparently mystified. He faced the back wall in the farthest booth from the front door. 'No,' he said.

Hardy was across from him, where he could see anyone who entered. 'You're asking me to believe she wasn't one of your credit card names?'

'I don't care what you believe, but that's right. Rita Browning?' There wasn't any humor in the moment, but Ron almost chuckled. 'Look, I might not be the most masculine guy in the world, but do you really think I could pass as a Rita Browning?'

This, Hardy had to say, was a reasonable point.

Ron amplified it. 'And what was I supposed to use it for?'

'To pay the mortgage on another apartment in your building.'

An expression of apparently real perplexity. 'Which one?'

'Nine oh two.'

Ron thought about it for second, and finally reached for one of the coffee mugs and took a sip. 'And why would I want to do that – have another apartment in my own building?'

It was a good question, but Hardy believed he had a good answer. 'So if you had a problem just like the one you're experiencing now, you'd have a place to hide out for a while, to take the kids until you could relocate.'

'Well, as you say, I'm having this problem now. You'll notice I didn't take them there. Doesn't that tell you anything?'

Hardy hated to acknowledge it, but it did.

'This is God's truth. I've never heard of Rita Browning in my life. She owns nine oh two?'

'Maybe. That's the name on the mailbox, on her checks. David Glenn – your supe? – he says he's never seen her.'

'How long has she been there?'

'Five years, a couple of months longer than you have as a matter of fact.'

'David came on after us,' Ron said helpfully. 'A couple of years later, I think. It's not impossible, I suppose, that he hasn't met her . . . She makes her mortgage payments for the year every January.'

'For the year?' Ron went quiet while he considered this. 'You think I've been paying for two apartments in that building for five years?'

'Let's say I don't think there's a Rita Browning. All your aka's have the initials RB—'

'Yeah, but I'll tell you something about those accounts, those lines of credit. If you studied them at all, you realized I never carried any balance in them. They were in case things here went to hell. A thirty-day parachute, maybe forty-five, to give me time to start out someplace else. That's all. Just out of curiosity, though, how in the world did you find out about those?'

'Bree's files from Caloco. Somebody over there shipped them to the DA to make it look like you'd premeditated this and planned your escape.' Hardy noted Ron's reaction – unfeigned, frightened. 'I didn't see any Rita Browning in those records, it's true. But I don't think anyone's living in nine oh two.'

'Can you find out? Have somebody check it?'

'Sure, eventually. With a warrant. They could take the place apart and might get lucky if that's where Bree . . . if that's where it happened. But any of that will take time and' – Hardy consulted his watch – 'that's in short supply right about now. We're in court in forty-five minutes.'

Ron swirled his mug a couple of times. His eyes met Hardy's. 'Bree,' he said.

'That's what I'm thinking.'

'She set up my accounts for me. It would have been cake to do one for herself.'

'Even if this one wasn't a credit card?'

Ron lifted his shoulders. 'Same thing, basically. Bogus numbers, false identity. There's nothing simpler, especially if your base account is a trillion-dollar multinational like Caloco. Banks are lining up to help you out.'

'But what would she have needed another apartment for?'

The answer came to both of them as Ron spoke. 'Love.'

'She met men there?'

'Why not? It's perfect when I think about it – discreet, close by, no hassles . . .'

'But for this, for the mortgage, there had to be real money somewhere. Did Bree make enough—'

421

Ron was saying no before Hardy finished. 'Up until this year, she made a lot, but not enough for that.'

'How much would it be?'

'In our building, the one-bedrooms go for like four fifty. Our place was seven and a half.'

Hardy whistled.

'Tell me about it. But she got enough bonuses to just cover us.' He hesitated. 'We're still house poor, to tell you the truth. And after she left Caloco . . .' He stopped, and stalled with the coffee. 'You might as well know. Maybe you do already. We were going to have to move.'

'And did you fight about that?'

Ron sighed wearily. 'I'll tell you, by the end, we fought about everything. It was terrible.' He hung his head for a long moment, then looked up. 'I'm just so tired.' His voice was almost gone. 'So incredibly tired.'

Hardy leaned over the table. 'Did you kill her, Ron? Did you kill Bree, maybe by mistake?'

Ron raised his head, his eyes reflecting the depth of his resignation and loss. 'You know, I didn't. She was my sister. I loved her. The kids loved her – she was their mother. I never would have even hit her, much less killed her. I didn't kill her. I really didn't. Even by mistake.' His hands imploringly crossed the table. 'I wasn't even there. I wasn't even there.'

Even with Freeman making sure at the bar, it made Hardy nervous as hell to leave Ron alone at the Greek's. He told him to have himself another cup of coffee or something and be at the back door to the Hall, by the entrance to the jail, at nine twenty. Hardy was marginally confident that he'd boxed him in adequately. Having come this far, with Cassandra held hostage, Ron wouldn't run now.

He hoped.

It was unusual, but Hardy had persuaded Glitsky to use some juice with the bailiffs so that they would allow Frannie to wear a respectable outfit for the hearing. So he had to get it delivered to her in time for her to change from her jumpsuit. Protocol, appearances, details.

But he couldn't have it both ways. She could take the time to change into pleasant civilian clothes that would subliminally humanize her to Marian Braun, or they could take a last few tense, private moments together in the attorney's visiting room.

There was no choice. After she was free, they'd have time to visit. Time for everything.

It left him with nearly a half hour and he was tempted to go back to Lou's and sit with Ron. But no. He'd worked that through. Ron would be at the back door at the appointed time. He had no other option.

Setting his heavy briefcase on the hard wooden bench just inside the entrance to the jail, he once again unsnapped the clasps, once again lifted his pages into his lap. He'd been through every scrap he carried at least once, except the final pages that Glitsky had delivered last night.

But now, unexpectedly, maybe he had just enough time to get through the rest of it – not that he thought he would discover anything. But if nothing else, he prided himself on his thoroughness. He wouldn't lose this thing out of sloppiness or fatigue. He would be prepared for his hearing when he walked into the courtroom. Scott Randall wasn't going to surprise him with something he should have read, should have noticed, should have figured out.

So he started where he'd left off – Canetta's autopsy.

And this time, he saw it. Went back and reviewed Griffin. Crossed the corridor to the coroner's and made sure. And then, finally, knowing where else to look, went back and found it.

Glitsky was in his office when Hardy called upstairs. He had sent his task forces out on Thorne's search warrant, which left him free until after the hearing, which he would be attending.

Hardy didn't want to say anything over the phone. He'd see Glitsky in five minutes and if they could get any privacy, he'd tell him then. In the meanwhile, they'd meet at the back door to the Hall.

As Hardy came out of the jail, he gave a surreptitious nod to Freeman, now loitering in the corridor that led to the morgue, and continued to the employees' back door to the Hall. The plan was that Ron and Hardy were going to take the little-used rear stairway to the second floor and make a break for Braun's courtroom, Department 24, when they got out into the hallway.

Glitsky opened the door for them. When Hardy introduced who they would be escorting, however, he could tell that it wasn't a pleasant surprise. But the lieutenant seemed to accept the situation, silently leading the way up the stairs until they reached the landing before the door into the main hallway. When they got there, though, he turned and faced them both. 'You guys just run into each other out front? Was that it?'

'Not exactly.' Unruffled, Hardy had guessed this moment was coming. He was ready. 'This time yesterday I had no idea where he was.'

'How about when I came to your office last night as a courtesy? The last time we talked, say?'

'Was he a suspect then?'

'Close enough, and you . . .'

'By the time you left, though? Honestly?'

The scar was tight on Glitsky's face, but Hardy had him. He kept pushing. 'OK, he's not a suspect. Had you ever seen him before now, a minute ago? Talked to him?'

'You know I haven't,' he growled.

'Right. Listen to me. And you had no idea that I had had any communication with him, ever, did you?'

'So what?'

'So when our dear pal Scott Randall asks you, maybe under oath, whether you have colluded with me and/or Ron here in any way, what are you going to be able to say?'

A vein stood out on the side of Glitsky's forehead, but

gradually his expression relaxed, though not quite into calm serenity. 'For the record, I still don't like it.'

'OK, noted,' Hardy responded crisply. 'But also for the record, you're going to thank me.'

Glitsky glared another second or two, then turned and pulled open the door. The three men stepped out into the open hallway together just as Randall, Struler, Pratt, and several of her minions rounded the corner from the elevator in a phalanx. The two groups nearly ran into one another.

'Well, well, well.' Randall made no effort to disguise his reaction. In a voice dripping with disdain, he adopted a theatrical tone. 'Lieutenant Glitsky, Mr Hardy, the elusive Mr Beaumont. How interesting that you should all be arriving together here at court.' He turned to Pratt, a portrait of smug satisfaction. 'Case study, Sharron,' he said. 'Exactly what we expected.'

Normally, in the minutes before the ascension of the judge to the bench, courtrooms pulse with a certain energy – attorneys and clients are getting settled at their tables, the clerks and bailiffs knot up, talking shop and trading banter, the court recorder warms up. If there is a jury, its members read the newspapers or study their notes.

In the gallery beyond the bar rail, the spectators and media types, if any, jockey for space with potential witnesses, with friends and relatives of victims or their alleged perpetrators. There is a constant, low hum of many unconnected conversations.

But generally, above it all hovers some small but palpable sense of restraint. Outside in the public hallways, hordes of unwashed and unruly animals often put on their raucous circuses, but once inside the courtroom doors, order often seems to impose itself over those assembled within.

Not this morning, though.

Many of the witnesses Hardy had summoned to this hearing had brought with them reinforcements, and they'd all apparently had time to get to know each other a little, to talk, to vent, finally to boil over.

As soon as Glitsky pushed the door open – Scott Randall and his team of prosecutors sniping behind them all the way – a wave of boisterous anger seemed to break over them. For the first time in his career, Hardy physically had to push his way through a mass of hostile humanity clogging the central aisle. Glitsky stayed with him, holding Ron Beaumont's arm above the elbow, moving them all forward.

Hardy pressed his way through, feeling no need to respond to any of the barbs he was hearing. He was sure that this was a staged demonstration either from Baxter Thorne, whom he recognized leaning against the side wall, or from the Kerry camp. Possibly both.

Scott Randall was a different story. He wasn't anybody's paid actor, and he was righteously angry for having to put up with this frivolous hearing, for being jerked around by an arrogant defense attorney who was probably a criminal himself.

Well, Hardy would deal with Scott Randall when the time came. He'd deal with all of them. He wasn't being drawn into a shouting match with a bunch of enraged witnesses and their friends.

Glitsky got them all through the bar rail and gave the high sign to the bailiffs, who came forward to ensure that the inviolability of the courtroom proper remained intact. David Freeman had somehow already gotten himself seated at the defense table and was watching the proceedings behind him with an amused and tolerant expression. The theatre of the law! He loved it.

'Good morning, Dismas,' he intoned. 'Looks to me like you might just have hit a nerve.'

And at that moment, the blessed voice of the clerk rose above the clamorous din.

'Hear ye, hear ye. Department Twenty-Four of the Superior Court of the city and county of San Francisco, State of

California, is now in session, Judge Marian Braun presiding. All rise.'

Since most of the people assembled were already on their feet, the judge's entrance didn't do much except provide a break in the hubbub. Braun, catching the tenor of what was transpiring below, refrained from taking the bench, instead preferring to remain standing. She reached for her gavel and slammed it several times until the silence was achieved.

Scowling down at her clerk, she whispered sharply. 'Mr Drummond. The members of the gallery will find seating in precisely two minutes, after which I shall return to the bench and mete out consequences to those who are unable to do so.'

When she returned, Braun adjusted her robes and sat. Hardy was next to Freeman at the defense table. Glitsky and Ron Beaumont had retired to directly behind them, the first row of the gallery. Turning in his chair, Hardy recognized Valens and Kerry and they recognized him. If looks could kill . . .

Freeman whispered to Hardy. 'Are all the players here?'

'Except one.'

'Who's that?'

'Jim Pierce,' Hardy replied. 'Caloco.'

'You think he'll show?'

Hardy's face was set. 'He'd better.'

When Braun returned to the bench, only one person remained standing. Sharron Pratt was in the aisle in the center of the gallery area.

'Madame District Attorney. Good morning,' Braun intoned. 'Do you have business before this court?'

'Yes, your honor. May I approach?'

'Mr Hardy has a hearing scheduled. I'm—'

'May I approach to discuss that hearing, your honor?'

Braun frowned at being interrupted. 'All right. Mr Hardy?'

Hardy knew exactly where this was going. After the groundwork he'd laid down which he believed would predispose Braun to a favorable ruling, he had gone a long way toward precipitating it himself by serving his papers on Pratt and Randall. Hardy was, in fact, so primed that he had to work to keep his face straight.

He stood up. 'I have no objection, your honor, but I presume my client is in the holding cell behind your bailiff, and I wonder if the court would call the case and allow her to enter the courtroom at this time, before we take up Ms Pratt's request at sidebar.'

Frannie wore a tailored pair of tan slacks and a dark brown V-necked sweater. The deep-green malachite necklace and tiny matching earrings heightened the beautiful shade of her eyes, and she had pulled the long red hair back, tied it at her neck, and let the rest hang halfway down her back.

When the bailiff opened the door to the holding cell, she stepped out and gave Hardy a nervous, embarrassed smile, then let the bailiff escort her to the defense table, where she sat next to him. He kissed her on the cheek. 'I love you. Don't worry. Everything's going to be all right.'

Then he stood and approached the bench.

Scott Randall got himself insinuated into the proceedings on Pratt's figurative coat-tails, and the two of them now stood before the bench with Hardy and Freeman. Randall was doing the talking, passionate and persuasive as always, and Hardy was content to let him dig a hole as deep as he wanted. Normally, no one would be permitted to discuss the internal workings of the grand jury, but today Randall would have to put his cards on the table to justify continuing Frannie's contempt citation.

'The grand jury is in session in this very building as we speak, your honor, considering evidence surrounding the death of Bree Beaumont as well as those of two policemen who were involved in the investigation into her murder.'

'Two policemen?' Braun, of course, had heard about the deaths of Sergeants Griffin and Canetta, but the news of their connection to this case was clearly a surprise.

428

'Yes, your honor. The state believes that there are three homicides related to the Bree Beaumont case currently before the grand jury. Because the homicide department under the direction of Lieutenant Glitsky has systematically refused to disclose evidence relevant—'

'Your honor.' Hardy was mild. 'This is a *habeas* hearing whose only purpose is to vacate the contempt citation levied against my client. The homicide department's handling of what might be other aspects of this case has no place in this proceeding.'

But Randall wasn't buying that. 'With respect, your honor. No part of this case belongs in this courtroom. This is a matter for the grand jury to decide. We shouldn't even be discussing it outside of the grand jury room.'

Braun's eyes were taking on a telltale flash that Hardy liked to see. 'If you want me to keep someone in jail, Mr Randall, you have to give me a better reason than your say-so.'

'With all due respect, your honor, you need no more reason than the witness refusing to answer material questions.'

Next to Hardy, Freeman's elbow twitched against him, and he cast a quick acknowledging glance at his old ally. They had maneuvered Randall into this spot and now he had just played into their hands, belittling the jurisdiction of Braun's courtroom, to which she would surely take offense.

And she did. Her eyes burned down at the young prosecutor. 'I'll decide what issues and what cases get resolved in my courtroom, Mr Randall. Do you understand that?'

Pratt decided to step in. 'Your honor, perhaps we could adjourn to chambers?'

The judge directed her displeasure toward the DA. 'We've only just gotten started here, Ms Pratt.' She lowered her voice. 'I'm sure you noticed that we've got several important people out there – among them possibly our next governor – and I'm not inclined to take any more of their time than is absolutely necessary. Anything we could say in chambers, we can say right here.'

But Randall, true to form, couldn't seem to let it go and after a short non-verbal exchange with his boss, he piped right up. 'We've got a very unusual set of circumstances here, your honor. I am at this very moment preparing grand jury subpoenas for Mr Hardy and Lieutenant Glitsky to testify on matters related to his case. They themselves may be open to criminal charges.'

Hardy shook his head, derision all over his face, but he remained silent.

'Additionally,' Randall continued, 'the DA's office has repeatedly requested an arrest warrant for Mr Beaumont, who is seated behind us in the courtroom today even as we speak.'

'It ought to be easy to serve the warrant, then,' Braun said drily.

'Except that the warrant is not forthcoming, your honor.'

'And why is that?'

Hardy finally had to say something. 'Because there hasn't been any evidence, your honor.'

'That's ridiculous!' Randall exploded. 'We have more than enough evidence for an indictment.'

'So get one,' Hardy snapped back.

Braun cast a stern eye. 'Counsel will address the court, not each other. Is that clear?' After accepting the nods of apology, Braun softened her tone. 'Now, Mr Randall, correct me if I'm wrong, but Mr Hardy's point seems to me to be well taken. If you have the evidence to indict Mr Beaumont, present it to the grand jury and it will order a warrant issued. That's how it's done. You should know that.'

Pratt spoke up in her assistant's defense. 'He does know it, your honor, but our investigation has been hampered at every turn in this case. Indeed, we believe that Mr Hardy has influenced Lieutenant Glitsky to use his position as head of the homicide department to engage in a systematic coverup of Mr Beaumont's activities.'

Hardy raised his hands theatrically. 'Your honor! This is really beyond the pale.'

But Braun, wanting to hear more, pointed him quiet. 'These are serious charges, Ms Pratt . . .'

Randall took over again. 'Which is why, your honor, we wanted to explore them with the grand jury, with the police department's office of management and control, and with our own department's investigative staff.'

'In other words, Mr Randall, it sounds like you want to do all of this investigating except you either haven't actually done it or you haven't found anything.'

Blindsided, Randall stammered. 'Well, no, your honor, of course not. We have strong evidence—'

Hardy cut him off. 'Your honor, they have nothing.'

'We are developing a case.'

Eyes on Braun, Hardy nevertheless was arguing with Randall. 'And bringing accusations before there is anything to support them.' Now he turned to look up at the judge. 'If I may, your honor, I have a suggestion that relates specifically to the hearing you have granted today, and will also address the very serious issues and charges raised by the district attorney' – he paused long enough to make the point – 'and her staff.'

Braun was getting impatient. She glanced over the lawyers' heads to the restless gallery beyond. This had already taken too much of the court's time, of everyone's time. 'All right, Mr Hardy, let's hear it, but make it fast.'

Hardy took a breath. He was in the grip of high emotion, but it would serve little to play to it. When he finally spoke, his was the voice of reason. 'The gravamen of the contempt charge against my client – the subject of this hearing – is her refusal to disclose to the grand jury information relevant to a murder investigation. I believe we are all in accord here?'

No one objected.

'Both Mr Randall and Ms Pratt have been clear and unambiguous that the information my client refused to disclose bears upon the motive Mr Beaumont may or may not have had to kill his wife. Isn't that correct?'

Neither Pratt nor Randall nodded – their defenses had by now come up – so Hardy decided to drive the point home more forcefully. 'Put another way, if Ron Beaumont didn't kill Bree, whatever secret shared by my client and himself is not the proper concern of the grand jury or their investigation.'

'All right,' Braun said thoughtfully. 'Where is this leading, Mr Hardy?'

'It is leading, your honor, to this. Mr Randall has made the point that the deaths of Sergeants Griffin and Canetta were pursuant to their respective investigations into the murder of Bree Beaumont, and I presume by extension that he concludes that all of these killings were committed by the same individual.'

'That's exactly our contention.' Randall was glad to be able to get in a word, and Hardy was happy to let him do it.

'And it's a reasonable one to which, for purposes of this hearing, you'd be prepared to stipulate,' he said.

Pratt saw the trap closing, and moved to stop it. 'Well, I don't know, your honor. This is a theory we've not yet . . .'

Braun stopped her cold. 'Ms Pratt, I've just heard Mr Randall say that this is *exactly* – his word – what your office believes. More importantly, if memory serves this is the theory upon which you both have based, and raised in open court, your accusations against both Lieutenant Glitsky and Mr Hardy. Now which is it? Did one man commit these murders or not?'

The two prosecutors exchanged glances. Pratt answered. 'That is our belief. Yes, your honor. Subject to contradictory evidence of which we may become aware at a later date.'

'I would think so,' Braun declared. 'Go on, Mr Hardy. You've got my attention.'

'Thank you, your honor. Therefore, it follows that if Mr Beaumont can be shown to be blameless in the deaths of either of the two police officers, it may be assumed that he is likewise blameless in the death of his wife.'

'That's a nice syllogism, Mr Hardy.' Braun remained

tolerant, yet unconvinced. 'But "blameless" is a tall order. Do you mean to say that you can prove he's absolutely innocent of one or more of these killings? Normally, that's why we have jury trials.'

'But we don't get to jury trials, your honor, until there is a grand jury indictment or preliminary hearing to ensure a threshold of sufficient evidence to where a jury might convict. In this case, we don't have that, and yet my client's continued incarceration is based upon Mr Beaumont's presumed guilt, and not his presumed innocence, as the law demands.'

'That's rather elegant, Mr Hardy, but—'

'Your honor, if new and damning evidence about Bree Beaumont's murder comes to light after this hearing, then my client will have the opportunity to testify again before the grand jury about Ron Beaumont. If at that time she declines to answer material questions, she will of course be subject to contempt charges again.'

Just when he might have been about to win one on the legal merits, to take the investigation back to the grand jury and hold Frannie until she decided to talk, Randall opened his mouth again. 'Your honor, with respect, you can't put Mr Beaumont on trial for murder right now in your courtroom.'

Braun's visage was terrifyingly benign. The pupils of her eyes were pinpoints, skewering Scott Randall. 'That's not what I was contemplating, counsellor. Rather, it seems to me that the question is whether, when faced with what you yourself admit would be compelling evidence of Mr Beaumont's innocence of the murder of his wife, you will seek to reinstate Mrs Hardy's incarceration for contempt, which is based upon his guilt. Do I have your argument correctly, Mr Hardy?'

'Perfectly.'

'So, Mr Randall?'

'Yes, your honor?'

'What is your decision?'

'I'm not sure I'm clear on what Mr Hardy is proposing.'

'I presume he is proposing to call some witnesses at this hearing. Am I right, Mr Hardy?'

'Yes, your honor.'

Sharron Pratt was struggling for whatever face she could save. 'And I presume that Mr Hardy proposes to show that Ron Beaumont is factually innocent of one or more of these murders? Is that the case?'

Hardy agreed that it was.

Pratt was thinking fast. On the one hand, she didn't have to reveal what was going on in the grand jury. Since the judge couldn't know what evidence they had, Hardy could never prove here that Ron Beaumont was actually innocent, only that it might be less likely that he was guilty. She could point that out and terminate Hardy's end run right here.

On the other hand, she knew that her office really had nothing. She wanted badly to know what Hardy knew. And the public appearance of reasonableness was increasingly important as the mayor and the media bashed her office.

She decided to let Hardy have his show. And of course, they could cross-examine whoever Hardy intended to call. 'We don't object, your honor, so long as it doesn't take too long.'

'All right,' Braun said. 'Let's get this show on the road.'

39

But Hardy found himself in an unexpected bind. Having convinced the judge and coerced the DA into pushing ahead smartly with his unconventional game plan, now he looked out into the gallery and realized that he had to stall. He had been planning to start with the testimony of Jim Pierce and had assumed that, like the other witnesses he'd served who were now sitting in the gallery, Pierce would show up on time.

While he'd argued with Pratt and Randall during sidebar, he'd expected to turn around when he was finished and see Pierce seated in the gallery. But now it was time to begin and Pierce hadn't yet arrived.

Having gotten to here, he couldn't very well ask Judge Braun for short continuance or even so much as a recess. He was going to have to juggle while doing a tap dance, and could only hope he could keep the balls in the air until it was time for the main event.

'My name is Abraham Glitsky. I hold the rank of Lieutenant in the San Francisco police department, and currently I am the head of the homicide unit.'

'And how long have you held that position?'

'Five years.'

'And before that?'

'Your honor.' Scott Randall was on his feet. 'We all know Lieutenant Glitsky.'

'Is that an objection, counsellor?' Objections, like so much else in a court of law, were part of the orchestrated ballet of justice, and had to be based on deviations from the evidence code. Telling the court that everyone knew Abe Glitsky didn't fall anywhere near that category. But, more, Braun's response reaffirmed Hardy's belief that Scott Randall no longer had any kind of friend on the bench. 'But Mr Hardy,' she added, 'let's move it along.'

'I'm trying to make the court aware of Lieutenant Glitsky's credentials, your honor.'

'All right, but briefly, please.'

It took less than two minutes. Five years lieutenant of homicide, twelve years a homicide inspector, steady rise through the ranks from street cop, through vice, robbery, white collar. Four departmental citations, one medal for valor.

People could always turn bad, of course, but Hardy wanted to show Braun that if someone predicted the next one to do so would be Glitsky, it would be a pretty wild – and bad – guess.

Braun had told him to keep it brief, and that was his intention with Glitsky – put him on the stand, establish him as a good and honest cop, and then see if Randall rose to the bait and tried to take him apart, discrediting himself in the process. 'That's all for this witness,' he said. 'Cross?'

The young prosecutor couldn't wait. 'Yes, I'd say so.' Randall strode up to the witness box and positioned himself squarely in front of Glitsky. 'In your position as head of homicide, lieutenant, were you originally involved with the investigation into the murder of Bree Beaumont?'

'Not in a hands-on way. Only in an administrative capacity.'

Comfortable after years of practice in the witness seat, Glitsky quickly took the opening Randall had provided and outlined his job description – he had a staff of inspectors who reported to him and who worked in coordination with a crime scene investigations unit, forensic specialists, lab technicians, and the city and country coroner to gather and collate evidence on homicides in this jurisdiction.

None of this had anything to do with Ron or Bree Beaumont, and Hardy could never have introduced a word of it during his direct question Glitsky. But he'd counted on the fact that Randall had an ax to grind. The young prosecutor wanted to prove to Braun that his unorthodox and even extra-legal tactics had been justified all along because the head of homicide was corrupt. Hardy could have objected all day and been sustained, but he was happy to let Randall hang himself.

'And when your staff assembles this evidence, lieutenant, and determines that there has in fact been a crime and they've identified a suspect, what do they do next?'

'We go to the DA, who decides if they want to charge the individual, and what the exact charge will be. First-degree murder, manslaughter, that kind of thing.'

'And how long does it take, roughly, from the commission of a homicide until you make this submission to the DA?'

'It varies widely. A couple of days to a couple of years.'

'OK.' Randall was covering ground familiar to every professional in the courtroom, but obviously he felt he was making his case to Braun. Now he became specific. 'In the case of Bree Beaumont, it's been over a month. Can you tell the court why that is?'

'The original inspector assigned to the case, Carl Griffin, was shot to death five days after Bree was killed. That slowed things down somewhat.'

A ripple of nervous laughter spread through the courtroom. Randall seemed oblivious to it and Braun let it pass.

'And at that point, did you get personally involved in the investigation?'

'No, I did not.'

'Did you interrogate witnesses?'

'No.'

'Did you have occasion to talk to the victim's husband, Ron Beaumont?'

'No.'

'But isn't it a fact, lieutenant, that this morning you escorted Mr Beaumont and Mr Hardy to this courtroom?'

'Yes, that's true.'

'But you say you had never before met or talked to Mr Beaumont?'

'No.'

'I remind you, lieutenant, you are under oath.'

A small lifting of the mouth. 'I understand that. The answer's still no.'

The questions went on rapidly, without interruption, as Randall walked Glitsky through the steps of his eventual personal involvement in the case. The proximity of Griffin's murder scene to the residences of Bree and the other suspects, and finally to Canetta and the ballistics test proving that both men had been shot with the same gun.

Hardy picked up no sense of impatience from the judge. Finally, Randall got to where he'd been heading all along. 'Now, lieutenant, after you had determined that Sergeants Griffin and Canetta had been killed with the same gun, did you immediately turn this information over to the district attorney?'

'No, I did not.'

'Can you tell the court why that was?'

Glitsky turned up to face Marian Braun. 'It is standard procedure to withhold information from the media so that potential suspects will not be privy to incriminating evidence we might have against them. That way, if they tell us something that hasn't been released . . . I think this is probably pretty obvious, isn't it?'

'But this wasn't the media, lieutenant. This was the district attorney's office, with which you are supposed to cooperate. Why didn't you tell them?'

'Two reasons. One, we've had a lot of trouble with leaks.' Everyone in the building knew this was a constant problem, although every department accused every other one of being the source of them. 'Second, a little more prosaically, I wasn't sure of any of this until last night. If I didn't have this hearing this morning, I might have brought the information to the DA already.'

438

Hardy couldn't believe that Randall still thought he was scoring points. But evidently he did, and now moved on to another area where Glitsky had allegedly failed in his duties. 'Lieutenant, do you know a Sergeant Timms?'

'Yes. He's a crime scene specialist.'

'Did he work with you on the cars of Sergeants Griffin and Canetta?'

'Yes.'

'And did you tell him about your suspicions that the two deaths of these policemen might have been related?'

'Of course. I'm the one who asked him to check ballistics on the slugs.'

'And did you tell him not to mention this suspected connection to anyone?'

'Yes.'

'Why was that?'

'It was premature. I didn't know if it was true. You have one person killing two policemen, it stirs up the force. I thought maybe we could avoid that if it turned out not to be true.'

Randall threw his hands up theatrically. 'But it did turn out to be true? Isn't that the case?'

'Yes it did.'

'And both men were investigating the death of Bree Beaumont?'

'Yes.'

Hardy was just thinking it was going to be too easy when Randall finally hit a nerve. 'Lieutenant, did Sergeant Canetta work in the homicide detail? Was he a homicide inspector?'

Glitsky threw a neutral look at the defense table, and returned to the prosecutor. 'No. He worked out of Central Station.'

'Central Station? Perhaps you can tell the court how he came to be working on a murder case?'

'He was connected to the case through one of the witnesses we'd interviewed.'

'Who was that?'

439

'Jim Pierce, a vice president for Caloco oil. Mr Pierce used to be Bree Beaumont's employer, and he'd also employed Sergeant Canetta for security at some conventions and so on.'

'And so on,' Randall aped. 'Isn't it true that Canetta was in fact working for Mr Hardy?'

'In what sense?'

'I mean the sense of working, he was his employer . . .'

'On his payroll? Not to my knowledge. No. Ask Mr Hardy.'

Randall had made the cardinal mistake, asking a question in court for which he didn't already know the answer. It left him speechless for a beat.

And into the silence, Marian Braun finally spoke up. 'Where are you going with all this, Mr Randall? Do you have any proof that Mr Hardy had hired Sergeant Canetta?'

'No, your honor, not yet.'

'Then find another line of questioning, establish this one's relevance, or sit down. This courtroom is not the old fishin' hole.'

It was a little after ten thirty and Braun called for a ten-minute recess. Jim Pierce had not yet arrived, but the way this free-form hearing was developing, Hardy thought that even without the oil company executive's testimony, there was still some chance that he could succeed in freeing Frannie and keeping Ron and his children out of the system. Randall's arrogance had played beautifully into his hands, and now Hardy believed that the judge was primed for his next revelation, which should erode the DA's credibility to the point of extinction.

As soon as Braun was out of the courtroom, the familiar bedlam began again.

At this point, all Hardy wanted was a few minutes to talk to his wife, and to get Glitsky to one side, but neither of those seemed likely.

The minute Glitsky left the stand, he paused at Hardy's desk, opined that he'd rarely had a better time in the witness box, then said the vibrating buzzer had been going off on his belt for the past hour. He'd better go make a few callbacks. He passed through the bar rail, back up the center aisle and out the back doors of the courtroom.

Meanwhile, Al Valens, apoplectic, was making a racket, demanding that the bailiff let him back to see the judge. All right, he and Damon Kerry – good citizens, respecting their subpoenas – had shown up after voting, but the candidate couldn't be expected to sit here all day. He had meetings, press conferences, fundraising . . . there were reporters out in the hallway already writing stories about his appearance here in a courtroom involved in a murder case.

Baxter Thorne sat in the pew under where he had been standing when they had come in. He was talking to a well-dressed young couple, evidently giving them instructions of some kind, and Hardy was glad that the dapper slimebag chose to remain near the back of the room. If he got too close to the man who he believed had set fire to his house, he thought there was still a reasonable chance that he might assault him, and that wouldn't further his case with Braun.

A wronged Ron Beaumont wanted to know what Hardy was doing. What was all this witness stuff? How long was this going to take? He'd thought that Hardy's idea was to argue for Frannie's release, and Ron would be there to make sure she no longer was bound by her promise to him. Then somehow he was going to get him out of here before Randall or Pratt could stop him. But he'd noticed the guards at the doors and now he'd seen Pratt talking to another one, who had come down to the end of his pew. What was he supposed to do now?

Hardy calmed him as best he could, explaining that he was laying groundwork for the judge. Glitsky's testimony of course didn't legally *prove* that a bullet from the same gun had killed both Griffin and Canetta. This proceeding wasn't about proof anymore, although Hardy still hoped that that might come later. It was about the DA's judgment and tactics and Braun's faith in them or lack thereof.

'That's the only thing that's going to get you out of this courtroom a free man, Ron. If Braun decides that Randall needs a stronger case to even consider you as a suspect. And now at least I've got her listening.'

Ron still didn't like it, but Hardy had never promised him that he would.

David Freeman kept Frannie chatting at the defense table. They didn't want her interacting with Ron Beaumont in any way, and it was Freeman's role to keep her entertained. By the time Braun re-entered the courtroom, he had her laughing quietly at one of his stories. During the recess, Hardy had barely had time to get a word in, but as they rose for the judge's entrance, he took her hand and squeezed it. She looked up at him and nodded. Confident in him, committed.

Hardy felt he had to establish a few more facts, and introduced into evidence the autopsy and coroner's reports on the two policemen. Pratt and Randall had no objections to Dr Strout's findings as to the causes and times of the deaths.

Hardy put it orally into the record. 'According to the coroner's report, your honor, Sergeant Griffin was shot between ten thirty and about noon on Monday, 5 October. Ms Pratt and Mr Randall both accept this timeframe. For the court's information, this was the same day of Bree Beaumont's funeral and burial.'

'All right, Mr Hardy. Proceed.'

'I'd like to call Father Martin Bernardin.'

The priest was in his cassock and collar. He came through the gallery and up to the stand. Somewhere between forty and fifty years old, Bernardin was a trim, gray man with an ascetic's face. After the clerk had administered the oath, Hardy spent a minute identifying him as the pastor of St Catherine's parish, the church where Bree had been buried. Then. 'Father Bernardin, do you know Ron Beaumont?'

'Yes, I do.'

'And do you recognize him here in this courtroom?'

'Yes.' He pointed. 'He's the gentleman in the green suit in the first row over there.'

Several members of the gallery strained to look at this key player in all these events. There was a low buzz of comment, but Braun rapped her gavel lightly and put an end to that.

'Now, Father Bernardin. On October fifth, the day of Bree Beaumont's funeral, did you have occasion to spend any time with Mr Beaumont?'

'Yes, sir. I spent most of the whole day with him.'

This brought the gallery to life again, but this time Braun let the noise die of its own accord.

Bernardin had already said it, but Hardy walked the priest through the day – the breakfast, mass, burial, lunch at the Cliff House. 'In other words, Father,' he concluded, 'it is your sworn testimony that you were continually in the presence of Mr Beaumont from before seven in the morning until at least two thirty in the afternoon on October fifth of this year?'

'That's correct.'

'Every minute?'

'Yes, sir.'

'And were there other people who you believe could testify to this as well?'

'Well, yes. His children, some friends. It was a long day, as funerals often are.'

Hardy stood a minute to let the import of the priest's words sink in, then whirled and faced Pratt and Randall. 'Your witness,' he said.

What could they do? Here was an absolutely credible man of the cloth providing an unimpeachable alibi for their main suspect. They conferred for a long moment at their table, then Pratt stood. 'No questions, your honor.'

Braun told Bernardin that he could step down, took off her glasses, put them back on, and looked from Hardy, in the center of the courtroom, to Pratt and Randall at their table.

'Mr Hardy?' she said.

'Your honor, it's clear from the testimony of Father

Bernardin – and there evidently are several other witnesses who can corroborate his statements – that Mr Beaumont could not have killed Sergeant Griffin. If that is the case, it follows that he did not kill Sergeant Canetta and, based on our earlier discussion, it can then be assumed that, for the purposes of this hearing, he did not kill Bree Beaumont.'

Braun's face was set. 'Counsel approach the bench,' she said.

When they got there, she turned a hard glare on to Pratt and Randall. 'It seems to me, counsellors, that you have wasted a great deal of this court's time – to say nothing of Mrs Hardy's – when any reasonably thorough investigation into Sergeant Griffin's death should have turned up this rather obvious alibi.'

'Your honor.' Randall was ready with an excuse. 'At the time I pursued the contempt charge against Mrs Hardy, we were unaware of any connection between Bree Beaumont and Sergeant Griffin's death.'

Hardy had to get it in. He worked to keep the gloat out of his voice. 'A connection provided by Lieutenant Glitsky, I might add, your honor.'

But Braun wasn't interested in excuses. She was furious. 'Turn around and look at this courtroom, Mr Randall. I said *turn around*! Ms Pratt, you might, too.'

They both half-heartedly did so, and Hardy did, too, noticing that Abe Glitsky had returned to the courtroom. There were other very welcome additions to the gallery as well. Mr Lee from Heritage Cleaners, even though Hardy hadn't subpoenaed him, had told Hardy when he'd called this morning that he'd try to make it to the courtroom, and now he had. So, too, at last, had Jim Pierce. He was even now edging his way into one of the rows of seats, accompanied by another of the city's well-known attorneys, Jared Wright.

And not a moment too soon, Hardy thought.

Pratt and Randall came back to facing the judge. '*Look* at the number of people you have seriously inconvenienced by this irresponsible pursuit not, apparently, of a murderer, but merely of one person whom the police had not yet seen fit to charge because they had not yet built a case. And now it appears that we know why that was, don't we?' She shook her head in disgust. 'This is appallingly irresponsible behavior.'

Randall stood silent. Pratt mumbled something.

As the gallery hummed, Braun dismissed them all back to their desks, then raised her voice. 'Mr Hardy,' Braun said, 'I believe I am ready now to rule on your *habeas* motion.'

Hardy was rummaging in his briefcase, arranging more papers in front of him on his table. He looked up and spoke in measured tones. 'If we can just take a few more minutes?'

This brought a perplexed frown to the judge's visage, another rumbling in the gallery. 'And do what, Mr Hardy?'

He came out from behind his table and stood in front of Braun's podium. 'We have been working on a limited assumption provisionally accepted by both the court and the district attorney that the killer of Sergeants Griffin and Canetta is the person responsible for the death of Bree Beaumont.'

'Yes?'

'That assumption, however, is not legal proof that Mr Beaumont did not, in fact, either commit the latter act, or contract to accomplish the former. Any suspicion that may one day fall upon Mr Beaumont leaves my client's future liberty at grave risk. I believe I can eliminate that risk with a few more minutes of the court's indulgence.'

The courtroom was stonily silent behind him. Braun removed her glasses and brought one of the earpieces to her mouth. Finally, she stole a glance at her wristwatch and made her decision. 'And what do you propose?'

'I'd like to call one more witness, your honor.'

'*One* more?'

'Yes, your honor. I'd like to call James Pierce.'

40

'This is ridiculous!'

Hardy heard Pierce's grumbled outburst from the back of the courtroom but as he turned he saw it was Jared Wright now on his feet, objecting. 'Your honor, Mr Pierce has spoken to the police and their representatives at least a half-dozen times. He has cooperated with every investigation related to the Bree Beaumont case, and he . . .' He was out of his pew into the aisle of the gallery, coming forward.

Braun gaveled him quiet. 'Mr Wright. If Mr Pierce has cooperated all that much before, he surely won't mind doing it one more time.'

'This is pure harassment, your honor.'

'And why would that be, Mr Wright?'

Wright had made it up to the bar rail. 'Because Mr Pierce's employer, Caloco Oil, has been a contributor to Ms Pratt's campaigns and a supporter of her administration. We have seen today the animosity between the police department and Mr Hardy here, and the district attorney's office. As a good citizen, Mr Pierce responded to Mr Hardy's high-handed, last-minute subpoena, but now to endure another round of questioning on these events will serve no purpose. He is not implicated. To imply such is reckless at best and criminal at worst.'

Braun heard him out, then eyed Pierce who was standing directly behind his lawyer. 'Mr Pierce. You've been properly subpoenaed to appear and now called as a witness. Come forward. Mr Wright, your objection is noted for the record.'

'Your honor.' Wright, not giving up.

'Yes, counsellor? What now?'

'I would ask the court's permission to accompany my client to the witness stand. He had endured several police interviews without the benefit of his attorney, and I believe . . .'

Braun held up a hand, interrupting him. 'Mr Hardy, do you object?'

Hardy didn't like it, but he wasn't going to say so. 'No objection, your honor.'

The oil man hesitated for another instant, then angrily stood up, and marched up the aisle, past Hardy, to the witness stand. Wright met him at the rail and now stood at his side. The clerk held the Bible out for him. 'State your name.'

'James Pierce.'

'Mr Pierce, do you swear to tell the truth, the whole truth, and nothing but the truth, so help you God?'

'I do.'

'Please be seated.'

'Mr Pierce, have we spoken before?'

The bailiff had pulled up a chair and now Jared Wright sat in it, next to his client. He wasted no time getting on the boards with an objection. 'Immaterial, your honor.'

Braun gaveled him quiet. 'Overruled. Mr Pierce?'

The witness spoke. 'You know we have.'

Hardy was all business. 'Your honor, would you direct the witness to answer the question?'

Braun did so, Hardy repeated it, and Pierce growled out a yes.

'And on that occasion, when you and I spoke, did you deny having a personal relationship with Bree Beaumont?'

'No, of course not. I had been her mentor and friend for several years.'

'Mr Pierce, did you have an intimate relationship with Bree Beaumont? Sexually intimate?'

Jared Wright spoke up again. 'My client has answered that question a hundred times, your honor. He's . . .'

Bam! 'Mr Wright, legal objections, please.'

'All right, immaterial.'

It *was* immaterial, but Hardy had already pulled a rabbit from his hat with Bernardin, and Braun was inclined at this point to let him go for two. 'Overruled.'

Hardy bowed slightly. 'Thank you, your honor. Mr Pierce, would you like me to repeat the question?'

This time, Wright whispered something into his client's ear, but Pierce brushed him aside. 'No, I heard it, and the answer, as it's been every time, is still no.'

'No, you did not have a sexual relationship with Bree Beaumont?'

'That's right.'

Arms crossed over his chest and sulking at the mistreatment he'd suffered at the hands of the court and his client alike, Wright sat back in the hard chair. Hardy noted the change in affect and took it as a good sign.

He spun and walked back to his table, fiddled with some papers, and left them where they lay. 'All right. Did you have a personal relationship with Sergeant Canetta?'

'No, I did not.'

'But you did know him, did you not?'

Pierce shifted in his seat, answered impatiently. 'I gather he helped to provide security at some Caloco events. I may have talked to him at those. I really don't remember.'

'You don't remember,' Hardy repeated. 'And how about Sergeant Griffin? Did he interview you?'

Pierce hesitated, throwing a quick glance toward his attorney.

This time, no reaction was forthcoming, so Pierce answered. 'Yes, I believe he did.'

'You *believe* he did? Don't you remember?'

'All right, then. Yes, he did.'

'And when was that?'

Another stutter. 'I'd have to check my calender. I don't know exactly.'

But Hardy was sure. 'Perhaps I can help you remember, Mr

Pierce. Wasn't it directly after Bree's funeral?'

'No. I don't think so.'

'You don't think so? Do you remember what you did do after the funeral, Mr Pierce?'

'Your honor!' Jared Wright's short fuse had lit up again. 'Your honor, I must protest. What is Mr Hardy's basis for any of these questions? Mr Wright isn't on trial here. He doesn't have to answer these questions.'

Braun pondered it for a moment. In actual fact, Pierce's attorney was right. And while she admired Hardy's point – he was treating this hearing the same way Scott Randall would conduct a grand jury proceeding – she should not allow this interrogation to go forward. The whole line of questioning was suspect.

But before she could even tell Wright that he was correct and make some kind of ruling, David Freeman stood and came to Hardy's rescue. 'Your honor, Mr Pierce can always take the Fifth.'

But things here were getting out of control. She tapped her gavel and glared over her podium. 'Gentlemen, sit down. This is my courtroom and I will instruct in the law.' She turned to look down on the witness. 'Mr Pierce, if you feel that your answers will tend to incriminate you, you may invoke the Fifth Amendment. Do you wish to do so?'

Sweat had broken on Pierce's forehead and seemed to surprise him as he wiped a couple of fingers across it. If he took the Fifth, he knew that his troubles with the law would only be beginning – the police investigation going forward would be relentless.

Everyone had lost track of Wright's objection that the original question was immaterial.

Hardy felt he could almost see the thoughts playing in the man's head, deciding to take his chances here and now – to put an end to the accusations and suspicions. It was a joy to watch. Successful, arrogant, insulated by money and position, Pierce's world view simply didn't include the notion that mere

449

mortals could best him in a fair fight. This was because there could never be a fair fight.

Pierce assumed a fighting pose – a palm down on the railing to the witness box – and spoke up to the judge. 'I have nothing to hide, your honor, though I deeply resent these questions.'

And Braun had to admit that by permitting Hardy to continue without any evidentiary base, she was opening herself up to rebuke. But lawyers can ask anything they want unless the other party objects, and Pierce was answering.

'Your resentment, which is not a legal objection, is noted.' Braun turned her attention to Pierce's tormentor. 'Mr Hardy,' she said sternly, 'I will tolerate more questions only if you can provide the court with some kind of evidentiary framework. Otherwise, I'm going to dismiss this witness.'

Hardy stood still for a moment. 'Of course, your honor.' He returned to his desk and this time brought a small handful of pages back with him. He first showed them to the judge, then handed a copy of one of them to the witness. 'Mr Pierce, do you recognize this document?'

Pierce gingerly held the paper out in front of him. His shoulders slumped visibly. Wright grabbed the paper from his client while Hardy kept talking. 'Would you tell the court what this document is, Mr Pierce?'

Pierce looked down, set his lips, looked back up. Couldn't find his voice. Nor, apparently, could his attorney.

Hardy kept up his onslaught. 'Would you please identify this document, Mr Pierce? For the court?'

Pierce seemed not to hear. Eventually, he sighed, seemingly unable to take his eyes off the document, reading the words silently over to himself.

Hardy: 'It's a letter written by you to Bree Beaumont, isn't it?'

More silence.

'Would you characterize the document as a love letter?'

Pierce did not answer.

'Mr Pierce, would you like me to read the first couple of lines to the court? Contrary to your earlier testimony, isn't it a fact you were having an affair with her?'

By now, Wright was whispering furiously to his client, who seemed not to hear.

Hardy had to give it to him. The gears shifted quickly and smoothly. Damning revelation went to damage control in the blink of an eye. Pierce flipped a hand, trying and failing to make the gesture appear casual. 'It was over long ago.'

'How long ago? A year? Five years?'

'Yes. Somewhere in there.'

Wright was beside himself with frustration and anger. 'Your honor, let the record reflect that anything Mr Pierce says is against my advice.'

But Pierce had decided on his own approach. He broke a cold smile. 'It was unimportant. A dalliance that I regret.' He turned again to the judge. 'Out of respect for my wife, your honor, I tried to keep this from coming out in public. It was a mistake.'

But if he thought he'd get some sympathy from Braun, he was barking up the wrong tree. 'Another mistake is perjury in my courtroom,' she said coldly.

Hardy kept up the press. 'Mr Pierce, I ask you again. When did this affair end?'

Perhaps unnerved by Marian Braun's negative reaction, Pierce took a moment to reply. 'I said I didn't know.'

'Actually, that's not what you said,' Hardy replied. 'You said it was something like one or five years. Would you like the court recorder to read back your earlier answer?'

'No, that's not necessary.' He appeared to be trying to recall, to cooperate. 'I don't know when we broke it off. Not exactly.'

'Not exactly? Isn't it true, Mr Pierce, that your affair with Bree Beaumont ended only six months ago, about the same time she quit her job with Caloco?'

'No, it was longer ago than that.'

'But you don't remember when?' he asked. 'Exactly?'

'No.' Pierce was striving to hold his ground. 'Just because I wanted to keep an affair private does not mean I killed her.'

'No,' Hardy agreed. 'No, it doesn't, but I haven't asked if you killed her. Did you kill Bree Beaumont, Mr Pierce?'

'No. Of course not.'

'But you did lie, under oath, about your relationship with her, isn't that so?

'Yes, I suppose I did. But I told you—'

'Mr Pierce, did you also lie about your relationship with Sergeant Canetta?'

A nerve started to twitch slightly to the side of Pierce's mouth. 'I've told you. I had no relationship with Sergeant Canetta.'

'Did you not ask Sergeant Canetta to report to you on Bree Beaumont's comings and goings after she broke off her relationship with you?'

'No, I didn't do that.'

'And did you not pay him for this service?'

Pierce's eyes strafed the courtroom, then settled back down. 'No.'

'No,' Hardy repeated. 'Mr Pierce, did Sergeant Canetta come by your house last Saturday night, the night he was killed?'

Again, the twitch, the recovery. 'No.'

'And did he not attempt to get more money out of you for misdirecting the investigation into Bree Beaumont's death? Away from you?'

'No.'

'And did you not then invite him into your house to discuss this, and then . . .'

Finally, a true rise. Pierce came forward in the box, his eyes ablaze now. 'No, no, no. I didn't do any of that. You're making all this up to discredit me.'

Marian Braun finally spoke up. 'The witness has a point, Mr Hardy. You're making a lot of accusations without any show of proof.'

Hardy sucked in a lungful of air and let it out. 'I have

proof, your honor,' he said coolly. 'Mr Pierce is holding it in his hand.'

Pierce still held his letter to Bree and now, in the suddenly silent courtroom, he held it up again. But this betrayed the shaking in his hands, and he quickly put them down on the railing.

Braun pulled her glasses down on her nose and glared over them. 'He's already acknowledged perjury regarding his affair with Ms Beaumont, Mr Hardy. But that is not murder.'

'No, your honor, it isn't. But there is evidence in the letters Mr Pierce has identified that directly relate to Bree Beaumont's murder.'

Braun hesitated – if Pierce hadn't already perjured himself, she'd have stopped this right now – but she found herself nodding. She wanted to know. 'But be careful, Mr Hardy.'

He nodded. 'If I may, your honor, I'd like to read to the court a portion of one of these letters.' Braun nodded.

> 'I live
> Longing
> Only for you.
> Vast love
> Eternal.
> Young again
> Overcome with it all
> Untamed.'

Hardy didn't wait for the treacly words to have any effect. They weren't his point. 'Nearly each of these letters has a similar poem in it, your honor.' He handed the letter he'd just read up to the podium. 'As the court will note, the first letter of each line of the poem spells another message – in this case "I love you." As your honor will see, this is consistent with every poem in these letters.'

Braun turned through a couple of the pages, nodding. 'All right.'

'The letter that Mr Pierce now holds in his hand contains another similar poem.' He came up to the witness, lifting the paper from his hands. 'May I?' He read, breaking the lines.

> 'Never have
> I touched or felt
> Never
> Even knew.
> Oh, the craving –
> Touching
> Wanting
> Only you.'

Again, he didn't pause. 'Mr Pierce, can you tell the court the significance of the phrase nine oh two?'

The sweat had broken heavily now on Pierce's face. 'I don't know,' he said. 'I don't remember.'

'You don't remember?'

'No.'

This was what Hardy wanted – to get him in a rhythm, saying 'no' before he'd considered sufficiently. 'Isn't it true, Mr Pierce,' he continued, 'that nine oh two was the number of the apartment in Bree Beaumont's building where you would conduct your trysts?'

'No, I . . .'

'And isn't it true that you and Bree bought this place together nearly six years ago?'

Pierce cast his eyes out to the gallery. 'No. She . . .' He stopped.

'She what, Mr Pierce? She bought it herself?'

'No. I don't know that.'

'Your honor!' Jared Wright couldn't stand watching his client self-destruct any longer. 'This is an outrageous . . .'

Hardy raised his voice over the interruption. 'But you do know, don't you, Mr Pierce, that apartment nine oh two is two floors directly below her penthouse?'

454

'No. I don't think it's . . .'

But Hardy, at high volume now, couldn't stop. 'Are you saying that it's *not* directly below her penthouse, Mr Pierce? When you know that to be false?'

Pierce was unable to answer.

Hardy leaned in to Pierce and all but shouted. 'Mr Pierce, don't you in fact know that nine oh two is the apartment from which she was thrown to her death?'

'*Your honor! Please!*'

Bam! Bam! 'Mr Wright, sit down. Mr Hardy!'

Fighting to slow his momentum, to regain control, Hardy looked up at the judge. His color was high, his breathing ragged.

Braun's voice was stern. 'I have to stop this now, Mr Hardy. It's gone on long enough. You've shown the court no evidence that puts Mr Pierce in apartment nine-oh-two, no evidence for any of these accusations. You said you had proof and presented these letters and this poetry, but neither rises to the level of proof. Mr Pierce hasn't admitted the truth of anything you've said related to Bree Beaumont's murder. If you have nothing stronger, I've got no choice but to let the witness step down.'

Hardy took a deep breath and let it out heavily. 'I do have physical evidence that places Mr Pierce in apartment nine-oh-two, your honor.'

The judge, too, had reached the end of her patience. This was clear from her tone. 'If that's true, the court needs to see it now.'

Hardy walked briskly back to his table and reached into his briefcase, and extracted the xerox copy of Griffin's note about the Movado watch that he'd picked up from Heritage Cleaners.

Coming back before the bench, he read it aloud and then handed it up to Braun. As she was looking it over, he was talking. 'Your honor, as you see, this note refers to a specific Movado watch which Inspector Griffin took as evidence in his investigation into the death of Bree Beaumont. I am prepared to call a witness, Mr Lee, who is in this courtroom today. Mr

Lee is the manager of a company called Heritage Cleaners, which cleans apartments in Bree Beaumont's building. Mr Lee will testify that this watch was found by his staff in apartment nine-oh-two of that building on the Thursday following Mrs Beaumont's murder.'

Braun looked down at Hardy, across to Wright and Pierce, then out over the courtroom. 'All right, but I don't see . . .' she paused. 'But where is the watch itself, Mr Hardy. Without the watch—'

Hardy nodded and pointed to the witness. 'Mr Pierce is wearing it right now.'

Suddenly, finally, there was a deep silence in the room. Hardy spoke into it, almost whispering. 'Mr Pierce?'

Pierce could not wrangle free. He knew that there was evidence of his presence all over that apartment. And though this wasn't prima-facie proof that he'd killed Bree, he knew what the police would find there once they started looking – glass of the type imbedded in Bree's hairline, evidence of the struggle which had ripped Pierce's watch off.

He fixed Hardy with an empty stare. 'I didn't mean—'

Jared Wright's voice boomed out in the courtroom. 'For Christ's sake, Jim, shut up! Don't say another word!'

And Braun's gavel pounded again and again over the resulting uproar.

Glitsky was good about it. The court bailiffs took Pierce into custody over Jared Wright's heated objections. Then there was the bedlam of the courtroom, and all of the wronged witnesses who'd been forced to waste so much of their day. Finally, the Ron Beaumont moment – apologies and thanks. Some not altogether light banter about Beaumont's daughter, who had gone back to school.

Waiting patiently, Glitsky accompanied Hardy, Frannie, and David Freeman as they walked through the steps, processing her out of the system. David Freeman left them to go back to work, and finally they got five minutes alone in the waiting area of the jail as the female bailiff took Frannie back to reclaim her personal effects.

But Frannie wasn't three seconds out of sight when Glitsky turned to Hardy. 'That's OK,' he said. 'It's not like murders are my job or anything.'

Hardy felt bad about the timing of it, but there hadn't been anything he could do. 'I only knew this morning, Abe, and I planned to tell you all about it, but you remember we had our little discussion about if you'd known Ron and then Randall and Pratt showed up in the hallway for their moment. I figured you'd survive.'

The lieutenant worked it around for a beat, still not thrilled, but more curious than angry. 'So what was it? It wasn't the poems.'

'No. That was after I already knew. It wasn't even the watch at first. It was Almond Roca.'

Hardy explained about the bowl of candy by the door to Pierce's home, the stomach contents of both Griffin and Canetta, and the square gold wrappers in both cars. 'I didn't see it at first because of that damned Almond Joy in Griffin's car. So I see almonds and chocolate, and an Almond Joy, I know where they came from, right?'

'Sure.'

'Except there wasn't any coconut in Griffin's autopsy, so he hadn't recently eaten the Almond Joy. I checked with Strout. Just almonds and chocolate. Also almonds and chocolate with Canetta, which made me think. Canetta came by Pierce's house to squeeze him, grabbed a couple of candies by the door, and ate them just before he got himself shot.'

'You think Pierce hit him at his own home?'

'That's my guess. They were alone. You'll find something if you look, but I'm also guessing Pierce is going to tell you. Once they start confessing . . . but you know this.'

Glitsky did know it. What he didn't understand was why Canetta had waited so long to start blackmailing Pierce. 'Why then? Why not earlier?'

In truth, Hardy wasn't sure. But. 'My guess is that Canetta originally – and marginally, I might add – was willing to buy the idea that the killer had been Ron. When it became clear to him that it hadn't been, from his perspective there was only one suspect left, and he happened to have deep pockets.' He shook his head sadly – Canetta might have been crooked and confused, but Hardy had liked him. 'He picked the wrong guy.'

Glitsky chewed his cheek for a while. 'Griffin had the watch when he went to talk to Pierce,' he said. 'He showed it to him.'

Hardy nodded. 'Right. And Pierce thought Griffin himself and not the cleaning people had found the watch. Only Griffin knew about nine oh two and the watch was the only evidence. So Pierce somehow got a hold of his gun and shot him and took the watch back and it almost worked. Except for the Heritage note.'

Glitsky could have gone on and on about the note that Hardy hadn't shown him, but he realized that he'd just be whining. His friend had done what he thought he had to do and nothing Glitsky said was going to change that. Or influence his future behavior, for that matter. But there was one last issue. 'So Frannie never had to tell Ron's big secret, did she?'

A sideways glance. 'Now that you mention it, I guess not.'

'And there's no chance you know what it was, is there?'

'What?' Hardy pulled at his ear.

Glitsky started to repeat the question, but Hardy held up a hand, stopping him. 'I can't hear you,' he said. 'I've got a banana in my ear.'

EPILOGUE

On Friday, 26 March, Governor Damon Kerry signed into law a bill outlawing the use of MTBE in California. The bill – nicknamed 'Bree's law' by the media – was the culmination of the governor's main legislative effort of his first three months in office, and was popularly viewed as a political and moral victory against the powers of big oil and special-interest lobbyists. Kerry was cleaning up the state house, cleaning the state's water supply. There was already talk of a national campaign in his future.

Al Valens saw to it that the results of Bree Beaumont's report blasting ethanol and all other oxygenates never made it to the governor's desk. In fact, the law's preamble praised the EPA for mandating the use of oxygenates in reformulated gasoline. The state's air had improved under the oxygenated formulas, and was now at its cleanest in decades. Oxygenates, such as ethanol and MTBE, had proven effective in reducing air pollutants. Unfortunately, the petroleum additive MTBE had been shown to be carcinogenic. Other oxygenates, notably ethanol, were available in sufficient quantity to supply the state's needs. MTBE's ever-increasing presence in the groundwater of California constituted a considerable and ongoing health hazard, and from this date forward, its use would be aggressively phased out.

Two weeks later, at the Spader Krutch Ohio shareholders' meeting, held in Cincinnati, CEO Ellis Jackson proudly read aloud from the annual report, embellishing for his audience where it seemed appropriate.

'Regarding ethanol production, I am delighted to report

459

that the latest battle in the war between the Middle East and the Midwest has turned for the moment in our favor. The increased demand for ethanol as a gasoline additive in many states, but particularly in the huge California market, has spurred the US government to continue its exemption of the federal fuel tax on ethanol. In addition, the government has guaranteed to buy every barrel of surplus corn-ethanol produced in this country well into the next millenium.'

This brought a huge round of applause.

'. . . of course has not come without its costs. The corporation's state and federal lobbying and education efforts on behalf of the ethanol subsidies during the fiscal year amounted to eight point six million dollars. Of course, last year was an election year. We supported political campaigns in all twenty-three states that held elections, and it is a great pleasure to report that seventy-two per cent of our candidates succeeded to elective office.

'As our political influence increases, so inevitably will our lobbying costs. But this figure pales in comparison to the forty-five million dollars *profit* – I repeat, this is a profit figure – generated by sales of ethanol last year in the United States. With its recent banning of MTBE, California's use of ethanol is expected to multiply exponentially in the short term. And we are seeing similar campaigns in many other regions of the country.'

Jackson refrained from reading the next sentences aloud. They read: 'Unfortunately, the markets in California and other states remain undersupplied because of our continued inability to provide ethanol in sufficient quantity and, without the government subsidy program, at a profitable cost. However, research on this problem is ongoing. Currently, without government assistance, real costs of producing ethanol – wages, refinery costs, tractor fuel to plant and harvest the corn – average about one dollar per gallon, or roughly twice as much as gasoline. Fortunately, governmental tax credits keep us competitive, but clearly, this is an area that needs improvement.'

But it was as though these lines had never been written. Jackson continued smoothly, his voice ringing with confidence.

'Ethanol profits next year will be in the range of a hundred million dollars, and if we can increase our production to meet the needs of the market, in the not-too-distant future, we can predict profits that may well reach half a billion dollars per year!'

Ellis Jackson waited as applause rocked the room. Finally, grinning broadly, he held up his hands and the noise subsided. The CEO leaned into the microphone. 'Ladies and gentlemen,' he crowed triumphantly, 'it's been one hell of a year!'

On the following Saturday, 17 April, the Hardy kids were spending one last day at their grandparents' house.

Now, an hour before dusk, Dismas and Frannie were working mostly in silence, finishing up the last of the unpacking in their newly designed kitchen. Skylights, white cabinets, and fifty additional square feet they'd borrowed from the rooms at the back of the house gave the space an airy, open feel.

They had finally come around to accepting the Chinese position that disaster and opportunity derive from the same symbol. And so, retaining the original home's footprint, they'd gone up. Over the first floor, they'd added a new master bedroom and bath. This freed up enough space to convert their old bedroom into a family room. This meant no more television in the living room, a long-awaited goal – now rational and uninterrupted conversation might have a chance to transpire there.

Hardy had installed a new, enlarged fish tank – sixty gallons – into the wall between the kitchen and the family room behind it, so that it could be enjoyed from either side. He'd bolted an old marlin fishhook into the wall above the new stove and on it – in easy reach – hung his cast-iron pan, which glistened black with reseasoning and a fresh rub with olive oil.

They'd stored as much as they could in the back rooms during the construction and over the past three days had done most of the heavy moving. Now, the new furniture graced the living and dining rooms. Three new ones and the one surviving Venetian glass elephant caravaned again on the mantel. The new bed upstairs sported a wedding-ring quilt they'd discovered together in an antiques shop on a family trip to Mendocino one weekend.

Tapped out, even with the insurance money, they were broke as newlyweds after the honeymoon.

Hardy finished stacking a load of dishes into one of the cupboards and turned around, surprised to find himself suddenly alone. He pushed open the door to the dining room and walked through it, passing the sturdy and graceful Shaker table and chairs. A dozen coats of lemon oil still hadn't completely eradicated the smell of carbon from the old sideboard, but the old piece was a comforting presence, some connection to what had been before.

The sun was low and its light streamed through the shutters in the bay windows, illuminating the living room. Frannie was sitting forward on the ottoman in front of what Hardy thought might become his reading chair, although it was still far from broken in, too new to tell.

'You OK?'

She smiled politely, quickly. 'Just taking a break.'

Standing in the opening between the two rooms, he studied her face for a minute, then pulled a chair from behind him and sat so that he was facing her.

'It's beautiful, isn't it?' she said.

Feet planted, elbows on his knees, Hardy took it in – the shining hardwood floors, the Navajo rug, the blond leather couch, a handful of tasteful new accessories, some art. With the addition over them, they'd been able to raise the ceiling to over nine feet. Frannie was right – it was a little eclectic, vaguely Santa Fe, but it all fit together well.

'We do good work.'

His phrasing struck her and the ambiguous smile returned, flitted, disappeared.

'What?' he asked.

'We do, you know. Do good work together.'

'That's what I just said.'

'Yes, but the difference is that I mean it.'

He looked levelly at her. 'I do, too, Frannie.'

She hesitated, then stood up and walked to the shutters, where she stood for another minute before turning back to him. 'Real life is going to start again here on Monday. Just the four of us.'

'I know that.'

'School, kids, all the household errands, your work. I don't want to get where we were before.' She gestured around their new home. 'If I don't have you, I don't want any of this – I mean it. I'd give it all away tomorrow if you start to feel now that you have to work every single minute to pay for it, if it's too great a burden.'

His hands had gotten clenched. 'It wasn't the work.' He blew out through his cheeks. 'The work was escape.'

'From what?' The next he barely heard. 'From me?'

He lifted his shoulders, then let them down heavily. 'I don't know. It was all of a piece. I think I forgot we were doing this together.'

This struck a chord and she broke a small laugh. 'Well, at least we did that together. But, you know, I never did lie to you. I never have.'

'I know that.'

'Do you, really? Because it's true.'

He considered it, then let out a long breath. 'I never really believed it, Frannie. It was just difficult to understand.'

'I know,' she said. 'I'm so sorry for that.' She took a tentative step toward him. 'So maybe we can start over? New house, new attitude.'

'I've been trying.'

She came the rest of the way to him. 'I know. I have, too.

463

These past few months with Ed and Erin – they've been good. But it wasn't the routine like the four of us at home. And I think the routine is what gets to you.'

Hardy eventually answered her. 'You think right.'

'So it's going to start again.'

He tried to make light of it. 'Not till Monday.'

But she wasn't giving it up. 'So what are we going to do?'

Another sigh. 'How about if you need to confide in somebody, you come to me?'

'I could try that. If you'd listen.'

'That sounds fair.' He met her eyes. 'But how about, also, a little balance between kid things and adult things? I'm not asking for the moon here – say seventy thirty, maybe a date every couple of weeks?'

Frannie had to acknowledge his point. 'I know. It got a little too much. That was me.' She straightened him up and sat on his lap. 'But I'm still going to have friends, and some of them are possibly going to be men.'

Now Hardy almost smiled. 'I wouldn't want to stop you. Friends are good. It's possible I'll have a few myself, females I mean. Though it's not as likely as you and men.'

'I don't know,' she said. 'Some women like that old, rugged look.'

'I don't think it would be a looks thing. And what do you mean, old?'

'Well, not real old, more like mature, stately.'

'Stately. I like that.' He kissed her, well and good. When it stopped fifteen seconds later, he pecked her again. 'Stately that,' he said.

'I believe I will,' she said.

And standing, taking his hand, she led him back past the dining room, through their kitchen, up the stairs to their new bedroom.

The next day, Sunday, a strong, sea-scented breeze blew in off the ocean, but the sky was a deep blue and the temperature was shirtsleeves.

All four of the Hardys and most of their friends and relatives had gathered to celebrate the move – Glitsky, his father Nat and his son Orel; David Freeman; Ed and Erin Cochran; Moses McGuire, his wife Susan Weiss, and their son; Pico and Angela Morales and two of their kids; Max, Cassandra, and Ron Beaumont, and his girlfriend, Marie.

The Hardys' backyard was a long and narrow strip of grass bordered by rose bushes. The area was between two medium-rise apartment buildings that, fortunately, caught the afternoon sun.

It was a pot luck, and everyone except Freeman had brought a pot of something – chili, spaghetti, cioppino, Irish stew. All of it, with salads and breads and the pony keg of beer, was on the picnic table. Now, after the house tour and the oohs and aahs, the drinks and first plates of food, Glitsky gave Hardy a look and the two of them went inside the house to admire the crown moulding. Or something.

In fact, they went all the way through the house and out on to the new porch, which was twice as wide as its earlier counterpart. Hardy sat on the new railing, but hadn't gotten comfortable yet when the front door opened and David Freeman appeared, brandishing a cigar.

'I thought I'd just step outside for a smoke.'

'You already were outside, David,' Hardy said. 'In the back.'

But the old man clucked at that. 'Children. Second-hand smoke. Hurts their young lungs. If you fellows want privacy, though . . .'

Hardy looked the question to Glitsky, who shrugged. It didn't matter. 'If you can keep a secret.'

'It's my life's calling,' Freeman responded, straight-faced.

'What?' Hardy was facing Glitsky.

'I've known about this for a couple of weeks now,' Glitsky said, 'but I wanted to wait until today to tell you. Something about the symmetry of it all.'

'Notice how he strings it out,' Hardy said to Freeman.

'I was just admiring that,' the old man responded.

Glitsky rarely smiled, but Hardy decided that the expression he wore now would qualify as a decided smirk. 'I will not beg,' he said soberly.

'It's about Baxter Thorne.'

'All right,' Hardy conceded, 'I might beg a little.'

Within a week of the election, during which time Glitsky's search task force had been unable to unearth even a shred of evidence relating the Pulgas Water Temple attack to Thorne or to his company, the FMC offices in the Embarcadero had closed for good. Although police investigators had asked Thorne to stay in touch, two days after FMC shut its doors, he was gone without a trace or forwarding address.

Hardy didn't know what he had planned to do with Thorne if he ever did catch up with him. Getting his wife and family resettled at the grandparents had kept him from seeking Thorne out until it was too late. By the time Hardy tried to contact Thorne again, the man had fled.

Glitsky, though disappointed that he hadn't gotten another crack at him, thought that all in all it probably was good news for Hardy that Thorne had left town. It had never been one of Glitsky's goals to arrest his friend for homicide, even justifiable homicide.

'There was an attempted burglary,' Glitsky said, 'two weeks ago tomorrow at the Georgetown home of a senator from the great agricultural state of New Jersey, who had recently announced his decision to lead the fight against the exemption on federal fuel taxes on ethanol. No one was supposed to be home, but the maid had stayed behind and was sleeping in her quarters upstairs when the break-in occurred. She kept a loaded gun in the nightstand by her bed. You might have read about it.'

'Thorne,' Hardy said.

Glitsky nodded. 'Unidentified for a couple of days, and by the time he was, it wasn't news anymore. It wasn't as if the senator's wife shot him or something to give it a profile, so it was just another bad-luck break-in. But since I'd put him on the wire as wanted for questioning, I got a call from George-town PD. Your man Mr Thorne is no longer, as they say, among the quick.'

Hardy eased himself off the railing. 'Well, there it is,' he said. Then, after a pause. 'How come I'm not happier about this?'

'It's a sad thing, that's why, somebody dying.' Freeman was lighting up his cigar. 'It's always sad when somebody dies.'

The sun had gone down. Ron and Marie and the two kids waved and shouted their goodbyes from the front gate on their way out and their laughter echoed back, bouncing off the apartment buildings, as they trekked to their car.

Hardy stood with his arm around Frannie on the porch. She leaned into him, and said that if she were him, she'd feel pretty good about the Beaumonts.

'They seem happy,' he admitted.

'That's not what I'm saying.'

'No, I know.'

In fact, he knew more than Frannie did. In the immediate aftermath of his investigation, to satisfy his own curiosity, he'd followed up on Ron Beaumont's story about his first marriage. The original custody hearing and eventual judgment had been big enough news in Racine, but the kidnapping itself had captivated most of the Midwest for a couple of weeks. It had been relatively easy to follow the story until it became by definition old news and disappeared from print.

Not so simple had been following the trajectory of Dawn's life. In all the newspaper reports on both the custody hearing and the kidnapping, Max and Cassandra's mother had been Dawn Brunetta. No one by that name lived anywhere near Racine any longer. Finally Hardy had called Ron and asked him if his ex-wife had used a professional name. Sure, he'd said – Amber Dawn.

A sergeant in Glitsky's detail named Paul Thieu had come up through missing persons and still prided himself on being able to find anyone in the known world. Hardy, keeping the reasons for his interest to himself – some client – bet Thieu a case of good wine that he couldn't find a pornographic actress who in the last ten years had worked under the name Amber Dawn.

And even for a motivated and experienced Paul Thieu, it had taken nearly a month. Amber Dawn, aka Dawn Brunetta, born Judy Rosen, had died of a speedball overdose in Burbank in 1996. In the last five years of her life, she had worked intermittently as an administrative assistant and actress with a now-defunct company called Bustin' Out Productions, which had done business out of a warehouse in Van Nuys.

Her birth certificate and other personal effects had been in the apartment she shared with a thirty-year-old actor named Dirk Balling, real name Jon Stanton. She had been forty-five years old – five years older, Hardy realized, than she'd told Ron.

Thieu wanted to know if Hardy wanted to get copies of any of her movies. He'd located seven of them in which she'd had supporting roles. He could probably find more for another case of wine, although getting the actual copies might take a little digging. Hardy thanked Thieu for his efforts, gave him his case of mixed Cabernets, and told him he'd take a pass. He had what he needed.

Now, on his porch, he tightened his arm around his wife. He heard his own children playing some made-up game back in the house. Laughing, running around, getting crazy and loud. It was going to get louder, out of control, any minute. He kissed the top of her head, and gave her a smile.

'My turn,' he said.

If you enjoyed this book here is a selection of other bestselling titles from Headline

THE BROKEN HEARTS CLUB	Ethan Black	£5.99	☐
WHITEOUTS	Michael Blaine	£5.99	☐
RESURRECTING SALVADOR	Jeremy Dronefield	£5.99	☐
CEREMONY OF INNOCENCE	Humphrey Hawksley	£5.99	☐
MOON MUSIC	Faye Kellerman	£5.99	☐
THE MERCY RULE	John Lescroart	£5.99	☐
THE SHADOW IN THE SANDS	Sam Llewellyn	£5.99	☐
CRITICAL MASS	Steve Martini	£5.99	☐
WHEN THE WIND BLOWS	James Patterson	£5.99	☐
UNDERDOGS	Rob Ryan	£5.99	☐
AN AMERICAN KILLING	Mary-Anne Tirone Smith	£5.99	☐
HELL GATE	Peter Tonkin	£5.99	☐

Headline books are available at your local bookshop or newsagent. Alternatively, books can be ordered direct from the publisher. Just tick the titles you want and fill in the form below. Prices and availability subject to change without notice.

Buy four books from the selection above and get free postage and packaging and delivery within 48 hours. Just send a cheque or postal order made payable to Bookpoint Ltd to the value of the total cover price of the four books. Alternatively, if you wish to buy fewer than four books the following postage and packaging applies:

UK and BFPO £4.30 for one book; £6.30 for two books; £8.30 for three books.

Overseas and Eire: £4.80 for one book; £7.10 for 2 or 3 books (surface mail).

Please enclose a cheque or postal order made payable to *Bookpoint Limited*, and send to: Headline Publishing Ltd, 39 Milton Park, Abingdon, OXON OX14 4TD, UK.
Email Address: orders@bookpoint.co.uk

If you would prefer to pay by credit card, our call team would be delighted to take your order by telephone. Our direct line is 01235 400 414 (lines open 9.00 am–6.00 pm Monday to Saturday 24 hour message answering service). Alternatively you can send a fax on 01235 400 454.

Name ....

Address ....

....

....

If you would prefer to pay by credit card, please complete:
Please debit my Visa/Access/Diner's Card/American Express (delete as applicable) card number:

Signature .... Expiry Date ....